Chispa

feminine noun • *Spanish*

---

1. one's passion
2. that which lights up the soul
3. an ignited fire

Ruby Fink

ISBN: 979-8-9917728-3-9 (print)

ISBN: 979-8-9917728-2-2 (ebook)

Cover design by Violet Fink
Published by fINK PRESS

For my dad and my sister, Violet. Who listened to me read the first chapter and didn't stop nagging until I finished the story.

Jerks.

I love you.

Table of Contents

Chapter 1: Natural Spin Turn

"The natural spin turn is used in the Waltz. It is typically used to advance a couple, although an underturned spin turn is also very useful for turning a corner."

Champion dancer Yamini Krishnamurthy once said: *"A dance performance is rather like going out into a battlefield."* After being a competitive ballroom dancer for more than a decade, seventeen-year-old Claire Beauchene understood this all too well. She approached every competition with the dedication and thoroughness of a seasoned general, ready to take down any opponent who stood between her and first place.

The Paxton Regional Championship was no exception.

First, the music. Claire waited, her heart beating wildly in her chest as the cheerful Tchaikovsky melody she'd chosen for their Solo lilted across the ballroom.

Second, choreography and technique. Claire's grin widened as she stepped forward into position, arms upraised, one glittering heel outstretched. Sebastian Alvah, her dance partner of five years and boyfriend of six months, met her and encircled her with his arms. Claire felt the familiar frame click into place like a key in the lock, the careful pressure from Sebastian's palm against her own, the delicate balance between the two of them seconds before Sebastian pushed off. The two of them spun effortlessly across the floor to a roar of applause, every movement perfect and precise.

Third, costume choice. Violin and harp music gave her feet wings, and as they whirled around, Claire felt herself transform. She was no longer the daughter of Natalia and Leon Beauchene of the Beauchene Dance School and multi-Dance champion. She was Sleeping Beauty, reunited with her Prince Phillip after awakening from her slumber. Claire beamed an easy smile at the crowd as she whirled past; the blue georgette material of her costume transformed during the dance into a magical gossamer given to her by the fairies. She smiled at Sebastian, blond, blue-eyed and resplendent in his matching blue suit and bowtie. He was the perfect handsome prince, the kind she could imagine fighting a dragon in order to rescue her.

Even now, Claire could hear the whispers, see the looks in their direction as she and Sebastian whirled past the spectators.

"They're the best dancers here."

"So talented. Look at their technique!"

"They win every competition they enter."

As Sebastian guided her by the judge's table, Claire saw him steal a peek at the men and women, scribbling on their scorecards.

"Focus," Claire murmured, barely moving lips that were perfectly outlined in blue lipstick.

"Relax," Sebastian whispered back, leading them through three pivots that had them both spinning even faster, like a pair of synchronized tops. "They like us, we're going to win."

"Celebrate later, dance now." Claire lifted a graceful arm, the rhinestones on her nails matching the tiara securely fastened to her elegant hairdo.

"You worry too much." The crowd applauded as Claire draped her arm around her partner's shoulders, and Sebastian lifted Claire into the air, her white-blonde hair gleaming, one leg wrapped around his torso, the other stretched out behind her.

This time Claire snuck a quick look at the judges as Sebastian set her down and guided her back into his solid frame.

"You really think they like us?"

"Babe," Sebastian assured her, "it's in the bag."

This, Claire told herself, this was going to be the year they graduated from gold medalists to world champions. She and Sebastian were going to come in first at the Paxton Regional Championship for the third year in a row. Then as soon as she turned eighteen next month, she would be eligible for the Amateur Rising Star Ballroom division of the Blackpool Dance Festival, one of the most prestigious dance competitions in the world. Claire had been dreaming of competing since she was six years old. It was their first win at Blackpool that had elevated her mama and papa's careers, and it was their three-time world champion status that made Beauchene Dance School the premiere dance studio in San Diego.

If—she corrected herself—*when* Claire and Sebastian won the championship trophy at Blackpool, they would make history as one of the youngest couples to achieve the award. The fame would propel them into a successful career full of prestige and sponsorships, allowing them to travel all over the world and compete with the best dancers in every country.

The last strains of the violins faded away, and Claire sighed happily as they finished their dance, bowing to thunderous applause. Even if she was no longer Sleeping Beauty, her life felt like a perfect fairytale. In a few years, she and Sebastian would get married, she decided, as he tucked her hand into the crook of his arm and led her off the floor. And once they had gotten tired of traveling around the world, competing in various International and National Dance Competitions, they would settle down and open their own dance school. Just like Mama and Papa.

"I'm going to change for our next heat," Sebastian said, kissing her on the cheek. "See you in ten." Claire watched Sebastian walk away, taking in his perfectly coiffed blond hair, the little dimple on his cheek that deepened as he smiled and greeted other contestants, the athletically tanned and toned package encased in a stylish suit by DSI London. She sighed again. Yes, indeed, her life was pretty much perfect.

Claire was so distracted she didn't see the muscled, lithe figure in black until she slammed into the chest as solid as a brick wall. A firm hand around her waist kept her from falling backward onto the floor.

"Hey!" said a familiar irritated voice. "Watch where you're going."

With rising dread, Claire's eyes tracked up the black V-neck dance costume, into the eyes of Luca Ortiz, the Beauchene School of Dance's Latin Champion.

Though Claire could admit Luca was a talented dancer, there was something intangible about him that she didn't like. Maybe it was the fact that even in three-inch heels she had to look up to meet his gaze. Or the eyes that were coal black and seemed to burn with their own hidden fires. Or maybe it was Luca's beautiful face, gifted by some unfair god and surrounded by a halo of dark curls. But probably the thing that annoyed Claire the most was Luca's tendency to mock her at every turn, ensuring every encounter was a series of sniping matches where Luca usually emerged with the upper hand.

Claire tilted her head back, giving Luca her best fake smile.

"Ortiz, I don't think those basic dance lessons have sunk in. I'm the follower, remember? That's not in my job description."

"Call it common courtesy then." Luca's grip around her waist tightened slightly, and Claire belatedly realized she was still pressed against his chest, one hand resting on the bare V of smooth skin.

"Just as I kept you from falling, you could be more aware of your surroundings and not crash into people."

"Well—" Claire opened her mouth to voice a pithy retort, but nothing came out.

"And while we're on the subject of courtesy," Luca's dark eyes mocked her. "People usually say 'thank you' when someone does them a favor."

She would sooner kiss a frog than say 'thank you' to Luca. Claire pushed herself away, tossing her head as she looked up at his smug face.

"Shouldn't you be waiting with the rest of the team for your turn?" Claire asked. "Maybe you wouldn't have been in my way if you were."

"And now, for the Latin portion of our competition," the announcer's voice echoed around the ballroom. "Would the contestants please take your places at the edge of the dance floor, we will be starting in two minutes!"

Luca smirked. "You were saying?"

"Well…" It was starting to feel like a losing battle, but Claire refused to back down. "What about your partner? Where is she?"

"I'm here! I'm not late! Oh, hi Claire!" Lily Cho, Luca's partner of the last four months, hurried on three-inch heels to take her place in line. She was petite and delicate, with huge doe eyes and straight dark hair. Her black and white salsa costume complimented Luca's all-black outfit. "Great job on your dance earlier."

"Oh, thank you." How the sweet but slightly scattered Lily had managed to tolerate a jerk like Luca was beyond her. Most partners quit after a month due to his rigorous practice sessions and perfectionism. "Good luck with yours!"

"Dancers, we will now start the competition for the Salsa, please step onto the floor!"

Luca cleared his throat and stepped around Claire, leading Lily onto the floor. "If you'll excuse us, we have a competition to win. In the meantime, you should really work on that awareness," he called over his shoulder, "it's very useful."

"Wha—" Claire stood, her mouth forming a silent 'O' of outrage as Luca and Lily took their positions.

The music started, a quick, pulsing rhythm that had everyone tapping their fingers and toes to the beat. With a sudden flash of sequins and a toss of his head, Luca's face was transformed by a charming smile and seductive look that set off a wave of enthusiastic applause from the crowd.

Philistines, Claire thought as she recognized the popular song. The Latin category of ballroom dance which included Salsa, Cha-Cha, Samba, Argentine Tango, and Pasa Doble typically garnered all the songs that were crowd pleasers, while the Smooth dance category which included Waltz, Viennese Waltz, Tango, and Foxtrot did not. Of course, most new students who came to her parent's studio wanted to learn something fun, while classical dances like the waltz were only learned for weddings and Quinceañeras.

She glanced towards the dance floor where Luca was moving between two other couples. His suede-soled shoes traced a pattern over the smooth floor as his hips rolled, while fingers that were lithe and full of energy snapped.

Luca turned his back to the spectators, his well-toned waist and butt gyrating to the delight of the audience. There were whistles and screams as Luca looked back over his shoulder, and his dark eyes met Claire's blue ones. Luca's lips curled into a smoldering smirk and he winked before Claire looked away.

They wouldn't be cheering if they knew what a jerk he was in real life, Claire thought, crossing her arms.

"Uh-oh, what happened this time?" said an amused voice on her left. Bella Price, one of Beauchene's star ballet dancers and Claire's best friend, sidled up to join her. Tall, slender, with skin the color of polished ebony and dark curly hair that had been tamed into an elegant bun, Bella attracted attention everywhere she went.

"What do you mean?" Claire watched as Luca spun Lily three times, muscles in his arms rippling as he dipped Lily so low her head almost touched the floor. He looked up and smiled flirtatiously at the crowd, and Claire saw several female onlookers whisper among themselves.

Bella and Claire had met years ago in a Mommy and Me class hosted by Claire's mother and bonded over a mutual love of unicorns, glittery tutus, and dance. In the past fourteen years, Bella had come to every one of Claire's competitions, and Claire had never missed a ballet performance.

"You and Luca are like...two electric eels," Bella chuckled. "Every time you meet, sparks fly."

"Because every time I see him, he irritates me," Claire scowled. "If I was an electric eel, I'd shock him every time he walked into the room so he'd stay away."

"Interesting fact: electric eels actually have very poor vision," Bella commented. "They use a type of echolocation where they release low voltages of electricity into the water to detect objects around them..." she yawned and rubbed her eyes.

Claire gave Bella's shoulders a sympathetic squeeze. "Another late-night watching nature shows again? I thought you'd have more time together now that Bianca is Dr. Honeybear."

Bella's girlfriend, Bianca Santos, was a medical student at the local hospital. A stocky, yet curvy woman of twenty-four, Bianca had seemed intimidating, until Claire discovered the soft interior underneath. After a year together, Bella and Bianca were devoted to each other, and in the process of finding an apartment to share.

Bella grimaced. "I got all dressed up because I was hoping to have a date for the first time in weeks. But a car accident kept her busy at the hospital until two AM. It was either the nature channel or that show that follows celebrities." She yawned again. "So, what happened with Luca?"

"I accidentally bumped into him, and he told me I needed to be more aware." Claire scowled. "He's so full of himself, isn't he?"

"He's the worst," agreed a voice on Claire's right. Bethany LaManna tossed her head scornfully, her dyed red hair dotted with rhinestones. Bethany held no Championship title of any sort, usually coming in second place or third to Claire's first. Still, she was a decent dancer and had been performing almost as long as Claire and

Sebastian had. "I asked him to help me with a dance move last week, and he totally blew me off."

"Is that *all* you needed help with?" Bella raised an eyebrow. It was a well-known secret that Bethany was a notorious flirt.

Bethany pouted. "*Okay*, so maybe I asked if he wanted to come over to my place to hang, but he was totally mean and said he had better things to do."

"Well, you wouldn't be the first girl he's turned down," Claire shrugged. "He had half the school swooning when he first started, remember?"

"Yeah, then he opened up his mouth, and everyone realized how rude he was."

"Maybe he's just a really committed dancer," Bella offered. "Don't forget, he's a scholarship student. He probably has to work really hard to keep his spot."

"Still, you'd think he'd take a few minutes to buy a few more costumes," Claire watched as Lily moved toward Luca in a sashay of sparkling material, and pressed herself to his torso, hips mirroring his, rolling from side to side. "Considering all the money he saves on classes."

"I know right?" Bethany snickered, "He's been wearing that same outfit for two years. I hope he washes it."

"I don't know, he might not have time to do that either."

"You know," Bella's eyes flashed in irritation, "I saw him teaching one of the kid's classes, and he was actually doing a really great job. He might be a little arrogant, but I bet he doesn't gossip about others behind their backs."

Claire stopped, mid-giggle, feeling a twinge of guilt in her stomach. Bella was right. She shouldn't be making fun of Luca. Even if he was a jerk.

"Ugh, why do you have to be such a buzzkill?" Bethany was scowling at Bella. "We're just talking."

"Bella is right," Claire interrupted, coming to her friend's defense. "Just because he's rude, doesn't mean we should stoop to his level."

"I thought you were on my side," Bethany pouted.

"We're all on the same team," Claire reminded her. "Team Beauchene, and it looks like Luca is going to win us another gold medal," she said, just as Luca finished his dance with an extravagant bow. "Besides," she said, changing the subject, "I shouldn't be focused on anything but the awesome routine I've got next with the best partner and the best boyfriend in the whole world."

"You better be talking about me," Sebastian teased, coming up from behind and kissing her on the cheek. "What'd I miss?" he asked.

"We were having a fun little chat about the school's charity case," Bethany complained, "but Claire and Bella had to ruin it by being noble and sweet."

"They are sweet," Sebastian said, squeezing Claire in a hug. "The sweetest girls in the entire studio."

"Aww," Claire cooed.

"Ugh," Bethany said simultaneously, rolling her eyes.

"Well, I might be the sweetest, but you are the cutest, nicest, and—" Claire suddenly realized Sebastian was dressed in his Oberon costume for their next dance solo. "Oh my gosh!" she squealed, "I'm supposed to be dressed like Titania right now! I gotta get changed!" She hustled off, skirts held high as she ran towards the dressing room in three-inch heels.

* * *

From his place on the floor, Luca saw the glances in his direction, the whispers, and giggles from the three girls.

He had enough experience to know they were talking about him. Not that he cared, he reminded himself, keeping a smile on his face as he led Lily off the floor. They might think they were better than the scholarship student because of their rich parents and easy life. And, of course, Princess Claire, the studio's pride and joy, expected everyone to fawn over her and treat her like royalty. Only the ballet dancer—Bella—treated him with the same decency she gave the other students, a brief greeting when they passed in the hall and a friendly nod during competitions.

Luca skirted the contestants at the edge of the floor and let go of the smile he'd been holding during the performance. His body was aching from the double shift he had worked the night before, but the bills were piling up at home, and he'd needed the second shift to pick up some extra cash. Just two more dance numbers, then he could take a nap on the battered couch in the men's dressing room.

"Lily!" Sebastian called out, stepping in their path, and Luca was aware of his partner curling her fingers tighter around his arm. "Looking good."

"Oh, thank you," Lily averted her eyes from the studio's golden boy. "I have to get changed." She hurried off and was quickly lost in the crowd. Sebastian watched her go until Bethany jabbed him with her elbow.

"Take a picture, why don't you. It'll last longer."

Sebastian immediately looked away, catching the eye of a pretty brunette dancer waiting for the next heat. Luca felt his stomach roll as the young girl flushed and smiled at the handsome, blond dancer.

"Hey," Bella gave Luca a friendly smile and a slight nod. "Nice job out there."

Luca relaxed slightly. "Thank you."

"Nice outfit," The redhead—Bethany, snickered.

Luca eyed her with distaste. "Excuse me," he said, brushing past her. Behind him, he could hear her whispering to Sebastian, the studio's golden boy, but he didn't care. He had more important things to think about at the moment. Like where he could find a gallon of coffee.

* * *

"First place in the Solo portion of our competition goes to…"

Claire gripped Sebastian's hand tighter, and he patted her arm.

"Claire Beauchene and Sebastian Alvah from Beauchene's School of Dance!"

Claire smiled in triumph as she and Sebastian stepped forward to accept their certificate and trophy.

Everything was going according to plan, she thought, as she and Sebastian took photos with the other finalists. After this, they would compete in the Blackpool Dance Festival, win numerous awards, and then… she sighed happily. The rest was history.

"Congratulations, darling." Natalia Beauchene limped forward to kiss her daughter's cheek. A blonde, stern-looking woman in her forties, Natalia Beauchene, formerly Natalia Ivanov, had been a promising ballet dancer for the Bolshoi Ballet Company until a hit and run accident cut her career short.

"Thanks, Mama," Claire replied as Natalia led her back to the Beauchene table, leaning heavily on her cane. "We worked really hard on that routine. I'm glad that it paid off."

"Hard work usually does," Natalia reached up to tuck an errant strand of hair back into place on her daughter's head. "I am glad they did not take off points for presentation. Your curl came loose halfway through."

"What is one curl when our daughter was the epitome of Sleeping Beauty on the floor?" Leon came to embrace his daughter and kiss her cheeks. A lean, dark-haired man in his forties, he exuded a kindness and youthful energy that charmed everyone who came within a hundred yards of his person. "*Ma belle princesse, bravo, bravo.*"

"First place for the Amateur Latin Dance Finals goes to… Luca Ortiz and Lily Cho from Beauchene's School of Dance."

"One moment, *chérie*," Leon held up a hand. He and Natalia joined in the applause as Luca and Lily stepped forward to claim their awards. After a moment, Claire joined in.

"He might be a jerk, but he makes our studio look good every time he competes," Claire muttered to Sebastian. Natalia's head whipped around, and she eyed Claire sternly.

"Don't be rude," Natalia scolded, her native tongue becoming more pronounced as she reprimanded her only daughter. "It is a great honor to receive the award." She waved a hand at the other dancers in the ballroom. "Everyone here work hard, put in time, money, sweat, for such an honor, especially Luca."

"I never said he didn't!" Claire protested. "I just don't like him personally."

Natalia's blue eyes, the mirror image of Claire's, were ice cold. "It would benefit you to be kinder." And with that, she turned and limped away, irritation seeming to radiate from every bone in her body.

"What's her deal?" Sebastian asked. Claire sighed.

"Who knows. All I said was I didn't like Luca as a person. Is it my fault he's such a jerk?" she huffed. She wrapped an arm around Sebastian, giving him a hug.

"Well, it doesn't matter. Now that we're done competing, we can focus all our attention on the Blackpool Dance Festival in May. Speaking of which, are you free to start practicing our routine tomorrow? I can bring our favorite smoothies," she added.

Sebastian sighed and pushed Claire away slightly, so he could look her in the eyes. "Here's the thing, babe… I won't be able to do the competition in May."

Chapter 2: Double Reverse Change

"The Double Reverse Spin has the distinction of being the only left-turning bronze figure where the dancers can complete a full rotation in just one measure of music."

"I still don't understand." Claire paced back and forth across the wood floor in Sebastian's bedroom. Outside the window of his parent's luxurious townhouse, life in the quiet San Diego neighborhood was going on as usual. A woman in pink exercise gear was walking her dog; two boys rode their skateboards down the street; a messenger with an Uber Eats bag sped by on his moped. But inside Sebastian's elegant house, Claire's world was being turned upside down. "You're throwing away our plans, a five-year partnership, and leaving to participate in some reality dance show in Los Angeles?"

"Look babe, I'm sorry I'm leaving you without a partner for the competition, but I talked with your dad, and he said it's okay. He understands this is a big deal for me,"

Sebastian said, placing a stack of neatly folded pants in his suitcase. Two suitcases and three garment bags full of suits were already hanging by the door, ready to be taken to the airport. Claire sat on Sebastian's bare mattress, the sheets already stripped away and packed in a suitcase. The rest of the room was in a similar state of emptiness, all his trophies and awards had been packed away in boxes, and there were faded squares on the walls where his certificates had hung.

Most of his belongings would be shipped to the house Sebastian's father owned in Los Angeles. A prominent TV producer, Joshua Alvah traveled often, depending on the project he was working on, and had multiple houses. "Besides," Sebastian continued, "aren't you glad I waited until after the competition to tell you? You would've totally lost focus if I'd told you before. Now we can say we finished strong by winning Paxton Regionals three years in a row!"

"But winning at Blackpool was our dream, Seb," Claire argued. "We've been planning this for three years now, are you really throwing it all away for some TV show contest?"

"No, babe, Blackpool was your dream." Claire's mouth fell open in shock. "Don't get me wrong," Sebastian continued hastily, "I would've danced with you in London, but I got onto *Dance Craze*! That's huge! My dad says I have a good chance of being recognized for my talent and making a name for myself as a dancer! Tell me that's not important!"

"If getting on the show was so important, why didn't you tell me about it?" Claire demanded. "I thought you were taking a break from TV shows."

"That was when I was a kid. I'm tired of living out here away from the action, I want to be a part of something again!" Sebastian insisted. "I have so many dancer friends in Los Angeles who've got solid careers while I've been what? Ballroom dancing for meaningless competitions no one cares about? People have forgotten who I am, I need to get myself out there again."

Sebastian thought the competitions they worked so hard for were meaningless? Claire bit back the hurt. "So when did you audition?"

Sebastian ran a hand through his blond hair.

"A month ago, when I said I was visiting my dad in L.A.."

"A month?" Claire echoed. "You've been hiding this from me for a month, but you decided to tell me you were leaving now?"

"I'm sorry about that," Sebastian sighed, "I wasn't even sure I'd get in, my dad had to call in a few favors to even get me an audition because I've been out of the game for so long. Besides, I was pretty sure if I told you early, you'd freak out."

"I don't freak out," Claire protested. Sebastian began meticulously packing his hair products and toiletries in an overnight bag.

"You kinda do, babe," he smiled. "Remember when we were two minutes late for that one event? I thought you were going to have a heart attack."

"I do not freak out," Claire insisted stubbornly. "I just like when things go according to plan." She watched as Sebastian put two pairs of dance shoes—one for practice, one for competition—in a shoe bag to be stowed in the last suitcase. "I guess I always thought that it was our plan to win Blackpool together," she muttered.

"I really was trying to figure out how to tell you," Sebastian insisted. "But I kept worrying you'd freak out right before our big competition so I kept putting it off and then suddenly…" Sebastian spread his hands helplessly. "It was time for me to go."

Claire felt her temper rise again. "Of all the things you decided to procrastinate on, this has got to be the worst one!"

Sebastian threw up his arms in frustration. "Look, I'm sorry. Okay? I know I messed up but all I can do at this point is say sorry."

"You could also quit your show!" Claire retorted.

Sebastian closed his eyes, pinching the bridge of his nose. "Well, sorry again, but I can't go back in time and change anything. Contracts have been signed and plane tickets have been bought and…and…I can't get out of this now! For once you just have to accept that you can't have your way!" Claire flinched as if he'd struck her and tears welled in her eyes.

"Claire…" Sebastian zipped up the final suitcase and came to sit beside her on his bare mattress. "I'm sorry, I didn't mean to yell," he apologized, digging out a handkerchief. "Don't cry, please?"

"I can't help it," Claire sniffled, taking the cloth and dabbing at her eyes. "It's a lot to take in all at once."

"I'm sorry," Sebastian tucked an errant strand of hair behind her ear. "Forgive me, please?" he begged. "Look, babe, this show will last six months, right? Maybe it's good for my career and I get more work out of it, maybe it's just something to add to my resume. But if it doesn't work out, and you still want to dance with me next year, then I'll do it, okay?" He leaned in to kiss her.

The moment was ruined as Bethany walked in the door without even knocking.

"Oh," she said, stopping in her tracks. "I didn't know you'd be here."

"Why wouldn't I be?" Claire asked a little resentfully as she and Sebastian pulled away.

"I don't know, aren't you teaching right now or something?" Bethany replied, blowing a bubble of gum. She fumbled in her purse. "I uh—just came to return this movie you lent me, Seb. Good flick."

"Oh—no problem," said Sebastian. "Glad you enjoyed it."

"Yeah, I'd have liked to watch it again, but I didn't want you to leave without it…"

"Wait," Claire turned to glare at Sebastian. "Bethany knew you were leaving too?"

Sebastian sighed, ran a hand through his hair. "She heard me talking about it to your dad, I asked her not to tell until I told you."

"Yeah, it wasn't my secret to tell," Bethany was still digging through her purse. "I was keeping it quiet because he asked."

"Having trouble finding it?" Claire felt her annoyance torn between Sebastian and Bethany as she watched the redhead continue to dig. If this was the last time she was going to see Sebastian for a while, she wanted that interrupted kiss.

Bethany yanked her purse closed. "I swear, I thought I packed it," she said with a little laugh, "this is so embarrassing, I'll just have to mail it to you later."

"No rush," Sebastian shrugged.

"Yeah, you totally didn't have to come over right this second to return it," Claire scowled.

"Claire, she didn't know," Sebastian chided her gently. "We're all having a rough day," he apologized.

"Some apparently more than most," Claire muttered.

Bethany shifted her weight in the doorway "So, I guess with Sebastian going you won't be competing for a while. Unless there's another partner who's available?"

"Not that I've heard of," Claire shot Sebastian another glare. "It sucks," she complained. "Everyone at my level is already taken."

"Babe, I can only apologize so many times," Sebastian groaned.

"Just stay here, then I don't need an apology!"

"Well, on the bright side, maybe now that you're benched, I've got a shot at winning something," Bethany interjected.

"You?"Claire winced as the question came out sounding more surprised than she'd intended. Bethany was a decent dancer, she acknowledged. But she'd never gotten the impression Bethany viewed her competitions as anything other than an enjoyable way to meet guys and wear expensive costumes.

Bethany's heavily-mascaraed eyes narrowed. "What's that supposed to mean? You don't think I'm as good as you?"

"No, of course you're not!" Claire said quickly. "You're a solid silver medalist."

"Claire!" Sebastian scolded.

"You don't have to be mean," Bethany crossed her arms. "It's not like I'm not horrible."

"I'm sorry! Of course you have a shot," Claire tried to placate her. "I bet you'll bring in a lot more gold medals for the studio."She managed a weak smile. "Go…Team Beauchene."

"Whatever," Bethany huffed and tossed her purse over her shoulder. "Good luck with your partner problem. Maybe you'll get lucky and someone will get injured or drop out."

"That's horrible!" Claire protested after Bethany's retreating back. "I don't want someone injured!" But Bethany was already out the door, showing a great deal of leg and a tattoo of a rose on her thigh as she went.

The door closed and Claire swallowed, feeling the emptiness of the room in the pit of her stomach.

"One day babe, you're going to have to learn not to be so blunt with people," Sebastian double-checked his carry-on bag. "There's a thing called diplomacy, you know."

"Being a silver-medalist isn't bad," Claire crossed her arms defensively. "But if she wants to be a winner she might want to consider…practicing more."Sebastian gave Claire a reproving look.

"Not everyone is as obsessed with dance as you are. You don't have to practice 24/7, you know."

"Not everyone is a champion dancer either," Claire watched Sebastian's hands as he checked every bag one last time. She knew those hands, those smooth, manicured hands that guided her through every routine. Sometimes Sebastian was late for rehearsals and sometimes he needed extra practice to learn the choreography, but she was used to it, they were a team!

Claire felt a lump rise in her throat as the finality of his decision weighed on her like a ton of bricks. What was she supposed to say? *Don't leave? Take me with you?*

"There's nothing I can say to convince you to stay?" She finally asked.

Sebastian shook his head. The slight jingle of zippers was practically deafening.

This wasn't fair. There was nothing in the plan about Sebastian leaving two months before Blackpool. She wanted to scream, throw a tantrum, but she forced down the bitter anger and grief and smiled as Sebastian turned back around, asking instead:

"Did I mention I'm proud of you?"

Sebastian offered her a brief smile as he slung his designer backpack onto his shoulders. "Not until now, but I appreciate it just the same."

He gently moved her out of the way as an alarm beeped on his smartwatch and he began gathering up his other bags. "I need to get my stuff outside; the Uber will be here soon."

Claire picked up a bag. "I'll help you."

She stayed with Sebastian until the Uber arrived and helped him load all his luggage in the back. Once every bag was neatly in place, Sebastian slammed the trunk closed and hugged her one last time.

"I'll call," Claire promised, clinging to him. "And I'll visit."

"Okay," Sebastian said, gently moving her and opening the car door, "just let me know in advance, and we'll work around my rehearsal schedule."

"Okay."

She stood on the curb, waving, until the Uber was out of sight. Then, carefully dabbing at her eyes which were definitely *not* teary, she turned around and climbed into her own car. There was someone she had to talk to.

* * *

"Papa!" Claire yelled, slamming open the door to her parent's offices. "Sebastian got accepted on some stupid show and you let him go?"

Leon Beauchene, looked up from the pile of papers on his desk; glasses perched precariously on the end of his bony nose.

The room was small, made smaller by the wall of filing cabinets behind him, meticulously labeled, from A-Z. Gleaming dance trophies rested on top, largest ones in the middle and smaller ones on the outside. Pictures of Leon and Natalia's past dance competitions covered the walls, mixed with gold and silver medals in frames.

"*Chérie,* this is a dance studio, not a prison. Believe it or not, students are free to leave whenever they want." He rubbed the bridge of his nose, signifying a brewing headache. "Not to play Devil's Advocate, but you should be proud of him. To be on *Dance Craze* is quite a feat, it wouldn't have been easy to be accepted."

"Why would I be proud of him when he knows I've wanted to compete in Blackpool for years and he walked out two months before the festival?" Claire almost kicked the corner of her father's desk in temper, then decided against it. "You should've talked him into staying. It's… it's not fair!"

"Claire, be reasonable," Leon stood up from his desk to put an arm around his only daughter. "You would have me deny a young man a once-in-a-lifetime opportunity to advance his career just because I want him to stay and compete with you? Now who's unfair?" He sighed and pressed a soft kiss on the top of her head. "Look, *ma chérie,* I know what this competition meant to you. If it makes any difference, I did my best to try and convince Sebastian to stay, but it is not my place to make his career choices. And while this is an unfortunate setback, what's done is done. Your mother is looking into replacements as we speak, but even if we can't find someone there is always next year."

"She won't be able to find anyone," Claire mumbled, tears of disappointment welling up in her blue eyes. "Everyone is paired up already. Why did this have to happen now?"

"Claire, everything will be alright," Leon reassured her. "*Ce n'est pas la mer à boire.*"

It's not as if you have to drink the sea. It was one of Leon's favorite sayings, and while Claire knew he meant it as a comfort, the words felt hollow. Maybe it wasn't as impossible as drinking the sea, but it felt close. Hours, years of practice, wasted because her boyfriend wanted his fifteen minutes of fame. But before she could say it out loud, an outraged voice could be heard through the connecting door of her mother's office.

"You can't be serious!"

"Papa? Is that Luca talking to Mama?"

"Yes, well," Leon winced as more irate words could be heard through the connecting door. "He's a very talented and passionate dancer but he does have a temper."

The door was suddenly wrenched open and Luca, wearing a tight tank-top, sweats, and a murderous expression on his face, stormed out. He froze as he saw Claire and her father.

"Good, you're here," Natalia said briskly, limping to the doorway. "Claire, I want you to meet your new partner."

* * *

Luca? Her partner? Claire stared at Luca in horror. Gone was groomed look he maintained for competitions. While Claire was outfitted in a stylish blue practice dress and heels, Luca's tank top had holes along the hem and his sweatpants were dotted with bleach. Claire's hair was swept up into an elegant bun while Luca's hair fell in messy curls around his face. And while Luca had been born with admittedly attractive features and a muscled physique that he no doubt got from hours in the gym, the entire image was ruined by his perpetual scowl.

"Mama, you can't be serious."

"That's what I said," Luca muttered, slouching against a file cabinet.

Claire ignored him. "He can't be my partner. What about Lily?"

Natalia gave a weary shrug. "Lily has been accepted to a prestigious dance school in Europe, she is leaving at the end of the week."

Claire instinctively bristled. "Papa taught in Europe; what can they teach in Europe that he doesn't already know?"

"*Chérie*, I love your faith in me but there is plenty she can learn that I cannot teach," Leon gently interceded. "However, this is wonderful news for you, it means you will have a partner for Blackpool!"

"But Papa, he's a *Latin* dancer," Claire protested. "I'm —"

"A snob?" Luca muttered. He winced as Natalia whacked him on the back of the head.

"Behave, that is my daughter you are talking about," she warned him. She aimed a glare at Claire. "That goes for you too, show some respect."

"Claire, you must decide what is more important. Competing at Blackpool with—as you say—a Latin dancer, or not at all."

"But—but—" Claire sputtered, "how would we even make it work?"

"There are two months until you have to leave for London," Natalia said. "You will practice for both the Latin and Smooth entries in the contest, perhaps even compete in a few competitions here beforehand—as practice," she clarified, "just to see how you would do."

"But that's impossible!" Claire burst out. "It's not enough time!"

"You are both talented dancers," Leon reassured her. "I am sure there is nothing the two of you cannot accomplish if you work together."

"But Latin dancing so undignified," Claire protested again. "I'll have to wear skimpy outfits and…and *shimmy*," Claire winced.

"Better than dressing up like a character from an old fairytale," Luca retorted.

Claire's eyes narrowed in disdain. "Titania and Oberon are not fairytale characters, haven't you heard of Shakespeare?"

Luca shrugged, crossing his arms. "It's hard to pay attention to something that's so boring it puts me to sleep."

"Boring?" Claire sputtered. "Smooth dancing is elegant and cultured, unlike all that… *booty-shaking* you insist on doing during your competitions."

Luca took a step forward, looking down his nose at Claire. "Latin dancing is full of passion and has just as much culture—"

"Enough!" Natalia's voice cracked like a whip, startling them both. "One more word out of either of you and I turn you both over my knee, I don't care how old you are."

"Sorry Mama," Claire glowered at Luca.

"Sorry Mrs. Beauchene," Luca said, looking away.

Natalia eyed them both sternly.

"I will say it one last time. Dance together, or not at all. Those are your only options."

There was a timid knock on the door and Zoya, one of the part-time dance teachers, poked her head in. "Excuse me Mr. Beauchene, I was wondering if you could come and supervise Mr. and Mrs. Hicks during their private lesson? They requested you personally."

"Did they really? How nice of them," Leon smiled. "I'll be right there," he said, placing his glasses on the desk.

"But Papa, what about London?" Claire protested.

Leon shrugged. "It is as your mother said, *chérie*, either you two dance together or not at all. We will leave it up to you to decide," he paused. "In the meantime, we have students to teach." He smiled at Natalia. "Darling, would you like to supervise as well?"

Natalia huffed impatiently. "I do not think I have time. There is work for me to do."

"One minute of your time, *mon amour*," Leon said, reaching for her hand and kissing it. Natalia looked away, lips twitching.

"I will watch for one minute. That is all," she acquiesced. Leon beamed.

"Excellent." He beckoned to Claire and Luca. "You two, come along as well, I could use some assistants."

Claire crossed her arms. "I don't have time to help, Papa, I need to find a new partner."

"Think of it as a trial period while you make up your mind, *chérie*," Leon said, leading the way out of the office.

The small group followed Leon down the hall to one of the smaller practice rooms, where Sheryl and Tony Hicks were waiting, looking a little nervous. Claire had seen them once or twice while assisting group classes, and knew Tony was a prominent lawyer while Sheryl worked in an office. They had been coming to the dance studio for the last few months because Tony had bought Sheryl six months' worth of couple's dance lessons as an anniversary present.

Claire decided they looked good standing together; Tony, tall and dark, Sheryl blonde and petite, and felt a slight twinge of sadness. People said she and Sebastian looked good together. She glanced at Luca who stood a few feet away, arms crossed, looking like he was ready for a boxing match rather than a dance class and shuddered.

Claire was going to have to put a lot of work into their costumes if she didn't want to lose points on presentation. No one would believe Luca was a fairy king.

Maybe she could add a donkey's head to Luca's costume and he could play Bottom instead of Oberon. Claire's lips curved at the thought of Luca attempting the graceful waltz steps, wearing a donkey costume.

Luca's eyes flicked away from the dance floor to meet hers. "What?" he demanded.

"Nothing," Claire looked away, biting her lip to hide the smile. She could practically see him stumbling around the floor with a donkey head. It'd almost be worth coming in second place to see him play an idiot.

"My friends, hello!" Leon's voice pulled Claire from her thoughts as he extended a hand for Tony to shake. "What are we going to be practicing today?"

"Well, uh—" Tony reached out a hand to Leon and flinched. It was an expected response for newcomers. Leon had lost part of his pinky and ring finger to a nasty case of frostbite when he was studying in France. Both fingers had been amputated to the first knuckle, and though his hand had healed, the sight of the two stubs on his right hand often startled the new students.

"They wanted to work on their waltz and rumba today, sir," Zoya supplied, filling in the awkward silence.

Leon beamed. "Excellent! Show me what you have learned so far."

Claire watched the Hicks perform the basic steps of the waltz, their movements somewhat stiff and awkward, their technique still beginners' level at best. *They should be bending their knees more*, she thought to herself. Sheryl had the timing correct, but Tony was too stiff with his frame and was trying to lead his wife too forcefully. When Tony started to maneuver Sheryl into a promenade with the woodenness of a toy soldier, Leon stepped in.

"Stop, my friends, stop. Tony," Leon said, putting a hand on Tony's shoulder. "Your wife is not something that should be turned forcibly in whatever direction you choose. She is the precious object of your heart and must be *guided* where you want to go. Observe." He held out a hand. "Natalia, *mon amour*, would you assist me?"

Natalia looked toward the door and back, gripping her cane fiercely. "No, I do not think today is a good day, husband…my leg…" she trailed off as Leon took her hand and kissed her fingers tenderly.

"I will support you, my dearest, as always."

Before she could object, he had handed her cane to Zoya, and led her to the middle of the floor. Then, taking Natalia's hand, Leon wrapped his other arm around her slender waist.

"Now, my friends, watch how I demonstrate this box step with my lovely wife. Tony, you must keep your frame strong, open, so that she knows what you want to do," Leon said, arranging Natalia in his arms as he did so. "At the same time, Sheryl, you must reciprocate so there is balance between you two. If you are too loose—loosen up, *mon amour,*" he instructed Natalia and she slackened her arms until he could jiggle them like spaghetti noodles. "There is no way you or she can understand what the other wants because there is no connection between the two of you. And if you are too tense—" At that, Natalia tightened her elbows and shoulders and woodenly moved through a box step. "Then it becomes a struggle to go anywhere. But it does not have to be, see?"

Natalia allowed her arms some flexibility and Leon guided her gently through an underarm turn, their movements graceful and fluid from decades of practice. "It is only when you both are open with your communication and allow the same flexibility and firmness you have in life to come into your dance that you will find true harmony."

Claire watched as her father led her mother effortlessly through a promenade, shifting his weight and frame so they were walking forward. "If there is equal balance between us, I barely need to do anything in order to tell my wife where I plan to go. And from there it is a simple matter to do something like this…" He pulled Natalia tighter and pivoted with her, adding on more and more advanced moves as they spun effortlessly around the floor.

As they continued to dance, Claire saw the stern lines drop away from her mother's face, her furrowed brow relaxed, replaced with a faraway look in her eyes. She looked serene and almost peaceful, as Leon guided her into another promenade, and she lifted her leg up into a developè. Claire felt a tinge of envy, wishing she could have what her parents had.

At first glance, you wouldn't think that the gentle Frenchman and the irritable Russian would have had much compatibility, but somehow, they had managed to take their partnership and turn it into twenty years of marriage.

Claire glanced toward Luca, sure that he would be looking bored or annoyed, but he was watching her parents dance; a rapt, almost awed expression on his face. She remembered her mother didn't dance much anymore. As Natalia had gotten older, the injury caused by the car accident ached more and more, so seeing Natalia and Leon Beauchene dance together was something not everyone got to see.

From the stories they'd told her, Claire knew Natalia and Leon had met by chance in Paris when Natalia was seeking treatments for her leg injury. Leon had convinced her to try ballroom dancing as a way to strengthen the muscles in her leg. He'd apparently pestered her for days— much to her mother's annoyance—before she agreed to take a few lessons, but it wasn't long before Leon convinced her to compete with him.

No one had expected the small-time dancer from Paris and the former ballet star from Russia to win the Blackpool Dance Festival and become World Champions. But they did, and two more times after that before they retired in order to open their dance school.

A lump rose in Claire's throat. Life was so unfair; she should be dancing with Sebastian. Instead, she was stuck with Luca, one of the rudest people in the world. Claire shook herself out of her thoughts in time to see Natalia pushing herself away from Leon, stopping the dance.

"Enough, *moya lyubov'*," she said firmly. "I think they have the idea." Leon took her hand and kissed it gently.

"Of course, *mon coeur*, forgive me. When I have you in my arms, I am lost in the dance." Natalia yanked her hand away, her eyebrows coming together in a frown in an attempt to look irritated.

"You are a shameless flirt, husband," she scolded, her lips twitching upwards into a reluctant smile. She grabbed her cane from Zoya and limped back toward the office.

"Only with you, *mon amour de mon vie*," Leon called after her with a smile. Natalia paused, the doorknob in one hand, cane in the other and Claire swore her mother's ears were bright pink.

"Shameless," Natalia repeated over her shoulder, before limping out and slamming the door behind her.

"Twenty years and she still does not believe the sweet words I say," Leon sighed dramatically as he turned back towards Mr. and Mrs. Hicks. "But I persevere, just as we must with our dance. So," he clapped his hands together eagerly. "Shall we try again? Perhaps my daughter and her new partner can assist this time."

"We're not partners, Papa, we never agreed to anything," Claire protested, folding her arms across her chest.

"Then, at least, will you help your Papa with his lesson?" Leon asked. He continued to smile, but his eyes contained a word of warning. Claire knew what that meant. Leon might not have the lightning temper that Natalia did, but her father was still a force to be reckoned with. She sighed and reluctantly walked over to join him, Luca tagging behind her.

"Excellent! Now, please take your frame, we'll be working on our rise and fall to give your waltz the flow that it requires. My friends," he said, turning his attention to the Hicks, "you've been dancing at the beginning level, we'll start with our knees bent on the count of one, step for two, up on three and hold for four. *Chérie*, Luca, would you demonstrate?"

He looked meaningfully towards Claire and Luca, and after a moment, Luca held out his hand to Claire. She took it reluctantly, and was unexpectedly yanked forward with such force, she slammed into his chest, simultaneously knocking the air out of her lungs.

"*Hurk*," she gasped, her face buried in Luca's broad chest. He smelled of soap and spice, not at all the sophisticated cologne that Sebastian used. Behind her, she heard Sheryl giggle quietly.

Claire glared up at Luca. "You don't have to pull so hard," she snapped.

"Sorry," Luca said, not sorry at all. She felt like a delicate doll in his arms, her head fitting just under his chin. "I am just a Latin dancer, but I thought a person with your *experience* would know enough to keep a little tension in your arm."

"I did have tension in my arm! You're the one yanking me around like a neanderthal!" Claire retorted.

"All right, you two," Leon stepped forward and put a hand on Luca's shoulder. "How about we demonstrate the box step with the rise and fall?"

"Yes sir," said Luca, and stepped forward, inadvertently stepping on Claire's foot.

"OW!" She yelped. "That was totally on purpose!"

"It was an accident," Luca insisted. "If you had a little tension—"

"Oh yeah?" Claire snapped and stomped hard on Luca's foot. "How's this for tension?"

"*Ow*," Luca hissed. "What is wrong with you?"

"Enough, you two!" Leon's voice cracked like thunder across the room, uncharacteristically louder than usual. "We are professionals, are we not? Apologize, both of you."

"You first!" Claire scowled at Luca.

"For what?" Luca returned. "You're the one trying to impale my foot with your heels!"

"You're the one yanking me around and injuring me on 'accident'!" Claire made air quotes with her fingers.

Claire's ice blue eyes met Luca's defiant dark ones, the animosity between the two of them palpable. After several seconds, Claire pushed away from Luca and stomped towards the door. "You know what, you can show them how to do this box step without me, because I'm not dancing with you!"

"Believe me, the feeling is mutual," Luca snapped.

"Claire, *chérie*," Leon sighed as she opened the door. Claire turned back towards her father.

"I'm sorry Papa," Claire said quietly, "but I'd rather wait a year than dance with this… pig!"

And as Claire slammed the door behind her with a bang, it occurred to her that once again, Luca had emerged from their altercation with the upper hand. But at least he hadn't won unscathed.

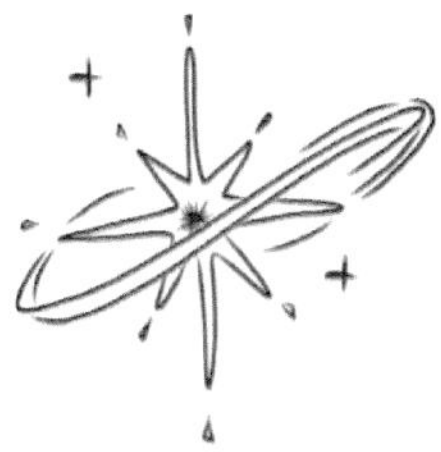

Chapter 3: Chaines

"French for 'chain', a series of quick turns along a straight line or circle."

Luca was still steaming when he got home.

"Crazy snob!" He muttered under his breath as he barged into his parents' old room, peeled out of his sweaty practice clothes and began to change into the slacks and polo shirt that was his work uniform. There was a nasty bruise forming on his foot where Claire had stomped on it, though thankfully it didn't hurt enough to impede his night shift at *Ragazzo's*.

Luca had gotten the job when he was sixteen and had gradually worked his way up from stockboy to bartender by the age of nineteen. His quick service and easy manner kept the tips flowing, even if the fees for competitions and costumes ate up any extra money he saved.

His boss, Chris Ragazzo, often said if it hadn't been for Luca constantly adjusting his schedule for dance, he would've been made manager years ago. It was at times like this, when Luca wondered why he didn't just quit dance, and focus on his steady, paying job. Things would be so much easier if he didn't have to practice so much, shell out money for competitions—and especially if he didn't have to deal with Claire. He could take classes at the community college, get a degree that would qualify him for a higher paying job, bring in more money for his family…

"*Mijo*, is that you?" A voice called from the kitchen. Luca gave his polo shirt one more adjustment and ran a hand through his dark curls.

"*Sí Abuela*," Lucca called, heading down the hall toward the living room. "I'm just getting ready for work."

The entire living area had been converted into Abuela's room almost five years ago when she had moved from her home in Argentina to the States, after the death of her husband, Hector. A recliner chair piled with blankets sat in the corner, while family pictures crowded every available surface in the room.

The kitchen, however, was her primary domain. Lina Martinez rarely left the kitchen, preferring to bustle around the stove in a brightly colored mumu, her gray hair piled high on her head, making her famous soups for people around the neighborhood. The sound of her beloved *telenovelas* blasted from the living room all day and all night, a comforting wall of noise Abuela worked and fell asleep to. Luca's father had complained at first, but Luca's mother had won him over eventually, saying her mother needed to be kept as comfortable as possible in her old age.

Two years later, Luca's parents had been driving home when their car was hit by a drunk driver. Abuela had suddenly, at the age of eighty, became the guardian of the

Ortiz boys, Luca and his younger brother Juan. Luca, who was in his junior year of high school at the time, had to start working to help Abuela keep a roof over their heads and food on the table. He'd been in the process of canceling his dance lessons when Leon Beauchene offered him the opportunity to continue with a dance scholarship. So long as he managed to juggle work and take care of Abuela and his younger brother, Luca could continue doing what he loved. But as the years went by, with more than a few sleepless nights, he began to wonder if his passion for dance was a worthwhile dream to hold onto.

"Luca?" Abuela looked up from a large pot she was stirring when he entered the kitchen. Her glasses were fogging up from the steam and she removed them, wiping them on the corner of her mumu. "I thought that was you," she said, standing on tiptoe to kiss his cheek. She switched to her native tongue, the words flowing easier than they did in English. "I have not seen you in two days, have you been working late?"

"I had to work early this morning before the competition and I'm starting another shift in half an hour," Luca replied in the same language. He spotted a stack of bills on the table and began to flip through them. The electric and water bills were due, as was the mortgage. Luca groaned. He'd spent almost two hundred dollars on some new dance shoes which meant he was short this month. He'd have to work a few double shifts next week to cover the rest of the bills and cursed himself for spending frivolously.

"You work too hard, and you're being stretched too thin."

"I'm fine, Abuela," Luca assured her, forcing a smile.

"Hmph." Abuela did not look convinced. "Try this soup I'm making for Elaina's family," she said, holding out the ladle. Elaina was a small, plump woman who lived next door with her husband Joe. Though she had her own two-year-old daughter to take care of, Elaina helped Abuela keep an eye on the youngest Ortiz brother when Luca was at work. "Her daughter Reina is sick, so I'm bringing them a batch of my mother's famous *locro*."

Luca obediently took a sip. The taste of corn, beef and pork, warmed his taste buds.

"You did not add as much paprika as you usually do," he observed.

"Reina is only a baby. She cannot handle spice the way her parents can. That is why I have made two batches." She indicated a large Tupperware already full of soup on the counter. "Would you be able to drop that off before work?"

"Of course," Luca's stomach rumbled. He hadn't had anything to eat since dawn.

"There is also more in the fridge," Abuela pointed. "Eat some before you go, you're too skinny."

"*Gracias,*" Luca went to the fridge, trying to ignore the newest photos on the off-white surface. Despite Luca making sure he'd gotten a haircut and was wearing a nice shirt for picture day, Juan glowered at the camera as if he was being photographed for a mug shot. Luca sighed. Ever since Luca had taken charge of the house, Juan had become surly and argumentative, staying out late, and only coming home to eat and occasionally shower.

"Luca?" Abuela was watching him with concern. "Is everything okay?"

"Fine, Abuela."

Luca grabbed the Tupperware and pried off the lid. Abuela handed him a bowl.

"Fill it all the way to the top," she scolded when Luca splashed a small portion of *locro* in the bowl. "I promised your mother, God rest her soul, I'd look after you, and you're fading away before my eyes."

"Abuela-"

"You are!" She insisted. "You work long hours, barely eat, barely sleep, I see you and think it's Day of the Dead, you're practically a ghost!"

"I got a video of my performance in the competition yesterday," Luca said, hoping to distract her. It worked. Abuela stopped, mid-lecture.

"Show me," she demanded, and Luca handed his phone to her. She held the screen close to her face and watched, rapt, the ladle forgotten in her hand until the end. "You are just like your Abuelo," she said, patting his cheek fondly as she handed the phone back. "That fire he had," Abuela indicated the large picture on the counter next to her. It featured Abuela and her husband in their early thirties, dressed in traditional dance costumes for a local dance festival. "*Tu chispa*, your spark is the same in your eyes when you dance."

"Yeah, well, I'm not sure how much longer I can keep it up," Luca ladled soup into his mouth. His whole body was aching from the competition, and he had to leave soon for an eight-hour shift at the bar.

"I know things are hard," Abuela laid a hand on his arm. "You have had to carry a lot on your shoulders to help take care of this family. But I have faith it will get better soon. You have the spark. You are meant to dance. Understand, Luca?" she asked. Luca shook his head.

"It's not just that," Luca let the spoon drop, his appetite lost. "I'm sick of being seen as a charity case. And since my partner dropped out to go to some European school, I either have to partner with the school snob or not compete at all." He sighed, rubbed at the headache that was starting to form between his eyes. "Maybe it's time to accept I should focus on other things."

"*Mijo*," Abuela stood on tiptoes to kiss the spot where the ache was concentrated. Like everything Abuela applied her special brand of magic too, Luca felt the tension immediately ease. "You worry just like your mama did. Always a choice between her dreams and her family. She loved to dance, remember? But she didn't believe she could make a good life for you and Juan as a dancer, so she got a job that would ensure you would. But let me tell you the same thing I told her." Abuela clasped Luca's hand in hers. "Do not give up your dreams. They are the things that make our lives worth living. One day you will shine like the star you are."

"Thanks, Abuela." Luca managed a smile and set his soup bowl on the counter, his appetite lost. His mother might have dreamed of being a dancer, but she worked long hours at a steady job to make sure he had food in his belly and a roof over his head. Maybe it was time he considered doing the same. "I should get to work."

"Before you go…" Abuela pulled a note out of her apron pocket. "We got a call about Juan yesterday while you were at work," Abuela said. "The principal said if Juan's grades don't improve, he'll have to take summer school." She handed him the note. "I took down the number so you could call him back."

Luca took the slip of paper. "He's failing his classes?"

Abuela nodded. "He's been skipping class for the past month and turning in homework that is either late or incomplete and always covered in—how do you say—" Abuela fumbled with the translation. "Those scribbles he likes to do, 'dooggles'."

"Doodles," Luca corrected her absentmindedly as he ran a hand through his hair. Juan had promised him the last time they'd talked that he'd work harder, but after only two months he'd fallen back on his old habits. Luca checked the clock. Juan wouldn't be out of school for another two hours, but Luca's shift started in twenty minutes.

"I'll have to have a talk with him before school tomorrow," Luca said. At that moment, the screen door banged, and Juan walked into the kitchen. He froze like a deer caught in headlights when he saw his older brother by the fridge. At sixteen, he was still going through his gawky phase, nearly three inches taller than his older brother and all elbows and knees. While Luca was all broad shoulders and graceful muscle, Juan was scrawny and uncoordinated. Dark, curly hair, which both brothers had inherited from their father, fell to Juan's shoulders and covered half his face.

Luca spoke first. "Hey," he said, switching back to English. While Juan could understand Spanish to a certain extent, he wasn't as fluent as his older brother.

"Yo," Juan stuck his hands in his pockets and bobbed his head in greeting. "Didn't know I'd see you today."

"Just about to leave for work." Luca took a step toward his younger brother. "Why aren't you at school?"

"Uh…" Juan cleared his throat. "It's not what you think, I asked to go home early because I wasn't feeling well."

"Oh, *pobrecito*," Abuela was immediately concerned. She laid a hand on his forehead. "Is it fever? Sore throat?"

"Yeah Juan," Luca faced his little brother, and for a second he felt like the sheriff in some old western movie, ready for a shootout. "Is it a fever? Sore throat?"

"Umm…" Juan fidgeted. "Sore throat."

"Really," Luca reached for his phone. "So, if I call the school, they're going to tell me you got a note from the nurse?"

"Umm, yeah, because I did," Juan's eyes darted, looking for an escape.

"Great, I'm just going to double-check, because I didn't get any calls that they were sending you home," Luca said, dialing. He held the phone up to his ear. "It's ringing… yes, hello, I'd like to speak to—"

"Wait!" Juan's shoulders slumped. "I lied, I just snuck out during lunch."

"—Chris," Luca finished. "Oh, he's in the back? No, it's okay, just tell him I'll be a little late to work. Yeah, got some stuff at home to deal with first." He flipped his phone closed and glared at Juan.

"*Juanito*," Abuela scolded. "You told us you weren't going to skip school anymore, you promised that you were going to do better, and *then* you come home and lie to our faces?"

"I was going to go back before the end of the day!" Juan protested.

"And how are we supposed to trust you if you've already broken your word?" Luca demanded.

For a second Luca heard the echo of his mother and father in his words and he desperately wished he was a young boy again and his parents were here instead. He glanced at the clock. He was going to be very late, and Chris was going to throw a fit.

"Come on, I'm going to take you back to school." He grabbed his car keys and headed for the door.

"Hey, we can't go back!" Juan protested. "I've got a test I didn't study for! Can't you tell them I'm home because I'm sick?"

"Yeah, I'm not covering for you just because you didn't study," Luca snapped. "Come on, we're going."

"Wait, wait!" Juan grabbed a battered duffle that was tucked behind a chair.

"What is that?" Luca demanded.

"Stuff," Juan slung the bag over one skinny shoulder, meeting his brother's eyes defiantly.

"For?"

"School project," Juan snapped.

Luca eyed Juan for a moment, then swung the door open, motioning for Juan to go first. "I'm late enough as it is, just get in the car."

"Whatever," Juan muttered, heading out the door.

"Wait! Eat some more soup first," Abuela held out his unfinished bowl. Luca shook his head.

"I'm not hungry." He picked up the Tupperware, kicking open the screen door with his foot. "I'll be back late. Don't wait up."

* * *

Luca had difficulty focusing as he went about his shift, mixing and serving drinks, collecting tips, and cleaning up after patrons. The bad mood that had started with being paired with Princess Claire, and ended with Juan's truancy, compounded into a nasty headache that pounded at his temples. Not getting enough sleep probably didn't help the issue, he decided, and wished he'd had time to grab a nap.

Ragazzo's was an unpretentious bar that had started out as an Italian restaurant back when the owner, Chris Ragazzo, was still optimistic about opening up his own business. Unfortunately for him, the food he produced from the kitchen was barely edible, and since he'd decided to open smack in the middle of a local motorcycle gang's territory, the bar was trashed within a week from bar fights.

If it hadn't been for the bar and pool table, Chris would've had to close shop within a year, but local patronage for pool games and booze kept the doors open. So, after a little reevaluation, Chris bought some heavier, studier tables, a dart board, and a second pool table to keep the customers from getting bored.

"You gotta be flexible with life, kid," he'd said to Luca that night while they were restocking shelves. He was a stocky man who kept his wispy brown hair short and a piece of nicotine gum constantly between his teeth. "Try and be stubborn and you're usually going to end up on your ass." He'd then gone on to lecture Luca again on how much more he could make if he gave up this dancing business and worked for him full-time. "I mean, what's the point, kid?" he'd asked Luca with a wave of his stubby hand. "So you get to hang out with rich, dolled-up chicks and win a few fancy trophies, there's not much of a financial reward to this gig, is there? Seems like it's more of the opposite."

Chris had a point, Luca thought despondently, as he polished glasses and stacked them under the bar.

"Hey kid, I'm heading home," Chris ambled towards the door, smelling lightly of beer. "Don't forget to lock up, I'll see you tomorrow."

Luca finished wiping down the counter and grabbed a broom, sweeping the pretzel and chip crumbs out from behind the bar. *Ragazzo's* seemed much bigger without the well-imbibed patrons filling up the tables and bar stools.

Luca usually liked the peace and quiet after a shift. Tonight, however, he felt restless. On a whim, he turned on the beat-up jukebox for a little music as he wiped down tables.

The catchy song made him move to the rhythm, his hips dipping and rolling to the beat.

One last dance before I quit, he told himself, pushing some tables back to make room for himself. The music pulsed and swelled around him, inspiring him to traverse across the room in a series of *chaines,* his work shoes squeaking slightly on the stained floor as he spun across the bar, throwing out his arms as he hit the far wall and executing a body roll. Luca spun back to the center of the room and snapped the damp rag in his hand like a matador, the sharp crack accenting the rhythm of the music. He turned, this time going down and spinning on his knees, then coming up into a pencil turn, spinning in place with his arms over his head.

Luca stopped when he caught a glimpse of himself in the mirror behind the bar, a lone figure standing tall and strong in the dim light.

"You have the spark, you were meant to dance," his abuela had said, and in his mind's eye he saw another figure—his abuelo—tall, dark, and dashing, his salt-and-pepper mustache perfectly waxed and wearing a glittering jacket. He danced with a fiery passion that seemed to command the attention of everyone around him, and in his eyes burned a light that was brighter than a thousand fires.

There is no future in dancing, he reminded himself, but the figure in his memory would not be deterred. This time Abuelo was joined by his abuela—younger, healthier, her grey hair in a stately bun as she snapped the skirt of her glittering costume. They danced together, so perfectly in sync with each other that they moved as one unit of glittering, swirling color.

"Tu chispa, your spark, is the same in your eyes when you dance," his abuela's voice echoed in his head.

Now Luca could see his mother joining the dance, wearing the red dress she only took out for special occasions, her long dark hair flowing to her waist as she spun around the room with his papa.

"Do not give up your dreams. They are the things that make our lives worth living."

"Stop!" Luca waved the damp rag as if to banish the dancing specters from his mind. "I'm done dancing!"

Furious with himself, Luca went to the jukebox, shutting off the music and plunging the room into silence. He had a family to look after. A younger brother who needed supervision to make sure he finished school. There was no time for dreams.

"I am done dancing," Luca repeated, taking the damp rag and scrubbing the tables with a feverish intensity.

The quiet was oppressive now as he moved around, stacking chairs on tables, turning off the lights that lit up the string of beer cans that Chris had hung around the pool table area. It was so still Luca could hear the beat of his heart in his ears in the deafening silence. *Ba-baum, ba- baum, ba-baum!* Couldn't he escape from the sound of music? *Ba-baum, ba-baum, ba baum!* Annoyed, Luca cracked the wet rag in his hand. *Ba-baum, ba-baum, ba-baum CRACK!* He did it again. *Ba-baum, ba-baum, ba-baum CRACK!*

Luca grabbed a broom, chasing after crumbs in every nook and cranny of *Ragazzo's*. *Ba- baum, ba-baum, brush.* He tried to go faster. *Brush, brush, brush, brush,* he was still following the rhythm of his heart.

Luca reached for a dirty paper napkin and as he turned away it suddenly became a pencil turn, then a lunge, a turn on his knees, and he was rising up again, cracking the wet rag twice. *Crack! Crack!*

A *chaine* somehow moved him in the direction of the jukebox to turn the music back on, and then he was whirling across the floor again, executing spins, lunges, body rolls, and shimmies.

In that moment, the only thing that mattered was the music, the rhythm that seemed to pulse through every fiber of his being, as much a part of him as his own heartbeat.

The last strains of the song faded away, and Luca was left, standing in the middle of the empty bar, chest heaving, and sweat running into his eyes.

"Damn it!" He slammed his fist down on the table. He could still feel his heart hammering in his chest, the rush from the intensity of the dance. It wasn't logical, and yet, that feeling, that need to keep dancing…

Luca closed his eyes. He could still see the people applauding, feel the rush from performing before a cheering crowd. He would work, day and night if he had to, practice until he dropped, dance with Princess Claire if it meant he could keep going, compete with the best dancers in the world at the Blackpool Dance Festival. He just had to convince Claire to accept him as a partner.

Piece of cake.

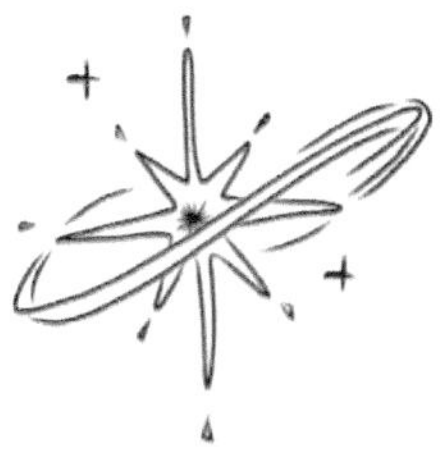

Chapter 4: Chase

"A figure where one partner pursues the other. A visual 'what-you-see-is-what-you-do' lead is used for this figure."

Luca found Claire in one of the practice rooms of the dance studio the next day after work. The classroom was considered one of the smaller ones, and yet it was still bigger than Luca's living room. Mirrors lined two walls, while the third was a full-length window, looking out onto the street below.

"He's so frustrating!" Luca could hear Claire complaining on her phone. "He was yanking me all over the floor, and when I complained, he said it was an accident!" She paced the small classroom in her heels, graceful in a leotard and practice skirt. One manicured hand flicked the heavy braid over her shoulder in a sharp, impatient movement. "No, I don't want to dance with him, but he's the only one that's available! And if I don't partner with him, I have to wait a whole year to compete! A year Seb! It completely throws off the timeline I had in place!"

Luca paused outside the classroom. On one hand, he hadn't meant to eavesdrop. On the other hand, Claire was talking quite loudly, and anyone passing by could hear. Students milled around him in the hallway, going to and from classes, carrying gym bags stuffed with their shoes, practice skirts, and tights. They chattered in small groups, a rainbow of different ages, races, and experience.

"Look, are you sure you can't—" Claire leaned against the wall, her back to the door, listening to Sebastian's voice on the other end. "I'm glad you're having fun but your timing was…I know we went out on a good note but…" She sighed, and Luca heard the resignation in her voice. "You're right. Of course, I'll vote for you in next week's performance, I can't wait to see you," Claire continued. "And I already made an announcement for everyone here to watch and support you. It's not every day someone from our school makes it on a television show." Claire sighed again. "I understand, I'll talk to you later. I lov—" she stopped, biting off the last word. Sebastian had already hung up. "Good-bye," she muttered, staring at the blank screen.

Luca waited a moment for Claire to put her phone away and begin her practice so it wouldn't seem like he'd been eavesdropping. In spite of his consideration, she still stopped in the middle of a turn and glared at Luca when he stepped into the room.

"Keep away," Claire ordered. "I still haven't recovered completely from you stomping on my toes."

Luca didn't move. "I've got a bruise from you trying to impale my foot with your heel. Do you suppose that makes us even?"

Claire opened her mouth to respond, then closed it. "What do you want?" she finally demanded. "I told you, I'd rather wait a year than dance with a pig like you."

"And while being rejected by someone of your considerable charm is heartbreaking," Luca replied, sarcasm dripping from his words. "Neither of us have the luxury of choosing anyone else."

Claire blinked, surprise in her ice-blue eyes. "Are you saying you want to dance with me?" she asked. Luca cocked his head, considering.

"No," he said after a moment. "If I had to choose between dancing with a burro on hind legs or you, I would probably go with the burro." Luca bit the inside of his cheek to keep from smiling as Claire Beauchene's pretty face turned pink with anger.

"Why…you…" she sputtered.

It was petty, he chided himself, and beneath him; the amount of satisfaction he got from irritating Claire. Luca restrained himself from needling her further. Like it or not, he needed her, and she needed him if they wanted to compete at an international level.

"However," he continued, "since I do not have the option of the burro, you will have to do."

"Am I supposed to be flattered?" Claire retorted. "You're still a pig. Oh, wait, that's an insult to all pigs." Luca caught a whiff of her scent when she turned away from him and began to practice a series of turns in the mirror, her perfume something that was both flowery and exotic at the same time.

"There is no rule that we have to like each other," he pointed out. "We just have to dance together." When Claire didn't respond, he persisted. "Are you really going to let your dislike for me keep you from competing for an International Championship Title?"

"I'm not giving up," Claire raised one arm and began to incorporate flowy arm extensions into the turns, her hand and wrist going out, then in, the indignation practically radiating from her. "I'm just putting it off for a little while. Sebastian said he'd dance with me next year if he doesn't get a job out of *Dance Craze.*"

"If?" Luca grasped the word. "If he doesn't get a job out of *Dance Craze?* So you might be waiting another year for nothing. He left you two months before the biggest competition of your life but he might be available next year if you wait for him? What makes you think he won't do it again? What happens if he abandons you and never comes back?"

Temper flared in Claire's eyes. "Hey! You can't talk about my boyfriend like that!" Claire jabbed a manicured finger into Luca's chest. "He had to work very hard to get onto that show and the fact that he had to drop our plans to compete in Blackpool is just…very bad timing," she finished weakly. "But it's going to be great for his career!" Claire insisted. "And he's going to come back and we'll compete together next year!" Luca gave her a look like she was a small, naïve, child.

"Look, you don't get it!" Claire burst out. "Sebastian and I were training for five years together, this was our dream!"

"Clearly," Luca raised an eyebrow. "Considering how fast he dropped you and left for Los Angeles. Are you putting your dreams on hold for him out of loyalty, or…" Luca let the sentence trail off.

"Because…" Claire faltered, thinking of what Sebastian had said to her before he left. To her horror she felt tears well up in her eyes. She bit her lip hard, forcing the tears away. There was no way she was crying in front of Luca, of all people. She'd die of embarrassment first.

"Look, be as skeptical as you want," Claire said, jabbing him again. "Even if I wanted to team up with you, you're nowhere near his level. I bet you don't even know how to waltz! We'd lose before we even got a shot at the championship award!"

Something very dangerous flared in Luca's eyes for a second, and Claire felt like she had suddenly awakened a tiger. Then just as quickly it was gone, and Luca's eyes were dark and unfathomable as usual.

"Tell you what," he said coolly. "We'll have a little contest. If I can impress you with what I know, you'll stop stalling and agree to be my partner."

"And if you don't impress me?" Claire asked cautiously. Luca shrugged.

"I'll stop asking. You can put off Blackpool as long as you like, waiting around until Prince Charming gets back."

"He's coming back," Claire insisted.

Luca shrugged again. "Believe what you want. But at least if I can meet your *standards,*" he said the last word with only the barest trace of scorn, "you won't have to wait as long."

The idea of being able to compete in two months instead of fourteen was appealing. And if Luca didn't meet Claire's standards, all she had to do was say she wasn't impressed and she would never have to deal with him again.

"Fine," she nodded. "It's a deal."

Luca walked over to the stereo system on the shelf and flipped through the options until he found the song he was looking for. The intro to a light, airy piece floated out of the speakers, violins and flutes playing a lilting melody. Claire frowned when she recognized the piece.

"You're playing the song I chose for Sebastian's and my solo."

"Yes," Luca nodded.

"Don't tell me you learned the choreography and plan to use it to impress me," Claire scoffed.

"Impress you? No. Convince you that our partnership deserves a shot…well," Luca shrugged. "That's up to you, isn't it?" Walking to the center of the room, Luca stood and held his hand to Claire. "What are you waiting for?"

Reluctantly, Claire crossed to join him, placing her delicate, manicured hand in his large, rough one and putting her other hand on his bicep, fingers just below his shoulder. Luca's other hand went to the spot just under her shoulder blade, cradling her in his frame as he held her close. For someone who'd probably never heard of moisturizer, he was surprisingly gentle, Claire thought to herself, then almost lost her breath when Luca suddenly pushed off, quickly moving through a series of advanced rotations and turns. His frame was solid, and the tension between them was so perfectly balanced that Claire found herself effortlessly whisked around the floor before she had time to be surprised. The music flowed around them while they spun and pivoted, with only the unspoken language of dance between them. Luca led Claire through hesitations, promenades, and reverse turns, their feet seeming to barely touch the ground.

This was not good, Claire thought as Luca gently but firmly sent them both spinning again like a pair of synchronized tops. She had known Luca was good, but not *this* good. Even Sebastian had had some trouble leading her when they first partnered up. But Luca… Claire felt like she'd been dancing with Luca all her life. And it seemed like the lightest touch between them was all that was needed to tell the other what they would do next.

When they came out of a double spin, Luca led Claire through a series of pivots, then easily lifted her in his arms, spinning them around effortlessly across the room. Claire stretched one arm out as she spun, her practice skirt swirling around her legs. It felt like flying.

As the music ended, Luca gently set Claire down, twirling her one last time and finishing in a dip.

"Well," he asked, gently lifting her back up. "Did I pass the test?"

Claire held up a hand, catching her breath. She was suddenly aware that she was covered in sweat and exhausted. She hadn't realized the dance had taken that much out of her. Luca's hand felt like a brand on her back, sending tingles of warmth to the rest of her body.

"How… how did you do that?" she asked.

Luca shrugged again. "Practice." *For six hours*, he thought silently. Watching Claire's routine on his phone again and again, practicing again and again in the bar with the chairs and tables pushed back against the wall until the sun came up. "So," he repeated. "Did I pass the test?"

"Well, uh…" Claire stammered; it was hard for her to think when Luca's eyes were so close, it was as if he could see right through her. "I think…" What was she going to say? Right! That she wasn't impressed, then he would leave her alone. "I think we can make this work," she heard herself saying out loud.

"Good," Luca said, and for a second Claire saw his lips twitch upwards in a slight smile. "Now that we have covered Waltz for the day, perhaps we should move on to Salsa."

He released his hold on Claire and moved back over towards the stereo, turning on something that was definitely more Latin in rhythm. Claire felt the first strains of panic when Luca moved back towards her and took her hand.

"Umm, I did not get the memo I was supposed to memorize your routine…" Claire started, feeling a little nervous. "If we could meet tomorrow—"

Luca smiled a little wider and this time Claire could've sworn there was a mischievous glint in his eyes. "I'll walk you through it." He pulled Claire close, holding her right hand in his left, and adjusted her arms so her forearm brushed against his. "Now, unlike your waltz routine, which needs to be light and airy to match your fairy characters, I need you to dredge up your fiery and passionate side for this salsa. This dance is supposed to be full of power and passion. A constant battle of dominance between the man and the woman."

"Not really my forte," Claire felt the beginning of nerves twist in her stomach. "Can't we just meet up tomorrow after I've learned the routine?"

"We only have two months to practice," Luca reminded her. "Time is precious."

"You learned mine in advance," Claire pouted.

"I was trying to prove a point."

"But—"

"Claire!" Luca cut her off, mid-protest. "You're a talented dancer. You'll be fine, just…pay attention." Claire gaped up at Luca, looking for signs he was joking. But Luca's eyes, usually full of scorn, were completely serious and sincere. A tingle of electricity ran down her spine.

"That's the nicest thing you've ever said to me," she managed.

"Well don't get used to it," Luca sighed. "We've got a lot of work to do."

Maybe it was the light in the studio, maybe it was hearing an actual compliment fall from his lips, but Luca seemed different. Now that Claire wasn't as focused on his scowl, she saw dark circles under his eyes, caught the whiff of espresso as he stifled a yawn. And now that she was looking for it, she could see a seasoned weariness, the kind that came from someone used to very little sleep. She'd seen the same look in Bianca after working long weeks at the hospital. The determination to remain upright, even when the body is running on fumes. How long had it taken him to learn the choreography? *Did he?* … Claire's heart skipped a beat. *Want to dance at Blackpool just as much as she did?*

"Shall we?" Luca asked, and Claire gulped, shaking the insane thoughts out of her head. This was *Luca* she was thinking about. Sarcastic, condescending, and insulting Luca, who never had a nice thing to say about anyone and always practiced by himself. He might have surprising depths as a dancer, but he probably scared small children in his spare time when walking down the street.

"Hey, are you listening?" Luca asked, giving her hand a little squeeze. Claire felt another quick tingle run down her arm. Not children, Claire told herself, he scared puppies. Luca was a pretty face with impressive dance skills that scared puppies every day. "We'll start off easy, and do the whole combo at half speed, starting with a triple turn to the left."

Luca's scent, a mix of spicy musk that she couldn't quite place and sweat wafted toward Claire as Luca adjusted his frame. What was it? Cinnamon? Nutmeg? Why did he have to smell so nice? "Puppies," Claire muttered.

"Claire!" Luca snapped.

"What?" Claire blinked. "I'm listening!"

"Clearly," Luca sighed.

Focus, Claire chided herself, she was a professional. "No, really, I'm ready. Half-speed, starting with the triple spin to the right."

"Left," Luca corrected her, "I said left."

"Left," Claire repeated, switching her weight back and forth a few times to loosen her hips. "Got it, I'm ready."

Luca rolled his eyes and took a deep breath. "You better be. Alright then, here we go."

* * *

"Let's take a break," Luca finally said. "Grab some water, we start again in five."

"Great," Claire gasped, staggering to the shelf where she kept her water bottle. Her leotard was soaked with sweat and wisps of hair had escaped her braid and clung to her face. Uncapping her bottle, Claire guzzled greedily, sliding down the wall into a sitting position.

She rarely felt this tired; years of training had built up her stamina but Luca's routine pushed beyond the limits of even her energy reserves. The cool, wooden surface of the dance floor had never felt so good to her in her life.

From his place by the stereo, Luca glanced covertly in Claire's direction. He'd never admit it, but he was secretly impressed by how long she'd held out. He'd pushed them both hard today, and Claire had danced continuously, without a word of complaint. A point in her favor, Luca acknowledged reluctantly.

"I didn't think I'd be so rusty," Claire spoke up. She put down her water bottle and started re-braiding her hair, loosening the tangle of gold strands wound together with deft fingers. "I help Papa teach basic Salsa to the beginning students, but it's been a while since I've had to do any advanced moves."

"Why not?" Luca asked.

Claire shrugged, starting to separate the curtain of hair into separate strands. "Sebastian always said it was best to specialize, and early in our partnership we decided we liked the more classical dance styles. And with all the competitions we've had to prepare for, there wasn't time for anything else."

"I see." The simple explanation was logical. Maybe that was why it bothered Luca so much, he decided, unscrewing his water bottle. "He's not wrong, there are a lot of dancers who choose to focus on one style of dance over the course of their career..." He paused.

Claire waited for a beat. "But?"

"But…you can also gain a lot of insight and experience from practicing different styles as well as finding the similarities and differences," Luca pointed out. "Not to mention, it's fun. Right now, we're still young enough to experiment and learn, we don't need to specialize."

Claire shook her head. "I'm not that young. In dance years I'm practically middle-aged. I can probably compete for another ten years, but once I hit thirty, I'll be ancient. That's why it's so important to compete in Blackpool now, I don't have time to waste. Once I've made a name for myself as a dancer, then I can relax a little and take it easy."

"And here I thought I'd been partnered with a nice young lady," Luca joked. "Are those highlights or grey hairs?"

Claire scowled. "That's not funny."

"What's funny is your Cuban motion," Luca continued, "I thought your hips were stiff because you're not used to moving them, but maybe you just have arthritis."

"Seriously," Claire's mouth twitched, "stop it."

"Or what, you're going to chase after me with your cane, Grandma?"

Something that was a mix between a laugh and a snort shot out of Claire's nose before she could stop it and her mouth quirked up slightly. "You're such a jerk."

"Well you're…" Luca opened his mouth for another insult and felt it dry up on his tongue. She was smiling at him, just a little, the smile carrying up to her eyes, wrinkling them in the corners. The sun hit Claire's hair, turning it into a rope of pure gold as it fell over one shoulder. "You're not that old, so you should try and make time for fun," he managed to say.

Claire finished her braid and tossed it over one shoulder. "Solid advice and two hours with minimal insults. Who are you and what have you done with Luca Ortiz?"

Luca took a gulp of water and wished he had ten gallons more. "Maybe I don't have the energy for it today."

"Well it's making you much more tolerable," Claire said, her smile widening.

He wished she would stop looking at him like that. Luca could handle Claire's scorn and condescension, heck, he'd dealt with it for more than two years. But that little smile was creating a warmth in his chest he wasn't completely comfortable with.

"We should get back to work," Luca said, fumbling to replace the cap on his water bottle.

Claire sighed but she got to her feet without complaint. Another point in her favor, Luca thought unwillingly. "We should work on the last part of the solo a few more times," Luca decided, leading Claire to the center of the floor. "It's still not perfect yet. Remember, triple-turn, dip, around the world, open break—"

"Chase, shimmy, shimmy. I know," Claire rolled her eyes.

Luca bit off the retort that sprang to the tip of his tongue. At least the smile was gone, it made it easier to focus. "Good, then I won't have to remind you during the dance."

He went to turn on the music and jogged back just as the first strains of the now familiar melody bounced out of the speakers. He reached her three seconds before their cue, pulling her in for the start of the routine. Claire caught herself with one hand on Luca's chest and they body-rolled together, torso, then hips briefly brushing against each other once, twice, before Luca grabbed both of her hands, spinning her twice before enfolding her in an embrace.

Claire was briefly aware of his warmth, feeling the damp places where sweat had soaked through his tank top, before he spun her out again.

Chase turn, shimmy, shimmy, Claire forced herself to keep track of the steps, her limbs aching from exertion. She was fighting years of practicing Smooth dancing and had to constantly remind herself to lead each step with her toe, not her heel. Lean her weight *forward* into the Cuban motion instead of backwards into Luca's frame. Where was the place where she kept messing up? There! Luca pulled

Claire in for a triple-spin, and as he did, she caught the sight of someone watching from the door. She crashed into Luca harder than she meant to, overbalancing and knocking them both onto the floor.

"*Merde*," Claire found herself splayed on top of Luca, her face buried in his broad chest. Somehow his arms had come up around her, protecting Claire from hitting the hard wooden surface.

"Well, this is cute," Bethany said, eyeing them both with a wicked grin. "You do know these rooms are for practicing *dance*, right?"

"It's not what it looks like," Claire protested, trying to extricate herself from his embrace. "He doesn't have a partner either and—and—"

"Oww!" Luca grunted as the heel of her hand dug into his solar plexus. "Careful!"

"Hey, no judgment here, girl," Bethany said calmly, "your man is gone, no reason why you can't add some spice to your diet."

"That's not what's happening!" Claire's ears flushed bright pink as she staggered to her feet. "We were just working on our routines!"

"I don't know," Bethany said, holding up her phone. Claire felt her stomach clench at the picture of herself on top of Luca, his arms around her. "You two look awfully cozy together. If I didn't know any better, I'd say you make a cute couple."

"We're not a couple, we're not even friends," Claire said desperately. "We don't even like each other, we just need someone to dance with for the competition in

Blackpool." She turned to where Luca was still lying on the floor. "Tell her, that we're not even…" and faltered, at the flash of emotion that crossed Luca's face for a moment. Was that…hurt? But then it was gone and Luca's lips curled slightly into a familiar smirk.

"Right," Luca agreed. "We just need each other for the competition."

"All right, if you say so," Bethany shrugged. "I'll see you guys around. But for the record, I wouldn't blame you if you decided to test the waters, you guys look good together." And with that, she strolled out of the practice room.

"Great, now she's probably going to tell as many people as she can what she saw," Claire groaned.

"I wouldn't be too worried," Luca said, pulling the practice door closed. Just to be safe, he locked it to prevent anyone else from strolling back in. "It'll feed the rumor mill for a few days but anyone who knows you won't believe her."

"She's got pictures for proof! Why didn't I grab her phone when I had the chance?" Claire groaned as he turned away from the door. "I'm probably going to spend the next week explaining myself against whatever rumors she cooks up." Another thought struck her. "What if she posts those pictures on social media? What if Sebastian sees them and thinks I'm cheating on him?" Claire began to pace back and forth across the floor. "I should call him and explain everything before he sees them. No, better, I should go see him in person."

"Los Angeles is a couple hours' drive from San Diego, are you really going all that way to explain yourself to him?"

"It's not that bad," Claire dismissed Luca with a wave of her hand. "I can drive down on Saturday; Papa will get someone to cover my dance classes for the day, and I'll be back Sunday. Plus, I'm sure Sebastian misses me as much as I miss him, it'll be a good opportunity to reconnect." She eyed Luca who was calmly drinking from his water bottle. "Why aren't you freaking out?"

Luca shrugged. "What Bethany says about me isn't as important. I'm already the poor scholarship student, it can't get any worse."

Claire's heart twisted a little in guilt. A few days ago, she'd been one of the people joining in on the gossip. "Luca…" she started to say.

"Hey, it's fine," Luca said. "You're worried about your reputation, do what you can do to make it right. If we end our session early, you can start prepping for your trip."

"Thank you," Claire gathered her bag and headed for the door. She paused as she unlocked it. "Are you sure you're okay?"

"Fine," Luca was already going over the routine in the mirror. "Enjoy your weekend."

"I'll make sure everyone knows neither of us did anything wrong."

"Claire." Luca gave her an exasperated look over one shoulder. "I genuinely don't care what she thinks of me. I'll be fine. Go."

"Okay…" Claire didn't like the feeling that was solidifying in her chest like a heavy stone. But she forced herself to put one foot in front of the other until she was out the door. The last thing she saw before she left was Luca practicing in front of the mirror with fierce intensity. As if it was the only thing that mattered.

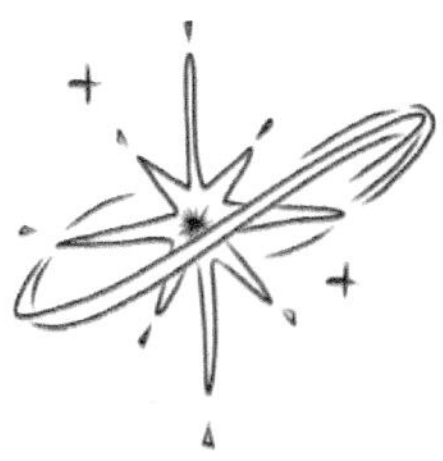

Chapter 5: Conga Line

"The conga line is a novelty line dance that was derived from the Cuban carnival dance. The dancers form a long, processing line, which would usually turn into a circle."

Luca arrived promptly at 8:15 on Saturday morning to substitute for Claire's dance class. Leon was hanging up announcements outside the classrooms, but he stopped and beamed when he saw Luca.

"Bonjour, mon ami," he said joyfully. "How are you this *magnifique* day?"

"Bon-jerrr, Mr. Beauchene," Luca replied and Leon had to shake his head at the mangling of his mother tongue.

"Bonjour, mon ami, bon-jour," he corrected Luca gently, "Your pronunciation is as terrible as your grasp of dance is exceptional." Luca looked down at his shoes.

"I'm okay," he muttered, pleased nonetheless. "I'm still working on the techniques you were helping me with last week." Leon nodded in approval.

"There will always be techniques that can be improved, no matter how much experience you get. Even I am learning new things every day! Last week, a friend of mine taught me a rain dance he learned while at a reservation in Arizona! I won't try it now because I am enjoying this winter chill, but in the summer, who knows?"

"Anyway, thanks for calling me in today, Mr. Beauchene," Luca said, changing the subject.

"No, thank you," Leon said, clapping Luca heartily on the shoulder. "You know how I appreciate your help," Leon said, returning to his task of hanging flyers. "And you are especially popular with the children."

Luca shrugged. "I'm just teaching them basic steps."

"Yes, but how you teach them is important. You break it down and make it easy for them to understand and follow, which is not something that our seasoned students can do as well as you do." He glanced at Luca out of the corner of his eye. "You know the job offer is still available if you want it." Luca stiffened slightly.

"Sir, you've been very kind, but I don't need any extra work, I'm doing fine."

"It's not charity," Leon frowned, his voice rising slightly in irritation. "I wouldn't offer you a position if I didn't think you deserved it."

"I just haven't really made a name for myself yet," Luca explained, "Maybe if I win Blackpool, I would be more qualified—"

"Luca," Leon interrupted, exasperated. "Whether you win ten, or a million competitions is irrelevant." He reached out a hand to Luca, then stopped himself at the last minute. "Your dedication, your *passion*, is something I wish for you to pass on in this school, not your success in competitions. I want you to teach *la joie de la danse*, not just to the younger students, but to everyone who walks through these doors."

Luca hesitated, tempted, then a wave of doubt washed over him and he shook his head. "I'm sorry," he said, "I don't think I'm ready yet."

Leon sighed, looking disappointed. "Well, perhaps you will change your mind soon. I can only keep the offer open for so long." He gathered up the last pile of flyers and nodded to Luca. "Thank you again for filling in for Claire today. I'm sure the class will enjoy seeing you. Speaking of which, I see one of your students now."

Luca had barely enough time to register the pitter-pat of tiny shoes when a ball of energy suddenly crashed into his leg, making him stagger slightly. Viviane Murphy, an enthusiastic five-year-old with honey-blonde hair clung to his knee like a burr.

"S'nortiz! S'nortiz!" she squealed, beaming like the sun, "are you my teacher today?"

"*Sí*, Viviane, I am," Luca said, bending down to gently detach her. "Do you remember what '*sí*' means?"

"It's when you look," Viviane said proudly and Luca couldn't help but smile.

"It does," he agreed, "but in Spanish, it means 'yes,' as well."Viviane crinkled her tiny forehead in confusion.

"How can it mean 'yes' *and* 'look'?" she asked curiously.

"Because *Señor* Ortiz is Mexican and in Mexico they speak Spanish, which is a different language, sweetie," said her mother, catching up to her daughter. A tall, busty, real-estate agent, Kathy Murphy shared her daughter's brown eyes, but her hair was the highlighted and styled blonde of a quality salon.

Luca treated her with one of his best professional smiles. "I am American, Mrs. Murphy. But my mother was born in Argentina and my father in Mexico."

"Ah," Kathy said, pulling out her phone when it buzzed. "But the language is pretty much the same, right?" Luca tilted his head in a half-agreement.

"There are similarities, but there are also parts of the language that are vastly different," he finally said.

"Oh. I guess it all sounds the same to me," Kathy said, her fingers flying over the tiny keyboard. She put down her phone long enough to give Viviane a kiss. "All right, baby girl, be good, I'll be back for you in an hour."

"Bye Mommy!" Viviane shouted, waving tiny fingers at her mom's retreating back. Kathy was already talking on her phone and gave only a distracted wave, weaving through the incoming parents and kids arriving for the morning class.

Children between the ages of three and five—mostly girls—clung to their parent's hands, wearing colorful leotards and tights, their practice shoes in small backpacks or already on their feet. They chattered between their parents and new friends, the talk and laughter mingling into an indistinguishable wall of sound. Luca welcomed them all into the class, leading the children toward the dance floor while the parents took their seats along the walls. Once everyone was inside Luca closed the door and took his place at the front of the room.

"*Buenos Días clase*," Luca said, and a smattering of students responded.

"*Bue-nos días* S'nor Ortiz," they said, fumbling over the Spanish pronunciation of his name.

Luca cupped a hand to his ear, frowning slightly. "I'm sorry, what was that? I couldn't hear you." Luca pretended to stagger back, holding his ears as every kid screamed at the top of their lungs: "*BUENOS DÍAS* S'NOR ORTIZ!!"

"Ah, *bueno*," Luca said, rubbing his ears and wincing. The kids and a few of parents smiled and chuckled. "Now, why are we speaking in Spanish?" He answered his own question before they could respond. "Because today, we are working on the *merengue*! A dance that originated in the Dominican Republic, where they *also* speak Spanish, just like *Señor* Ortiz," he said, pointing at himself. "All right, who wants to tell me what they know about the merengue? Raise your hand if you know the answer!" he added hastily, and fifteen hands shot up. He picked a young redhead named Kyle at random.

"Umm, it's like butter, but it's not?"

"Not quite, Kyle," Luca said, smiling. He chose a blond-haired girl named Kelty.

"So, um, my mom makes really good pies and some are really, really good, like apple, and cherry, but then there are some that are yucky, like pumpkin pie, because it looks like cat food in the crust—"

"Good Kelty," said Luca, trying to get her to the point. "And how is that related to this dance?"

"Well, she's got a yellow lemon pie that I think is called the merengue…" Kelty said, playing shyly with her braids.

"That's meringue, sweetie," Kelty's mom called from her seat. "I don't think it's what *Señior* Ortiz is talking about."

"No, but it sounds similar, doesn't it?" Luca said gently, before Kelty could feel embarrassed. He began walking in place, lifting his knees waist high. "What am I doing right now?"

He picked another blonde girl named Alexandra who raised her hand.

"Walking?" she asked hesitantly. Luca shook his head.

"No, but close." He moved around in a circle. "How about this. It's something that soldiers do."

"Marching?" asked Viviane.

"*Bueno*! Good, Viviane, I am marching. The merengue is a marching dance. Can everyone march with Señor Ortiz?"

One by one the young boys and girls began to lift up their little knees and march in place with Luca.

"*Excellente*! Keep marching!" Luca said encouragingly. He crossed to the stereo and turned it on, filling the room with a fast-paced, bouncing melody. He went back to the front of the room, lifting his knees in time with the music and clapping his hands.

"March, march, march! *Bueno*! Keep going, move around the room!" he yelled over the music. Luca joined three kids together, putting their arms on each other's shoulders so they formed a conga line and pulled the leader gently along by her hands. "All right *clase*, join the choo-choo train! Keep marching!"

Excitedly, the rest of the class ran to join the marching train, putting their hands on the shoulders of the student in front of them.

"Parents! Come join in!" Luca yelled, waving to the parents sitting on the sidelines. A few, encouraged by their children, got to their feet and joined the train of laughing kids while Luca guided the whole line around the room, letting it curl and coil like a snake, everyone following behind, marching to the beat of the music.

When the song ended, Luca stopped the train, clapping loudly, and the students reluctantly let go of the person in front of them.

"*Excellente! Magnifico*! You have learned the basic step for the merengue, well done!" Parents joined in the applause, smiling proudly at their progeny, who, slightly baffled, began clapping their tiny hands with everyone else. "As you can see, the merengue is a very simple dance to learn, and it can be a lot of fun at parties. Now, we are going to move on to something that is *still* a lot of fun but will require a partner. The under-arm turn! So pair up everyone, grab the person next to you and let's give it a try."

Luca began organizing the children into groups of two, unaware of Leon watching from the doorway, a smile of approval on his face.

* * *

Behind an abandoned apartment complex at the edge of town, Juan put down the spray can to admire his creation. Vivid reds, pinks, blues, greens, and yellows had turned the crumbling brick wall into a tropical forest. Flowers bloomed, birds flew across a half-finished sky, and animals were starting to take shape in the trees and shrubs. The mural had taken nearly a month to fill out, hours of work in the hot sun, his face covered with a mask to keep him from breathing in the fumes from the spray can.

Once it was finished, he'd leave it there for someone to find, and move on to find a new canvas. Word of his work would spread, slowly at first, then quicker as more and more murals were found in remote, abandoned places. He would be *Lejano*, a mysterious and unknown street artist who left his work in far, out-of-the-way places. People would wonder who he was, comb the city looking for his paintings, study and theorize about his process and inspiration. One day when his mystique had reached its peak, he would reveal his identity and accept the fame and accolades worthy of his talent. Juan grinned at the thought and checked his watch. He needed to get home before Luca returned from work, pretend as if he'd been sleeping most of the morning. Juan tucked the spray cans back into his duffle, along with his mask and gloves. He shucked off the paint-speckled shirt and bandana that protected his clothes and hair. He checked his watch again. He had about half an hour to get home. He'd better hurry.

* * *

The house was quiet when Juan came home, but he still eased open the screen door as carefully as possible, moving quietly as a cat as he toed off his shoes and crept toward his room, holding the duffle so it wouldn't make any noise. Like most Saturdays, Luca was occupied with work and dance and only came home for short intervals. Juan knew from experience he had twenty minutes to sneak back into his room before Luca came home to take a two-hour nap. He'd check on Juan, make sure he was doing his schoolwork before picking up his night shift at *Ragazzo's*. Juan was looking forward to climbing into bed and catching a few blissful hours himself before starting on homework when he heard a weak voice from the kitchen.

"*Mijo*? Is that you?"

Hiding his duffle behind an armchair, Juan detoured toward the kitchen. "*Sí*, Abuela, I just went out for a little exercise—"

He stopped in horror when he saw Abuela lying in a crumpled position on the floor, the stool she usually sat on knocked on its side some distance away. Her dress stank of urine—obviously, she had been there for some time. Abuela's eyes met his, and he saw both shame and embarrassment etched in her face before she looked away.

"Juan… I had… *un accidente…*"

Juan was already bending down beside her. "Abuela, what happened? What hurts the most? Does anything feel broken?" His grandmother shook her head.

"My hip hurts, but I do not think it is broken."

"Is there anything else that hurts?" Juan asked, struggling to find her pulse on her wrist. He frantically tried to remember the First Aid class he'd had to take for school. How was he supposed to count the beats again? Her hand was too cold, and her skin felt as delicate as paper. "What happened?"

"I…" Abuela hesitated. "I felt dizzy. Next thing I know, I am on the ground."

"It'll be okay, Abuela," Juan assured her. "I'll call 9-1-1 and someone will come and help."

"No," Abuela's voice gained a little of her strength. "We… can't afford it. Call your brother, he can take me to the hospital."

"Luca's at work, and he has the car."

"I… can wait… a little longer…" Abuela groaned.

"No, we can't, you need help," Juan protested. "Don't worry Abuela, I can take you."

Abuela gave him a skeptical look. "I can," Juan insisted. He bit his lip in frustration, pulled out his phone. "I'm going to call us an Uber."

"Wait," Abuela struggled to sit up, and Juan tried to help. "I need… to change… can't go like this."

"Okay," Juan strained to lift her up, wishing he had more muscle. He was going to start working out, he promised himself as he finally got Abuela on her feet. "Let me get you cleaned up, then I'll call someone to pick us up. The emergency room is only a few minutes away. I'll figure something out, Abuela, don't worry."

* * *

Juan held her hand all the way to the ER, only letting go to call his brother and tell him where they were. Luca arrived just as Dr. Reynolds, a wiry man with steel grey hair, was finishing his examination.

"Abuela?" Luca burst into the examination room of the doctor's office. He found her sitting quietly with Juan by her side and rushed to her. "Are you okay? How bad was your fall?"

"It is nothing, Luca," Abuela smiled faintly. "I was making *sopa* for Elaina and tripped."

"Abuela…" Luca sighed.

"*Mijo*," Abuela looked at him sternly. "I do not want to hear you telling me that I am old and need to look after myself."

"Your grandmother is in remarkably good health for her age, though I am concerned about dizzy spells," Dr. Reynolds said. He checked the medical information on his clipboard, frowned and turned to Luca and Juan. "I don't see any information from a previous visit, what hospital was Mrs. Martinez examined at for her last fall?"

"Last fall?" Luca echoed.

"Yes," Dr. Reynolds nodded, "Besides the new bruises Mrs. Martinez has on her hip and elbow, there are some older ones that are at least a week old on her knees and shoulder, that look like a previous accident."

Luca looked between his brother and grandmother. Juan looked completely blank, but Abuela was examining her hands on her lap with extreme interest.

"Abuela," Luca knelt and took her hands gently. "Did you have a fall last week and not tell me?"

Abuela bit her lip and avoided her grandson's eyes. "It was just a little *accidente*, I did not want to worry you. I got a little dizzy while cleaning Juan's room but I got right back up."

Dr. Reynolds frowned and flipped through his notes. "Regardless of how little you thought it was, you should have still come in for a check-up, Mrs. Martinez," he said. "If you're having dizzy spells, there is good reason to be concerned about possible future accidents."

"They are nothing," Abuela insisted. "*Mijo*, I don't need to be here, these doctor's visits are so expensive."

"Well, it's a good thing your grandson brought you in instead, Mrs. Martinez, because I am here to tell you those dizzy spells are not nothing," Dr. Reynolds corrected her. "If you don't take care of yourself, the next time you fall you could actually break something. It's a miracle you only have a few bruises. It's my professional opinion that you need to have someone nearby at all times to keep an eye on you." He checked the clipboard again. "Is there anyone else in the house? What about your grandson's parents? Could they help—"

"Our parents are dead," Luca cut him off. "It's just the three of us."

"Ah," Dr. Reynolds cleared his throat. "I'm sorry."

"I could watch her—" Juan started to speak.

"You need to focus on school and passing your classes," Luca reminded his younger brother. "I can take care of Abuela."

"No, your work, your dance, is also important, *mijo*."

"I can take more night shifts and stay with you during the day," Luca insisted. "As for dance, maybe—"

"No," Abuela's dark eyes blazed. "You are not giving up your gift. I can take care of myself if necessary."

"It would be beneficial if someone is there to help monitor your grandmother's fluid intake as well," Dr. Reynolds spoke up. "At her age she is more susceptible to kidney failure, urinary tract infections, kidney stones—"

"Maybe Elaina can keep an eye on you, Abuela?" Juan suggested.

"Yes, Elaina," Abuela's eyes lit with relief. "I will ask her to check up on me while you're at work. You don't need to worry about me, *mijo*."

Dr. Reynolds looked relieved. "Fantastic. Sounds like you've gotten it all worked out."

The door behind them opened and a young nurse poked her head in. "Excuse me, Dr. Reynolds? I have those information packets you were asking for."

"Yes, thank you, Joy." Dr. Reynolds said, stepping out of the way to let her in. "I'll let you handle it from here. Take care, Mrs. Martinez," he said, and left the exam room.

"I, uh—have Mrs. Martinez's treatment packet," Joy said, and after a slight hesitation held out the neatly stapled stack of paper to Luca. "There's instructions on how to keep her on a regular hydration schedule and a prescription for some pain medication for her bruises. Dr. Reynolds would also like to see you in a few weeks for a follow-up."

Abuela started to shake her head. "No, no follow up —"

"It's fine, Abuela, I'll handle everything," Luca interrupted, taking the packet and prescription slip. He glanced at the bill at the bottom and winced. He would be working a lot of extra shifts to pay this off. "Let's go make an appointment, then get this filled, and then I'll take you home."

Joy looked from Luca to Abuela. "Oh… you're going to take care of this?"

Luca barely spared the nurse a glance as he and Juan gently helped his grandmother off the examination table. "I take care of everything."

Chapter 6: Free-Spin

"In dance, a free-spin is performed without partner contact."

Claire was bored out of her mind.

When she'd had the idea to make the drive from San Diego to Los Angeles, she'd hoped for various things. First, that even though she was going primarily to erase any doubts about her loyalty to him, Claire was hoping for a scene straight out of a romantic movie. She wanted Sebastian to be overjoyed at the sight of her and scoop her up into a passionate kiss. And she wanted him to tell her how much he missed her and promise her an amazing night on the town after rehearsal.

As she pulled onto the tree-lined street where Sebastian was living, she checked her make-up in the mirror and re-tied her hair into a neat bun at the nape of her neck. *He's going to be so happy to see me,* she told herself as she practically skipped up the path to the modern-looking house that was all steel and glass windows. Instead, the first words out of Sebastian's mouth when he opened the door were:

"What are you doing here?"

Dressed in a stylish jacket and jeans, his blond hair was perfectly coiffed, and Sebastian looked like he was about to step onto a photo shoot. Claire suddenly felt underdressed in her leggings and top.

"Killing two birds with one stone," Claire had said, swallowing disappointment. Couldn't he be just a little happy to see her?

"Don't get me wrong babe, it's a nice surprise," Sebastian had said, giving her a hasty kiss on the cheek. "But isn't this something that you could've called about? Or texted?"

"I didn't want to send a text message that would be misinterpreted," Claire protested. "I wanted to talk to you face to face, so you know there's nothing going on between me and Luca before Bethany's viral post took on a life of its own and turned you against me," she said and explained what had happened during rehearsal. "You have to know, Luca and I are just partners, he was the only one available to perform at Blackpool, nothing more. Plus," she added, giving her boyfriend a once over. "I really missed you."

"Okay," Sebastian said, locking the door behind him and heading towards his sleek car. "I think you've been watching way too much reality TV."

"There are way too many conflicts on TV that could've been solved face to face," Claire insisted, chasing after him.

"Okay, well I appreciate you driving down, but I have a full schedule ahead of me," Sebastian said, unlocking the car. He paused, his hand on the door handle. "So...bye?"

"Seb—" Claire felt disappointment twist like a knife. "We haven't seen each other since you left, can't I come with you?"

Sebastian sighed. "Babe, I have a full day. I can't really be hanging around; I have to practice."

"It's fine," Claire had assured him, "I've been wanting to see what it's like to be on a TV show, so I'm happy to watch, and maybe afterward we can do something together."

Sebastian sighed again. "I'll make some calls."

It had taken a few calls on the way to the TV studio, but when they arrived, there was someone waiting to give her a stack of legal forms to sign. "But I'm going to be practicing until four with Lisa, and there's not a lot you can do except watch." Sebastian reminded her as she was escorted inside.

"Don't worry," Claire said, "I'll be fine."

She'd said that two hours ago with a smile. Now, after sitting on the bench, in one of *Dance Craze*'s rehearsal rooms, watching Sebastian and his partner practice their routine again and again, she was wishing she had something else to do.

The space looked a lot like her parent's studio, with the same shiny wood floors, mirrors, and a barre lining two walls. A camera man wearing black with a *Dance Craze* cap over his balding head and wearing a Steadicam harness sat on the bench next to Claire, looking just as bored as Claire felt. A tiny woman, also in black, her hair bleached and dyed in crazy tiger-like stripes, sat on Claire's other side, a microphone on a long pole—which Claire found out was a boom mic—across her knees. For the first hour, both crew people had filmed and followed every detail, but after it became clear Sebastian wasn't making any progress, they had turned off their equipment and taken a seat.

They were practicing the salsa, and it amused Claire to see that Sebastian, who could handle every smooth dance imaginable, was having the same difficulties she was having with the dance. His weight should be more forward, she thought quietly, and he keeps leading with his heels when he should be stepping forward with his toes.

"No rise and fall! Do it again!" the dance choreographer, Jesse, barked. He was a stocky man of medium build who chose to dye his hair in bright rainbow hues to match his colorful sweatsuit. Claire had watched enough episodes of *Dance Craze* to know he was a talented up-and-comer from Texas, who had already put together several high-scoring dance numbers. The fact that Sebastian had gotten him as a choreographer should've been a huge coup, but instead he was sulking and arguing with Jesse every five minutes.

"Loosen up your hips more," Jesse shouted, and Sebastian scowled.

"I'm trying!"

"Try harder!"

Claire sighed and looked toward the window, which had a third-floor view of the busy L.A. street below. Cars crawled by, stuck in mid-morning traffic, belching exhaust fumes and honking at the people in front of them. A homeless man dressed in a filthy coat shambled by, pushing a shopping cart full of cans and bottles.

Sebastian hadn't even glanced at her once during the entire two hours, merely focused on his routine—and Jesse—the entire practice. At least Lisa, Sebastian's assigned partner seemed friendlier. She was a pretty brunette with caramel-colored skin and curves Claire would've traded her entire wardrobe for, and she glanced at Claire from time to time and gave her a sympathetic smile.

"Stop! Stop!" Jesse held up a manicured hand to halt the practice. "Sebastian, you did a great Waltz last week, but this is Salsa. You're stepping forward with your heels instead of your toes, and your steps are too big. Shorten them up, make them half that size, and show me some hip movement."

"I was doing that, you just weren't paying attention!" Sebastian insisted, his pale cheeks pinking slightly.

"Fine, then show me," Jesse insisted, hands on his hips. Sebastian scowled and took a step forward, heel first. "Stop, do it again. Toes first, Alvah. Toes first!"

"You need to throw your weight forward, Seb," Claire suggested, getting up from her seat. "Because it pushes your bottom and hips out more and you can't step with your heel if you're—"

"Excuse me, who are you?" Jesse demanded, whipping around to glare in Claire's direction.

"I'm sorry, I'm Claire," Claire stuttered, uncomfortable with the pairs of unfriendly eyes looking at her. Even the cameraman and boom operator were glaring in her direction. "I'm—I'm with him," she said, pointing at Sebastian.

Jesse sighed, running a hand through his styled rainbow hair. "Jesus, Alvah, who said you could bring one of your groupies to rehearsal?"

"I'm not a groupie," Claire bristled. "I'm his girlfriend!"

"Ah," Jesse's expression softened slightly and he gave Claire a sympathetic smile. "Look, I'm sorry, sweetie. If you're not part of the show, I need you to keep quiet while we're rehearsing."

"Oh, sure, sorry," Claire said, feeling mortified. "I'll just go to the green room and wait." She gathered up her purse, her cheeks burning.

"She was right about your technique, though," Jesse said to Sebastian, watching Claire head for the door. "Hey, cupcake!" he called after her. "Do I know you from somewhere? You're a dancer, right?"

Claire turned back toward him. "My name is Claire Beauchene," Claire said, lifting her chin proudly.

Jesse's eyes lit with recognition. "Beauchene. That's where I've seen you. You did a competition in Texas a few years back. Brilliant choreography."

Claire flushed with pleasure. "Thank you, it took me a month to put together. I can't imagine having to come up with a new one every week."

A small smile tugged at the corner of Jesse's mouth. "You know what?" He turned to Sebastian. "She can stay, I like her."

"Great," Sebastian's smile looked tight.

"So, Claire Beauchene," Jesse turned his attention back to her. "You do Salsa now?"

"Latin dancing isn't really her forte," Sebastian interjected. Claire glared at him, and he shrugged. "Sorry to be blunt, babe, but it's the truth."

"Actually, I've been working with Luca on his Salsa routine for Blackpool," Claire corrected him, feeling irritation curling in her gut.

"Blackpool huh?" Jesse raised an eyebrow, impressed. "I'd have thought you'd give yourself more than a few months to prepare for that. That competition is intense."

"Well Sebastian and I had been training for the past year but he decided to do this instead," Claire shrugged. "But it's okay, I'm adapting."

"Wow, someone is playing the victim," Sebastian forced a laugh, moving closer to Claire. "Uh, babe, can we not air out our dirty laundry here?" he whispered, indicating Jesse and Lisa slightly with his head.

But Jesse already had other ideas. "I'd be interested in seeing what you've learned so far," he suggested, a gleam in his eye. "Why don't you show us what you got, sweetheart? Lisa, Sebastian, take five."

"I'm sorry, what?" Sebastian looked taken aback. "We're in the middle of practice."

"You heard me, take five," Jesse said.

Sebastian scowled and stalked off the floor, Lisa trailing behind like a small, bewildered puppy.

"So, what are you, a size seven? Eight?" Jesse asked Claire quietly.

"Sorry what?"

"Your foot size, hun," Jesse said, grabbing a pair of rhythm practice heels from a cubby. "Hmm, these are six," he said, putting them back.

"Umm, s-seven," Claire stuttered. "Listen, are you sure this is okay? I didn't want to get anyone in trouble."

"First you interrupt my rehearsal, now you want to hide?" Jesse checked another pair. "Here, put these on," Jesse thrust the shoes at her.

"Okay," Claire juggled the shoes in one hand as she slipped out of her sneakers. "But I can't promise the routine will be perfect."

"Hun, if you're a tenth as talented at Salsa as you are at the Waltz, you're going to wipe the floor with him," Jesse's grin was wicked. "And maybe between the two of us we can motivate him to actually put some effort into practice."

She wasn't doing this to make Sebastian look bad, Claire reminded herself as she slipped on the practice shoes, re-tied her bun to make sure it was secure. But she'd learned more than a few things from Luca. If Sebastian assumed she couldn't handle this dance just because she had struggled with it in the past, maybe he deserved to be proven wrong. She tested out the shoes, shifting her weight back and forth to loosen her hips.

"Ready?" Jesse asked, holding out his hand.

She saw the camera man standing, the red light on his camera blinking, as the boom operator pointed the mic in her direction. Claire gulped, feeling her stomach begin to twist in knots. Performing in front of an audience was one thing, but usually she had a few hours to prep beforehand.

Did her hair look alright? Why couldn't she have chosen a more flattering top this morning? What if she messed up and it was used on the show as a blooper reel? What if Sebastian got mad at her and never wanted to talk to her again?

Claire forced herself to take a deep breath. *Don't think about Sebastian, don't think about falling on your butt with the camera recording,* she told herself. Maybe she should call it off before it was too late. She took another breath, willing her stomach to settle. Unbidden, an image of Luca popped into her head, dark shadows under his eyes, his mouth set in a grim line. *Claire, you're a talented dancer,* she heard Luca's exasperated voice in her head. *Just pay attention and you'll be fine.* Claire shook her head, baffled as her nerves immediately lessoned. This was ridiculous. Why did Luca, of all people, suddenly have the ability to make her feel better?

"Puppies," she muttered.

"Sorry, what?" Jesse's voice brought her back to reality.

"I mean I'm ready," Claire said quickly, taking Jesse's hand. "Start the music."

Jesse led Claire to the center of the floor, then pointed a remote at the music system in the corner. The song started—a pulsing, dynamic beat that seemed to vibrate through the floor.

Out of the corner of her eye, Claire saw Sebastian's eyes narrow as he recognized the song from his routine. She forced herself to focus on the music, the rhythm that was working its way into her blood, into her bones.

Then she was lost in the middle of the dance. Turns, spins, body rolls, Luca's hours of training were really paying off, Claire realized as she executed a series of shimmies. She chased Jesse across the floor, hips rolling, her feet light as Jesse lifted her onto his shoulder, then brought her down into a perfect split. Jesse pulled Claire to her feet as the camera man and boom operator applauded enthusiastically, crushing her in a bear hug.

"You were magnificent! Oh, I would kill to work with someone as talented as you!" Jesse squealed, lifting her off her feet.

"What the hell was that?" Sebastian demanded, striding across the floor towards them. Jesse stepped in front of Claire, hands on his hips.

"That, is what the routine *could* look like if you actually *tried*." Jesse snapped. "But no, you're too good to show up for practice on time, you're constantly half-assing or talking on your phone and honestly I'm at my wit's end with you! Keep it up, and you won't get enough points to make it through the next round on Friday."

Sebastian's face flushed bright pink. "How dare you talk to me like that! Do you know who my father is?" Sebastian jabbed a finger at Jesse, practically drilling a hole in his chest. "He is one of the executive producers on this show, one call to him and you're back to teaching senior citizens in the middle of nowhere."

"Seb!" Claire gasped, horrified. "He was just trying to help. Don't you want to do your best during the competition?"

"Stay out of this Claire, you're just making it worse!" Sebastian snarled. He stopped, his face unreadable as his eyes flicked toward the camera man, the red light still blinking. Then he smiled, the sunny, brilliant smile that Claire was more familiar with. "I'm sorry, that was incredibly rude and unprofessional. I shouldn't have said that." He turned to Jesse, clasping his hands, the image of contrition. "You know what Jesse, you're right. I have been a little lax, but I promise, I'll work harder and give the routine a hundred and ten percent."

Jesse raised an eyebrow, looking skeptical. "I'll believe it when I see it," he said, turning away.

"And Claire." Sebastian grabbed both of Claire's hands. "Thank you so much for being here to explicitly point out what needed to be fixed and showing me how the routine should be danced. I know it'll make me a better dancer. You really are the best." He hugged her so tightly Claire had to fight to breathe. "Actually," Sebastian faced the camera. "Since Claire is such an *exceptional* dancer, why doesn't she take over for a bit and help with the choreography? I bet there are so many things we can learn from her. Doesn't that sound like a good idea?"

"I mean," Jesse hesitated, shifting uncomfortably, gaze darting between Claire and Sebastian. "It's not a *horrible* idea, but—"

"Excellent! Claire," Sebastian prostrated himself in an elegant bow at her feet. "Would you grace us lowly dancers with your superior technique? Shine your light of genius upon us ignorant souls?"

"Well…" Claire's stomach roiled. Sebastian was smiling, the same way he always did, but something felt different. Something beneath the surface of that smile that made her wary. "I don't know if I'm a genius…" she said cautiously.

"After that brilliant demonstration?" Sebastian waved a dismissive hand. "You're too modest. Please, Claire," Sebastian clasped her hand in both of his. "We need you desperately. I don't know how we'll be able to make it to the next level if you don't help us."

Claire was aware of Sebastian's hand gripping hers a little too tightly. The blinking red light of the camera over his shoulder. Claire forced herself to smile. "I can't say no to you."

"Excellent," Sebastian kissed her hand, the image of a perfect Prince Charming and Claire felt her stomach clench even tighter. "And if we have to go overtime, there's no worries, it's all in the name of our craft, right? Let's not leave until this routine is perfect!"

Chapter 7: Outside Change

"The outside change is a simple figure which consists of three steps, all danced in-line with a basic waltz rise-and-fall."

By the time they had finished, six hours later, Claire's legs ached. For the first time in years, Sebastian had been relentlessly focused, driving everyone to practice the same choreography over and over again, until every move of the routine was flawless. Even Jesse was forced to admit, "if Sebastian doesn't win, he'll be one of the top three contenders."

After such rigorous exercise, the luxurious seats of Sebastian's car felt like heaven. Claire couldn't help a sigh of relief when she settled back against the headrest.

"You sound tired, was today too hard for you?" Sebastian slipped into the driver's side and started the car.

"I've had worse," Claire shrugged. "Remember that competition we did in Vegas last year? We must've been on our feet for ten hours straight."

"Vegas?" Sebastian's lips twitched for a split second. Was it Claire's imagination, or did he look disappointed? "We did so many competitions, it's hard to keep track."

"We did that solo performance where I dressed up in that wedding dress I got from a thrift store and you wore that ugly suit," Claire prompted him.

"Oh yeah," Sebastian slowed to a stop for a red light. "I hated that costume, why did we do that again?"

"Because we were supposed to look like we just had a Vegas wedding…" when Sebastian didn't respond, Claire elaborated. "Because people get drunk and have impulsive weddings in Vegas all the time?"

"Oh yeah." Sebastian's expression didn't change. "Funny." The light changed from red to green and the car glided forward again. "Still, you probably have easier rehearsals now that you're paired up with the charity case."

Claire stiffened at the familiar nickname. Why did it bother her so much now? Maybe because she knew Luca a little better? "You know, he surprised me. I thought it would be awful, but he's not that bad once you get to know him. I bet the two of you would get along if you talked."

Sebastian snorted, turning at the next light. "About what? Where to get another ugly suit?"

"Don't be mean, he's passionate, Seb," Claire heard herself coming to Luca's defense before she realized what she was doing. "And he's as committed to dance as we are, maybe more."

"Whoa, babe, chill!" Sebastian glanced in surprise in Claire's direction. "It was just a joke."

"Well I'm telling you it's not funny," Claire responded. "He…" She had a sudden flash of Luca leaning against the wall, hair in sweaty curls around his face. He was smiling slightly, the edges of his eyes crinkled in amusement. "Doesn't deserve all the crap we give him," she finished.

Sebastian eyed her as he waited to turn. "Maybe there was some truth to Bethan's post. I don't have to worry about Ortiz stealing my girl, do I?"

"Of course not!" Claire objected. *Why did she feel the sudden urge to defend Luca?* "He's just a decent guy and a really good dancer and I think we should stop making fun of him!"

"You're kinda making my case for me, babe. You sure there's nothing going on?"

"Excuse me?" Claire sputtered. "I came down here despite my *very busy* schedule preparing for Blackpool to make sure everything was okay between us and you alternated between ignoring me and telling me I can't Salsa!"

"Oh, is that how you see it?" Sebastian retorted, "Because it seemed like you hijacked my day. I jumped through hoops so you could come along, and you called me out in front of everyone and told me I could do better."

"You *can* do better!" Claire insisted. "We were *champions* together and then you give up our plans to come out here, and you're not even taking *Dance Craze* seriously! What happened? You told me this was a once in a lifetime opportunity for you, but you're not trying hard enough; you're making threats toward Jesse—"

"Not everyone is you, Miss I Can Do Everything Perfectly On The First Try. At least I'm not busting my butt for some obscure ballroom dance—" Sebastian was so preoccupied he almost slammed into the car in front of him and he honked the horn angrily. The driver ahead of him flipped him the bird out the window.

Claire took a breath. "It just—it feels like—when we were partners," Claire struggled to find the words. "We were so good together, I guess I still don't understand why you had to abandon everything and come here." Claire turned her head so she could see Sebastian's profile in the dim light of the car. "The worst part about all of this is I'm so used to having you around so not having you around— I've just missed you so much. I had to see you, and I didn't think about the fact it might disturb your schedule, I just drove down at the first excuse."

Silence followed her words. Then after a moment, Sebastian reached out to squeeze her hand gently. "I missed you too." Sebastian stopped at the red light and leaned over to kiss her. Claire sighed happily when her lips met his. They were warm and familiar and tasted slightly of mint, as usual. "Look, I'm sorry we both had a rough day," Sebastian said as they broke away. "Let's start over, the night is still young. I'll take you somewhere fun…" he added coaxingly.

"Actually, Seb," Claire said, "I was hoping we could just relax with a movie at your place. After that workout, I'm exhausted."

"A movie?" Sebastian scoffed. "That's boring! You'd rather sit on a couch and stare at a screen when you could be out, taking advantage of hundreds of fun opportunities? Look, babe, my buddy Josh is throwing a party at his house. Let's go and hang out for a bit and have a good time. And if you don't like it, I promise we'll go back to my place."

Claire hesitated. She liked parties as much as the next girl but the thought of walking around on her aching legs, talking to strangers while music pounded around her just didn't sound appealing. She much preferred the idea of snuggling up on the couch with Sebastian, watching one of their favorite movies and eating kale chips together.

Sebastian seemed to sense her reluctance because he continued. "You just said I'm not trying hard enough with this lifetime opportunity and you're right. I need to get out there and make more connections for my career. And this party is a great way to do that."

Claire frowned, her curiosity piqued. "How do you mean?"

"Just that everyone usually knows someone who can help get my foot through the door. You want that for me, don't you babe?"

Claire bit her lip and sighed. Felt the fantasy of a relaxing movie night slip away. "All right, fine, but just a little while. I'd really like to get some sleep before I drive back tomorrow."

"You mean you want to get some sleep or you want to get some *sleep*?" Sebastian waggled his eyebrows suggestively.

"I mean sleep," Claire insisted, though she felt her cheeks flush hot pink. Now that she thought about it, she was going to be spending the night alone at his house. Not that that had been her plan. She'd driven down to save their relationship and spend time together, that was it. But if something else happened…

"Tell you what," Sebastian kissed her hand, nibbling at her knuckles in a way that sent shivers through Claire's body. "We'll stay for an hour, and when we get back to my place…" he grinned at her in a way that had Claire blushing even hotter. "You can decide the kind of sleep that you want."

* * *

The house was packed when Sebastian and Claire drove up. Young adults of varying ages milled around, red cups and beer bottles in their hands as they chatted and joked with friends. A haze of vape and marijuana smoke seemed to have wafted through every room, creating a slightly sweet and earthy smell that made Claire's eyes water.

Sebastian moved through the crowd confidently, saying hello, grabbing guys into one-armed-hugs, and kissing girls on the cheek while Claire limped miserably behind. It's not that she didn't enjoy parties, she had gone to plenty with Sebastian. She loved having social events with friends, but she usually knew more than one person at the party and had never been interested in the ones that involved alcohol.

They moved through the masses into an area that Claire assumed had once been the living room, but now had all the furniture pushed against the wall to make room for a beer-pong game and a foosball table. Claire tried not to notice several couples occupying the various couches and armchairs, who were either too stoned to realize they were making out in public, or too drunk to care.

"Josh, dude, how's it going?" Sebastian said, high-fiving a gawky-looking teen with curly hair and an abundance of acne. "Great party here!"

"Thanks, man," said Josh, taking a swig from his drink. "Thought I'd live it up a little while the parents were out of town. I've even got a maid service who's going to come in tomorrow, so I don't have to worry about clean-up."

He spotted Claire next to Sebastian and gave her a look up and down that had her skin crawling. "Who's this pretty lady?" he asked.

"Claire. I'm his girlfriend," Claire said curtly, linking her arm with Sebastian's. Josh quirked an eyebrow but shrugged.

"Well, Claire, welcome. Any friend of Seb here is a friend of mine, and as they say in Spanish, *mi casa is you casa*, so grab a drink from the bar and have a good time!"

"Thanks. You got anything non-alcoholic?" Claire asked. Josh seemed amused by the question.

"Don't worry, no one cares what age you are."

Claire forced herself to smile. "Well, I do. I'm not interested in drinking."

Josh laughed. "She's so cute," he said to Sebastian. "Where'd you find her?"

"Huh?" Sebastian seemed distracted. "Oh, she's just visiting." He gave Claire an absent kiss on the cheek. "I'm gonna go find the restroom. Be right back," he said, heading off into the crowd and leaving Claire with Josh.

"So… where are the non-alcoholic drinks?" Claire asked.

"In the coolers by the fridge." Josh indicated the open door over her shoulder. "Just walk that way, you can't miss it." His head whipped around when there was a resounding crash from the hall. "Hey, dudes, take it outside!" he yelled, moving toward two muscled guys who had started pushing each other. "Come find me if you need anything!" he called over his shoulder as he rushed to push the two drunk jocks apart. "Come on guys, I can clean up the mess, but if you break anything, my mom will kill me. Just take it outside."

Claire wandered through the crowd toward the door Josh had indicated, finding herself in a wide kitchen full of white cabinets and checkered tile floors. The counters were littered with bottles of every shape and color, but against one wall, Claire spotted three large white coolers. Claire knelt in front of them and lifted up the lids.

The first was full of beer, the second more beer and a couple bottles of vodka and hard cider, but the third had a few cans of soda. Sebastian had always warned against having too much sugar since it would make her break out, but it was either that or beer. Claire chose a Sprite and cracked it open, thrilling in the taste of overly sweet lemon and lime.

"Hey."

Claire spun around towards the unfamiliar voice. "Hey," she answered. Like Josh, this new stranger was tall and gangly, but with greasy brown hair hanging almost to his shoulders. Eyes the color of mud stared out of a face that was thin and freckled, with patches of stubble on his chin and cheeks.

"I'm Tommy. Can I get you anything to drink?" he asked, finger-combing his hair back from his face. Claire wordlessly held up her opened soda. "Right," Tommy laughed nervously. "You've already got something. Well, how about to eat? You want pizza? We got pizza." He gestured to several large white boxes sitting on a table in the backyard. Claire shook her head.

"Got it, trying to watch your weight? Though, I gotta say, you look great already." He laughed again and took a gulp from the bottle in his hand.

"No, I'm not watching my weight," Claire said, mildly irritated by his assumption. "I'm just not hungry."

"Cool, cool." Tommy leaned on the door frame, blocking her exit. "So what have you been in? I swear I've seen your face in something."

"What?" Claire blinked at him, completely baffled.

"Like what movies or TV shows have you been in?" Tommy asked. "These parties are a great way to make connections, I've been an extra in a couple TV shows because of the people I've met here."

"I'm…not in anything," Claire answered, her gaze sweeping over the party guests gathered in the living room. For the life of her, she couldn't understand how they were all making connections given their state of intoxication.

"Oh, well, don't worry," Tommy assured her. "There are plenty of people here that are just getting started in the biz, and like I said, you already look great, so it should be easy to get some auditions—"

"I'm not interested in getting started or being in anything," Claire cut him off. "I'm a dancer, that's it."

She moved past him, intending to find Sebastian, but Tommy followed behind like a puppy.

"So if you're not here to make connections, what are you doing here?" Tommy asked, drinking from his beer bottle.

"I'm just here with my boyfriend," Claire said, pushing through the crowd. The house seemed to be full of drunk, smelly teenagers.

"Oh, that's cool, where is he now?"

"I don't know," Claire said, yanking open the first door she saw. Five boys who couldn't have been more than eighteen years old stopped in the middle of passing around a bong and looked at her blearily.

"Oh hey," said one with greasy curls and a ripped t-shirt. "You wanna join us?"

"No, thank you," Claire said, slamming the door. The next door revealed a girl bent over the toilet, puking out her guts. The third featured two half-naked boys making out in what appeared to be a guest bedroom.

"Do you mind?" shouted the boy on top with spiked blue hair.

"Sorry, just trying to find someone," Claire apologized, closing the door quickly.

"So, what's your boyfriend's name again?" Tommy asked, following Claire as she took the stairs to the second floor.

"Sebastian Alvah," Claire said, opening another door. To her disappointment, it was just a linen closet.

"The name doesn't ring a bell, what's he look like?"

"Blond, blue eyes," the pounding music really wasn't helping, Claire's head was starting to ache. "Really cute…." *Deserves to have a drink thrown in his face for bringing her to the party and leaving her alone*, she thought to herself. "Sebastian is focused on his career as a dancer, that's why he's here."

Tommy blocked the doorway Claire was standing in, leaning against the doorway.

"So, you want to make out?" he asked, indicating the empty bathroom.

"What? Why?" Claire responded, too baffled to be mortified. "Why would I want to do that? I'm here looking for my boyfriend."

"Yeah, you said that," Tommy said, with what could've been interpreted as a charming smile if his breath didn't smell like a distillery. "But you've been looking through these rooms for a while, and I'm starting to wonder if he really exists."

"He's here!" Claire snapped, temper adding color to her cheeks. "I just haven't found where he is yet. And if he was here," she added, "Sebastian would not like knowing you were hitting on me." Tommy didn't seem worried, but then again, he was pretty drunk.

"Well, I don't see him here, so this seems like the perfect opportunity," Tommy said suggestively. "And I won't tell him if you don't." He tried to lean in for a kiss, and instinctively, Claire slapped him.

"You bitch!" Tommy shoved her, his cheek flushed with a bright pink handprint. Claire stumbled back, smacking her hip painfully against the bathroom counter. "If you weren't interested, you should have said so!"

"I said I had a boyfriend," Claire shoved him back, fear and adrenaline giving her strength. "How much clearer could I get?" Tommy went down swearing and sloshing beer all over his shirt. Claire didn't wait to see him get up.

"Sebastian! Sebastian!" Claire started yanking doors open and closed as fast as she could, the pain in her hip throbbing as she rushed down the hall. Just as she reached it, the door at the end of the hall opened, and Sebastian came out, shirt and hair slightly mussed and a scowl on his face.

"What's going on? Who's yelling?" he demanded.

"Seb." Claire clung to him like a drowning swimmer clinging to a life preserver. He smelled of alcohol and weed, but he was there, and now she was safe.

"Babe? What's wrong?" Sebastian asked, putting his arms around her. The door was slightly open behind her, and Claire could see a mixed group of teens lounging on the furniture, smoking and drinking.

"I want to leave. Now. I don't like it here," Claire pleaded, mortified she could hear her voice shaking.

"What? Why? We just got here."

"I don't like it here," Claire repeated. "Please, can we just go?"

Sebastian sighed and patted her on the shoulder. "Sure. Just let me say my goodbyes. You want to wait in the car?"

Claire looked back down the hall. Tommy was nowhere to be seen, but she wasn't willing to take the chance that he was still lurking around somewhere. Claire shook her head firmly.

"No, I'm staying with you," she said, keeping a tight grip on his shirt.

Sebastian sighed again. "Okay, fine, we'll go."

***

"Look, I'm sure the dude was just messing around," Sebastian said.

They were in his classy new car, Claire at the wheel, finally driving back to his parent's condo. "Seb, I know what I heard. He wanted to make out, even though I told him you were there."

"All right, babe, I get it, that kinda sucks, but you got away and you're fine now, right?"

"Yes, I'm fine, but it would've been nice if you'd stuck with me instead of going off alone!" Claire snapped.

"Whoa, since when do you need me to stay with you?" Sebastian demanded.

"Since you thought it was a good idea to bring me to a party where I didn't know anyone!"

"Look, I was going to come back, but I ran into some friends, and I lost track of time," Sebastian shot back. "I told you this party was an important place to make connections. Don't you want me to have a career as a dancer?"

Claire's hip ached as she merged into a new lane. "It didn't look like you were making connections, it looked like you were drinking and getting high."

"Woah, excuse me, do I drive down to San Diego to criticize your life?" Sebastian demanded. "You drove down here without telling me, forced your way into my rehearsal and made me look bad in front of everyone, then when we went to the party where I had a good chance of landing a couple of auditions, and you want to leave after half an hour! Now maybe I was partying a little bit, but you're the one who came down here because you were worried I'd think you were cheating. But I didn't! I believed you! So could you cut me some slack?"

Claire felt her stomach clench. Maybe she was overreacting a little. "Okay, I'm sorry." Claire sighed. "I'm just feeling a little overwhelmed. I guess I wish you'd be mad if someone was harassing your girlfriend."

Sebastian sighed. "No, I'm sorry, I'm sure that situation sucked. But you also didn't have to come down here to explain yourself over one of Bethany's stupid posts. I would've believed you if you called or texted me about what was going on."

"Really?" Claire shot a quick look in his direction, trying to see his expression in the dim interior of the car.

"Lucky for you, I'm a very understanding and trusting boyfriend," Sebastian said, leaning against the window.

A silence fell over the car, interrupted only by the click of the indicator as Claire turned down the quiet, tree-lined street where Sebastian lived and into his driveway. Claire's Prius was parked nearby, looking small and in need of a wash next to the other gleaming luxury vehicles on the street. Claire turned off the car and Sebastian opened his door. "So, do you want to come in and watch a movie? I've got some of our favorite kale chips, and we could snuggle. My dad's in New Zealand so we have the house all to ourselves."

Claire could see from the look in his eyes what he meant by 'snuggle'. "Movie, yes, as for the snuggling…" Sebastian's face fell slightly.

"You want to wait," he groaned. Claire leaned over and lightly kissed his cheek.

"I'll be eighteen in a week, remember? And I still plan to—"

"Have a proper celebration with me?" Sebastian teased.

"It's my first time," Claire flushed and felt something twist inside her, simultaneously terrifying and exciting. "You're going to be my first. And I want it to be special. We're going to wait until my birthday, and rent a room at a nice hotel and…and…I—I just want to make my first time perfect."

"You don't want to reconsider?" Sebastian laid a trail of tingling kisses along her neck. "We have three bedrooms to choose from." She gasped and arched her back, her fingers finding purchase in his hair as Sebastian found a particularly sensitive spot behind her ear. "Not to mention several couches and a very comfortable carpeted floor if we can't wait to get upstairs."

An empty house, just the two of them—it was the stuff Claire had fantasized about more than once. She could picture Sebastian carrying her inside, up the stairs, clothes falling away behind them. The way his bare chest would feel under her hands, the way his hands would feel on her.

She could feel her heart hammering frantically in her chest, thoughts of what could happen if she bent her dream just a little. After all, nothing was going to plan, she was going to Blackpool with Luca, not Sebastian, why couldn't she lose her virginity a week early?

Desire screamed at her to give in.

Just one more week, she reminded herself, but it felt so far away as Sebastian's hand slid down to the hem of her shirt, his thumb brushing the bare skin underneath. What was one week? Claire moved to allow Sebastian's hands better access. As she did, the weight on her hip shifted and a twinge of pain cut through the lust clouding her brain.

"Merde!" She hissed. With every last bit of willpower she possessed, Claire pushed Sebastian's hands away. "Not tonight," Claire whispered, her voice unsteady. "I need to take it easy on my hip."

"Fine," Sebastian sighed. "Who am I to argue with Claire Beauchene's Grand Master Plan? If you want to make it into a special night, that's what we'll do," he said, exiting the car. Claire waited for him to walk around to her side and open the door for her. "I'll put your overnight things in the guest room," he said, taking her duffle from the trunk of the Prius.

Claire slipped her hand into his as they walked up the driveway, grateful for the familiar feeling of his hand in hers. She still wanted him, but she could wait. She would wait. At least one of her plans was going to happen as planned. And it was going to be perfect.

"One more week," Claire reminded him cheerfully.

"Yeah, believe me, babe," Sebastian said, hunting for his keys. "I'm counting down the days."

113

"Yeah, believe me, babe," Sebastian said, hunting for his keys. "I'm counting down the days."

Chapter 8: Toque

"(Touch). Short touch of the leader's instep by the follower's foot."

A creature of habit, Claire was up with the sun and had washed, dressed, and stowed her overnight gear in the car by the time Sebastian had stumbled downstairs to make his morning protein shake. Her hip was a little stiff and showed signs of bruising, but other than that, she felt fine. She had a three-hour drive ahead of her, and she fully intended to be back in time for her practice session with Luca.

Claire kissed a drowsy Sebastian goodbye and drove off, rolling down the window to let the wind whip her hair as she sped down the highway. The first hour flew by. Claire cranked up the music in her car and sang tunelessly along at the top of her lungs, rejoicing in the freedom of the open road.

She was half an hour from home when, out of nowhere, her car rattled, sputtered, and died.

"No, no, come on! You can't do this to me!" Claire pleaded, slapping at the console.

Fortunately, her car had stopped in an area of town that didn't seem to have a lot of traffic; instead, featuring a long street of run-down-looking bars, cafes, and vacant lots. *Unfortunately*, this meant she wouldn't be getting help from a good Samaritan anytime soon. She stepped out of the car, resigning herself to the arduous task of pushing her Prius over to the side of the road. Her hip felt stiff after sitting in the car, and she carefully stretched her legs and rolled her hips to loosen everything up.

But first, just to say she did, Claire lifted the hood and examined the engine, as though the wires and other car parts weren't completely alien to her. She even poked gingerly at one or two pieces, though there was no chance that all her car needed was a random touch to get it started again.

Wishing for a hot bath to soak her aching muscles, Claire limped behind the Prius and tried to push it to the side of the road. The tiny car didn't budge an inch.

Resigned, she dug in her purse for her phone to call for a tow truck. She hoped someone could come get her car before she became an obstruction in the middle of the road. And if she could get it fixed before her practice session...

"Claire?"

Claire turned at the sound of the familiar voice and saw Luca standing at the entrance of one of the bars, two bulging trash bags in each hand. "What are you doing here?" Luca asked, putting down the bags and crossing the street to meet her.

"I, uh—was coming back from visiting Sebastian when my car broke down," Claire managed to reply, gesturing to her car. "What are you doing here? Is that where you work?"

Luca shrugged. "Sometimes. You need a hand?" he asked, rolling up the sleeves of his light jacket and exposing his muscled forearms.

"Yes, please," Claire said gratefully. She put her hand on the bumper to help push, but Luca waved her away.

"I'll push. You steer," he directed, putting his shoulder to the bumper of her Prius. "Any day now, *princesa*," Luca commented dryly when she hesitated, and Claire hurriedly slipped behind the wheel of her car.

"I couldn't get it to move, maybe we should wait—"

"Did you release the brake and shift into neutral?" Luca asked.

"Umm…" Claire looked at the gearshift. "No."

"Put your car in neutral and release the brake at the count of three. One, two…"

As Claire released the brake, Luca shoved it easily over to the curb while Claire struggled to steer. Between the two of them, they managed to line it up neatly with the sidewalk.

"You can put the parking brake back on now. And I'd engage the emergency brake," Luca told her, and Claire obeyed. "Now, let's look at your engine," he said, walking to the front of her car and peering into the engine.

"You know anything about cars?" Claire asked curiously, climbing stiffly out of the driver's side and standing beside him.

"When you've got a crap car like mine that breaks down once a week, you learn how to fix it," Luca commented, untwisting a cap to some foreign car part and checking inside. Claire's chuckle had his head snapping up in surprise, and she quickly covered her mouth to stifle her mirth.

"Sorry, I didn't mean to laugh," she apologized, mistaking the look on his face for insult.

"No. It's fine. It really is a piece of crap," Luca managed to say. "I spend more time fixing it than driving it."

Claire chuckled again, and Luca ducked beneath the hood, the corners of his mouth twitching up.

"So you work around here?" Claire asked, leaning against the side of the car. She caught sight of herself in the window and wished for a brush. Her hair was a mess.

"Ragazzo's, for about three years now." Luca popped his head up for a second. "You should get an oil change when you get a chance," he informed her before going back to inspecting the engine. "Your levels are getting low."

"Don't you have to be at least eighteen to work in a bar?" Claire wanted to know, trying to finger-comb out the worst tangles.

"I'm nineteen," Luca replied. "So it's not a problem."

"Nineteen?!" Claire echoed, forgetting her hair for a moment. "Why didn't I know that?"

"You didn't ask," Luca said simply, standing up and wiping his hands on a rag he had in his back pocket. He moved around to the driver's side, where Claire was standing. "Pardon," he said looking down at her.

Maybe it was because he was a lot taller when Claire wasn't wearing her practice heels. Maybe it was the smudges of grease on his hands or the black polo shirt—with the bar's logo—tucked into the trim waist of his jeans. A polo shirt should not be that flattering, Claire thought to herself. Her heart did a quick cha-cha anyway.

"Oh, it's fine. I'm not mad. I mean, it's not like we spent much time swapping personal information with each other…" She was babbling but couldn't seem to stop herself while he was looking at her with those unfathomable dark eyes. "We're actually only a year or so apart, did I mention my birthday is in one week? Yep, the big eighteen, I'll finally be an adult. Which means I can finally start competing in much more challenging divisions."

The corner of Luca's mouth twitched. "And what a formidable opponent you will be. But I was actually asking you to move so I can get inside and try starting your car."

"Oh! Right!" Claire felt her cheeks flush pink as she moved out of the way, allowing Luca to slide inside. He grunted in annoyance upon sitting down, as his knees jammed up against his chest.

"*Pequeño coche estupido,*" he muttered, adjusting the seat to accommodate his longer legs. Claire giggled quietly and Luca's mouth twitched upwards as he turned the key in the ignition. The engine started, sputtered, then died.

"See? I was driving, and the car did that and just… stopped working."

Luca raised an eyebrow at Claire, who flushed, feeling her lack of car proficiency.

"Nothing ever just 'stops working,' as you say," Luca admonished her gently. "There is always a reason." He unfolded himself from the driver's side and stretched. "If your car stopped while you were driving, it's either your battery or your alternator. I'll go grab the jumper cables." He started to head towards Ragazzo's, then stopped and turned back around. "Would you like to come inside and grab a drink?"

* * *

"I haven't finished cleaning up, so excuse the mess," Luca apologized, holding the door open for Claire.

"It's not that bad," Claire replied, scanning the dim room curiously. Chairs had been flipped upside down onto tabletops, and while there was a sizeable pile of peanut shells and crumbs in the middle of the floor, the bar counter and surrounding floor gleamed. The air smelled of alcohol and stale cigarette smoke, with undertones of Lemon Pledge and air freshener. In the corner, the battered pool tables were lit by a collection of Christmas lights mixed in with cheap shamrocks from some bygone St. Patrick's Day, though a few looked a little worse for wear.

"Water? Soda?" Luca asked, stepping behind the bar and setting a clean glass on the counter.

Claire decided it was a little strange to see Luca in his work uniform, his black hair combed neatly back from his face. His profile caught the light as he tied a grubby apron around his waist, highlighting his sharp cheekbones, the strong jawline which was showing a sprinkle of stubble.

"Water," Claire requested, taking a seat on the barstool. Her hip twinged, and she bit her lip quickly to hide a wince. "With lemon if you have it."

"We have lemon," Luca reported, holding up a bowlful. He took out a cutting board and a knife, his hands deftly slicing the fruit into perfect paper-thin circles. He filled her glass with water and squeezed in some lemon juice, then rested another slice on the rim before placing it in front of her.

"Thanks," Claire said, taking a sip of refreshing, cool water. Luca's eyes bored into hers.

"You're injured," Luca observed, and Claire looked up in surprise. How had he seen that? He had seemed to be occupied with her drink.

"Just a little…it's nothing," Claire said evasively. "Really, I'm fine. I was at a party with Sebastian yesterday, and I hurt my hip."

"What happened? Do you need some ice?" Luca asked, coming out from behind the bar. "I have a First Aid kit—"

"No, it's fine, really," Claire protested, "I'm pretty sure I'll be okay. Sebastian said it was just a minor bump—" *despite the fact it ached all night*, Claire thought treacherously. "It only happened because I got separated from Sebastian at the party and that jerk shoved me—"

"Stop," Luca held up his hand. "Who shoved you?"

"It was just some drunken guy..." the words came out in a rush. "He tried to kiss me and I slapped him and then he shoved me and I smacked my hip on the bathroom counter." Saying it out loud brought the memory back accompanied by a wave of mortification and fear. The sickly-sweet smell of Tommy's beer, the way he'd leaned toward her, mouth open, made her stomach churn. The sting of her hand slapping Tommy's cheek, the sharp pain of the counter as she was shoved. How could she have let herself get in a situation like that? She should have seen the warning signs, but she'd been so preoccupied looking for Sebastian, she hadn't realized Tommy's intentions until it was too late.

Luca's features looked like they had been carved from stone. "And why were you in the bathroom?"

Claire hesitated. Was Luca going to criticize her for not being more careful? "I was trying to find Sebastian," she finally admitted. "We got separated because he wanted to make connections at the party and that jerk Tommy kept following me and—"

Luca's eyes glittered like black ice in his striking face. "So, just to be clear," he said, his voice dangerously calm, "you went with your...*blanquito novio* to a party where he abandons you, and while looking for him some drunken *pendejo* tries to kiss you and you get injured fighting back?"

"He didn't abandon me, he was making connections... for his career," Claire protested, the excuse sounding weak, even to her ears.

"Mhmm..." Luca took a breath. "And what happened when you told this connection-building career man that you were sexually harassed and injured by someone at the party?"

Claire felt her hip throb and bit her lip. "He got me out of there and took me home."

"He didn't go after the person that injured you?"

"Why would he? He's a gentleman!"

"Yes, he sounds like the perfect gentleman," Luca's lip curled in contempt, his hands clenching and unclenching. "He doesn't stand up for you, he doesn't protect you, he just throws you into the lion's den to be eaten alive."

Claire flinched; he might as well have slapped her. "Are you saying I'm helpless?"

"No, I'm saying…" Luca hesitated. "I'm not saying you're helpless, I'm saying…" His voice trailed off and he looked away, as if struggling to find the right words, then something like resignation flitted across his face. "Nevermind," he muttered. "Just let me see your hip."

"What? No!" Claire slid off her stool.

"Let me see your hip," Luca repeated, moving forward, and Claire took a step back, covering her hip defensively with her right hand.

"I'm fine; you don't need to look at it!" She insisted.

"We've got a competition in a week, you can't perform if you're badly injured," Luca said.

"I don't need to rest," Claire's chin jutted defiantly. "I'm fine."

"You're babying one side and you can't sit without wincing," Luca disagreed, crossing his arms over his chest. "Let me see."

Defiant blue eyes met burning dark ones, a clash of ice and fire. "I'm fine," Claire repeated.

"If you're fine," Luca took a step closer. "Then it shouldn't be a problem to show me how fine you are."

He was too close, Claire was aware of the scent of cut citrus surrounding him. She could see the lines of annoyance in his forehead, the dark shadows under his eyes that hinted at another late night. But his actual eyes... Claire blinked, caught off guard. The eyes that were usually full of irritation and scorn were filled with concern.

"It's nothing," Claire muttered, looking away.

"Claire." It would've been easier if he'd yelled, she didn't know his voice could be gentle.

"Fine, but it's no big deal," Claire reluctantly lifted her shirt an inch. "I'll be all better in a day."

But Luca had already seen the ugly purpling bruise under the hem of the shirt that was spread across her hip.

"*Puta de madre*," he swore, stepping away from her. "That *cabrón* did this to you?"

"I slapped him. And I shoved him back," Claire yanked her shirt back down protectively. "His beer spilled when he fell."

"A slap and a shove," Luca repeated, his voice thickening with temper. "Did your boyfriend the perfect gentleman at least take care of your bruise?"

"I put some ice on it, but he was really tired..."

"*Tu novio es un pedazo de mierda.*"

Claire's eyes narrowed. "Say that in English, I dare you."

"I said your boyfriend is a piece of shit," Luca snapped, and rounding the bar, retrieved a First Aid kit. He yanked out an ice pack, crushed it in his hands then slapped it on the counter with a *BANG* next to Claire. "And he does not know how to treat a lady with respect."

"Oh, so your way is better?" Claire demanded, her voice rising. "Suffocate a girl by never letting her out of your sight and beat up every guy who looks in her direction?"

Luca's jaw tightened. "No, I wouldn't do that either."

"Well, what would you do?" Claire leaned on the counter, challenging him.

Luca's dark eyes burned into hers, like two glowing embers. "I wouldn't have left you to feel scared and abandoned," Luca chose his words carefully. "I wouldn't have been so focused on making connections that I couldn't come when you called. And if someone had *dared* to hurt you half as much as *cabrón* did…" Luca's voice was the low growl of a tiger as his hands clenched into fists. "I would make sure he understands why he should never, ever, do that again."

"Oh." Claire took a breath. She wasn't sure she liked this feeling in her chest. The tightness that made it hard to breathe, made her very aware that her heart was beating faster than it should. "I guess that's better…" she managed. She snatched up the ice pack and pressed it to her hip, trying not to sigh with relief as the coolness eased her aching side and wishing she had another. The room was suddenly stifling hot. "It would've been nice to be with someone who stuck up for me."

Luca's hands were balled into fists at his side, looking like he was dangerously close to taking out his temper at the next thing to walk in the door. Unexpectedly, his hands relaxed.

"Well," he said quietly. "Maybe next time you will be." Before Claire could respond, he turned on his heel and went into the back, returning with a small car repair kit. "I'm going to go out and check on the car. Just stay here and keep that ice on your hip."

* * *

He was back within fifteen minutes, looking a little sweaty, dark curls starting to spring out wildly from his neat hairstyle.

"Hot outside," Luca reported, putting the repair kit on the counter and going to the sink behind the bar. He scrubbed his hands furiously in the sink, avoiding Claire's gaze, then wiped his hands dry on a paper towel and tossed it in the direction of the trashcan. It bounced off the lip and hit the floor. "You've got a dead alternator," he told Claire, finally meeting her eyes. "Basically, I can't charge your battery, and you'll need a new one. You might want to call an Uber or someone to pick you up because it often takes a while to get a replacement."

"Bella might be free to pick me up," Claire said, digging into her oversized purse for her phone. "It's in here somewhere," she muttered, pulling out items to make the search easier. Luca watched curiously as she unearthed a mixed bag of nuts, a giant bottle of water, a rumpled practice skirt, her practice heels, a couple of scrunchies, a date book, a large lanyard of keys, and finally, her phone.

"Do you really need all that stuff in your bag?" he asked, eyeing the small mountain on the counter.

"It always pays to have a couple things in case of an emergency," Claire said, selecting Bella's number from her contacts. She waited patiently for it to finish ringing, nibbling on a few dried raisins. Luca watched a smile light up her face when Bella picked up, and her voice became much more animated. "Hey, Bells, it's your girl. Are you busy? I need a favor." She laughed at something Bella said. "No, I swear it's legal. Listen, I'm stranded at this bar called Ragazzo's. It's on—" She covered the phone with one hand and whispered to Luca. "What street is this on again?"

"Fourth and Paxton Lane," Luca said, putting away the repair bag.

"Fourth and Paxton Lane, yeah, I owe you lunch for this," Claire hung up and blew out a breath. "She'll be here in about ten minutes, though I still need to call a tow truck for my car."

"I have a friend who works in a repair shop," Luca offered. "He can get it towed out of here and fixed up for a good price."

"Really?" Claire's eyes lit up. "He can do that?"

"Probably," Luca shrugged. "I've known Ramón since middle school. He does good work and can get you the parts you need in a week or so."

"And yet he can't keep your car running?" Claire's lips curved in a slight smile.

Luca chuckled. "Ramón is the reason it's lasted this long." He refilled Claire's water and began wiping down the counters. "You should go home to rest and ice that hip instead of dancing today."

"No way!" Claire protested. "I have a full day! Practice with you—"

"We can reschedule for another day," Luca interrupted.

"Okay, well, besides practice with you, I have to teach two private classes, and Mama is fitting me for my new costume in the competition."

"If you don't rest, your hip could get even worse," Luca argued. "Then it might take you even longer to recover."

"It's not going to get worse!" Claire scowled. "Look, I feel fine!" She stood up to prove her point, but her leg was stiff from sitting, and she stumbled. Luca caught her gently before she hit the floor, effortless as if it was another dance move.

"You sure about that?" he asked. Without her heels, Claire's head barely came up to his chest. Once more, she caught the scent of spice and freshly cut lemons. Felt the steady beat of his heart under her fingertips.

"Yes, I'm sure," Claire insisted, pushing him away. "See? I'm fine." Claire wobbled, and Luca steadied her again.

"You're not fine," he argued, gently scooping her up and placing her back on the seat. "Sorry. I know you don't like it when I make you do something, but you should at least rest until your friend gets here."

"Fine," Claire scowled, putting the ice pack back on her hip. "Happy?"

Luca inclined his head in a nod. "Yes." He picked up a broom, which was leaning against the wall, and started to sweep. Silence fell over the room, with only the slight *swish, swish* of the straw bristles over the floor filling the bar.

"How come I have to rest when you're the one who's working here all night?" Claire demanded after a minute.

Luca stopped sweeping and stared at her in surprise. "How did you know I was working here all night?"

Claire pointed at the shift calendar behind the counter. "Have you been working here every night this week? Do you get any sleep? How have you not dropped dead yet? Why didn't you tell me?"

Luca held up a hand to stop the barrage of questions. "It didn't seem necessary since I don't let my lack of sleep affect practice."

A worried crease showed on Claire's forehead. "This can't be healthy, though. You really need more rest."

Luca laughed, and Claire thought she heard a touch of bitterness in his voice. "I don't really have a choice."

"There's always a choice."

Luca looked down at his hands, stained with grease from her car, despite his best efforts to wash it away. "Not for me," Luca said, returning to sweeping. Before he could reach for the dustpan, Claire was off her stool and kneeling on the questionably clean floor, holding the dustpan steady for him.

"I told you to rest," Luca reminded her.

"You helped with my car. Besides, this job is a lot easier with two people," Claire pointed out. Rather than comment, Luca swept the rest of the debris into the waiting dustpan.

"There, done. Now go back and rest." He held out a hand to help her to her feet.

Claire winced but gripped his hand and hauled herself up. Her pants were smudged with dirt now, and some dust had gotten onto her sleeve. Claire brushed it off easily without complaint.

"Thank you," she said, sky-blue eyes meeting his. She hesitated for a second, then continued. "Not just for helping me up, thank you for helping me with my car, and for making me comfortable and looking after me…" She paused, looking down at the ground. "I know I haven't been the easiest partner to work with. I had this perfect plan of going to Blackpool with Sebastian and when he just left…" Claire shrugged ruefully. "I should've been grateful to have a partner instead of upset that you didn't fit into my plan."

Claire looked up at Luca, expecting a response. There was exasperation hidden in those eyes, but also surprise. "You're welcome," she heard Luca answer. He was still holding her hand, staring into her eyes, but she couldn't bring herself to look away. He...didn't seem to mind and was looking right back.

"Hello? Is anyone here?" Luca and Claire jumped as Bella opened the door, her long curly hair twisted up into a bun and a pair of jeans thrown on over her leotard. She stopped in her tracks, eyeing the two of them, the identical guilty looks on Claire and Luca's faces.

"Am I interrupting something?" She asked, lips curving in amusement.

"Uh, no!" Claire said, flushing pink. Bella raised a skeptical eyebrow but said nothing.

"Good, 'cause we gotta jet, girl. I need to be back in time for my next class in twenty minutes."

"Right, coming," Claire said, moving over to the counter. She shoved everything back into her purse and slipped out the door. "I'll see you later, Luca."

"Wait—" Luca grabbed for the ice pack Claire had left on the counter, held it out. "Take care of yourself."

Claire eyed the ice pack for a moment.

"Woah, ice pack, are you okay, hun?" Bella asked in concern.

"I'm fine." Claire shot Luca a pleading look. "I just had a little accident." She snatched the ice pack from Luca, her fingers brushing his as she did. The momentary touch was enough to send tingles up her arm, Claire tried to ignore them as she hurried to the door. "Let's go, don't want you to be late."

Bella started to follow, then paused in the doorway, giving Luca an appraising look up and down.

"Is there something she's not telling me?" she asked. Luca hesitated.

"I don't want to betray her trust but…try to get her to rest today, will you?"

Bella nodded. "I'll do my best." She started to head out again then stopped. "Thanks for helping her. You're good people." With that, Bella was out the door, leaving Luca standing dumbstruck behind her.

Good people, Luca considered the phrase as he went back to cleaning the bar. He caught the lingering scent of Claire's perfume in the air and shook his head. He might be good people, but was he good enough for her?

Chapter 9: Open Break

"The Cross Body Open is a dynamic way to begin your patterns where you move away from your partner to create a strong BOING or rubber band effect."

"Wow, Viviane, I'm so impressed with your progress. You've really improved since the last time I saw you." Claire applauded as Viviane Murphy finished demonstrating her Cha-cha routine. "I especially liked your arm extensions on the open breaks. You look like a real professional."

"S'nortiz taught me that," Vivian said proudly. "He said when I'm doing my arm 'stentions to pretend I've got a little bouncy ball between my fingers like this, see?" She held out her little, dimpled hand, fingers stretched out, thumb and index finger in position as if there was some invisible golf ball being held there. "S'nortiz gave me a ball to practice with, but now I can do it all on my own."

"Well, S'nortiz was very smart to help you use your imagination to create the correct shape. I've seen some kids in our older class who still have trouble with that, so maybe you'll have to teach them." Viviane's face lit up at the thought of teaching the older students something they hadn't learned yet. "Did… S'nortiz just start teaching you, Viviane?" Claire asked, mentally flipping through the roster of instructors who taught the children's class. She didn't think she knew anyone called S'nortiz, but then again, Viviane had called her Miss Eclair for a few months when she had first joined the class.

"Nope!" Viviane's brown curls bounced as she shook her head back and forth. "He's been here almost forever. Longer than me!"

So it wasn't a new hire, Claire puzzled, racking her brain. "Well, what does he look like?" she asked, hoping to get a clue.

"He's tall," Viviane stretched her arms as high as she could to demonstrate. "And he has hair like macaroni, but it's not pasta color, it's candy bar color. And Mommy says he's an alien like from space even though he lives here now." She cocked a head at Claire. "If he's an alien, why doesn't he have green skin? Or make things float in the air without holding onto them?"

Claire swallowed a laugh. "Maybe he can do other things, like show you new ways to dance. And I'm sure if you ask him nicely, he'll help you with other 'alien' dances too," Claire said as she took Viviane's small hands in hers. "Now let's see how your East Coast swing looks. Remember, you want to do a rock-step, triple-step, triple-step—"

But Viviane was already doing so, tiny brow furrowed in concentration as she stepped nimbly, rocking back, then taking three steps to the right, three to the left, then repeating the sequence again. Her knees were actually coming up, and she was developing some hip movement, a huge change since the last time she had practiced.

"Wow, Viviane, that was amazing!" Claire enthused. "Did S'nortiz teach you that, too?"

"Uh-huh," Viviane's curls bounced as she nodded. "He taught me a trick where I pretend I'm digging with a 'normous shovel." She exaggerated the digging movement, bending her knees again and pushing as if she were stomping something into the ground. "S'nortiz didn't have a shovel, but we practiced with a broom," she explained.

"Unorthodox, but it works," Claire agreed, feeling a wave of respect for this mystery teacher. Most of the students at this age – understandably—had difficulties with coordination, but Viviane's movements were as smooth and clean. Claire would definitely have to ask Papa who this 'S'nortiz' was when she had the chance.

"Miss Claire?"

"Yes, sweetie?" Claire turned her attention back to her student.

"Why are you walking funny?"

"Oh…" Claire floundered, trying to think of an acceptable explanation. "It's just a little boo-boo; I had an accident yesterday."

"Oh." Viviane considered this news seriously. "Did you ask your mommy to kiss it better? Sometimes that helps me."

"No… I didn't." Claire couldn't imagine her stern mama doing anything as tender as kissing an injury.

"Mama doesn't really kiss boo-boos," she explained to Viviane. "That's usually Papa's job. It's really just a little thing, though. I was at a party and someone was a little mean and pushed me."

Immediately, Viviane's face clouded over. "That's not a little mean, that's VERY mean Miss Claire! Did you tell his mommy to put him in time out?"

Claire tried to imagine an older female version of Tommy putting him in a time out and had to bite her lip to keep from laughing. "You know, I never thought of that. Sometimes adults think they have to handle everything themselves."

"Next time you go to a party, you should bring S'nortiz with you," Viviane advised her seriously. "One time, Charlie was trying to wipe a booger on the rest of the class, and S'nortiz got him to stop."

Claire chuckled. "You really like S'nortiz, don't you?"

"S'nortiz is the best," Viviane boasted. "He makes sure that I never get hurt or covered in boogers ever."

"You're very lucky to have him as a teacher then, aren't you?"

"He's the best teacher in the whole un-i-verse," Viviane stated emphatically. "He NEVER yells if we're doing it wrong, and sometimes he teaches us new words from where he comes from, and he's always making the classes fun."

Viviane looked around to see if anyone was listening, then crooked a finger at Claire, indicating she wanted her teacher to bend down to her level.

"Miss Claire," she whispered. "I'm gonna marry S'nortiz when I grow up."

"Really?" Claire couldn't stop a small smile from breaking through. "You're not going to wait for Prince Charming to come for you?" Viviane gave an exasperated sigh and put her hands on her hips.

"Prince Charming's are only in movies, Miss Claire. S'nortiz is real."

* * *

Claire was still chuckling over Viviane's confession when she was being fitted for her Latin dance costume an hour later.

"Hold still, *dorogoy*," Natalia scolded, her mouth full of pins. "Do you want to dance with uneven seams?" Claire was being fitted in the dance studio's costume room, a space not unlike a large, Hollywood costume room her mother set up next to the studio office. Costumes in every color of the rainbow hung on racks, shimmering with rhinestones and sequins. Many of the dresses had been worn by Natalia herself in her younger years, and some had been donated by others. Most of the costumes could be lent out to students who couldn't afford to buy their own. Leon was never one to deny a dancer a costume when they had so many to spare.

But Natalia had made all of Claire's dresses herself. Years of repairing her own tutus and ballet slippers had left her with deft hands, even if they were starting to get stiff and sore as she got older. The sudden need for a Latin costume at the last minute had meant Natalia had to spend a few nights in front of her sewing machine, but after a week of work, the dress was almost done. She just needed her daughter to stand still for ten minutes.

"*Prosti*, Mama," Claire apologized. She tried to stand straight, but her hip tinged painfully, and she winced, automatically shifting her weight back off her injured hip. She was unused to wearing this sort of dress for competitions. In the past, her dresses had long, ankle-length skirts. This costume was a skimpy, shimmery number that accentuated her toned figure, covering her torso in a semi-sheer material that flowed down until it stopped abruptly, barely skimming her thighs and showing a lot of leg.

"Stand straight!" Natalia repeated, a line of irritation creasing her forehead. She adjusted a pin along the hem of Claire's skirt, keeping an eagle eye out for wrinkles along the seams. She watched as Claire obediently moved herself into an upright position, then just as quickly shifted her weight back, letting out a barely audible hiss of pain. She knew the signs well enough to know her only daughter was in pain but trying to hide it.

"Relax a while. I'll be right back." Natalia ordered, rising stiffly to her feet. Her leg seemed to ache more and more as she got older, and she hobbled into the small adjacent kitchen, leaning heavily on her cane. There, she filled two clean cups with hot water and the special stash of tea she kept for when her leg was feeling particularly painful. Setting both cups on a tray, she limped back towards Claire but stopped when she heard voices.

"I thought I said you should rest." That was Luca's voice, sounding like he was concerned.

"And I told you, I had a costume fitting along with two private lessons," Claire countered. "What are you doing here? Our rehearsal isn't for another hour."

"Mrs. Beauchene called me for a fitting, she said my costume for the competition was finished."

"Oh," Claire sounded a little flustered. "It might actually need a few tweaks; I had an inspiration when I got back so now it's not ready."

What? Limping to the closet, Natalia searched for Luca's costume on the rack. There it was, the donkey head and outfit so Luca could play Bottom to Claire's Titania. Natalia frowned. Was it possible her daughter was having second thoughts about the performance for next week's competition?

"Does this inspiration mean redoing the routine?" Luca sounded irritated. "Why can't we just be two people, doing the waltz?"

"I like having a little story in the routine," Claire sounded like she was pouting. "It gives the performance nuance."

"Nuance or not, you should be resting, not redoing an entire choreography last-minute."

"I have come first in every competition for the past five years, I'm not about to lose now," Natalia could practically see her daughter's arms crossed, the stubborn tilt to her chin. "I can rest after Blackpool."

"You trying to dance with that injury that *idiota* gave you is not going to improve our chances of winning," Luca snapped. Natalia pricked her ears in interest. Had Sebastian been the cause of her injury in Los Angeles?

Leon would have a fit if he heard someone had harmed a hair on his daughter's head.

"Fine," Claire sounded irritated, too. "I'll rest if you get some extra sleep."

"I'm used to getting less sleep; I'll be fine." Luca snapped as Natalia limped back into the room. Neither noticed as she set the tray down on a table, so engrossed were they in their argument. "There's a difference between being tired and being injured."

Claire said nothing, merely raised a single, perfectly plucked eyebrow.

Luca clenched his fists. "Look," he sighed. "You need rest more than I do. I can handle my workload."

"For how long?" Claire demanded. She barely registered Natalia shoving a cup of tea into her hands but continued her argument as she sipped her tea. "You might be 'handling your workload' now, but at some point, you need to take a break before you collapse."

Natalia stood off to the side, sipping her own tea and watching them. For some reason that she couldn't explain, it pleased her to see them together, the fiery and passionate Luca against her elegant and driven daughter, a combination that seemed to be in complete opposition but simultaneously seemed perfectly balanced. Cool elegance to chill fiery heat. Determination to temper passion. Fire to warm ice, like one of those American poems Leon had read to her. They probably didn't even realize how perfectly they complimented each other, Natalia mused as she sipped her tea, didn't notice the sparks that seemed to fly and charge the space around them.

On the other hand…Natalia's eyebrows raised as Luca handed Claire another ice pack, holding it out insistently until Claire rolled her eyes and pressed it against her hip. Perhaps only Claire was in the dark. Could Claire not see the way Luca looked at her? Standing with one hand on her hip, wearing a skimpy Latin costume of blue and silver that fit her like a second skin? Perhaps it was because Natalia knew that look, had seen it on men's faces many times during her illustrious ballet career. Her daughter was a beautiful girl, just as she had been, though far more innocent. Leon had seen to that, making sure their daughter had lived a life full of love and support, without wanting anything, encouraging her to have friends and an education outside of the dance studio. He'd made sure that their lives had been full of family adventures outside of work, had dragged them to amusement parks and museums, visited all fifty states and most of Europe on their vacations.

"What if she doesn't want to be a dancer?" Natalia had fretted when Claire came home from a trip to the Roy Rogers Museum, whooping and waving around the cowgirl hat that Leon had bought her from the gift shop.

"Then we will support whatever she chooses to do," Leon had said. "She should have the freedom to be whatever she wants to be."

But Claire had taken to dancing like she took to breathing air. And if Natalia had been a little disappointed that her daughter had followed her father's love of ballroom dance more than her mother's love of ballet, she had never said it out loud.

Now, looking at her daughter and Luca, Natalia had never seen the young man so concerned for the condition of his partner before. And as for her daughter, Natalia remembered when Claire had decided to specialize in Smooth dances at the age of thirteen, right after she'd been paired with Sebastian. She knew the reason Claire had chosen to specialize had been all that boy's influence, just as she knew that boy had only done so because he was too lazy to experiment with other categories. They might have done well by specializing, bringing in award after award for their category, but she's always felt Sebastian had dragged her daughter down to his level rather than attempting to rise to hers. And no matter how much she and Leon had urged Claire to continue to practice other styles, Claire had been determined to follow Sebastian's lead.

However, in the past few days, Claire had thrown herself into practicing dance styles like she hadn't in years, working to hone techniques that were rusty from disuse. Natalia nodded her head in approval. Luca, it seemed, was already pushing Claire to greater heights. She liked this partner a lot more.

"Look," Claire sighed. "You want me to rest, and I want you to get some more sleep. So, how about a truce? I'll go home and put some ice on my hip if you use our practice time to get a nap. Deal?" She held out a hand for Luca to shake.

"Deal," Luca agreed reluctantly, clasping Claire's hand in his. Natalia could practically feel the air fizzle around them. She slipped out of the room, muttering something about needing more pins in case either Luca or Claire noticed her leaving. "Have you ever been to a salsa club?" Luca blurted out. Natalia peeked back out of the kitchen, surprised. Luca rarely interacted with students while he was inside the studio, and he NEVER interacted with them outside. Claire stared at him, clearly just as surprised.

"Uh, no," she stuttered, "why?"

"Well, since we won't be practicing today, it might be a good idea to get in a little extra practice later this week… like a field trip," Luca said quickly. "There's a place a few blocks from here that plays Latin music on Fridays. You don't have to have a lot of experience, and it's for all ages. One of the disadvantages of only dancing here is that you don't get the opportunity to improvise. It might be useful to see how you can handle dancing Salsa that is not part of a routine- just in case one of us has to adapt while we're on the floor."

The boy was actually blushing, Natalia noted with some amusement.

"All right," Claire said after a moment.

Her daughter was a little pinker than usual, too.

"If it's for the sake of practice, why not?"

"Really? Uh—good," Luca stammered. "I can meet you there, maybe around eight-thirty?"

"Sure."

They smiled at each other. The moment was ruined when Claire's phone rang, and she stooped to dig it out of her bag with an apologetic smile. The smile faltered briefly as she saw the caller I.D., and Natalia felt a stab of annoyance as she recognized the photo of the handsome blond-haired boy on the screen.

"I should take this…" Claire was eyeing the phone with some trepidation.

"Sure, I get it," Luca turned toward the door with a look of disgust.

"Uh… hey." Was it Natalia's imagination, or did Claire's smile look a little forced as she answered? "Oh yeah, I got home safe." There was a pause. "You're coming to visit next week? That's great!" Now Natalia was sure her daughter's cheery voice was fake. She looked as excited as if she was making a trip to the dentist. "I can't wait to see you! Hang on a second, babe." She covered the phone with one hand and whispered to Luca, "I'll see you Friday at eight-thirty?"

Luca shrugged, his face back to its usual impassiveness. "Sure."

"I'll see you then!" Claire smiled and waved, turning back to her phone. Natalia turned and went back into the kitchen. So, her daughter's boyfriend would be coming back into town. She did not like the way such news turned her stomach into knots.

Chapter 10: Cari Cias

"A term describing caress like rubbing thigh, calf, or foot down the follower's body or leader's leg."

"So, how's the practice going? Luca driving you crazy yet?" Bella asked as she sprawled on Claire's flouncy, queen-size bed.

Two years before, Claire and Natalia had decorated the whole room, painting it a classic cream and gold trim, with furniture, bedspreads, and curtains to match. They had argued the entire time, but after two long months, the entire room had been refurbished beautifully. Claire's medals and awards dominated the whole wall closest to the bed, with a computer study area occupying the far side of the room next to the walk-in closet that Claire was currently digging through.

"He's actually really good," Claire commented, her voice muffled as she searched her shelves. "You gotta respect him for taking the time to practice while working his full-time job. Plus, he can also Waltz well, which I was not expecting."

"Mhm…" Bella eyed her best friend curiously while Claire examined a frilly shirt, then tossed it away. "So, what's this I hear about you and Luca doing a little something more than practice last week?"

"Where did you hear that?" Claire demanded.

"Bethany. That girl loves to spread gossip," Bella rolled her eyes. "Don't worry. I made sure everyone talking about you remembered that you were still one of the school's best dancers, and if they wanted to be half as good as you, they should exercise something other than their mouth."

"The same could be said for Bethany," Claire muttered. "Still, thanks, Bells."

"Girl, you know the saying. Sisters before gossipy-biatches-with-more-boob-than-brains."

"I'm pretty sure that's not how it goes," Claire laughed as she discarded another fancy top.

"It does where we're concerned," Bella smiled, stretching one leg over her head. "I got your back no matter what."

"You're the best," Claire smiled, coming out of her closet. "So, what do you think of this shirt?"

Bella examined the blue, filmy top Claire held up to her chest.

"Pretty," she decided, before going back to her stretches. "You going somewhere?"

Claire flushed and ducked back into her closet. "Luca asked me to meet him at this local Salsa club tonight," she explained. "Apparently, it'll help me improve my technique if I practice outside the studio?"

"Uh-huh," Bella touched the bottoms of her feet together into a butterfly pose and pushed her knees towards the ground. "So, you need help deciding what to wear on your date?"

"It's not a date!" Claire flushed, a frilly top in each hand. "It's a professional night out with my dance partner with the objective to learn new techniques… in the wild, so to speak." She held up a pink crop top in one hand and a blue number with voluminous sleeves in the other. "Which do you like better?"

Bella transitioned to a half-pigeon stretch and looked over the options carefully. "The pink one shows too much skin, and the blue one makes you look like a disco queen," she declared firmly. "Actually, I'm pretty sure that top is from when you did that 70's themed competition three years ago. Claire-bear, do you understand the importance of cleaning out your closet?"

"You never know when they'll throw another one," Claire pointed out. "Logically, I'm saving myself money by hanging onto it."

"Tell me that in two more years when your closet takes over the rest of your room," Bella predicted, pulling one leg back so far, her foot touched her head.

"Fine, well, maybe this?" Claire dropped the rejected tops on the growing pile and dove back into her closet with an air close to desperation. She held up a red, glittery corset that looked like it was from a burlesque show.

Bella eyed it, then studied Claire. "So… you're sure this is a professional thing, right?" she asked.

"Of course," Claire snapped, dropping the corset and continuing to dig through her clothes.

"So, why are you freaking out so much? Just wear whatever you want."

"Because!" Claire sputtered. "I should make a good first impression!"

"A good impression on Luca," Bella repeated, just in case she had missed something.

"Yes!" Claire grabbed a dress off the clothes rack that looked like it belonged in a Fred Astaire movie and a skimpier one that seemed better suited for the beach. She looked at Bella pleadingly.

"Help me!" she implored.

Bella sighed in resignation and swung her legs gracefully off the bed. "Okay, but we're going to need to have a talk later about organizing this closet."

She surveyed the mess for two minutes before selecting a blue halter top and jeans from the chaos. "Here. These will be easy to dance in, but they're also nice enough for a first date."

"It's not a date!" Claire repeated, running for the bathroom to get changed. "I'm with Sebastian, remember?" The door slammed behind her.

"Yeah, whatever," Bella hollered at the bathroom door, flopping back onto the bed. "Wear your new earrings! They'll look good with your top! And keep your hair down!"

The door opened again after a minute, and Claire emerged, self-consciously tucking her waist-long hair behind her ears. She held out her arms and did a turn. "Well, how do I look?"

"Like you need a little eyeliner to make those baby blues pop. C'mere, girl." Bella gestured to the bed and patted the bedspread to indicate where Claire should sit.

Pulling a blue eyeliner pencil out of her purse, she held it out to Claire. "I was going to give this to you on your birthday but consider this an early present. It's supposed to be really good, and it's all natural."

"Aww, Bells, thank you!" Claire wrapped Bella in a hug.

"Yeah, I'm the best. Scoot back; lemme see how well it works."

Obediently, Claire moved back on the bedspread, closing her eyes so Bella could do her make-up like she had done a thousand times before. Bella gently traced the outline of Claire's eyes, patiently following the eyelashes before going back and smudging it lightly with her fingertip.

"So, Claire-bear, in all seriousness, I know I'm joking a bit, but how are things really going with Sebastian?"

She stopped applying for a second so Claire could open her eyes and look at her.

"Things have been a bit… strained since I went and visited, but we both knew this might happen," Claire admitted. "Long distance is hard, but we'll do our best to make it work."

"Claire, I know you're doing your best, but…" Bella hesitated before continuing. "I'm not sure he's doing the same. I mean, abandoning you like that at the party? If my

Honeybear did that to me… well, let's just say she wouldn't be my Honeybear anymore. At the very least, we'd be having a serious talk about what we expect from each other."

"Well, excuse me, but not everyone can have the best girlfriend in the world." Claire chuckled, closing her eyes so Bella could continue applying her eyeliner.

"Would it really be that bad if you two broke up?" Bella pressed. "No one is pressuring you to keep this relationship together. Can't you just… take a break?"

"But I want to make it work, Bells," Claire sighed. "We're so good together… I just feel like it's a shame to throw something like that way without even trying."

"Sweetie, he barely calls you; you drove all the way to see him last week and the way he left you alone at that party… I don't think he wants this as much as you do."

"That's not true!" Claire protested. "He called me a few days ago. He's coming into town for my birthday next week!"

"Well, that's a start," Bella muttered, finishing applying the eyeliner. "Keep those eyes closed; I also got you some new eyeshadow. You're going to love the color."

"You're a goddess among us mere mortals, Bells," Claire murmured as Bella brushed the deep blue powder over her eyelids.

"I know I am, but I hope your man showers you with flowers and presents when he comes to town. Because if not, I am kicking him in his stupid, white ass," Bella huffed, eyeing her handiwork critically.

"He's really not as bad as you think," Claire argued, keeping her eyes closed as Bella cleaned up a smudge on her cheek.

"No, you're too nice," Bella insisted, turning Claire's head from side to side. "I just hope he's worth your effort because there is a certain gorgeous hunk that has his eye on you."

"Luca is just my partner," Claire objected.

"Who said I was talking about Luca?" Bella asked slyly, and Claire flushed again.

"'Cause… you've been teasing me that this is like a first date," she muttered, squirming.

"You're also putting a lot of effort into looking nice for him," Bella teased. "Not that he's not worth it. If I was straight, I would nab that man in a second."

"Bells!"

"Okay, I'll stop," Bella chuckled. She pulled a small compact mirror from her purse and opened it up. "All right, girl, check it out. What do you think?"

Claire's eyes fluttered open, and she stared at her reflection in the mirror for a second before a broad smile broke out on her face. "I absolutely love it! Thank you!" she said, giving Bella a hug.

"You're so welcome," Bella said, kissing her on the cheek. "Now you're totally ready for your very professional outing that is definitely not a date."

Claire gave her a dirty look as she rolled off the bed, collecting her new eyeliner and tossing it in her purse. "I'm gonna ignore that because this make-up is really, really cute." She glanced at her phone display and blanched.

"And I'm going to be late if I don't leave, like, right now. Can you let yourself out?"

"Sure thing, Claire-bear," Bella said, flopping back on the bed. "Bianca will be here in ten to pick me up. She's finally got a day off and we're going to our favorite restaurant for dinner."

"Sounds fun," Claire slung her heavy purse onto her shoulder and dashed from the room. "Send her my love, I'll see you later!"

Half a minute later, she was back again, a little breathless. "Before I leave," she asked, holding out her arms. "How do I really look? And be serious."

Bella propped herself up on her elbows and gave Claire a thorough once-over. "Honestly, sweetie? If I didn't have my Honeybear, I would take you out for a night on the town myself."

"So… good?" Claire asked. Bella winked.

"You look better than good. You're going to be breaking hearts right and left."

Chapter 11: Fricction

"Argentinian Tango move that involves pulling the follower, typically dragging her on her toes."

La Casita Bienvenidos was a small, out-of-the-way restaurant only a few miles from Claire's home. She had often passed it while driving but had never thought to stop and was pleasantly surprised to find it was a charming little place with the dining area set up out front and a dance floor tucked in the back.

A live band played, and the dance floor was packed with dancers when Claire's Uber dropped her off at precisely eight-thirty.

Luca hadn't given her much in the way of where to meet him, but the bar area looked open, so she circuited the mass of moving, sweaty bodies packed onto every inch of the dance floor and took a seat on an available stool. The music was blasted from speakers set on all sides, a pounding, upbeat rhythm that vibrated through every bone of her body, while colorful lights illuminated the dimly lit room.

"Can I get you something, miss?" asked the bartender, a glass in hand. He was tall, dark, and lean, his curly hair tamed into a bushy ponytail at the nape of his neck.

"No, thank you," Claire found herself shouting to be heard over the music, "I'm just waiting for a friend."

The bartender slid a plastic cup full of water toward her with a smile.

"It's on the house," he assured her, "you're going to need it."

"Thanks." Claire took tiny sips and turned her attention back towards the sea of dancers moving under the multicolored lights. Men and women of every size and age seemed to be on the floor; in one corner, she saw a boy who looked barely old enough to drink, dancing with a woman she assumed was his mother, while two boys who looked like they were in college danced together in a separate corner. A tiny man who appeared to be in his seventies led a woman in her thirties through a series of complicated spins while another couple in their twenties seemed to be fused together.

A Latino man in his thirties slid onto the seat beside Claire, his shirt damp with sweat. He glanced at Claire, then held out his hand.

"You dance?" he asked in heavily accented English. Claire hesitated, then remembered. Luca had invited her to see what Latin dancing was like outside the studio.

"Sure, why not," she replied, taking his hand and letting him lead her onto the floor.

* * *

Luca peered out the bus window at the darkening street and cursed under his breath. His car had broken down again, and he'd barely caught the bus that would pass by the bar. Claire was probably throwing a fit that he was late, but there was nothing he could do about the lethargic speed of public transportation.

As if on cue, the bus groaned to a stop, and a homeless man with a long, tangled beard and ratty coat shuffled on board, dragging a threadbare suitcase behind him. From the pockets of his garment, he produced a tattered purse and began to ponderously drop coins into the meter as the door closed behind him.

Luca checked his watch. It was eight-forty, and he was still five blocks away. At this rate, he'd be there by nine. He'd make better time running.

Moving down the bus aisle, Luca squeezed past the homeless man who was still feeding coins into the meter and jumped out onto the sidewalk, hitting the ground at a sprint. With any luck, he'd be there in fifteen minutes.

* * *

Claire was dancing with her third and sweatiest partner of the night. Her halter top had actually become damp from him while in a closed hold, and despite her best efforts to stay as far as she could, she was feeling suffocated from the scent of cigarette smoke that made his body odor smell even worse. Sweaty Man sent her into a turn, and Claire used the opportunity to scan the dance floor. Where was Luca? She felt like she'd been there for hours as her partner tipped her backward into a dip. Sweaty Man smiled at her, displaying a wide mouth of discolored teeth, and the prior pungent smells were augmented by the eye-watering stench of his bad breath. Claire flinched as a bead of sweat rolled off Sweaty Man's forehead and landed on her bare shoulder.

"I'm so killing Luca when he gets here," Claire muttered as she was pulled to her feet. She pushed herself away from her partner, not wanting to wait until the music ended. "Thank you!" she shouted over the music. "But I think I'm going to take a break now." She started to walk away, but her partner grabbed her wrist in a damp grip.

"You stay for dance!" he insisted. Claire shook her head and tried to pull away.

"I'm sorry, I… really need to get some water," she lied.

"You very pretty, you stay for dance!" Sweaty Man argued. Claire pulled against his grip, feeling a mixture of panic and irritation rising in her chest.

"That's flattering, but I'm going to the bar. I need a break!" Her wrist was aching now, and it felt like the dancers were pressing in on all sides, leaving no room for escape. "Look," Claire shouted, "I really have to go. I said I would meet my…boyfriend here at eight-thirty, and I want to check and see if he's here yet."

Sweaty Man's grin widened. "You stay here and dance. He find you, *if* he is looking—"

His gaze landed on someone behind Claire, and his grin faded.

"Sorry I'm late," Claire caught a whiff of Luca's scent as he dropped an arm around her shoulders. "Are you okay?"

"Fine," Claire wrapped her free arm around Luca's waist. His shirt was damp with sweat, and he was breathing as if he'd been running.

"Hey, man," Luca glowered at Sweaty Man, who still hadn't released his grip on Claire's arm. "The song is over. Why don't you find a new partner?" Sweaty Man scowled and moved away into the crowd.

"You're trembling." Luca guided Claire off the dance floor and to a quiet corner away from the music. He lifted Claire's wrist to examine it under the colored lights. "Did he hurt you?"

His touch sent tingles up Claire's arm and she jerked her hand away. "Why do you care? You're the one who's twenty minutes late."

"My car broke down, and I had to take the bus," Luca said.

That would explain why he was late, but Claire wasn't prepared to forgive him right away. "Ever heard of Uber?" she snapped, and Luca shrugged his shoulders.

"I don't really have the funds to pay for it."

"Oh, right," Claire felt her irritation fading. "Did the bus just arrive?"

Luca shook his head. "It was taking too long, so I ran the last couple blocks."

"The last couple…" Claire gaped. "Because the bus was taking too long?"

Luca nodded. "I was already late, I didn't want you to be here by yourself, considering the last party you went to."

"You ran because…" Claire took in Luca's sweat-soaked shirt with new appreciation. "Thank you."

"So," Luca gestured expansively. "Do you still want to dance?"

Something inside Claire warmed. "We are already here," Claire said, taking his hand. Luca led her back onto the floor, guiding her to a spot that wasn't too crowded. Claire slipped into his embrace, taking the familiar hold. "By the way, any sweat you feel or smell is not mine," she insisted. "That last guy soaked me. I feel disgusting."

Luca chuckled, and the vibrations sent tingles down Claire's spine. "You don't smell sweaty, you smell…" Luca hesitated. "You don't smell sweaty," he repeated.

"Thanks, I feel so much better," Claire deadpanned.

Luca chuckled again, his right hand moving to the small of Claire's back. He clasped her right hand in his left, thumb brushing lightly over her knuckles.

"Anyway…" Claire fumbled. The light pressure of his thumb on the back of her hand was making it hard to think clearly. The song changed from a Salsa to something quicker, and she changed the subject with it. "What kind of dance is this?"

"This is a bachata song," Luca was already drawing her closer. "Just relax and follow my lead."

The frame was very different from the waltz, Claire realized as Luca took both her hands and looped them around his neck. She caught another whiff of spice as her cheek brushed his shoulder, and he began to move, Luca's hips rocking against hers, Claire's legs straddling his. She peeked at the other dancers around her, as Luca pivoted them around, trying to get an idea of how she should be moving. Men and women, women and women, men and men were pressed against each other, arms and legs twining around the other, breaking apart to spin, to roll, coming back together to rock against each other, moving in sensual dance. It was beautiful and intimate, sweet and provocative all at the same time.

Luca turned her head back towards him.

"Don't worry about looking like them right now," he instructed her. "Just work on trying to be in sync with me."

"But—" Claire tried to protest, but Luca gently pushed her head back onto his shoulder. "Just relax," he repeated. He was so close Claire could feel the vibration of his voice, smell the warm, spicy scent that seemed to envelop him. "Just relax and dance."

Easier said than done, Claire thought, annoyed as she tried to relax her head comfortably on Luca's broad shoulder. How the heck was she supposed to 'follow him and just relax?' She needed to watch and observe others. She had to ensure she was doing it correctly so she didn't stand out on the dance floor as the outsider. She tried to lean her head on Luca's shoulder while still watching out of the corner of her eyes.

"Claire," Luca gently covered her eyes with his hand and she instinctively reached up to yank it away. "Don't watch them. Keep your eyes closed and just focus on me."

Claire hesitated, her hand wrapped around his. "Trust me," Luca continued. "Just for a few minutes."

"Fine," Claire released her hold on his hand. "A few minutes." Claire returned her head to Luca's shoulder, keeping her eyes closed.

"Now just relax," Luca's voice was warm in her ear, "and follow my lead." He began to move again, and Claire forced herself to focus entirely on him, the feel of the shift of his torso, the roll of his hips, his legs between hers. The music pumped all around them, and Claire was vaguely aware of dancers on each side of her, but her world had narrowed to the feel of Luca's arm around her waist, the heat of his breath on her cheek.

Claire let her hand stray slowly down Luca's back, feeling the dampness between his shoulder blades. Feeling the muscle that didn't come from expensive physical trainers like Sebastian, but hard work, as a dancer and bartender. Feeling the solidness of *Luca*, who had run 'the last couple blocks' to meet up with her after his car broke down. Despite the sweat, Claire could smell hints of laundry detergent and shampoo. The mingled aroma of different soaps was strangely comforting, and Claire felt herself relaxing in Luca's arms.

"That's better." Claire lifted her head off his shoulder. Her heart gave an unexpected flip-flop as his dark eyes met hers, only a couple of inches away. "You're doing much better," Luca told her.

"Thanks…" Claire managed, suddenly feeling tongue-tied. "You're a good teacher." She started to drop her head back on his shoulder and paused. "Could I see your phone?"

"Sure?" They broke apart and Luca reluctantly pulled an outdated flip phone out of his pocket. "I can't really afford anything else—" he started to explain.

"I'm not judging," Claire took it and began pressing the small keys with difficulty. "I'm just putting my number in here for emergencies." She finished and hit the call button, showing Luca the read-out on her phone screen as it went through. "There," she said, handing the phone back. "Now the next time you're stranded you can call me, and the next time I get hassled I can call you. Not that I really needed you to," she added. "Your timing for showing up right when I needed you was perfect. I did not want to have to deal with that creep."

Luca blinked, surprise flickering in his eyes, then a rare smile briefly lit up his face, so radiant Claire was momentarily speechless.

"It's nothing," he answered and Claire could only nod, as every coherent thought in her head turned to mush. A man should be arrested for a smile like that. One lip twitch had transformed his already striking features into breathtaking.

"Shall we?" Luca pulled her back into frame and Claire immediately buried her head on his shoulder, hoping her blush couldn't be seen in the dark. Focus, she told herself sternly. He was still just Luca, she tried to remind herself. The same Luca who had criticized her at the last competition for not paying attention. Who in the two years she'd known him rarely gave her a compliment and was always scowling...

Someone bumped into them, hard enough to make Claire stumble and she was aware of Luca arms tightening protectively around her, pivoting her away and using his torso as a shield. "Watch it!" He glared at the offending couple, and they moved away, mouthing apologies. "Are you okay?" Luca ran a hand down her back, eyes full of concern. "Did they hurt you?"

Claire felt herself smiling up at him. "I'm fine," she reassured him, laying her head back on his shoulder and closing her eyes. Somehow, him being just Luca was exactly what she needed.

Chapter 12: Lock

"When moving, the foot approaches the standing foot and crosses in front."

"Come on, girl," Bella complained, her mouth full of hairpins. "Are you seriously not going to tell me what happened?" She pushed another pin into the elaborate bun of curls gathered on top of Claire's head and doused it heavily in hairspray.

"What's to tell?" Claire was meticulously gluing on her fake eyelashes, and she blinked rapidly as the glue made her eyes water slightly. "We met at the club, we danced for a few hours, and then I drove him to work for his overnight shift. It was the least I could do after he helped me chase off the creep who was bugging me."

It was a week later and they were in the women's changing area of the Revire Regional Dance Competition. All around them, women of various ages and ethnicities were applying make-up, hairspray, or squeezing into their skin-tight dance costumes.

Claire had always liked the feeling of solidarity that came from preparing for each event with the other women. They clustered around mirrors, applying lipstick or checking their seams or their hair. The more self-conscious ones ducked behind costume racks to change while others stripped down to their underwear without embarrassment. Some helped each other with the fasteners at the back of their costumes, and the sound of chatter as old friends and friendly competitors caught up while applying fake eyelashes and rhinestones filled the room. In these moments, it didn't matter who had the prettiest dress or who had been dancing longer. For every newcomer, there was a veteran with a can of hairspray and extra pins to help tame their updo; for every woman who needed help squeezing into her dress, there was a veritable sisterhood willing to lend a hand at a moment's notice.

"Uh-huh. And after you dropped him off, you dumped that sorry piece of ass you call a boyfriend and got an upgrade, right?"

"Bells!" Claire sputtered, almost gluing her eyelash on crooked.

"Don't 'Bells' me," Bella turned Claire's head from side to side, admiring her handiwork and checking for stray hairs. As was Claire's preference, Bella had styled Claire's white-blonde hair in an elegant updo, the bun a mass of intricate curls and surrounded by a formidable fence of pins and blue and silver clips. In the front, Bella had shaped a segment of Claire's hair into a graceful wave that cascaded in a curve over her forehead and was held in place by half a can of hairspray and more pins. A line of rhinestones flowed along the wave of hair and started down the edge of the razor-straight part. "You were being harassed, and Ortiz pulled the Prince Charming routine like a real man is supposed to. In fact, I'd go out on a limb and say he's got more man in his pinky than Sebastian has in his whole body. So why in God's name are you still giving that man-child a second chance?"

"I can't just break up with Sebastian over one little thing," Claire protested. "Besides, he made a mistake, and he said sorry. Didn't you mention that you and Bianca had a few rough patches in the beginning?"

Bella surveyed her masterpiece one last time, giving the whole thing an extra spritz in case it decided to rebel and fall apart in the middle of the dance. Satisfied, she put down the can and began to meticulously glue the rest of the rhinestones along Claire's part.

"Bianca and I have had a few rough patches, sure," Bella agreed, carefully gluing the glittery plastic in place. "But most of our arguments are usually about how our schedules make it hard to have a date night or what to buy for dinner." She finished with the larger rhinestones near the front of the part and selected some smaller ones for the back. "I also know my Honeybear would go after anyone who put a move on me and made me uncomfortable, and I would do the same for her because we love each other, and that's what you're supposed to do when you care for someone." She sighed and put down the tiny glue bottle. "Look, I know I shouldn't speak for every couple and that no one is perfect, but people in relationships should try and share their burdens, not make them more difficult, right?"

"Bells, I—we—" Claire fumbled, trying to find the right words. "Sebastian and I have been together for a long time. I can't just… end it."

Bella had finished Claire's hair, and now she moved around so she could be face-to-face with her best friend. "Claire-bear, listen to me, sweetie," she said, putting a hand on the shoulder of her sparkly dance costume. "Aside from my boo, you are the sweetest, kindest, most loyal girl in the whole world. You've been doing everything possible to make this relationship work, and Sebastian isn't even trying to meet you halfway. You deserve someone who can be there for you—"

"Like Luca?" Claire interrupted with a sigh.

"It doesn't have to be Luca," Bella brushed some stray glitter off Claire's shoulder, "but you deserve happiness with someone reliable, respectful, who doesn't make you do all the work."

"Sebastian can do all those things!" Claire protested.

"He can, but he's not, sweetie," Bella argued. "Has he called you in the last week? Or is he too busy?"

"Claire? Is there a Claire Beauchene in here?" called a dancer as she peered into the changing room.

"Yes! Right here! I'm Claire!" Claire shouted, waving her hand.

"Thank goodness I found you," the woman sighed, coming in and closing the door. "I've been to two rooms already, and I was worried you were already out on the floor."

The dancer walked over and deposited a bouquet of delicate white roses in her arms.

"These are for you, hon. And I'm supposed to tell you that your boyfriend is waiting in the lobby with a very special message for you."

"He's here!" Claire squealed, hugging the flowers to her chest. "See, Bells, I told you he cares! He came all the way here for my competition! Oh! I have to go see him right now!" She leaped out of her chair and practically zoomed out the door on three-inch heels, dodging dancers who were still getting ready.

"That special message better start with 'I'm sorry,'" Bella muttered to herself as she started cleaning up Claire's area, packing up hairspray cans, extra rhinestones, and spare pins. "Because if not, I know a special place where we can shove those roses."

* * *

Claire spotted Sebastian near the entrance of the lobby and threw herself in his arms.

"You're here! You're here!" she shrieked.

"Woah, careful babe," Sebastian said, gently pushing her away, "your hairpin almost poked me in the eye."

"Oh! Sorry!" Claire reached out a hand to stroke his face. "Are you okay?"

"Yeah," he said, smiling and taking her hand. "Just be careful."

"Looks like I got some glitter on you, too," Claire giggled, reaching up and brushing some blue glitter off his cheek. It was strange; she could've sworn that Bells had used silver glitter in her make-up to match her trimmings, but maybe she had thrown in some blue as well.

"So, I'm guessing you're excited for today?" Sebastian asked.

"Absolutely!" Claire enthused, "I know Salsa isn't really my strongest style, but Luca and I have been practicing a lot, and I'm confident we can get to second place at least."

"Well, speaking of your new-found Salsa talent, Jesse was talking to the producers of *Dance Craze*, and they'd be interested in making you a part of the show as a guest star!" He handed Claire a thick packet. "Now, I know it's a little short notice, you'd have to come down next week, start learning a new routine for the Friday after that, but this could be huge for your career! You'll just need to fill out these forms first—"

"Wait, wait, hang on," Claire interrupted. "This is a lot to take in, they just want to make me a part of the show? What about the audition?"

"Well, they were against it at first," Sebastian explained, "but once they saw the footage of you dancing with Jesse and heard who your parents were, they were falling over themselves to bring you on board. Isn't that great?" Was it Claire's imagination? Or did Sebastian's smile look a little tight? "If they really like you, there's a chance you could be brought on for multiple episodes, which means we can be partners again and we won't have to travel back and forth to see each other!"

"Sebastian..." Claire looked down at the heavy envelope in her hands. "This is flattering, but as much as I want to be closer to you again, I don't want to be on a TV show."

Sebastian stared at her in disbelief. "You're serious. You're really throwing this once-in-a-lifetime chance away for some contest no one has heard about?"

"Blackpool is one of the most prestigious competitions in the world!"

"And unless you're living in a tiny little ballroom dance world, no one knows about Blackpool and no one cares about it either!" Sebastian shot back. "But if you do *Dance Craze*, everyone will know your name! You could be famous overnight! You could be on other dance shows, or in music videos—"

"But that's not the life I want!" Claire burst out. "Look, you were right when you said we had different dreams. *Dance Craze* is yours, and Blackpool is mine. I want to go to London and compete on the international level, just like my parents did, and I can't throw it all away when it's only a few weeks away!" She looked pleadingly into Sebastian's eyes. "You understand, don't you? I still want to support you doing *Dance Craze*, I just don't want to compete with you."

Sebastian stared at her for a moment, his expression unreadable. "You're really selfish, you know that?" he said quietly.

Claire's mouth snapped open in shock. "What?"

"I vouched for you; I pulled strings to help get you on the show. And you're just not interested because it's not your dream?" He gestured expansively. "Do you know how many dancers would kill to have the opportunity that was just handed to you on a silver platter?"

"I didn't ask to be on the show!" Claire objected. "And I didn't ask for you to vouch for me! Why didn't you talk to me first before you went through all this trouble?"

"Because I thought you'd be excited!" Sebastian said, his voice rising. "I thought I'd come here and surprise you with the news, and…" He closed his eyes and took a breath, then pulled a hotel room key out of his pocket. "Since it's your birthday tomorrow, I thought we'd find somewhere to celebrate."

Claire felt her cheeks burn bright red. She hoped no one was listening. Was he really asking her to go to a hotel with him right now? "Sebastian, this is not a good time. My first heat starts in ten minutes."

"You can blow it off, can't you?" Sebastian coaxed. "And maybe I can make you reconsider moving to L.A. with me."

"No," Claire put a hand against his chest to stop him coming closer. "I'm not leaving. You can't just ask me to uproot my life and move elsewhere at a moment's notice, and I'm not blowing off a competition! This is important to me!"

Sebastian stared at her, open disgust on his face. "You really are selfish."

"Well then, she's selfish, but at least if she hurries, she won't be late," said a cold voice on Claire's right. She turned and felt her knees go weak with relief at the sight of Luca, dressed in his usual black. His curls had been combed back into a gleaming black helmet, and someone—Claire suspected her father—had pinned a blue feather to Luca's lapel that perfectly matched her costume.

"You can't give us a few minutes?" Sebastian snapped, aiming a glare sharp enough to cut. "You're interrupting a private conversation."

Luca raised an eyebrow, unfazed. "Contestants have been asked to report to the ballroom immediately," he informed Sebastian, holding out his hand to Claire. She didn't hesitate, and reached for him, but was held back by Sebastian's grip on her other arm. Claire found herself caught in a staring match between the two men, both who looked like they were willing to engage in a tug-of-war over her.

"Sebastian…" Claire could feel a headache building at the base of her skull. "I should go." People were looking in their direction and whispering. She could practically see the rumor mill starting to churn. Was Claire Beauchene stuck in some love triangle with her previous partner and her new partner? Sebastian seemed to notice the stares, and he released his grip.

"Whatever," he muttered. "I'll see you after your dance."

Claire couldn't even meet his eyes. "Sure," she said, as Luca led her away.

"You're trembling," Luca murmured as they moved towards the check-in table to pick up their entry number. "What was he saying to you?"

"I don't want to talk about it," Claire whispered.

"All right. But if you ask me, that *cabrón*—"

"I didn't ask you," Claire snapped, pushing away from Luca and stepping up to the table by herself. Never in her life had she been so mortified. She could feel the stares of the surrounding dancers, hear the whispers, the speculation all around her and she felt her cheeks flushing bright red. Today was just supposed to be a trial competition to prepare for Blackpool, a chance to test Claire and Luca's new partnership, not some drama-heavy episode fit for reality TV. She just wanted to make it through the next couple hours of scheduled dance and go home.

"Claire Beauchene and Luca Ortiz checking in," she informed the heavy-set woman with vivid red hair.

"Beauchene, Beauchene…" the woman's thick bracelets jangled on pudgy wrists while she checked the list of names on her clipboard. "Ah yes, here you are!" she chattered cheerfully, "number 115! Oh!" Her sunny smile dropped into a worried frown. "You'll be competing in the 5th heat today, which means you should get a move on!" She handed Claire a laminated card with their number on it and some pins, then shooed them toward the dance floor on her left. "Good luck, my dearies! Next in line!"

"Thank you!" Claire managed a smile as Luca ushered her into a different line. With the ease of an expert, Claire neatly attached their number to Luca's back with the supplied safety pins without pricking him. This would allow the judges to identify them during the dance among the other contestants.

"Did you get enough sleep last night?" Claire asked Luca as she moved to stand by his side.

"No less than usual," Luca said with a shrug. Claire caught his arm and peered at his face, ignoring the whispers and glances from the other dancers around them.

"I thought you said you would try and get more sleep! Are you sure you'll be able to perform at your best?"

Irritation flashed in Luca's eyes. "I always give my best."

"Your best on four hours of sleep?" Claire shot back.

"And you?" Luca countered. "Do you think you can focus after whatever your *novio pendejo* said to you? And speaking of that *cabrón*, how's your hip? Is that all better?"

"It's all better!" Claire's voice rose defensively. "And even if it wasn't, I am a professional! I never let anything bother me when I'm dancing!"

"Neither do I!"

They glared defiantly at each other, neither willing to back down. The tension was broken when a polished-looking emcee, a chosen representative from the Fred Astaire Dance Academy, tested his microphone and then spoke to the waiting assembly.

"Attention, dancers! Heat number five for the Salsa will be starting now. If you are participating in heat number five, please make your way onto the floor now!"

Chapter 13: Soltada

"Breaking Embrace to do figure on his/her own."

The line in front of Claire and Luca began to move forward. Luca shook out his shoulders, rolled his neck to loosen up, then held out his arm to Claire.

"Shall we?" he asked courteously.

Claire took his arm. "You better not fall asleep on the floor."

"You better focus on the dance instead of whatever that *cabrón* you call a boyfriend was talking to you about," Luca retorted.

"That is none of your business!" Claire hissed as they walked out onto the floor. She fixed a perfect smile on her face and waved at the watching audience.

"If it's going to keep you distracted during the competition, it is my business!" Luca shot back, attaching a dazzling grin on his face as they stepped onto the floor to a roar of applause.

"It won't, I'm fine!" Claire insisted. She hesitated for a second. "He said he got me a guest spot on his show so I could be with him in Los Angeles."

"He…what?" Luca paused, in the process of waving to a group of female dancers waiting their turn. Irrationally Claire felt her temper rise as they giggled, glancing shyly in his direction. "What did you say?"

Claire scowled at the girls and they stopped, mid-giggle. "I said I'd think about it," she lied.

"Are you insane?" Luca demanded, yanking her around so she was facing him. "After everything he's done, you're still going to give him another chance?"

"You're one to talk," Claire indicated the waiting dancers with a toss of her head. "Sebastian doesn't *flirt* with his groupies."

Sparks of irritation flared in Luca's eyes. "No, he—"

"Dancers, please find a spot on the floor." The MC seemed focused on a few stragglers who were rushing onto the floor. "Your dance will begin…."

"We'll talk later," Luca stepped behind her to take his position.

"Fine," Claire shifted her weight, alternately bending her knees to loosen up her hips. She hadn't been lying *exactly* to Luca when she said she was all better – her hip was still a little stiff – but it didn't hurt enough to bother her. She *wouldn't* let it hurt enough to bother her, she promised herself. She held up her hands for Luca to take. "Stay awake."

"Don't make stupid choices," Luca retorted, clasping her hands in his.

Claire tuned out the rest and focused on taking slow, deep breaths to calm her racing heart. This was no big deal; it was just an easy competition to prepare for Blackpool. Her eyes scanned the crowd for Sebastian's familiar blond hair and light skin. She couldn't see him among the spectators but maybe that was for the best.

Claire saw Bella watching from the crowd and smiled warmly. At least she could count on her best friend to be there when she needed her. Bella smiled back, and shot her a thumbs up. *Are you okay?* she mouthed. Claire smiled her best smile and managed a thumbs up in return. She might not be a hundred percent okay, but whatever she was feeling would have to wait until later.

The music began, a quick bouncing rhythm that had everyone tapping their toes. Luca started the dance with a double-hand spin from their choreographed routine that made Claire whirl like a top, her blue and silver costume glittering. She was unaccustomed to having so much leg showing during her routines, it felt a little breezy and free without her ankle-length skirt. For once, Claire wasn't an elegant princess, caught up in a fairy tale with her charming prince. She was a 1920's flapper, finally free of her restrictive corsets and skirts. Claire was a modern woman, seeking her own freedom in a new world.

The audience responded with cheers and applause as Luca caught her after two spins, wrapping her in a sweetheart embrace. Claire smiled flirtatiously over her shoulder at him, sinuously moving within his arms before rolling out, keeping a firm grip on his hand. The tension between their fingers stretched like a rubber band, then

Luca rolled her in again, turning the spin into a dip that had her head inches off the ground.

Luca leaned in close, and the crowd roared its approval. "Let's give them a show, shall we?" he murmured. In that moment, he didn't look tired and his dark eyes danced as he smiled. *He loves this*, Claire realized, *just as much as I do*.

"Let's," Claire whispered back, cupping his face with her free hand.

Luca pulled her up, leading her through the section of their solo that had always given her problems in the past. She flowed into the chase, one foot in front of the other, Luca's back in front of her, then turning and giving Luca a flirtatious beckon with one hand while he followed behind her. She didn't need a prince to rescue her anymore, Claire thought as she led Luca across the floor. She could have whatever future she wanted.

Shimmy, shimmy… the triple free-spin was coming up and she forced herself to breathe. She could do it, she and Luca had practiced it a hundred times. A flash of blond caught her eye and she turned…

Sebastian had found himself a spot behind the stage that, until a few minutes ago, had been hidden by a curtain. Now it had moved, and he was partially visible, his mouth fused with Bethany LaMana's as he pressed her up against a speaker.

A few spectators also noticed the couple and started tittering, but all Claire could see was Sebastian's hands as they moved hungrily down Bethany's torso, and over the bare thigh that was wrapped around his waist.

"No," Claire whispered. Her heart was thudding painfully in her chest, and try as she might, she couldn't look away. From across the room, Bethany seemed to feel her gaze and she opened her eyes. The blue glitter on her face was smudged but she met Claire's gaze, tipped her head back as Sebastian turned his attention to her neck… and smiled.

Luca, not noticing Claire's distress, wound her up for the triple-spin… and let her go.

The world around Claire blurred in a haze of color. She could see Bella, the judges making notes, the crowd cheering, the other contestants watching from the edge of the floor, and above it all, Bethany, a smug and vicious smile on her face.

One of Claire's feet caught on the other, her poised spin wobbled, and Claire pitched toward the floor as the crowd gasped and her own scream echoed in her ears.

"Claire!"

With a curse, Luca lunged forward and caught her before she hit the floor, cradling her head to his chest. His elbow sang as it came in contact with the wooden stage, but he ignored it, rolling and pulling Claire up into a sitting position.

"*Dios Mio*," he swore, taking Claire's head in his hands, "what were you-" Luca stopped, the angry words dying in his throat as Claire stared back at him, her blue eyes swimming with tears. "What happened?" he whispered, and Claire bit her lip, covering her face with her hands.

"I'm sorry, I ruined our chance of winning."

"Claire," Luca tugged at her hands, but she only tightened her grip. "Claire, I don't care that we lost, I just want to make sure you're okay."

"Excuse me," one of the judges moved towards Claire and Luca. "At this point, I need to ask you two to leave the floor."

"Can you give her a minute?" Luca demanded. "She just fell, I want to make sure she's okay."

"Luca!" Claire lowered her hands. Her make-up was smudged slightly and her cheeks were bright pink with embarrassment. "People are watching."

Luca glanced around. Most of the contestants had stopped dancing and a few were coming to assist them. "So?"

Claire struggled to get to her feet, waving off the offered hands of the other dancers. "I'm fine, thank you, really I'm fine," she insisted with a tight smile. She tried to take a step, wincing as her ankle throbbed. She took another step, wobbled and Luca caught her before she fell again. "So sorry to be an inconvenience, thank you, I'm fine," Claire said, smiling tightly at the onlooking dancers. "Would you quit babying me?" Claire hissed, pushing away Luca's hand. "You heard the judge, we need to get off the floor."

"Claire, tell me what happened."

Claire shook her head, brushing off his hand, forcing herself to keep moving. All she wanted to do was curl into a ball and hide in a small dark corner. She could see people talking, practically hear the whispers. Perfect Claire Beauchene, the golden girl who never made a mistake, had fallen during a competition in front of everyone. She had never fallen, never embarrassed herself like this before in her whole *life*.

She could feel the eyes of every audience member burning into her, but she forced herself to hold her head high and keep walking.

"Claire, *enough*!"

With another curse, Luca scooped her up in his arms and carried her off the floor.

"Put me down!" Claire wriggled, trying to break free, then yelped as her injured ankle twinged in protest. "I can walk by myself."

"No, you can't," Luca snapped. "And I'm tired of watching you torture yourself because it's some stupid way to maintain your dignity."

Luca's scent wrapped around her like a blanket, the scent of him, warm and spicy; the feel of his shoulder under her head the only solid thing as her world crumbled around her. A heavy wave of shame washed over Claire and she stopped struggling, burying her face in his black tunic, suddenly exhausted. "But it's the only thing I have left," she whispered, her voice breaking. "Because I fell, we're not even going to place in the top three, and now I'm too hurt for us to do our solo and I really wanted to do well because—" She bit back the last sentence before it could come out. *Sebastian is here. Except he's cheating on me.* "—because it's my birthday tomorrow," she said instead.

Luca felt the damp tear as it rolled down her cheek, soaking into his skin.

"Claire-bear, are you okay, sweetie?" Bella had run up alongside. "What happened? Are you hurt? Can I get you anything?"

Luca gently set Claire down in a chair at the edge of the dance floor.

"She could use an icepack," Luca told Bella.

"I'll be right back." Bella rushed off into the crowd. Already, dancers were lining up for the next event, as if Claire's accident was already a thing of the past.

"Last year I won three first place medals," Claire reflected. "This year I won't even place."

The memory of Bethany's smug smile flashed in her mind's eye and Claire fought to hold back the tidal wave of tears.

"So what if we lost?" Luca asked. From his pants pocket he retrieved a tissue and held it out to Claire. "Today was not about winning, we were just practicing for Blackpool."

"I never lose," Claire blew her nose.

"Well, now you've learned what it's like to lose and we know we still need to practice that triple spin," Luca offered her another tissue. "And possibly that dip," he added. "You could use some more control. So at least we didn't walk away empty-handed."

"My control is fine," Claire retorted, and Luca noted a little of her old arrogance was back in her eyes. "My control is exemplary, actually."

"It could still use some practice," Luca replied, fighting not to smile as Claire's chin jutted out haughtily.

"You know," Claire snapped, "I was going to thank you for being gentleman enough to carry me off the floor, but now I take it back."

One of Luca's genuine, rare smiles lit his face like a beacon. "And I was going to say you're not a princess anymore, but that's clearly not true." He patted her knee.

A sound halfway between a sob and a giggle escaped Claire's mouth. "Jerk."

"Snob."

Claire laughed, kicking at him lightly with her heel. This turned out to be a mistake as her injured ankle cried for mercy the second it connected. "*Merde*," she winced, reaching for it.

"Let me help," Luca pulled over another chair for her to rest her foot on.

"Here's your ice, sweetie." Bella was back with an ice pack and a bandage. "Thanks for elevating her foot, Ortiz," Bella said, kneeling next to Claire.

"It's nothing," he replied, hovering while Bella removed Claire's shoe and loosely secured the ice pack to her ankle.

"I called Bianca, there's a lot of perks to dating a doctor," Bella said, finishing her wrapping, "She'll be done with her shift soon and can take a look at your ankle when you get home."

"Thank you," Claire signed, leaning back in her chair. The ice was already dulling the ache in her foot, and she felt much better now that Bella was at her side.

"So, are you going to tell us what happened?" Bella asked.

"I…tripped," Claire said, avoiding her friend's eyes.

"Uh-huh. That's a first," Bella retorted. "Good thing this man here caught you or it could've been worse. You should buy him a coffee for saving your skull."

Luca shifted, looking embarrassed. "It was no big deal," he muttered.

"He shouldn't have more coffee anyway, Bells, he needs to get more sleep, not stay up later," Claire said absently.

"Maybe some dessert, then," Bella was undeterred. "My mom has a great recipe for cobbler. You like peach cobbler, Ortiz?"

Luca shrugged. "I like peaches."

"You'll love cobbler, then. Back to you, Claire-bear. What. Happened."

"I—" Claire suddenly turned at the sound of a familiar voice.

"This is ridiculous, where does it say that in the rules?" Bethany and Sebastian were being escorted out of the ballroom by a pair of security guards. "We weren't bothering anyone, we were just having *fun*. You know what *fun* is?"

"Ma'am, you were performing an act of public indecency at a competitive event and several witnesses reported seeing you and complained to the front desk."

"Public indecency, what are you, Puritans? We were just making out!"

"Ma'am, if you continue to make a scene, we will call the police. Please leave now and conduct your activities elsewhere."

"No…" Bells looked at Claire, her eyes wide with shock. "She didn't."

"Behind the stage," Claire looked down at her skirt. "I saw her."

"That——" Bella was at a loss for words. "And he… I knew he was stupid but…" Her hand closed around Claire's and held it tight.

"I'm sorry Luca," A tear splashed down on Bella's hand. "I said I wasn't going to let Sebastian affect our performance but——"

"No, sweetie, no," Bella wrapped Claire in a tight hug. "None of this is your fault." She shot a hopeless look to Luca who was standing frozen, his hands closed into fists, "he's just an idiot with no self-control."

"He wanted me to come to L.A. with him," Claire sniffed, "He said *Dance Craze* wanted me to be a part of the show, and this would be a big opportunity for both of us, and I told him that I couldn't uproot my life right before Blackpool. I said *Dance Craze* was his dream, not mine, and he was so… angry that I didn't want to go. He said I was… selfish." Claire wiped her eyes. "If I said I'd go with him, this wouldn't have happened, right? And we might've still won today."

"Sweetie, no. In fact, you should be proud you didn't go with him," Bells crooned, stroking Claire's head. "He doesn't deserve you, he *never* deserved you."

Sebastian caught sight of Claire and froze. "Claire, this isn't what it looks like——"

"Sir, it's time for you to leave." The security guard tugged on his arm.

"How could you?" Claire struggled to stand, not caring that her make-up was running, or that bystanders were casting curious looks in her direction.

"Claire, you have to understand, you turned me down and I thought—"

"Thought what?" Claire demanded, her temper rising. "That that made this okay?"

"Whoa, hang on a second," Bethany interjected. "You make it sound like this was an impulsive rebound." Her mouth twisted up into a smirk. "This is definitely not our first rodeo."

"Bethany!" Sebastian turned back to Claire, panic in his eyes. "She's lying!" He insisted. "I've never—"

"Please, can we be done with the secrecy?" Bethany rolled her eyes. "Though if I'd known all it would take to see you face plant during a competition was catching one of our make-out sessions I would've tried it weeks ago."

"Weeks?" Claire stumbled forward and felt Luca's hand, steadying her. "You've been doing this behind my back for weeks?"

"This is actually pretty mild compared to what we usually do oh—" Bethany held a hand to her mouth in mock realization. "That's right, I heard you had a whole virginity ceremony planned." Bethany's red mouth with its smeared lipstick twisted into a sneer. "Real sweet. Well, you can still have it, if you don't mind *my sloppy seconds!*"

Everyone was staring now. Claire would've happily melted into the carpet of the ballroom if she could. First her professional reputation as a champion, now her personal life was on display for everyone to see.

"Claire—" Sebastian started to speak.

Claire held up a hand. "Shut up."

"But—"

"She told you to shut up," Luca said quietly.

Claire took a limping step forward, so she was eye to eye with Sebastian. "We're done." She said quietly. "I never want to see you again. Don't call me, don't text me, don't speak to me. If you do any of those things, so help me, I will punch you as hard as I can."

"Claire, I swear, I never meant to hurt you—"

His words were cut off as Claire's fist smacked solidly into Sebastian's nose with a satisfying crunch. He staggered back, blood streaming between his fingers.

"You bitch!" Sebastian gasped. "I'm performing a Samba in two days!"

Claire considered the sniveling boy boy before her, red staining his cashmere cotton shirt. Once, he'd been her Prince Charming. Vivianne was right. They only existed in movies. "If your Samba is anything like your Salsa, it sucks. I did you a favor."

"Miss, you'll need to come with me as well," the security guard said, his eyes glinting with sympathy.

"She can't go anywhere, she's injured!" Bella protested.

"She still committed assault, she needs to come with us," the security guard apologized.

"She warned him not to speak to her, him getting punched is his fault!" Bella insisted.

"Still, she's going to have to come with me until we get this sorted out."

"That's right, there are consequences for your actions," Bethany snickered.

Claire eyed her with disgust. "You want me to break your nose next?"

Chapter 14: Solo

"A solo dance is danced by an individual dancing alone, as opposed to couples dancing together but independently of others dancing at the same time."

Claire's birthday was a somber affair. The original plan had been for an extravagant party in the largest practice room at the studio, with an invitation for all of the students to participate in a night of social dancing. But in light of what had happened the day before, the party had been canceled in favor of a quiet evening at home.

"Claire, you've hardly touched your food," Natalia scolded, eyeing Claire worriedly. "Can't you have a few more bites?"

"I'm not hungry, Mama," Claire picked up her plate and went to scrape the contents into a Tupperware tub.

"If you're not hungry for dinner, you won't be hungry for dessert." Natalia responded, hoping to galvanize her daughter into eating a few more mouthfuls. "Are you telling me this chocolate cake your father has worked so hard on is to be wasted?"

"I'll eat some tomorrow," Claire hobbled to the couch and sank onto the cushions, easing her foot into an elevated position.

Bianca had given her a splint to wear and told her to stay off her foot for a few days, but Claire hadn't really been listening. Every time she closed her eyes, all she could see was Bethany and Sebastian behind the curtain, and the smug smile on Bethany's face full of triumph when she saw Claire watching.

Out of habit, she pulled out her phone, but just as quickly put it away. There would be no more messages to Sebastian, no more time painstakingly choosing photos to get his attention or conversation starters sent between rehearsals. Her life was full of holes now, huge gaps of time that for the last five years, he had filled. She fought back the wave of emotion that threatened to break through and took a few deep breaths. This was good, Claire tried to convince herself. There was now more time to focus on Blackpool, practice her dance, to really work on the choreography for the solo routines and perfect it. She was still trying to find the right music, but now she had more time to do so, and to make modifications to the costume she was sewing with Natalia. Once her ankle felt better, she would meet with Luca and go over their routines; she was sure he had some insane salsa dance planned, and she would be so busy focusing on that there would be no room to think about her ex-boyfriend.

Ex-boyfriend. The finality of that title hit her hard and even though it made her feel weak, she pulled out her phone, hoping for something, anything. A text, a voicemail that she'd somehow missed giving her an explanation, telling her that it was all a mistake, a misunderstanding, or maybe just waking her up from this nightmare she was in. But there was nothing.

Oh, there were dozens of messages from friends, relatives, and fellow students, wishing her a happy birthday—but from the one person who had been a constant part of her life for so long, there was nothing. The phone screen seemed to mock her, denying her silent wishes.

With a sigh, Claire put the phone down again, then grabbed for it as it rang shrilly.

"Hey, Claire-bear," Bella's voice sang cheerfully through the phone, "how's my birthday girl?"

"Oh, hey," Claire responded, trying to keep her voice from sounding too depressed and failing. "I'm fine."

"Oh, sweetie." Bella's voice instantly softened with sympathy. "Would it help if I said I'm bringing ice cream?"

"Bells… I'm really not in the mood."

"Can we at least come in for a few minutes then? I'd like to give you your present and Honeybear wants to check your ankle."

"Fine, a few minutes," Claire sighed.

"Great! 'Cuz we're standing on your doorstep," Bella chuckled.

"Mama! Bells is outside," Claire called, "can you let her in?"

The doorbell rang as if in agreement.

"Fine, what is two more?" Natalia pretended to grumble, limping for the door. "Maybe they will eat something." She opened the door and Bella stepped in, plastic bags in one hand, to give Natalia a kiss on the cheek.

"*Dobryy Vecher,*" she greeted her ballet teacher in Russian. Natalia gave a small smile to her star pupil.

"*Dobryy Vecher,*" she responded. "You are preparing for your audition in spring?"

A local ballet company was performing *Giselle* for their spring performance, and Bella was determined to get the lead.

"I've been practicing every day," Bella smiled.

"Well, I look forward to seeing it," Natalia responded. A student of old traditions, she would never dream of showing partiality, but Bella's beautifully danced solos had won her the leads for the last three years.

"Hey girl, no hello?" Bella said, turning her attention to Claire. Claire looked up from her phone and forced a smile.

"Hey, Bells." She started to get to her feet.

"Woah, no need to get up." Bella rushed to her side and helped Claire sit back down. "And look, I brought ice cream! Mint chip, your favorite. The calories will go straight to my hips, but it's your birthday, so let's live a little."

"The way you've been practicing you can eat as much as you want," Bianca spoke up, slipping an arm around her girlfriend's shoulders. Dark, intelligent eyes were set above a prominent hooked nose and delicate mouth. Her arms and legs were all toned muscle, and despite the fact she was dressed in blue scrubs and comfortable shoes, she looked less like a doctor and more like a pro-boxer. "Hey hun," she said, crossing towards her friend and sitting carefully next to her. "How's the ankle?"

"Sore," Claire hissed as Bianca began to unwrap the bandage.

"That's normal." Bianca said, gently examining it. "Looks like the swelling has gone down, have you been icing it?"

"I made sure she did," Natalia reported. "We also put it in an ice bath for ten minutes every hour."

"Good." Bianca nodded, satisfied. "Can you try rotating it for me?" Claire sighed and complied, wincing. "Okay, so still painful. How about pointing your toe?" Claire winced again as it twinged painfully when she tried.

"What's the diagnosis, Doc?" Bella asked, hovering over Bianca's shoulder.

"She needs to stay off her foot and keep icing it for at least three days," Bianca reported. "Do you hear me, Claire? No dancing!" She turned to Natalia when Claire didn't react. "You're my witness, Mrs. B. She stays off her feet for three days."

"Understood," Natalia nodded, but her eyes were focused on her only daughter, who didn't even protest.

"Well, how about I get us some ice cream, then?" Bella suggested, breaking the tension. "Claire, how many scoops do you want?"

"I'm not really hungry—" Claire started to say.

"Ten scoops it is," Bella joked, heading toward the kitchen. Natalia followed.

"And I'll bring some cake."

"Has she been like this all day?" Bella murmured when they were out of earshot.

"*Da*. She just sits and stares at her phone. Waiting for messages from that *zasranets*."

Bella stared at her teacher, surprised at the fury in her voice. "Do I want to know what that word means?"

Natalia looked guilty. "When you're older."

"You know I'm twenty, right?"

"Much older," Natalia said firmly.

* * *

"While I'm here, let's take a look at your hip," Bianca said kindly. Claire obediently shifted on the couch, lifting her shirt so her friend could examine the bruise. "Still a little tender?" Bianca asked as she moved her fingers over the bone.

"Little bit," Claire admitted.

"That's because you didn't tell me about this right away, naughty girl," Bianca teased. "See what happens when you don't go to a doctor right away?"

"Does Bells ever tell you when she hurts herself?"

"Oh no, my baby girl would try and dance on the stumps of her feet if she thought she could get away with it," Bianca chuckled fondly. "I have to tie her down to get her to rest, but that's what keeps our lives interesting."

"What about when you're sick?" Bella demanded, coming back into the room. She held a plate of ice cream and cake in each hand. "Remember when you had that fever last winter? I practically had to force-feed you soup."

"It wasn't that bad," Bianca chuckled.

"You had a fever of a hundred and four. I swear, doctors make the worst patients," Bella said, handing Claire a plate. "For some reason they think they're above the illnesses of us mere mortals. Hey, hands off, this isn't yours," Bella held the plate of cake and ice cream out of reach as Bianca reached for it.

"Then where's my cake?" Bianca asked plaintively.

"In the kitchen," Bella said. "Claire and I need some girl time."

"Oh, all right." Bianca gave a world-weary sigh, standing up from the couch. "I'm done with my examination anyway." As Bella moved to take her spot, Bianca's arm shot out and pulled her girlfriend in for a quick smoldering kiss. Claire was surprised the ice cream on Bella's plate didn't melt. "You're lucky you're cute, Legs," Bianca said, releasing her. She winked in Claire's direction and headed toward the kitchen.

"Almost two years, and she's still got it," Bella sighed happily and settled down on the cushions.

"How do you do it?" Claire asked as Bella forked up a mouthful of cake.

"How do I do what?" Bella asked. "Eat cake? It's easy, you use this thing called a fork..."

"You know what I mean," Claire sighed, exasperated, "how do you make it work with Bianca without it... you know... falling apart?"

Bella looked thoughtful.

"Well, I'm not going to lie, hun, it's not always easy to get along with my Honeybear. For starters, she's messy and always leaving her scrubs and gear all over the floor and I prefer to keep things neat and organized. Also, she's usually at the hospital when I'm home from dance rehearsal, and sometimes I don't see her for days at a time because she's working crazy shifts but…"

She looked at Bianca, who was in the kitchen, scooping the ice cream into a bowl with a slice of cake as she chatted with Natalia.

"Even on my worst days when I'm cranky and tired, I know she loves me. All of me, the good and the bad. And trust me, on the days when I'm surviving on coffee and three hours of sleep because I've been practicing all night, it's *all bad*. Because even if I wasn't as a gold-digging ballet dancer leading her to sin—like her parents seem to think," Bella paused. "It'd be a lot easier on Bianca if I wasn't who I am. I mean- well, you know what it's like." Bella shrugged.

"As a ballet dancer, I have a very short window to become a success. While Bianca can take her time getting her medical training and setting up her practice, I need to be performing at some prestigious ballet academy and have a solid career under me by the time I'm twenty-two. She'll be just starting out and paying off all her school debt and I need to be some famous ballet dancer already." Bella sighed, looked down at her plate. "But whether I become a principal dancer or someone in the background, she's still there, supporting me no matter what. And that makes me want to be the kind of person who deserves to stand at her side." Bella looked in Bianca's direction again, the love in her eyes so pure, Claire's heart ached. "I'm going to make sure I become one of the best damn dancers in the state," she declared quietly. "So when she's an established doctor and I'm retired at thirty-four she can show off my awards and say, 'that's my wife.'"

"I wanted to be all those things for Sebastian, too," Claire said quietly. "We were going to compete together, maybe win Blackpool next year after he finished his show, and travel the world, dancing. I really thought we would have the perfect life together."

Bella looked sympathetic. "I know you did, sweetie. But even if you want those things with all your heart, you can't force him to want those things, too. And that's okay. Someday, you'll meet someone who will want the same things you do, and everything will fall into place."

Claire fought back the urge to cry and Bella held out her arms.

"C'mere hun, get it all out. It'll be good for you."

Claire put her cake on the coffee table next to the couch and scooted over onto Bella's lap, leaning on her solid shoulder as Bella wrapped her arms around her. "Sebastian never liked when I cried," she sniffed. "He said it made me look blotchy and puffy."

"Well, that should've been your first clue he was a jerk," Bella growled, stroking Claire's head. "I think you look beautiful no matter what."

Claire could feel the tears welling up, and this time she let them fall.

"If he was such a jerk, why does it still hurt when I think about him?"

"Because you cared about him, and he hurt you." Bella sighed. "And it's okay to feel sad, okay? Cry those tears, get angry, whatever you need, sweetie. He is a major scumbag for messing around with other girls but that's his issue, not yours. He probably will never be happy with any one person, while I'm sure there is someone in your future that is a hundred times better for you."

"Is my heart ever going to stop hurting?"

"Yes, of course it will."

"When?"

"I don't know, sweetie. But I promise, one day it will."

Claire's tears had thoroughly drenched the front of Bella's blouse. "I'm sorry I'm getting your shirt wet."

"Trust me, hun, there's nothing you can do that can't be fixed with a quick wash."

Bianca stepped into the room, three flutes of sparkling cider in her hands. "Legs, I know you wanted girl time, but I just wanted to…" She stopped when she saw Claire's tear streaked face.

"Aww girl, need some tissues?" she asked in concern. She put down the crystal flutes and held out a box that was resting on the nearby coffee table.

"Probably," Claire managed a smile. "I've been using Bella's shirt."

She blew her nose on a tissue Bianca offered. "Thanks."

"As a doctor, I should tell you chocolate's good for sadness." Bianca handed Claire her plate of cake, which was sitting untouched on the coffee table. "Also hugs." She wrapped her arms around Claire and squeezed tightly. "It is my medical opinion you need an endless supply of both until you feel better."

"If I eat an endless supply of chocolate, I won't be able to fit into my dance costumes." Claire rested her head on Bianca's shoulder, feeling the comforting solidity.

"You're an eighteen-year-old dancer with zero percent body fat," Bianca pointed out, releasing her. "A week or two of comfort food won't hurt."

"Okay." To placate her friend, Claire took a bite of cake and chewed. The chocolate tasted like ash in her mouth. She shoveled down more cake, not tasting it, just eating for the sake of having something to do.

"Claire? Earth to Claire?"

Claire looked up as she heard her name.

"Sorry, Bells, I missed that. What did you say?"

"We were thinking you might want to watch a movie. Bianca is in the mood for something with a lot of action, but I know you love your cheesy Fred Astaire rom-coms."

"They're not cheesy," Claire forked up the last bite of cake. "You just don't appreciate the king of movie musicals."

"We can also go home, sweetie," Bianca assured Claire, "you do not have to keep us around if you want to rest."

"No, a movie sounds fun," Claire said, putting down her empty plate. "But no romance, whatever Bianca has in mind sounds good."

"Action it is." Bianca smiled.

* * *

Only when Bianca and Bella had left and the house quiet, did Claire allow herself to cry in earnest. She would be fine, she told herself. She would move forward from this. Bells was right, Sebastian was too much of a scumbag to deserve her tears. He was a stupid, cheating worm, she reminded herself fiercely, sneaking around with Bethany— and who knows who else—behind her back. Bella had told her that she wouldn't feel this way forever. But tears continued to flow until she cried herself to sleep.

* * *

Down the hall, Natalia and Leon were having a difficult time sleeping as well.

"She is too quiet, you should check on her," fretted Natalia.

"She might be sleeping, what if I wake her up?" Leon replied.

"It is her first heartbreak; how can she sleep?"

They were quiet for a moment as their sensitive parent ears, honed from years of experience, picked up a small sound that seemed to come from their daughter's room. Only when they were sure that it was their old heating system, did they relax.

"You talked to the boy's parents?" Natalia asked. "You make nice so they don't press charges for assault?"

"Make nice, I almost broke his nose myself." Leon growled. "I always knew he was trouble; I just wish I'd tossed him out on his ear sooner."

For some reason that seemed to placate Natalia. "Control yourself, husband," she said, patting his hand.

Their fingers, one hand white and delicate, the other tanned and stubby, linked together on top of the blankets.

"His parents knew this was not a lawsuit they wanted to pursue anyway. She'd discovered him cheating, she was upset…" Leon's mouth twitched in a grim smile. "Less embarrassing to just walk away."

"I wish she had listened when I told her that dating that *zasranets* wouldn't work," Natalia sighed.

"You also said marrying me wouldn't work, *mon coeur*," Leon said gently. "Sometimes a relationship will succeed and other times it will not. But our daughter has to learn and make mistakes on her own."

"She will be all right," Natalia whispered, but it sounded more like a question. Leon drew her close, kissed her head, which smelled faintly of peroxide. A vain woman, his wife tried to hide her gray hairs with dye she secretly applied when she thought no one was home. Leon, who loved Natalia, gray or blonde, pretended not to see the dye boxes hidden in the trash or smell it in her hair.

"She is our daughter." Leon kissed Natalia's head again, repeating what he had said the day Claire was born. "She will be exceptional."

Chapter 15: Palanca

"Argentine Tango lever move in which the man helps the woman to jump or lift."

Juan studied the blank wall of the abandoned grocery store in front of him, then the sketch on the paper in his hands. Since his abuela's recent fall, he was taking his career plan in a new direction. No longer was he going to work in secret for the next few years before revealing himself. He needed to become famous overnight, not to mention successful and wealthy, which is why he'd chosen a place that was still off the beaten path, but easier to find.

Over the past few weeks, Juan had started noticing the bills on the kitchen table get higher and higher. He had seen the way Luca and Abuela viewed the arrival of more envelopes with worry and concern. Juan was going to become a famous artist so he could help out and show his brother he was just as much an adult as everyone else in the house.

Juan considered the wall again, the places where the concrete was chipped and cracked. This mural would be based on a picnic place his parents had taken him and his brother when they were younger. There would be a giant oak tree in the foreground, with leaves so lush and green that passersby would feel the cool of its shade. In the background, sand leading to a beach, the waters so blue it would meld into the horizon.

The last time Juan had been there was shortly after his parents' accident. The tree had been cut down and the beach was under construction. Someone was building luxury beach houses. Building houses over the memories of his childhood. But here, on the wall, he could still remember how it looked back then. He could see the way the branches swayed in the wind, smell the salt air, and hear his parents laughing as they unfolded the threadbare picnic blanket. He'd paint them at the foot of the tree. His mama and papa, unpacking the food from the picnic basket; Abuela, sitting in the shade with her fan to keep cool; Luca on the edge of the grass, frozen mid throw, a football spiraling through the air towards a younger version of himself, running to catch it. One happy family, together at last.

Juan wiped at his eyes, which were definitely *not* tearing up, and picked up the spray can. He started with the outlines, the tree, the beach and water behind, consulting the sketch in front of him. His can ran out of paint and Juan stooped to pick up another from his bag. He could see the entire mural in front of him, even if it was still a bare outline. The tree, the beach, the happy family beneath. It was going to be beautiful. Juan raised the spray can and jumped when a strong hand clamped down on his arm.

Juan whirled to find himself face to face with a skinny man in his seventies, round glasses balanced on a bulbous nose and a thinning crop of white hair.

"Who are you?" Juan blurted out.

"I'm the one who should be asking you that, sonny," the old man's voice rasped. "Who are you, and what are you doing to my store?"

* * *

It had been a few days since the disaster competition when Luca spotted Claire in her favorite practice room.

Music pounded through the speakers, not her usual choice, but some sort of melancholy song, full of anguish and heartbreak. Claire danced, barefoot, in the middle of the room, her back to Luca. Her long skirt seemed to float around her as she kicked, leapt and moved her lithe body to the melody. Claire's blonde hair flowed to her waist, catching the light from the window and seeming to glow.

Like the music, her dance did not follow her usual style of reserved elegance but seemed to express sadness, grief, and frustration all at once.

Claire stopped the second she spotted Luca standing in the doorway.

"Hi," he said, but his voice was drowned out by the music. Claire crossed to the stereo and turned it off.

"Hi," Luca said again.

"Hello," Claire replied. Her eyes looked red, as if she had cried not long ago, and there were dark circles and bags under her eyes that spoke of sleepless nights.

She wasn't wearing any make-up, Luca realized. He didn't think he'd ever seen her without it, and she looked younger, paler, and more vulnerable all at once.

"I was going to practice…" Luca offered by way of explanation. "But then I saw you in here… how is your ankle doing? Do you want to go over our routines?"

Claire smiled wryly. "Good as new, and Dr. Honeybear gave her blessing for me to start dancing again as long as I take it easy."

"Dr. Honeybear?" Luca cocked his head inquiringly.

"Bianca's girlfriend, she's a doctor."

"Ah, right," Luca nodded. "Bella called her after…" his voice trailed off and he looked away, unable to finish. *After you fell. After you saw your boyfriend cheating on you.*

"Yeah," Claire couldn't meet his eyes, either. "Which is why I'd rather practice by myself today."

"Okay," Luca said quietly, turning towards the door. "I'll leave you alone."

"Luca," Claire called after him and he paused. "Am I an idiot?"

Luca turned back.

"Why do you ask?"

"I'm just coming to terms with the fact that my boyfriend was cheating on me with Bethany. And the fact that I had to find out in the middle of a competition isn't making it any easier," Claire sighed. "Am I an idiot for not seeing the signs? Because when I look back, there were signs all over the place, I just..." She opened her mouth, closed it. Cleared her throat. "I didn't want to believe he would ever do something like that."

Luca felt his temper rise. "Are you seriously trying to blame yourself for this? He was a *cabrón*, with no respect for you, who didn't care about your feelings, and was not worth your time at all!"

"Yes, I'm aware of that." Claire turned away. "Sebastian was vain and selfish, and arrogant, and he always had to say he did better than I did—"

"Again," Luca snapped, "he was a *cabrón*, so why do you care?"

"Because I loved him!" Claire burst out, and a tear ran down her cheek. "I loved him," she repeated, wiping her eyes with the heel of her hand. "Sebastian might have been selfish and insecure, but there were also times when he was sweet, and funny, and gentle..." her voice broke, and Luca felt something twist in his gut as she began to weep. "We used to talk for hours when we first started dating, he was the person I went to when I was frustrated, or sad, or happy...I used to think he was the one guy who knew me the best, and when I thought of the future, I could always picture him with me and that just made me feel so... secure and happy. And now..." She sniffled, started to wipe her eyes with her practice skirt. Without a word Luca handed her a crumpled tissue. "I don't know what's going to happen. Mama, Papa, Bells, Bianca... you..." Claire blew her nose. "You... are all saying that Sebastian is a jerk and I should move on with my life because there's someone out there better for me, but can't I feel sad for a little bit? *I loved him. I miss him.* I know that he's no longer in my life, but can't I just be miserable?"

"Okay… okay." Luca approached Claire like he would a wounded animal. He'd seen her angry—stubbornly bulldozing everyone in her path more times than he could count. And given the choice, he'd choose angry over this tearful, vulnerable version of Claire any day. The sight of her crumbling in front of him was breaking his heart. "You're right, I'm sorry. Cry as long as you want." He hesitated, awkwardly held out his arms. "You uh…" he cleared his throat. "Need a hug?"

Claire hesitated. "I'm going to ruin your shirt."

Luca shrugged. "It was four years old to begin with."

"What the heck," Claire sniffled, took a step forward and buried her head on his chest. "I'm ruining a lot of shirts this week."

"I doubt you can do anything that can't be solved with a good wash," Luca chuckled. Her hair was kitten-soft under his hands and cascaded down her back, fine and delicate as gossamer silk. Luca caught himself as his thumb lightly stroked her back, pulling back to keep his touch neutral. There was strength within that fragile frame; he knew she could dance tirelessly for hours without breaking a sweat, but at the moment he wanted to handle her as carefully as he would a butterfly with a crumpled wing.

"Bells said the same thing," Claire murmured, her voice muffled. "I'm so tired, I just wanted to be able to compete in Blackpool and yet in the past couple days, I've lost my boyfriend, injured and embarrassed myself in a competition and didn't win any gold medals."

"Of course, losing a competition would be the thing that bothers you most," Luca commented wryly.

"One of the things I could take pride in was no matter what happened in my personal life, I could always win." Luca could feel a damp patch growing on his shirt as Claire's tears soaked through. "I could dance when I had a fever, after staying up all night practicing, one time Bella and I were fighting for a whole month…I still won. But apparently seeing Sebastian cheat on me was the thing I couldn't overcome. Is it me or is my whole life falling apart more and more each day?"

"No of course not…" Luca considered and discarded several answers and decided to avoid the subject altogether. "Come on, let's go sit by the window."

He guided her over to the floor-length window of the studio, and they sat on the floor in a pool of warm sunlight.

Down below, cars zoomed down the streets, pedestrians walked or ran past on various errands. It looked like an ordinary day, but to Claire it wasn't.

"I was looking down at the people passing by earlier," Claire started, "going around like they don't care about me, and then I realized, of course they don't. They've all got their own lives, some of them have it worse off than I do, some have it better than I do, depending on the person… it just pissed me off, though. Because I feel like I have a giant hole in my chest, like the biggest event of my life just happened and… that woman is walking by with her poodle like she does every day."

She turned her attention to Luca. "Did you know that when you're in love, it activates the reward center of the brain? I'd get the same feeling if I was on pain medication or won the lottery." Luca gave her a questioning look, and Claire shrugged. "I thought if I could understand the physical part of love and heartbreak, it might hurt less. It turns out when you're in love, your body starts pumping in all sorts of happy chemicals, endorphins, dopamine, oxytocin… and when your heart is broken, the chemicals… stop." Claire massaged a spot under her collarbone. "You go into withdrawal. That ache in your chest? Is basically the same pain a drug addict feels when they can't get their fix anymore." Claire shrugged again. "That's the theory, anyway. I kind of took a trip down a rabbit hole looking at a lot of different websites, but it seems like there's still a lot about love no one understands."

"Maybe because not everything to do with love and heartbreak can be broken down into chemicals," Luca remarked.

Down below on the street, the poodle barked and tried to chase a squirrel up a tree.

"Luca?"

"Yeah?"

"Have you ever… had to deal with something like this?" Claire asked hesitantly.

Luca thought of the few girls he had dated briefly, the easy, but uncomplicated interactions they'd shared before either he or they had drifted away. If he'd felt a brief pang now and then for their absence, it was quickly lost in the daily hustle to and from work and dance.

"No," Luca shook his head. "Never."

"Lucky," Claire sighed. "'Cause this sucks."

"I never cared for them that much either," Luca admitted. "I could let them go because it didn't affect my life when they left. But you're hurting because you cared."

"Bella says over time I'll forget him."

"She's right."

Claire leaned against the glass, her blue eyes seeing something other than the street below.

"I just wish I could stop thinking about him *now*," she sighed. "The only thing that makes it hurt less for a little while is dancing."

Luca pushed himself to his feet. "So, let's dance, then," he held out a hand to her. "Unless you'd prefer to dance more on your own?"

Claire considered. She could say no, and she knew Luca would simply accept that and walk out the door. There would be no pressure, no expectations. He would walk and she could keep sitting by the window, watching the world go by if she wanted to. Somehow that seemed to help make up her mind. Claire took his hand, feeling the steady, solid grip of his fingers around hers as he pulled her to her feet. "Actually, I wouldn't mind having a partner."

* * *

The Argentine tango is considered a walking dance, with the partners in either an open embrace or chest to chest as the leader moves the follower around the floor. Techniques can involve complex kicks and various Latin styles. The dance relies heavily on the follower's ability to feel the leader's weight change and improvisations.

But neither Claire nor Luca were in the mood for a quick, frenzied dance that day. Luca selected a slow song and Claire rested her hand on his shoulder as they circled the floor. Even if the shirt was four years old, it smelled clean. And the shoulder beneath was solid and comforting. Luca wrapped an arm around her shoulders, and Claire felt herself relax. The music flowed like water around them as Luca gently guided her around the room. Claire felt the security of his right hand in the small of her back, his left enclosed around hers. Her world shrunk, until the only thing left was the music, the feel of Luca's strong shoulder, his heartbeat under her cheek, and her feet on the floor as they moved between his.

There was no Sebastian to cry over, no competition to stress about, and no judges to please. There was no need for fancy *cortes*, for kicks or *ganchos*, they simply moved with the beat. Claire breathed slowly, trying to match the in and out of her partner. Luca's scent, a unique blend of spice and sweat, and the sound of his heartbeat, soothed her. She could feel some of the tension, some of the grief, some of the hurt melting away as she continued to dance. And for a little while, there was only Luca to lean on, the feel of the wood under her bare feet, and the music.

The spell was broken as the shrill ringtone of a phone disrupted the song.

"That's mine," Luca said, releasing Claire from his arms. He dug his phone out of his pocket and answered. "Abuela? What is it?"

Claire watched with growing curiosity as his face changed from alarmed to furious in an instant.

"I'm coming," he snapped, hanging up. He ran a hand through his hair, meeting Claire's eyes, exasperated. "I have to go. Apparently, my brother was caught vandalizing a wall and he's in police custody, so I need to go bail him out." He strode to the door, wrenching open. "And on top of that, my car broke down *again*, so I'll have to take a bus to get him. We'll have to practice some other time."

"Wait!" Instinctively Claire hurried after him, and blurted out, "why don't I give you a ride?"

* * *

"You vandalized a wall? You vandalized a wall!" Luca strode into the police station where Juan was sitting next to Abuela and watched by Elaina's husband, Joe.

"He was caught spray painting a wall behind an abandoned grocery store," Joe spoke up. He was taller than both the brothers, with a wiry build dressed in police blues, his dark hair cropped short. "Since the store's been closed for months, the owner is not concerned about pressing charges, as long as Juan pays for it to be repainted. He's trying to sell the building and doesn't want gang graffiti on the side of the store."

"You're in a gang?" Luca demanded. "Is that why you've been missing school?"

"No!" Juan scowled. "I'm not stupid."

"Then what were you painting on the side of that building?"

Juan hunched lower in his chair. "It was supposed to be a mural," he muttered. "I want to be a street artist."

"A street artist," Luca rolled his eyes. "First you're failing your classes, now you want to be a street artist. Am I the only one in this family that has a sensible career?"

"Sensible?" Juan snorted. "You mean pouring drinks all night for bikers?"

Luca took a step towards his brother, then realized too late, his younger brother had a couple inches on him. "I make enough to keep a roof over your head and mine," Luca pointed out. "And I'm covering most of Abuela's medical bills! All you have to do is stay in school, and graduate! Why is that so hard?"

"Stop it! Both of you!" Abuela stood up. "You are brothers, family, you should not be fighting, especially in front of your old grandmother and…"

She spotted Claire hanging back, looking shy, and was immediately interested. Such a pretty young girl. Abuela was sure she had seen the girl somewhere and she seemed to have come with her grandson.

"I would never call you old, Abuela," Luca was saying.

"You're sweet, *mijo*." Abuela patted him on the head. "But I am more interested in that lovely young lady you brought with you." She pointed a gnarled finger at Claire, who flushed and waved hesitantly. "Come here, *querida*," Abuela beckoned. Claire obeyed nervously. She felt very self-conscious in her sweaty leotard and practice skirt, her hair piled into a messy bun on her head. She wished she had had time to change, though it looked as if Luca's *abuela* had hurried out of the house in a similar state of panic. Her gray hair was twisted up into a braid and she was wearing a housecoat over a colorful mumu. Dark eyes that somehow seemed youthful and full of ageless intelligence, danced in a heavily-lined face the color of parchment.

Abuela held out a hand to shake and Claire took it, feeling surprising strength in the bony fingers.

"Hello, ma'am," she said politely.

"Such good manners," Abuela was instantly charmed. "What's your name, *querida*?"

"Claire, ma'am." She turned her attention to Luca. "I'm sorry, this is clearly a family matter, I'm going to wait in the car. Just call me when you're ready to go."

"*Ay, que linda!*" Abuela murmured to Luca as Claire hurried away. "Is this the princess you were talking about?" she asked her grandson. Now that she'd heard the name, she recalled Luca talking about her more than once. "How long were you going to hide her from me?"

"Abuela!" Luca could feel the eyes of Juan and Joe boring holes into the back of his head. "We need to focus on Juan right now."

"I'm okay talking about Luca's new girlfriend," Juan spoke up.

"Shut up," Luca swatted his brother absently on the back of his head. "You're the one who's in trouble for vandalism. How much is the repaint going to cost?"

"Five hundred dollars."

The amount had Luca cursing under his breath. "I could repaint the wall for half that."

"Pay it and the charges are dropped," Joe reminded him.

"Fine," Luca ran a hand through his hair. He could always pull a few more double shifts to pay for it. On top of the shifts he was working to pay Abuela's medical bills. He groaned and turned to Juan. "But the next time you're arrested for vandalism, I'm not bailing you out."

"So you can waste money on shoes and competitions but I can't do what I want? That's totally not fair!" Juan protested.

"I pay for those things," Luca snapped. "You want to get in trouble for vandalizing—"

"Street art!"

"Fine, you want to get in trouble for street art, you better have a job so you can afford to pay the fines!" He started toward the door and stopped. "Where am I supposed to go to pay for the paint?"

"I'll take you," Joe followed Luca to the door. "It's this way. Abuela, we'll be right back."

***

"You're a dancer, yes?" Abuela probed as Claire helped her into the passenger seat, then rounded the car and slid into the driver's seat. "You dance at the same school as my grandson?"

"Yes, ma'am," Claire checked the rearview mirror to make sure Juan and Luca were buckled. "He's my partner."

"Partner?" Abuela turned to glare at Luca who was sitting behind her. "He didn't tell me he had a lovely new dance partner," she scolded.

"There were other things to worry about. Your health, for one thing, Abuela," Luca muttered. "Juan getting arrested—"

"So much bad news," Abuela shook her head. "You could've given me good news to balance out. You must invite her to my *cumpleaños* on Friday."

"Abuela!" Luca protested, "I'm sure she doesn't want to —"

"Ask her!" Abuela demanded.

"If you don't, I will," Juan interjected.

"Uh…" Claire was sure her face was bright red. Luca's certainly was. "Claire, would you be interested in coming to my *abuela*'s party?"

"Umm… sure." Claire was grateful she could keep her eyes on the road so she didn't have to meet Luca's eyes. "If she wants me there."

"*Sí.* I do." Abuela sat back in her seat, satisfied. "Also, *querida*, I do not want any presents, only bring yourself."

"Yes, ma'am," Claire said obediently.

"Call me Abuela," Abuela corrected her gently. She liked this young girl. Kind, polite, and a skilled dancer from what she'd gleaned from her grandson.

Claire's car had turned into their neighborhood, and already Abuela could see the dilapidated houses, kids playing in the streets or walking home from school.

"Turn here." Luca was directing Claire. "Pull up to the curb right… here."

Claire pulled to a stop and parked in front of Luca's house with its untidy garden, blooming with flowers in every color.

"Wow," Claire could barely take her eyes off the different blooms as she opened the door for Abuela.

"My daughter planted those flowers," Abuela smiled fondly. "She had, as you say, a grass finger?"

"Green thumb," Claire murmured, as she helped the elderly woman slide out of the car.

"Green thumb, that's right," Abuela nodded. "You will forgive my bad English. I have not been in this country as long as my grandson."

"I completely understand," Claire smiled. "My mama is Russian and my papa is French. They need my help with words sometimes too."

"Oh! They do?" Abuela's eyes widened with delight and she patted Claire's cheek. "I like you so much more knowing that."

"Abuela…" Luca winced.

"Her family is just like us, *Lucito*," Abuela came to her own defense. "I can't like her for that?" She smiled once more at Claire. "Feel free to take a few flowers home, *querida*," Abuela said, letting Luca help her slowly up the driveway to the house. "I hope to see you soon."

"You're very kind." Claire smiled. She was already feeling very fond of the spirited elderly woman.

"Thanks again for the ride," Luca added. "I guess I'll see you… Friday?"

"I'll be there," Claire promised, watching grandmother and grandsons make it safely to their door before getting in her car and driving away.

Chapter 16: Doble Frente

"The woman is in front of the man. Both are moving together in one direction."

"I can't believe Luca invited you to meet his family!" Bella squealed, her voice sounding tinny over the speaker in Claire's car.

"Well, technically his grandma made him invite me," Claire explained. It was Friday and she was driving to Lucas' house, a plate of her mother's *sharlotka* on the seat beside her.

"Girl, you sure there's nothing serious going on between you two?" Bella teased.

"Positive," Claire said firmly.

"You sure?"

"Legs, give her some time to heal before you shove her into a new relationship."

Claire smiled as Bianca scolded her girlfriend in the background.

"Fine," Bella sighed. "But I reserve the right to celebrate when you finally decide to try some sweet *dulce de leche*."

Claire could feel her ears turning bright red.

"Bells, I think I'm about to lose your signal," she lied. "I'll call you back later."

"Hey, don't you dare——" Bella's protest was cut off as Claire hung up.

"Whew," Claire sighed and let the welcoming silence of the car wash over her. She loved Bella, but there were days when her best friend was a little too enthusiastic about her love life.

This was not a date, she reminded herself. It was just like when Luca had invited her to the club. It was a field trip, a chance to experience dancing outside the studio. Claire frowned. Would there be dancing? She hadn't thought to ask.

* * *

"Luca, take these empanadas out to the tables!" Elaina called from her kitchen. Luca dropped the jumble of lights he had been struggling to untangle outside with Juan and stepped through the open door into a cloud of delicious smells and steam. Elaina's kitchen was normally neat and tidy as a pin, but today bowls and platters covered every surface along with a dusting of flour.

At the stove, Elaina, wearing a stained apron over a floral dress, had finished loading a pile of savory pastries onto a platter while Abuela sat at the kitchen table, playing with Elaina's two-year-old daughter, Reina.

"Careful, it's hot!" Elaina warned Luca, handing him the plate.

"Hot!" gurgled Reina, bouncing on Abuela's lap.

"That's right, *ranita*." Elaina smiled fondly at her daughter. "Joe and I are speaking to her in both English and Spanish so she can grow up learning both," she explained to Luca. "She can already say so much. What's this, Reina?" Elaina asked, holding up a piece of potato.

"Tato!" Reina bounced.

"What about this?" Abuela held up a carton of milk.

"Milt!"

"She's still working on her 'k's," Elaina whispered. She put a hand on Luca's shoulder. "Who's this, Reina?"

"Lutta!"

"See what I mean?" Elaina chuckled. "We'll keep working on it, I want her to be bilingual by the time she starts school."

"She'll be fine," Abuela smiled. "My daughter did the same thing with Luca and his brothers. If I remember correctly, Luca couldn't say his 'L's for the longest time." She winked at Luca, eyes twinkling with merriment.

"Abuela!" Luca flushed, embarrassed.

"Just enjoy it for now, Elaina," Abuela chuckled as Reina cooed. "One day she'll say all her words properly and you'll miss the days when she was still learning."

"You've got plenty of time," Luca agreed, smiling at the jiggling toddler. "She's a smart girl, just like her mama."

"Ay, you charmer," Elaina swatted him lightly with a dish towel. "Keep away, I have a husband."

"Hubband," Reina echoed happily. "Lutta! Hot! Tato!" She leaned forward in Abuela's arms, a dark-haired cherub in a floral print dress. "Up! Lutta, up!"

"Not now, Reina, *carina*," Elaina said gently, "Luca has to take some dishes out to the table."

"Lutta! Up!" Reina demanded.

"I'll be right back, Reina," Luca said soothingly, but her cherub face was already crumbling, her lip was quivering, and tears glistened in her dark eyes.

"Lutta, up!" Reina whimpered and she began to wail.

"Reina, you know that's not how we get things." Elaina admonished her. But Luca was already reaching for the crying toddler, balancing the plate in one hand.

"I can take her with me, Elaina," Lucca said, scooping Reina up and balancing her on one hip.

"That's sweet, *mijo*, but I'm not sure I want to encourage her," Elaina sighed. However, the second Reina noticed Luca was holding her, the tears ceased and Reina's smile came out, like the sun from behind the clouds.

"You're spoiling her," Elaina muttered, but she looked relieved that the crying had stopped.

"She's a little sweet pea," Luca chuckled, "come on Reina, let's go put these empanadas outside for your mama."

Luca carried the little girl outside, weaving through neighbors carrying tubs of ice, paper lanterns, and food platters. The entire street outside Abuela's house was a riot of color. Paper lanterns and banners swung from the trees, while fake flowers and streamers decorated the tables and chairs. Mariachi music played over a speaker system someone had set up, and the air smelled of cooking meats, sweet pastries, and chocolate. Children, dressed in their best clothes, ran from table to table, laughing and stealing samples from the different food dishes.

Everyone was laughing and joking as they set up extra chairs, speaking in a mix of Spanish and English that was pleasant to the ear and almost impossible for a casual bystander to follow. The scene was that of a tight-knit community; more than that, it seemed like one giant, extended family.

Abuela had become a beloved member since she moved to the neighborhood after the death of her husband. Any time someone was feeling sick or needed a helping hand, she was the first to knock on their door with a bowl of soup or volunteer. That was why, every year on her birthday, the whole street became the scene of a giant *fiesta*, with colorful decorations, and tables of food and drink from every house and music and dancing that went all day and long into the night.

"This is impossible," Juan complained as Luca came within earshot. He was wearing, rather begrudgingly, floral shirt and slacks for the occasion. "Why do I have to do this?"

"Because it's Abuela's party and she deserves to have her whole family here," Luca explained, feeling like his father. "And considering you got arrested for vandalism, I can't trust you to go off on your own."

"Own!" Reina babbled, clapping her hands.

"It wasn't vandalism," Juan protested. "I was…" he stopped, looking down at the tangle of lights in his hands. "Never mind. You don't get it."

"'And'lism." Reina tried to grab one of the empanadas on the plate Luca was holding, and he held it away from her chubby fingers.

"You're right, I don't get your need to pursue a career that could land you in jail, when the only thing you need to focus on is schoolwork," Luca said, bouncing Reina on his hip to distract her. "Because when I was your age—"

He stopped speaking when he saw Claire approaching through the chaos, a plate of food in her hand.

"Who's that?" Juan asked, following his brother's gaze. "Wait, is that the hot chick who gave us a ride home from the jail?"

"She's my dance partner. And don't call her a' hot chick'," Luca corrected him.

"Ha'chick!" Reina echoed.

"That goes for you, too," Luca told her, hurrying forward to greet Claire.

"Well, she is," Juan muttered, going back to untangling lights.

"Claire. Hi," Luca said.

Claire turned towards the sound of his voice and relief showed on her face.

"Hi," she answered, shifting the plate of food in her hands. "I… I was just about to call, I wasn't sure if I was in the right place."

"I should've warned you, my *abuela* likes a big party," Luca apologized. He couldn't take his eyes off her. She was dressed with her usual casual elegance, a beautiful blue sundress which brought out her eyes, matching heels, with half of her hair pulled back into a bun while the rest flowed free like a golden waterfall to her waist.

"I sorta figured, considering she invited a complete stranger," Claire smiled wanly.

"Party! Ha'chick!" Reina babbled.

"And who's this?" Claire turned her attention to the little girl on Luca's hip.

"She's my neighbor's daughter," Luca explained, hoisting the toddler higher up on his hip with one hand. "Reina, do you want to say hi?" Suddenly shy, Reina buried her chubby face in Luca's shirt.

"She's adorable," Claire cooed.

"She might need a moment to get used to you. In the meantime, let me show you to the food tables. What did you bring?"

"*Sharlotka*. My mother's recipe," Claire answered, holding up her plate. "It's sort of like a Russian angel food cake but with pieces of apple and walnut in it."

"You really didn't need to bring anything," Luca said as he led her to the refreshment tables.

"I know," Claire shrugged. "But it felt too strange showing up empty-handed. Besides, it's easy to make."

Claire set her dish down on the heavily laden dessert table. Luca set his empanadas on the table next to hers.

"What are those, by the way?" Claire asked.

"Empanadas, but they're not mine," Luca explained.

"Nadas. Na-mine," Reina echoed, peeking out.

"Elaina, Reina's mama, made them. There's actually more in the kitchen that I have to get. We made enough to feed an army." He started to head back toward Elaina's house, then stopped when he noticed Claire wasn't following. "You can come, too," he told her. Claire hesitated.

"Are you sure?"

"Yes of course," Luca beckoned her with his free hand. "Come on."

"'Mon!" Reina mimicked Luca, gesturing with a chubby hand.

"See? Even Reina thinks you should come."

"All right, then," Claire followed Luca up the path, around to the kitchen door.

"Luca!" Elaina looked up with a scowl as they walked into the kitchen. "I sent you out with that plate ten minutes ago. Did you have concrete shoes on your feet?" She caught sight of Claire and understanding dawned on her face. "Luca," she exclaimed, "who is this? *Ay, que linda, hola, querida…*" She dusted flour off her hands and held them out to Claire. "I'm Elaina, nice to meet you."

"Claire," Claire replied, taking Elaina's small hand in hers. It looked delicate, but the grip was firm, hinting at the underlying strength within the tiny frame.

"Taire!" Reina giggled in Luca's arms. She'd learned another new word.

"Claire, nice to meet you. I don't think Luca mentioned you were coming." She shot a glare in Luca's direction.

"Well, I'm just his dance partner…" Claire stammered. "Luca's grandmother technically invited me…" She spotted Abuela in her chair and smiled shyly. "Hello, ma'am. Happy birthday."

"*Querida*, I thought we agreed you'd call me Abuela," Abuela reminded her, mixing the filling for more empanadas.

"Yes, ma—sorry… Abuela," Claire said hesitantly.

"Well, find a seat and relax, Claire," Elaina smiled, nudging her into a chair. "Luca, why don't you see if you can help with anything outside. And take Reina with you," she said, scooting Luca and her daughter out the door again and slamming it shut behind her.

* * *

From her seat, Claire looked curiously around the room. The kitchen was small and cozy, with worn wooden cabinets, and a black and white stove that Elaina was currently cooking something on. Pots of basil, rosemary and mint lined the windowsill, their scents melding with the smell of delicious meats and pastry filling the air. The fridge to Claire's right was covered with photos of Reina as a newborn baby and continued through her infant years to her present toddler state. There were also a few photos of Luca as well, dressed for his dance competitions, looking slightly uncomfortable in front of the camera. Claire moved closer to take a look at one in particular where Luca was dressed in an old-fashioned red frilly shirt.

"That was Luca's first competition," Abuela said proudly. "He didn't have anything to wear, so I gave him his grandfather's old costume."

"That was the first time he brought home a medal," Elaina chimed in, scooping up the finished filling for the empanadas. "Ay, he was so nervous, I think he stayed up all night, practicing."

"I remember that performance," Claire murmured.

It had been almost two years ago; her Papa had entered a "surprise star" in the rhythm division. No one had ever seen Luca before in class; he seemed to be an unsmiling, scrawny boy with his dark bangs getting in his eyes. She remembered Sebastian and some of the other dancers snickering at the new kid in his weird outfit… and then the music started, and Claire saw him light up, as if from within. The way he moved… with such effortless grace… and that smile… no one could take their eyes off of him. He blew the rest of the competition away that day.

Claire remembered watching him dance and feeling a strange mix of respect and envy for the boy in the strange shirt, battered dance shoes, and fire in his eyes. He had been teased by some of the other students for his clothing, despite the fact he had won first place for his division. Claire remembered her father had tried to secretly give Luca a new costume, but he had refused.

"He was always one of the best, I used to be jealous because he made it look so effortless. It's only by practicing with him I've realized how hard he tries," Claire said out loud as guilt twisted her stomach. She had heard Sebastian teasing Luca for wearing a funny costume and hadn't done anything to stop it. It had been his grandfather's outfit, and yet Luca never wore it to a competition again. Instead, he'd bought a simple, all-black outfit with no frills or embellishments that became his standard costume for the next few years.

"My Luca has the gift for dancing, just like my husband," Abuela said fondly. "You know, Luca came home that day after the competition, put his medal on my lap and said to me, 'Abuela, I have finally found the thing that makes sense to me.' He started working extra shifts at the bar soon afterward, so he could keep taking lessons."

"He really loves to dance," Claire murmured, studying the photos.

"It is his *chispa*, his passion," Abuela explained. "His mama had the same, she taught him how to dance when he was only this big." She held a hand up to her knee.

"So, she was a professional dancer?" Claire asked.

"No, she worked as an accountant. But every time we had a party, she would let down her hair and dance so beautifully everyone would stop and watch." Abuela's eyes took on a far away look. "My Serena has been gone for several years, but it warms my heart to see one of her sons dance as she did."

"She passed away?" Claire's heart softened. "What about Luca's father?"

"They were both killed by a drunk driver," Elaina said. "The police never caught the driver."

"Ah." Claire suddenly recalled how quiet Luca had been during the last three years. He hadn't been surly; he'd been exhausted and grieving. How he had managed to drag himself to work and school and dance after losing both parents, she couldn't even begin to understand. "I'm so sorry, Luca never mentioned it."

"My grandson does not—how you say—open himself to emotion," Abuela sighed. "Neither of my grandsons do. I have watched them grow up without speaking about their parents, throwing themselves into work to ignore how they are feeling."

"I didn't know that he had a brother until last week." With renewed interest, Claire studied the photos on the fridge.

"Juan is still in high school. He is finding his way," Abuela indicated a picture of the skinny teenager Claire also remembered from the police station. Juan had a thinner face and lean build, but Claire could see he had the same sarcastic quirk to his eyebrows Luca did when he was annoyed, the same striking nose and mouth. "Which is why he's helping with decorations today."

"From what you said, Juan knows what he wants, he's just getting in trouble for it," Elaina snorted.

"He said he wasn't going to make trouble anymore." Abuela's brow quirked slightly. "His grades have improved, and he hasn't missed any school, but Luca is still keeping an eye on him."

"He has to. If Juan is arrested again…" Elaina sighed. "Luca already works so hard."

"I have faith Juan will not make the same mistake twice," Abuela said firmly. "Just as I have faith that someone will see Juan's work for the talent it is and give him an opportunity to shine. My husband and I were dancers,

Serena was a dancer, Luca is a dancer, and Juan is a painter," Abuela told Claire. "We are a family of artists, trying to make a living in a world where only money matters. My daughter had to put aside her dreams to provide for her family, but I can always hope that my grandsons do not have to choose between their dreams and their family."

"You're such a dreamer," Elaina chuckled, kissing Abuela on the cheek. She picked up the plate of finished empanadas, balancing it on one hand. "I'm going to take these outside and try and steal Reina back from your favorite grandson," she told Abuela. "It's time for her nap."

"Good luck," Abuela chuckled. "She clings to him like *el diablillo*."

"Make sure she stays off her feet," Elaina told Claire, slipping out of the kitchen. A sudden hush fell over the room as the screen door banged shut behind her.

"You dance very well." Abuela broke the silence. Claire looked at her, surprised. Abuela shrugged. "I have seen videos of your competitions. Luca…" She hesitated before continuing. "I think he has a great admiration and respect for you as a dancer, even if he doesn't say it."

Claire thought of the way she used to treat Luca, calling him a show-off, arrogant, rude… He might've been curt and anti-social, but she hadn't been kind to him either.

"He shouldn't respect me," Claire said, shame-faced. "He shouldn't even like me."

"*Querida*," Abuela said gently. "I am just an old woman. Do I know what is in my grandson's head? No. But I do know that when he talks about his dance studio, your name comes up first."

Claire felt her cheeks flush with pleasure. "Really?"

"Really," Abuela patted Claire's hand. "Now, if you would help me outside," Abuela said, hoisting herself to her feet, "I would like to see how the rest of my *fiesta* looks."

Chapter 17: Outside Change

"The Outside Change is a lovely and simple figure which consists of 3 steps, in-line with basic Waltz rise and fall."

Joe, who had gotten the afternoon off of work for the occasion, stole a glance at Claire as she and Abuela stepped outside, and joined his wife by the refreshment tables.

"Is that your date?" he asked Luca. A silver wedding ring gleamed on his left hand as he unpacked another tangle of lights from a cardboard box. Despite the large straw hat protecting his head, Joe's white dress shirt was already damp with sweat. "You've never brought anyone to a party before."

"He says she's just his dance partner," Juan teased, setting down another table and unlocking the legs.

"Abuela asked her to come." Luca placed Reina in her baby swing so she could watch without getting in the way.

"Buela come," Reina repeated, and began kicking her chubby legs in the air.

"That's right, *mi carina*, 'Buela come,'" Joe cooed at his daughter as he began wrapping the colored lights around a tree. "I guess if 'Buela' asked her to come, you don't really care either way that she's here. She's just your dance partner, you probably have your usual complaints about her techniques, right? Tired all the time, doesn't practice enough or-"

"Her technique is amazing and she rarely needs a break," Luca defended her before he could stop himself. "She's actually one of the best dancers in the school."

"Wow," Joe raised an eyebrow. "You actually like her."

Luca pretended to be focused on the table he was unfolding. "She's not a pain to work with," he muttered.

"High praise from the King of Perfection, you sure she's not here for other reasons?" Joe asked.

"'Fection!" Reina babbled and tried to catch a sunbeam in her hands.

"Abuela invited her," Luca repeated, unfolding tables and laying out plastic tablecloths like his life depended on it.

"Uh-huh," Joe didn't sound convinced. "Then I guess you don't mind that she's getting attention from some of the guys?"

Luca allowed himself a glance towards where Claire was sitting and saw two of his neighbors had stopped their work to shoot Claire admiring gazes. Luca made eye contact with both of them, glowering, and they hastily returned to work.

"Yeah, she's just your partner," Juan snickered.

"Shut up," Luca muttered.

"Hey, careful with those words around my baby," Joe warned. "Her mama will have me sleeping on the couch if Reina starts repeating them."

"Sorry Joe," Luca and Juan chorused.

"It's okay, just be careful—"

Luca glanced in Claire's direction again and his heart warmed as he watched Claire bring Abuela a drink. She moved with the unconscious grace of the dancer as she handed over the plastic cup, smiling, a breath-taking figure in blue. Claire must've felt his eyes, because she glanced in his direction, and waved. Luca quickly looked away, face burning.

"Heads up, Romeo, she's coming this way." Juan elbowed Luca in the side.

"Would you—" Luca swallowed the rest of the retort as Claire approached him with a tray of lemonade.

"I thought you boys could use a drink; you've been working really hard." She smiled, holding out the tray to Juan, Joe, and Luca.

"*Gracias*—thank you," Joe said, taking one. "We haven't actually met, I'm Elaina's husband, and that's my daughter Reina."

"Aina," Reina cooed, clapping her hands.

"Oh, it's so nice to meet you," Claire said. "Your daughter is adorable."

"Dorable," Reina agreed.

"Yes, thank you," Luca echoed. His hand brushed Claire's as he took the cup from her, and he felt a slight jolt of electricity pass between them.

"Luca was just telling me how you're one of the best dancers at his studio," Juan said, taking his own cup with a wicked grin, and Luca desperately wished he could kick him quiet.

"Oh," Claire's smile was sunshine itself. "I'm sure he's being kind; we have plenty of talented dancers at the studio."

"Udio," Reina bounced in her swing.

"Luca doesn't say anything unless it's true," Joe's grin broadened. Luca focused on the cup of lemonade in his hand, unable to meet Claire's eyes. "The two of you will have to show your stuff during the dance later."

"Sure," Luca forced himself to look up. "We'll show these amateurs how it's done."

"Who are you calling an amateur?" Juan demanded, draining his lemonade. "Mama taught me some moves, too." He stepped into a turn and grabbed Claire's hand, kissing it with a wink, a charming, younger copy of his brother. He grinned at Luca, who was eyeing him, irritated. "I got skills you wouldn't believe!"

"Sure you do," Luca's mouth twitched up in the corners. "Do they involve getting out of a headlock?" He grabbed his brother before Juan could react, slipping skillfully into the hold and pulling him away from Claire.

"Hey! No fair!" Juan protested, wriggling in Luca's grip as Reina squealed and clapped her hands. "I wasn't ready!"

"You're never ready!" Luca grinned and enjoyed the feeling of petty revenge. "That's why it's noogie time!" He rubbed his knuckles roughly across Juan's scalp, and for a moment, the years fell away. To the golden days when Papa would've joined in the horseplay, before Mama coaxed them onto the dance floor so she could show off her talented boys. Juan was still wriggling in his grip, but he was laughing, a sound Luca hadn't heard in a very long time.

"Well… I'd better see if anyone else needs a drink," Claire said as they continued to wrestle, turning and running lightly back to the cluster of women handing out cups.

Luca found himself watching, still holding Juan in his grip. After a few seconds, he was aware of a tapping on his arm.

"Hey bro?" It was Juan.

"What?" He looked down at his prisoner.

"Take a picture, it'll last longer," Juan smirked.

"Shut up," Luca said again before he could stop himself.

"Ut up," Reina echoed, and Joe winced.

"Well, now I'm in trouble."

* * *

"You're such a good girl," Abuela said, as Claire helped make her more comfortable. "But you shouldn't worry about me, go an have some fun. Try the food!"

"Mama would be furious if I did otherwise," Claire replied, handing Luca's grandmother a paper fan. "Besides, you're the birthday girl. People are supposed to fawn over you today."

"My Luca is always helping others, as well," Abuela glanced over to where her grandson was hanging up several colorful piñatas. "He is not so good at asking others for help though." She smiled fondly as several children crowded around Luca, jabbering excitedly in Spanish. One by one, Luca handed every kid a whiffle bat so they could smack the papier mâché animals. "I know he is a young man, but sometimes I worry about him," Abuela continued. One of the piñatas broke, and the children scrambled to pick up the colorful candy that had spilled out onto the street. "Sometimes he is so busy taking care of others, he forgets to take care of himself." She grasped Claire's hand in a surprisingly strong grip. "*Querida*, I am not long for this world. Will you… make sure that Luca takes time for himself?"

"Abuela, I'm sure you have many, many—"

"Promise me."

Her eyes, dark yet full of intense energy, burned into Claire's, reminding her of Luca. Claire covered the woman's worn, bony hand with her smooth, slender fingers.

"I will keep an eye on him for you," she promised.

Abuela nodded. "That is all I ask." She released Claire's hand and sat back in her chair.

"All these kids, *familias*, coming together to celebrate, it is just like my home in Argentina." Abuela sighed happily. She eyed Claire, "have you ever been to South America, *querida*?"

Claire shook her head. "I traveled with my parents growing up, and I've gone to a couple different states for dance competitions, but I've never really had the opportunity to really go out and explore. I just promised myself that I would make time for it after I won Blackpool."

"You're so young, *querida*," Abuela frowned. "You should be enjoying living life."

"Dance is my life," Claire answered. "I've been preparing for this competition most of my life. I even took my GED test last year so I could focus solely on practicing. My partner-" she corrected herself. "Ex-partner Sebastian and I were all set to compete when…" She looked away. "He made it clear he had other priorities. But it's fine," she assured Abuela. "Luca and I have been doing really well. I think we have a solid chance of winning."

"You're only young once," Abuela said, taking Claire's hand again. "You should of course make goals and work hard to achieve them, but do not forget to live your life as well. If you wish to travel, travel. Visit other cities, experience the culture! You can even learn of the dances they have there."

"Once Blackpool is over, I will." Claire said firmly. "In the meantime, I have a lot of work to do."

* * *

"…*Cumpleaños, cumpleaños, cumpleaños, cumpleaños feliz…*"

Everyone cheered as Abuela blew out the candle on her cake. Elaina moved in to take the large, multilayered confection that Abuela had explained to Claire was an Argentinian Rogel Cake. Unlike the traditional "American" cake, this was made with several thin layers of pastry and separated by dulce de leche, with a topping of meringue. An old family recipe, Abuela had had the same cake for every birthday since she was a baby. Claire watched as a few women set up a line of plates and forks so that everyone could have a slice of the enormous dessert.

Music started playing as everyone mingled, talking and laughing, some with plates while others waited. Joe picked up a microphone and tapped it, making sure it was on.

"*Atención, atención!*" he said over the crowd. Catching sight of Claire, he switched to English. "It is everyone's favorite part of the day… when we all get a dance with the birthday girl!"

Cheers and whistles ensued as Abuela got to her feet, and after a moment's deliberation, took Luca's hand, choosing to dance with him first.

Joe changed the music to one with a bouncy, Salsa rhythm, and Claire watched as Luca tenderly pulled his grandmother close. The years seemed to fall away as Abuela danced, following as Luca spun her around, her silver hair flowing around her as he rolled her out, then pulled her back into an embrace. Her feet stepped easily around her grandson as he let her out again, then brought her back into the embrace, kissing her lightly on the cheek as he did so. She chuckled, and reached for Juan next, letting her youngest grandson lead her around the dance space as well. Juan did not have the training and experience Luca had, but Claire saw him carefully twirl Abuela, his face set in concentration, to the sound of applause.

"Well done, *mijo*." Abuela kissed his cheek as Juan's turn ended and he flushed, trying not to look pleased. But before one of the men waiting in line could take Juan's place, she waved them off, taking the microphone from Joe instead.

"I'm sorry," she apologized, speaking to the group. "But I am no longer as young as I used to be and I do not have the stamina to dance with all of you." A few groans of disappointment could be heard. "However," she continued, "since I do not want to stop the festivities early, I have chosen someone to take my place. Claire, *querida*…" She beckoned to Claire, who came forward hesitantly. "She will dance for me." Cheers and whistles came from the crowd as Claire waved shyly.

"Are you sure you want me to take your place?" Claire whispered to Abuela.

"I am certain," Abuela whispered back. She grabbed Luca, placing Claire's hands in his. "This young lady and my grandson will go first!" she announced. There was more cheering, and another upbeat song started up.

"Any way I can get out of this?" Claire asked Luca nervously.

"Not unless you want to make a run for it," Luca said, pulling her close and pivoting her around. "Relax," he said kindly. "Think of this as more practice in the wild." He spun her twice, Claire's skirts flaring out as he did so. "I promise to step in if you need help," he assured her as he pulled her back. He glanced at the line of dancers waiting to cut in. "I'm going to give the next person a turn. Don't worry, you'll be fine."

Claire's next partner was a white-haired gentleman almost a foot shorter than she was, who barely moved his feet, but he spun Claire around him with the dexterity and control of someone who had years of experience. Then she was passed to a pot-bellied man who sang to the song as he danced, then another who was as thin as a rail and had no sense of rhythm.

It was liberating to dance with no choreography in place, having only to follow her partner and the rhythm of the music. Claire moved from one partner to another, young, old, thin, fat. The faces blended together, the songs flowed around her, lifting her feet, regardless of how tired she was. More partners were dancing in the streets now. Husbands and wives, some with silver in their hair, others that still seemed to be newlyweds, were twirling and laughing together. Blushing teenagers swayed together, some more clumsily than others, while little ones, some clinging to skirts or simply toddling happily between the forest of legs, clapped their little hands and gurgled.

"Having fun?" Juan caught her as Claire was twirled from one partner to another, and she clutched him, willing herself to keep down the cake she'd eaten before the dancing started.

"No… more… spinning…" Claire gasped, holding him tightly as her head continued to whirl.

"No spinning, got it," Juan chuckled, choosing to dip her instead.

"I see Luca's sense of humor runs in the family," Claire managed as he pulled her back up. Juan led her through some simple steps, his lead careful and controlled. "And your dance skills."

"Nah, Luca's the professional, I just do this for the ladies," Juan winked, and Claire found herself charmed by the younger Ortiz. "I got my own plans for my life that have nothing to do with dancing."

"You want to be a street artist, right?" Claire asked as Juan led her around an elderly couple shimmying to the beat.

"You probably think that's stupid," Juan muttered.

"On the contrary, I love whenever I see a mural someone has painted," Claire stepped around a toddler who spun wildly in a circle, giggling. "It's art that everyone can enjoy and there's usually a beautiful message that I can appreciate. But," she paused. "You need to be careful about where you paint. You don't want your family to keep bailing you out, do you?"

"I was trying to help," Juan suddenly looked very young. "I thought if I could get famous, I could make money off my work to pay Abuela's medical bills."

"You're too young to worry about stuff like that." Claire started to laugh then stopped when Juan's chin jutted out in a very Luca-like expression of stubbornness.

"In two more years, I'll be an adult. Luca was helping pay bills when he was my age," Juan scowled. "But I guess I'm just the screw up." He stopped dancing, releasing his hold on Claire. "I'm gonna go…" He walked away, leaving Claire standing in the middle of the dancers.

"What happened?" Luca stepped in and took Claire in his arms.

"I don't know, I thought he was opening up and then he just left me." Claire winced as Luca pivoted around.

"Are you doing okay? How are your feet?"

"A little squashed," Claire admitted, "there's some people here with some serious left feet, but I can keep dancing if someone wants a second dance."

"I'm sure there are plenty who would like a second dance." Luca glanced around at the circle. "But you can take a break if you want, someone can fill in for you."

"Your grandma chose me," Claire muttered. "I didn't want to be rude." She looked at the people surrounding her. "It also seemed like everyone was having a lot of fun, and I didn't want to spoil it."

"They were. And you were an integral reason for why they had fun."

"Good," Claire allowed herself to relax slightly. "I'm glad."

Unlike the many competitions Claire had been a part of, no one seemed to care about the style or expertise of their partner but seemed to just be content to move with the music for the simple enjoyment of it.

It was paradoxically wild and serene at the same time. There was the chaos of everyone laughing and moving where they chose, but it was also freeing in a way, not to have to worry about who was watching, analyzing her every arm extension and hip roll. For the fun of it, Claire added a pirouette to a turn that caused Luca's eyebrows to raise in surprise and appreciative cheers from a few onlookers. Emboldened, she lifted her leg high enough in the air to rest her foot on Luca's shoulder, not caring what dance it was from. After all, who was judging her?

She giggled, thrilled by her new-found liberty. Luca took her cue and lifted her up, spinning both of them around before letting her down into a dip.

The late afternoon sun warmed her face, and a lovely breeze played with her hair, and as she twirled Claire felt…

free. There were no rules, no restrictions; they weren't practicing the choreography for any competition, she could just dance for the joy of dancing. She shrieked with laughter as Luca lifted her up one more time, whirling her around, the street fiesta a blur around her.

"You should smile like that more often," Claire giggled as Luca set her down.

"What?" Luca looked confused. "I smile."

"I know," Claire answered. "But… this was different…" She cocked her head, feeling as if she was seeing him for the first time. "You just look… happy."

"You saying I don't look happy all the time?" Luca tried to look annoyed and failed.

"Most of the time you have a look that says you've been up all night and have a headache," Claire informed him. Luca's lips twitched into a smile. "There! Like that!" Claire pointed. "If you smiled like that more often, you'd have all the girls asking to be your partner."

Luca's smile vanished and he considered her statement seriously. "I already have the partner I want, though. Why would I want another?"

She looked up to meet his eyes. They were the same dark eyes she'd looked into a hundred times but now they were filled with warmth, like the amber glow of a fire.

"I don't know…" Claire found herself stuttering. "Maybe there's someone else you'd rather dance with?"

Luca leaned in and Claire shivered as his breath tickled her ear. "Never going to happen."

The sun felt so warm, but not as warm as Luca's hand around hers. His right arm circled behind, securing, framing, holding her gently in a way that made her feel so supported, so safe.

Claire was aware of the solid muscle under her left hand. Muscle made from picking up Reina and swinging her onto his shoulders, supporting Abuela when he was at home and putting out tables for the fiesta. Muscle that carried her when she was injured during her last competition, lifted her into the air no matter how tired he must've been already. It was…Claire bit her lip as she felt a lump rise in her throat, overwhelmed by the surge of emotion that swept over her.

"Claire? Claire?" Luca was looking concerned. "Are you alright? Do you want to stop dancing?"

And then there was that. The gentle, compassionate heart Luca had beating, hidden just beneath his sarcastic comments and unsmiling facade. No, that wasn't true. Claire corrected herself. Luca may have never smiled as easily as the others at Beauchene Studio, but he'd never started off as aloof and surly. The other students had pushed their prejudices and assumptions onto him, criticized his clothing, and Luca had isolated himself into his practice. Not just the other students, Claire reminded herself, and felt a twist of guilt. *I made fun of him, too. I thought he was rude and mean. So it's my fault he felt excluded.*

"Claire?" Luca was still looking worried.

"I'm sorry," Claire whispered, and she flung herself forward, her head almost slamming into Luca's chin as she wrapped her arms around him. "I'm so sorry for every single insulting or stupid thing I ever said to you."

"It's nothing," Luca finally managed, gingerly enfolding his arms around her.

"It's *not* nothing!" Claire protested, her mouth muffled in his shirt. "I was really rude to you for a long time and you didn't deserve it."

"Ah…okay." Luca still seemed baffled. "What brought this on?"

"I was standing in Elaina's kitchen and she showed me a picture of your first competition. It just took me back to when you first started." Claire looked up to meet his gaze. "Even in the beginning, you were…so full of raw talent, just this insanely good dancer; and I think I felt threatened," she admitted. "Up until that point, I was the best dancer in the studio, so it annoyed me that you could be so good without the years of practice I had." Claire winced, thinking of all the things she'd said to Luca over the years and felt guilt viciously twist her stomach in a knot. "I wanted so badly to be the best. And while I was trying so hard to prove I was the better dancer, I lost out on nearly three years of knowing the real you because I was so focused on winning."

Claire looked down at their joined hands. Her hand fit so easily in his, but all she'd focused on in the beginning was how rough they were. "Once I decided I didn't like you because you were a threat, it was easy to judge you because you didn't socialize, for always seeming to be in a bad mood —"

Luca's dark eyes were unreadable. "It's hard to engage with people at the studio. And being the charity case didn't help much."

"Plus when you're sleep-deprived you get cranky," Claire agreed.

The corner of Luca's mouth twitched. "I was under the impression you were trying to compliment me, but it seems like you're not anymore. Maybe we should keep dancing."

"Wait!" Claire protested. "I'm trying to say I'm sorry!" She took a breath. "For everything. You were right, I'm a snob, and a princess and and..."

"You forgot stubborn," Luca supplied.

"Yeah," Claire nodded.

"Fiercely competitive."

"I really hate to lose," Claire admitted.

"You'd rather walk with a sprained ankle than show any sign of weakness."

"All of that is true," Claire sighed, feeling miserable.

Luca looked down at Claire, and this time there was a definite twinkle in his eye. "But those are the qualities that make you, you. You're also a dedicated and patient teacher. A kind and loyal friend to Bella, nothing but respectful to my Abuela-"

"I want to be her when I grow up," Claire interjected. "If I can have dance parties at her age, I'll be happy."

Luca chuckled, pulling her into a tight hug and Claire felt the rumble of the vibration tingle through her. "And you dance because it is an integral part of you, not for fame or fortune. My point is that I didn't take the time to know you either," Luca said. "And I'm sorry for that. Because I would've liked to know this side of you as well." His mouth quirked up a little more and one of Luca's radiant smiles broke through. "Even if I had to deal with lectures every day about how I'm not getting enough sleep."

"I'm not the only one, Abuela thinks you need to rest too!" Claire glared, but Luca was grinning now and it was hard to stay annoyed. "The brain eats itself when it's sleep deprived you know," she muttered.

Luca chuckled again. "You're worried about my brain now?"

"I just want you to be able to remember our choreography for Blackpool," Claire huffed.

"Oh absolutely," Luca agreed, resting his chin lightly on her head. "Got to keep the brain in tip-top condition for Blackpool."

"I'm trying to get you to take care of yourself and you're being so mean!" Claire wriggled in his arms, trying to get free. "I take back all the nice things I just said."

Luca tightened his grip, his fingers brushing over her hair. "Oh no, I guess my half-eaten brain will just have to remember them forever," he teased.

"Workaholic," Claire retorted.

"Control freak."

"I am not!" Claire protested. "I just—"

"Like when things go according to plan, yes I know. That's my *princesa*," Luca murmured and Claire felt her heart skip a beat. In the past, she had disliked his referral to her as a princess. But for some reason, she didn't mind the nickname so much when she knew she was *his* princess.

She relaxed against his chest, feeling the thrum of his heartbeat in her ear.

"*Dios mio*! Abuela!" Claire and Luca jerked apart at the sound of Elaina's shout. She was leaning over Abuela, furiously fanning her.

"Abuela? Abuela? Can you hear me?"

Chapter 18: Contra Check

"The contra check is a phase V figure used in all the smooth rhythms. Contra-body action occurs when one steps with one foot but leads with the opposite side of the torso."

"Thanks for coming on such short notice, Bianca," Claire said as her friend stepped out of Elaina and Joe's bedroom. When Abuela couldn't be roused, the *fiesta* had come to an abrupt halt and Luca and Joe had carried the unconscious Abuela inside the air-conditioned house.

"Pay me back for the Uber ride and we'll call it even," Bianca said. She eyed Reina who was dozing on Claire's shoulder, oblivious to the distress around her. "It seems like you've made a lot of new friends."

"How is she?" Luca asked anxiously. He was pacing around the living room, unable to sit down and wait.

"She's resting," Bianca reported. She had been on her way to start her shift when Claire called, so she was already dressed in clean scrubs, her dark hair plaited into a neat braid. "At the moment, her pulse is a little fast, and she's having difficulty taking deep breaths. Who was with her when she passed out?"

"I was," Elaina raised her hand like a schoolgirl.

"And what was she doing?"

"Nothing," Elaina spread her hands helplessly. "She was just sitting, watching the dancers. Usually, she's a part of the party, but this year she was trying to take it easy and she still…" Her voice broke and Joe wrapped a comforting arm around his wife.

"Don't worry, *mamasita*," he soothed, "she's going to be okay." He looked to Bianca for confirmation. "Right?"

"You should still get an official check-up and make sure there aren't any underlying problems," Bianca said carefully, "but based on what you've told me, I think she is just experiencing heat stroke. It's actually very common with people her age. The older you get, the harder it is for your body to regulate heat, so being outside on a hot day can be dangerous."

"I'll remember that," Luca ran a hand through his hair. "So what can we do in the meantime?" he demanded.

"Keep her comfortable, make sure her feet are elevated, and that she gets plenty of fluids," Bianca advised. "Do you have any electric fans?" She asked, turning her attention to Elaina.

"*Sí*, yes, we have two."

"Put at least one in the room to help keep her cool. Abuela will need to rest for at least two days. And please take her to the doctor for more tests. It looks like a simple heat stroke, but it could also be the warning signs of something more serious—like a heart attack, kidney problem, or even a stroke."

"Would she be alright if I move her so she can rest at my house?" Luca asked suddenly. "I can't ask Elaina to keep my grandmother here for two days."

"*Idiota!*" Elaina whacked Luca lightly on the back of the head. "Abuela made me soup every day while I was carrying Reina. She helped look after my daughter so I could rest while Joe was at work. Never once has she not been there for me when I needed her. She's *familia* and welcome to stay as long as she likes."

"Then let me at least look after her when I'm not at work," Luca insisted.

"Well, whoever is looking after Abuela, just remember to keep her cool and hydrated," Bianca spoke up. "Claire, I'm going to need to get to work soon, do you think you can give me a ride?"

"Sure thing, be right out," Claire said as Bianca headed for the door. She looked at Elaina. "Is there anything else I can do before I leave?" Claire asked.

Elaina smiled at her. "You have done more than enough, *mija*," she assured Claire. "You called your doctor friend over, you helped pack up leftovers, and you've kept Reina happy this whole time. You should go home and rest."

"Oh," Claire flushed, feeling pleased. "It was no problem really, Reina's a sweetheart."

"Sweee-har!" Reina echoed sleepily, stirring slightly at the sound of her mother's voice, her chubby hand holding tight to Claire's dress. Her eyes drooped shut again and she yawned, showing off a tiny baby tooth.

"She looks like she's ready for her nap," Elaina murmured. "Reina, would you like mama to take you?"

"No, let me," Luca reached for the little girl. "You've been looking after Abuela this whole time."

"No, Taire!" Reina snuggled deeper onto Claire's shoulder, clinging tighter to her dress strap.

"Ooh careful," Claire said, grabbing for her dress as Reina almost pulled it too low. Luca's hand met hers, his fingers brushing against her bare skin as she tried to disengage the toddler's grip. "Reina sweetie, I have to take Bianca to work, but can Luca or your mom take you for your nap?"

Reina's face was turning red, the clear warning signs of a temper tantrum on her tiny face. "Want Taire!" she insisted. "Taire nap!"

"Maybe some other time, Reina, I have to go now," Claire tried to soothe her, but Reina wrapped her arms around her throat in a toddler chokehold. "Careful sweetheart," Claire managed to gasp, "that's too tight."

"I got her," Luca carefully untangled Reina's arms from Claire's neck and tried to lift Reina free. The little girl's response was to latch onto Claire's waist with her legs like a monkey pulling all three of them together into a tangle of limbs. Claire stepped on Luca's foot as Luca's chin smacked her in the forehead.

"Ow!" They said at the same time.

"That time really was an accident," Claire muttered, rubbing her forehead.

"No kidding," Luca grunted as he flexed his sore foot.

"Reina, that's enough," Elaina said sharply. "Let me or Luca take you, but Claire has to go now."

"No! Taire!" Reina's lip quivered. "Taire swee-har."

"*Sí, querida.*" Luca said gently, "but as sweet as she is, Claire needs to go home now. Do you think you can let go, please?"

"Please, Reina, I'll come back later, okay?" Claire promised.

Reina pouted. "Kay," she sulked, loosening her grip. Claire took advantage of the opportunity to unhook Reina's legs from her waist, allowing Luca to scoop the toddler up and settle her on his hip.

"Bye-bye, Reina," Claire waved at the tiny girl. "I hope to see you again."

"Wait! Nogo!" Reina protested. "Peso!"

She patted her cheek expectantly. Claire looked at Elaina, baffled.

"What does she want?"

"*Beso*, it means a kiss," Elaina explained. "Reina wants a kiss good-bye. Probably because my husband and I usually give her one when we leave."

"Peso!" Reina bounced wildly in Luca's arms. "Peso! Tiss!"

"You really don't have to…" Luca started to say.

"I'm happy to give her a kiss," Claire stepped closer to both of them, and her hair brushed against Luca's arm as she leaned in to place a gentle smooch on Reina's chubby, dimpled cheek. "Good-bye again, Reina. Or as my Papa would say, *au revoir*." She winked conspiratorially at Luca.

"She already knows more Spanish words than I do, why not teach her a little French? Can you say *au revoir*, Reina?"

"Arvor!" Reina giggled, looking delighted.

"Good enough," Claire chuckled. "*Au revoir*, Reina, I *definitely* hope to see you in class one day."

"Arvor!" Reina repeated, waving her tiny hand.

However, as soon as Claire started to move for the door, she cried out again. "Nogo! Lutta Tiss!"

"Reina, it's fine," Luca said quickly, though Claire noticed his ears were turning pink. "Besides, Claire has to go."

"Taire! Lutta Peso!" Reina demanded, patting Luca's cheek insistently. "Peso Bye!"

"You can go, I'm sure Bianca has been waiting long enough," Luca winced as the toddler's pudgy hand continued to whack his face. "I'll see you tomorrow for practice."

"Peso! Tiss!" Reina's lip trembled and she looked like she was on the verge of tears.

Claire hesitated, glancing from Reina's pout to Luca's increasingly pink ears. "Does she want…"

"Mhmm…" Luca ducked slightly as Reina's hand almost smacked his eye.

"Is she going to cry if I don't give you a kiss?" Claire asked, watching the toddler with a mix of alarm and amusement.

"Probably," Luca admitted, adjusting Reina on his hip. "It's fine though, she should learn she can't always have her way."

"Peso Tiss!" Reina repeated, her voice taking on the beginnings of a wail.

"It's fine, it's just a kiss." And saying so, Claire took two steps forward, raised herself slightly on tiptoe, and light as a butterfly wing, brushed her lips lightly against Luca's cheek. His skin felt soft, and she was aware of the slight prick of stubble against her lips, like the thorn of a rose. Anne Brontë said something about thorns and roses, Claire thought vaguely. How you shouldn't grasp the rose if you can't handle the thorns. And she supposed Luca was a wild exotic rose in his own right. Prickly to anyone he didn't want getting too close, only opening up to those he loved and trusted. He smelled of his usual spice and laundry detergent, the scent as fragrant as any cologne, and Claire felt her head swimming slightly as she stepped away. Luca, for his part, hadn't moved, just stood frozen, staring at Claire with an expression on his face she couldn't quite read.

"Yay!" Reina broke the silence, clapping her pudgy hands together. "Lutta tiss!"

"Well," Claire swallowed. Her lips were tingling and she was aware of her pulse pounding in her ears. "Glad she's happy," she managed and Reina cooed in response. Her face and neck were on fire and Claire desperately hoped her pale skin wasn't beet red. "I need to get Bianca to work… I'll see you tomorrow, Luca," Claire said, making a beeline for the exit.

"Bye-bye!" Claire heard Reina's cheerful response before the door banged shut behind her.

* * *

"'Bout time. I was going to come in after you," Bianca remarked as Claire hurried down the driveway to her car.

"Sorry," Claire muttered, fishing out her keys and unlocking the doors. Her lips still tingled and as she brushed her fingers against them, she felt a warm ticklish feeling spread all the way down to her toes.

"You look happy," Bianca commented, sliding into the passenger seat. "You want to tell me about it while you drive me to work?"

"Not really," Claire started the ignition.

"Can I guess?"

"No."

"Okay then," Bianca held up her hands in surrender as Claire pulled away from the curb and drove down the street. Colorful streamers and balloons fluttered disconsolately from branches, making the empty party scene look even more deserted. If Abuela hadn't fainted, everyone would still be dancing and having a good time, Claire reflected.

"Too bad the *fiesta* had to end early," Bianca commented, mirroring Claire's thoughts. "Looks like it had the potential to be a lot of fun."

"It *was* fun, while it lasted," Claire replied. She looked one last time at the festive, lonely street before turning onto the main road, remembering the people, young and old, gathering together to laugh, eat, and drink. "There was a lot of dancing, I see how Luca was able to get so much experience."

"His grandparents were big dancers, too, right?" Bianca asked.

"I—how did you know that?" Claire looked at her friend in surprise.

"Whoa, eyes on the road, Claire-bear," Bianca advised. "I want to get to the hospital, but not in an ambulance."

"Sorry."

"Elaina put a few pictures on the bedside table for Luca's Abuela to look at," Bianca explained. "I don't know what dance style they were doing but they were wearing some pretty fancy costumes."

"Abuela mentioned that she was a dancer, and Luca's mom was, too," Claire recalled. The conversation felt like it had happened centuries ago. "It's a shame that she passed away, it sounded like she was really talented, even if she didn't pursue dance as a career."

"Well, not everyone can follow their dreams," Bianca pointed out.

"Luca is," Claire argued.

"And I'm sure there are more than a few people who think he's a little crazy," Bianca said.

"Being a dancer isn't crazy!" Claire protested.

"Come on, I've seen Bella's dance bills," Bianca rolled her eyes. "It's super expensive to take lessons if your parents don't own their own studio."

"Dancing is about more than just winning a prize!" Claire said defensively. She thought of her first competition, the nerves in her belly as she danced to the routine, the feel of her skirt swishing around her legs as her partner twirled her across the floor, the roar of the crowd, and knowing that all her training and practice had paid off. "It's about the dance! How it feels in that moment, not material stuff —"

"Hey, you don't have to tell me, I'm living with a committed dancer myself, remember?" Bianca replied. "But dancing for the sake of the dance, paying for all the equipment you need to compete… especially when you're struggling to make ends meet… some people would consider that a little crazy."

There was silence in the car as Claire mused over Bianca's words. She recalled all the times Luca had staggered into the studio, dark circles under his eyes after a long night of work. *He has more passion than I do if he does all that and still comes in to dance*, she realized with a twinge of envy. Maybe if he had a better-paying job he wouldn't have to work as hard.

I'll ask Papa if he has any openings for new dance instructors, Claire decided. *Luca has done such a great job teaching me I'm sure he could help others.* She remembered how good he had been with Reina. *And he definitely likes kids. He'd be perfect to teach the children's classes. Maybe he'd even be as good as S'nortiz.* She chuckled at the thought.

"Something wrong with your lip?" Bianca asked. "You've been fussing with it for the last few minutes."

"Huh?" Claire pulled herself out of her reverie and realized Bianca was right. Her fingers were hovering around the edge of her mouth. She quickly put the traitorous hand back on the wheel. "It's nothing," Claire tried to brush it off. "It's just sorta tingling."

"Tingling?" Immediately Bianca was all doctor. "Is it itching as well? You might be having an allergic reaction."

"No, I think I just scratched them on his stubble or something."

"Who's stubble?" Bianca asked curiously. Claire was silent, her eyes fixed firmly on the road in front of her. Bianca gave a sigh of exasperation. "Girl, you can't just mention you scratched your lips on someone's stubble and expect me to let it go."

Claire bit her lip.

"I kissed Luca," she admitted.

"What?" Bianca yelped.

"On the cheek!" Claire added hastily, feeling her own growing hot. "Reina kept saying *tiss Lutta, peso bye* and it looked like she was going to cry, so…"

"So you kissed him because a little girl made you," Bianca finished.

"Yes!" Claire insisted, then hit the brake as she almost ran a red light. Someone behind her honked angrily.

"Uh-huh." Bianca looked intrigued. "And now your lips are tingling?"

"Yes…" Claire muttered reluctantly. "Could we talk about something else now?"

"Sure." Bianca was fighting not to smile now. "But as a doctor I feel it's my duty to give you various hypothesis about what it could be. Number one." She held up a finger. "As I said before, you might be experiencing an allergic reaction. Could've been something you ate, or maybe they became irritated by something on Luca's face, like soap. Number two." She held up a second finger. "It's unlikely, but there could be an interruption of blood to your brain and you're about to have a stroke. Relax." Bianca soothed Claire when she looked at her anxiously. "Do you feel weak? Any numbness or trouble speaking?"

"No!" Claire insisted. "Well… maybe a little numb…" She added nervously, "but mostly I feel happy. That's not a symptom, is it?" Claire asked. Bianca shook her head, looking amused.

"Oh it's one hundred percent a symptom," Bianca grinned.

"What?" Claire hit the horn on accident. "Does that mean I'm about to have a stroke?"

"No sweetie, most likely it was the third option: you were kissing someone you like."

"But I…"Claire felt her cheeks flush. "We just got to be friends."

"A kiss can bridge the distance between friendship and love," Bianca said sagely. She looked at Claire, exasperated. "Look, I know I told Bella off for teasing you about a new relationship, but come on girl, I could see the way you were looking at each other. And before you tell me you're not interested, you're touching your lips again."

"I am not—" Claire looked down at her hand and realized Bianca was right. It wasn't her fault, she thought, quickly placing it back on the wheel. Luca's touch was electric, thrilling, a fuse connected to dynamite. If that was how she felt kissing his cheek, what would his lips feel like? She quickly tried to push the thought out of her head. "But I can't be feeling things like this already, right? It's too soon after Sebastian, I can't just go hopping from one person to the next—"

"Sebastian did," Bianca interjected and winced. "Sorry, that just sort of came out. But it's true," she added. "Look, I can understand that you feel you have to take time to breathe after that whole thing with Sebastian, even though he…" she hesitated. "He really wasn't the best person for you." Claire was silent. "But I also think spending this time with Luca has given you the opportunity to see the kind of guy you deserve to be with, who is kind, respectful, challenges you as a dancer…and isn't trying out various girls like ice cream samples."

"Bianca! We don't know what!"

"Well sorry sweetie, but I trust your ex-boyfriend being faithful as far as I can throw him. And look, I'm not trying to rush you or make a decision for you." Bianca continued. "And I don't want to make you feel like you did anything horrible. Life gave you a bad experience and you dated someone who hurt you. But if you're worried you'll be judged for being attracted to someone new, and maybe wanting to see what kissing him on the lips might be like…" At this point, Claire was sure her ears were bright red. "Don't be," Bianca chuckled. "Anyone who truly cares about you, just wants you to be happy. Okay? Because you deserve to be this happy."

Claire couldn't trust herself to answer. Her heart was beating a mile a minute in her chest. Bianca sighed. "Message received; I won't bring it up again." She glanced out the window. "Could you drop me here? I want to get a sandwich before work." Claire wordlessly pulled over to the curb. "Think about it at least, would you, girl?" Bianca asked, opening the car door. "I'll see you later."

"Hey!" Claire stuck her head out the window.

Bianca stopped. "What?"

Claire hesitated. "It's really okay? It's not too soon?"

Bianca rolled her eyes. "Do I need to write you a prescription to go lock lips next time you see him?"

Claire shook her head.

"Good. But as your friend, I suggest you do it anyway." And with that, Bianca strode off down the street, quick strides eating up pavement as she headed for the nearby store and stepped inside.

"I can't just lock lips with Luca next time I see him," Claire muttered to herself as she pulled away. But she still touched her lips one more time.

* * *

"You idiot!" The words were out before Luca could stop them. As the day had turned to evening with no appearance of his little brother, he'd left Abuela in Elaina's capable hands and had driven around looking for Juan. The address that had been on Juan's arrest report had been his last stop. And there was his brother, a bandana on his head, mask on his face, and a can of spray paint in his hand.

Luca got out of his car, slamming the door. "You idiot! I waste all that money to bail you out, and you come back to the scene of the crime?" He was fully prepared to haul his brother back to the police station and toss him in jail when he stopped and took in the image that was taking shape on the concrete wall. He knew that place. It was still rough in places, some parts of the mural only outlines and rough sketches, but he *knew* that place.

It was the place by the sea their parents used to take them on their days off. And now that he was looking, Luca could see his mother and father sprawled in the shade, on top of that raggedy blanket they always kept in the trunk of their minivan. Abuela sat off to the side, a fan in her hand. He could see himself running barefoot over the grass, Juan in hot pursuit, a familiar-looking orange nerf football tucked under his arm. They always played football, running back and forth across the grass until the sun sank below the horizon. Sometimes when he felt like it, Papa would join in, tossing one son or the other over his shoulder to carry over the goal line for a touchdown, while Abuela and Mama cheered.

Luca felt a lump rise in his throat. He'd seen sketches, drawings his brother had done as he'd gotten older. But he'd never realized how talented his brother was until now. Luca could almost smell the sea breeze, mixed with the aroma of his mama's special picnic lunches. He felt the shade from the large oak tree that looked too real to be painted on a wall, hear the rustle of the leaves, his parent's laughter. There had been a time when the house was full of laughter. When Luca didn't have to worry about paying bills or making enough money. Before the accident, before the laughter was taken away by one drunk driver.

Luca looked toward Juan, who was watching him warily, the can upraised in his hand, like he was prepared to spray Luca with Sunrise Red if necessary.

"You did this?"

"Yeah?" Juan adjusted his stance, still wary. "So?"

Luca looked back at the mural. All this time. He'd thought Juan's actions had been acts of rebellion, but instead, his brother had been sneaking out to paint memories. This wasn't an act of anger, this was how he had been grieving.

"It's good," he said. "It's not even done, but I can tell it's going to be really, really good."

"Oh," Juan lowered the spray can. "Thanks, I guess."

"Too bad you can't finish it."

Juan looked up, baffled. "Why not?"

"You don't have permission. It's why you were arrested in the first place. You can't just go painting some wall even if it's part of an abandoned grocery store. It's illegal."

Juan stuck out his chin. "I want to help pay the bills."

"Then come work at the bar with me," Luca said. "I'll speak to Chris about a part-time position."

"I don't want to work in a bar though," Juan objected. "And neither do you!"

Luca felt a headache building. "Sometimes you have to do jobs you dislike to earn enough to pay our bills," Luca explained. "I'm doing it for our family!"

"You could make a living as a dancer if you tried," Juan argued. "I was watching you during the fiesta, you are one of the best dancers I've ever seen in my life!"

"I can't—" Luca started to say but Juan cut him off.

"Yes you can! Dancing your *chispa*, this is mine!" He pointed at the half-painted wall. "Abuela says it's important to do what you love. I don't want to graduate and get a job that just makes me money. I want to live my life doing something that makes me happy—and makes me money."

"Excuse me." Luca turned and his heart leapt to his throat at the sight of a skinny man in his seventies, round glasses balanced on a bulbous nose and a thinning crop of white hair. "Who are you and why are you here?"

"I—uh…" Luca gulped. Thoughts of another arrest, not being able to go to Blackpool because he was in jail flashed through his mind. "I'm sorry, we didn't mean any harm—"

"Luca, this is my employer, Mr. Lopez, he's the one who owns this grocery store," Juan interrupted, grinning. "He hired me to finish this mural."

"You can't really claim to be in my employ if you're not getting paid," Mr. Lopez rasped. He jerked a wizened thumb in Juan's direction. "This young man came knocking on my door after I caught him and begged for permission to finish his artwork, since he's not actually trying to vandalize my wall." He shrugged. "There's a very good chance any new owners who buy this dump will paint over it, but he convinced me that his mural would increase the value of the sale."

"If I'm right, I get a percentage," Juan spoke up.

"And if he's not, he gets nothing," Mr. Lopez nodded.

"Trust me, Mr. Lopez, this mural is going to make us both money," Juan said confidently.

"It's your time to waste, sonny," Mr. Lopez shook his head. "I have a soft spot for crazy artists; my first wife was a sculptor," he explained to Luca. "Got one of her uglier pieces… somewhere," he waved a hand vaguely. "And considering my store has been on the market for two years, I could use something to make it stand out. So it's a win-win for me either way." He ran a hand through his wispy white hair. "So, again, who are you?"

Luca couldn't help but smile. "I'm this crazy artist's brother."

Chapter 19: Reverse Embrace

"Reverse embrace is where both partners face the same direction;
occasionally to perform tango figures."

"Missy Claire! Missy Claire!" Viviane Murphy squealed, hugging Claire's knees. "I missed you!"

"We both did." Viviane's mother Kathy smiled and whispered conspiratorially to Claire. "There was a new teacher filling in for your last group class, but he didn't seem very qualified."

"Really?" Claire was surprised. "What made him seem unqualified? Were his classes bad?"

"I mean, they were fine," Kathy shrugged, "but he was using such unorthodox methods. And when I asked Mr. Beauchene where he'd learned to dance all he would tell me was that Señor Ortiz was the school's Latin Champion and that made him experienced enough to teach the children's class."

…Señor Ortiz… Claire felt her heart skip a beat. *Was Kathy Murphy talking about Luca?*

"Maybe you can talk to your father?" Kathy smiled hopefully at Claire. "After all, if we're paying *a lot of money* to have our children learn to dance, wouldn't it make sense to have someone teach who has an actual degree?"

"Mommy…" Viviane tugged on her mother's coat. "I like S'nortiz. He's nice and he makes classes super fun!"

"Well, I'm sure he does, dearie," Kathy smiled at her daughter, "but just because he's nice and fun doesn't mean he's teaching you properly. I mean…" she lowered her voice, "Can he even legally be here? I hear he can't even afford the actual classes; he just got a job filling in for the qualified teachers."

Claire felt her temper rise and she struggled to keep it in check. How *dare* Kathy Murphy decide Luca was unqualified just because he couldn't afford classes? And how dare she think Papa would randomly pick someone with no experience to teach the younger students? Leon was at times eccentric and impulsive, but he was no fool when it came to running his business. If he chose someone for a task, he had a good reason. And as for whether Luca deserved to be here…

"I assure you, Mrs. Murphy," Claire said as calmly as possible, "my Papa doesn't hire anyone who isn't capable of doing their job. And as for Luca… Papa is right in saying that he is our champion Latin dancer. I'd even go so far as to say he's one of the best dance students in the school."

"But as you said, he's a *student*," Kathy Murphy interjected. "Shouldn't a *teacher* be in charge of the class?"

Claire lifted her chin defiantly. "I've been giving Viviane private and group lessons for a year and a half and

I'm a student," she reminded Kathy. "Do you have a problem with *me* teaching your daughter, too?"

"Well yes, but you've been a student here for your whole life," Kathy Murphy sputtered. "And you're—you're not…"

"An illegal? No, I'm not, and neither is Luca," Claire said firmly. "He's a first-generation immigrant, as am I."

"What?" Kathy's eyes widened. "But—"

"My parents emigrated here from Europe twenty years ago," Claire cut her off. "My mother is Russian, and my father is French. Or didn't you remember?"

"Well yes, but…" Kathy fumbled. "If you don't mind me saying, you seem a lot more American than he does."

"*L'habit ne fait pas le moine,*" Claire cut her off. "I can say the same thing to you in Russian, I've been trilingual since I was Viviane's age." She smiled down at the little girl who was watching the whole exchange with wide eyes. "And despite the fact I was raised in America, my parents wanted to make sure I never forgot where they came from."

Claire paused, giving Kathy her best professional smile. "Now, of course, as Viviane is a student here, you are allowed to ask for a teacher that you think is more qualified. But if you don't like Luca based on his background, I probably shouldn't be teaching Viviane either. Do you want to request a different teacher?" Kathy was silent, her lips pressing in a thin line.

"Alright then." Claire took a breath. "Ms. Murphy, you enrolled your daughter in this studio because regardless of where my parents came from, this was the best dance school in the state. But if you want your daughter to be a champion dancer, Luca is one of the best teachers you could ask for. He's been teaching me for two months, and he's made me a better dancer as a result."

"Mommy?" Viviane tugged on her mother's coat. "Is everything okay? I don't have to get a 'nother teacher, do I?"

"No, sweetie," Kathy Murphy patted her daughter's head, guilt briefly flickering over her face. "Everything is fine. I'm sorry I made such a fuss," she said, her eyes meeting Claire's. "I just want what's best for Viv."

"Of course you do." Claire said, meeting her gaze evenly. "Just as I hope you understand that as a Beauchene of Beauchene Dance Studio, it's my job to want the best for *everyone* who comes here." She managed a smile, changing the subject. "Now if I can have a minute, I need to get the classroom ready. I'm going to teach the kids some techniques that Señor Ortiz taught *me*."

Claire turned on her heel and rammed into a muscled chest she knew all too well.

"How is it I'm always running into you?" Claire tipped her head up to meet Luca's gaze. She tried to keep her voice light but inside her mind was whirling. How long had he been standing there? Had he heard what she said about him?

"As I've said before," Luca replied, his tone laced with amusement. "You need to be more aware of your surroundings." Up close, he smelled of spice and cleaning supplies, meaning he had just come from a shift at the bar. How was it that that combination suddenly made her heart beat faster? She could still remember what it felt like to kiss his cheek, the rough stubble scratching her lips.

"Do I need to write you a prescription to lock lips?" She heard Bianca's exasperated voice in her head. Claire fought back the rush of heat at the thought.

"You weren't supposed to be here for an hour," Claire scolded him. "You could've gotten some rest—"

"On the contrary, I seem to have come at the perfect time." Luca's mouth quirked up in a smile. The way he was looking at her should be illegal, Claire decided. Everything —from the unruly curls framing his face to the look in those dark eyes—both thrilled and terrified her.

"S'nortiz!" Viviane latched onto Luca's leg like a burr. "Are you giving me a lesson today, too?"

"Not today," Luca chuckled, kneeling down to smile at the young girl. "I'm just here to practice."

"But you're my teacher," Viviane wrinkled her nose in confusion. "Why do you still need to practice?"

"Because no matter how good you are, it's always important to go over what you know," Luca advised her. "Even if you're one of the best dancers in the school." He looked up at Claire and winked. Claire felt her cheeks flush bright red. *He* had *been listening!*

"Oh, that makes sense," Viviane said cheerfully. "If I keep practicing, then I'll become the best, too!"

"Exactly," Claire agreed.

"I'm going to rehearse like S'nortiz every day then too!" Viviane said excitedly, dashing into the classroom. Kathy Murphy followed her daughter in, having the good grace to look embarrassed. Claire and Luca found themselves alone outside the classroom.

"I don't think I've ever seen Viviane so excited to see one of her teachers." Claire was the first to speak. "She must really like you."

"It's easier when kids are young," Luca said absently, a half-smile on his face as he watched Viviane twirl, giggling in front of the classroom mirror. Her mother sat off to the side, texting furiously. "They don't care if you're a little different as long as you come to class with something fun to learn."

There was a little sadness in his voice when he said that, and Claire had to wonder how many people had treated him like Kathy Murphy had. And yet, despite her mother's prejudice, Luca still smiled for Viviane. The actions of the mother didn't affect how Luca treated her daughter.

"I'm sorry," Claire blurted out as Luca got to his feet.

Luca shot her a look that was a mixture of surprise and exasperation. "You're doing a lot of apologizing these days. Did I miss something? It sounded like you were defending me a minute ago."

"You didn't deserve to be judged. I could've made things easier for you if I'd stopped it sooner."

"Claire," Luca's voice was firm. "I can't force people here to like me and neither can you. But-" Luca reached out to tuck a strand of hair behind Claire's ear, sending a tingle of warmth through her at the light brush of contact. "It's nice knowing you're on my side."

"Okay." Claire stared up at Luca, feeling somewhat tongue-tied. "I—I need to prepare for my class," she murmured, edging for the doorway. "I'll see you afterwards for rehearsal?"

"What did you say to her?" Luca asked as she turned away. "That thing you said in French."

"*L'habit ne fait pas le moine?*" Luca nodded. "Don't judge a monk by its habit," Claire translated. "It's one of my dad's favorite sayings. Americans have a similar one about not judging a book by its cover."

Luca's smile was like a lovely ray of sunshine. "It's beautiful."

* * *

"I didn't realize you were the mysterious S'nortiz," Claire said as she entered the practice room. "Viviane has been singing your praises for weeks." Luca looked up in surprise. His tank top was streaked with sweat, he'd been working on a series of footwork exercises.

"It wasn't really a secret," he shrugged, crossing the floor to grab his water bottle. "I was just helping out where I was needed."

"I was going to ask Papa if he'd consider training you for a teaching position," Claire murmured, feeling foolish. "But I guess he beat me to the punch."

"I told him I'm not good enough to be a full-time teacher yet," Luca said, taking a swig of water. "But I feel very privileged when he asks me to fill in as a substitute."

"You're kidding, right?" Claire stared at him in disbelief. "I've seen how much better Viviane has gotten after taking your class. I—" Claire fumbled, feeling shy. "I know I've gotten better from your training, too. What makes you think you're not good enough to teach?"

Luca's mouth twitched up in a smile and he fidgeted with the cap on his water bottle. "I didn't realize you thought so highly of me," he muttered.

It's hard to admit there's someone who's a better dancer than me," Claire crossed her arms. "Especially when that person tends to hold it over my head."

"Don't sell yourself short," Luca put his water bottle back on the shelf. "You're just as good as I am."

"And *I* teach," Claire said pointedly, "so logically, if I'm experienced enough to stand in front of a group of kids and show them how to do basic steps, you should be, too."

"It's not that simple." Luca shook his head.

"What do you mean?" Claire protested, "of course it is! You're a great teacher and an incredible dancer! What's stopping you from taking the job?"

"Because *I* need to believe I'm good enough!" Luca snapped. "Not you, not Mr. Beauchene. *Me.* Because if I don't believe I am capable of being a good teacher, how am I supposed to listen to complaints from parents like Mrs. Murphy and not feel like a fraud?" Luca ran a hand through his hair, suddenly looking tired. "You have your own reasons for competing in Blackpool, but as for me…if I win…maybe they'll finally take me seriously. And if they don't…at least *I* can know I'm the best." He ran a hand through his curls. "We leave tomorrow, can we just focus on getting ready for the competition?"

"But—"

"We can talk next week," Luca cut her off.

"Okay," Claire huffed out a breath. "But I'm going to hold you to that."

"Let's take it from the lift one more time," Luca said, changing the subject abruptly. He motioned Claire to the center of the practice room. "Ready? Five, six, seven…" Claire gripped one of his hands and stepped into the other, hoisting herself up onto his shoulder and posed, one arm in the air, a practiced smile on her face. After a moment, Claire leaned back into a controlled fall, flipping off his shoulder while Luca grabbed her leg, allowing her to come down like a pendulum, Luca spinning her off the ground. Luca pivoted once, twice, before he set her carefully down on the floor.

"*Fabuleux*." Claire and Luca turned to see Leon watching the practice from the door, dressed in a comfortable polo shirt and slacks. "Even if you two don't come in first, you have a good chance of placing in the finals."

"Well then, we should go through the routine again," Claire said, grasping Luca's hand. His muscles bulged slightly, but he pulled her to her feet with little effort. "Because Luca's teaching career is riding on us winning."

"Really?" Leon swung to face Luca. "You're taking the position?"

"I'm considering, I'm not committing to it," Luca muttered. "Can we go over the routine again?"

"You two have come so far." Leon approached the two of them. "Take the time to appreciate your progress and just-"

"Papa," Claire interrupted. "Do you have any notes?"

"*Petit à petit, l'oiseau fait son nid*," Leon sighed.

"What did he say?" Luca asked.

"Little by little a bird builds a nest," Claire translated. "But the nest has to be finished by tomorrow, Papa, we can't appreciate it until it's done."

"You do not need to finish something to appreciate the journey," Leon shook his head. "But since you want notes…" He considered the two of them seriously. "Claire," he said after a moment. "Your technique and footwork is perfect, but you are still missing a little something that is necessary for your performance. You are too used to the Waltz. The Waltz is elegance, precision, and composure. The Salsa is fire, energy and – I know this is not something that you are used to, but it is passionate."

Claire felt her cheeks flush. "I am too, passionate."

Leon shook his head. "Your expression, your mannerisms are still too reserved."

"Okay, so how do I fix it?" Claire demanded.

"If you would give me one moment…" Leon disappeared from the doorway for a moment. "*Mon cœur*, would you come here?"

"What's he doing?" Luca asked.

"He's calling my mother," Claire replied.

"What is it?" Claire could hear her mother's grumpy voice accompanied by the tap of her cane as she approached the practice room. "I was terrifying airline agent into changing our seating so we're on the same row." Natalia limped into the room, scowling. She wore a leotard and practice skirt in complementary shades of purple, her hair in its usual elegant twist.

"He will still be terrified when you get back," Leon reassured her. "We are just adding a little extra polish to their routine and wanted your expertise."

Natalia's scowl relaxed. "She needs more passion?"

"She needs more passion," Leon agreed.

"Why is my passion the thing that needs the most work?" Claire protested. "I've been dancing for years; you never had a problem before—"

"*Cherie*, it is not a question of technique, it is what is inside that needs to come to the surface," Leon explained.

"In every dance you do, you tell a story, do you not?" Natalia limped forward. "You are a princess in her 'happily ever after', someone at the end of her story who has found love."

Claire felt her cheeks flush. "So?"

"So? The passion of the Salsa is not the end of the 'happily ever after,' it is the beginning." Natalia handed Claire her cane. "Let me show you." Her practice skirt was knotted at one hip, but Natalia untied it, tossed the ankle-length material to one side, revealing muscled legs encased in dark gray tights. The scar that had ended her ballet career ran from Natalia's thigh to her calf, making the material bulge in irregular lines. Natalia took a limping step forward and took Leon's hands. "Let's show them our Blackpool routine," she commanded. "You still remember?"

"How could I forget?" Leon took her hands. "I asked you to marry me the first time in the middle of the choreography."

Natalia harrumphed. "And I said to focus on the routine."

"You asked me to marry you in the middle of our heat at Blackpool," Leon arranged her carefully in his frame, to support her weight. "What does that say about your focus?"

"I got caught up in the heat of the moment," Natalia's chin jutted in a very Claire-like expression of defiance.

Leon winked at Claire and Luca. "She's still mad we got disqualified for causing a disruption."

"Enough flirting," Natalia scolded. "Play something fast," she ordered Luca and nodded toward the stereo. "Keep the music on low."

"Yes Ma'am," Luca said, hurrying to obey.

After a moment, the energetic beat of a Salsa began to play. Natalia rolled her hips and her mouth curved into a flirtatious smile as she looked over her shoulder at Leon.

"When you dance the Waltz," Natalia said, and seized Leon's hand, bringing it to her hip in a sharp movement. "Your love has already bloomed; you have found love and you are content in it. But the Salsa is all about the beginning, the chase." Claire's mouth dropped as her mother expertly performed her routine, her movements confident, fiery… sexy.

"It's that spark at the beginning, the flirtation when you just meet." Leon dipped her and Natalia arched sensuously and came up, her hands on his chest. "You don't know if things will work, but you don't care, it's all about the feeling." Natalia's hand caressed Leon's cheek. "A feeling that you want to enjoy, as long as it lasts." Leon started to lead Natalia through another sequence but immediately stopped when she paused and grabbed her leg, expression twisting in pain. Rather than continuing the dance, Leon scooped her up and carried her to a chair.

"Wait! I was not done teaching," Natalia wriggled in his arms.

"You are today, *Mon cœur,*" Leon said firmly. "Your leg cannot take as much exertion as when you were younger."

Natalia's eyes narrowed. "Are you calling me old?"

"We both are," Leon took her hand and kissed it tenderly. "And as your husband, it is my privilege to make sure that you take care of yourself."

Natalia sighed, resting her hand lightly on her husband's cheek. For a moment, her expression softened and her face blazed with a love fierce enough to traverse to an unknown country and strong enough to withstand twenty years of marriage. "You spoil me," she scolded, smacking Leon lightly. "I can still supervise from my chair even if my leg hurts."

"It's okay, Mama," Claire hurried to her side with the discarded skirt and cane. "You can rest. I understand now. I need to dance like I'm starting to fall in love." She watched Luca as he knelt by her mother and felt something inside her flip-flop. "Feeling the potential and excitement —"

"—And while you don't know how it's going to end, you're still willing to try," Luca finished, his eyes meeting hers. Claire felt her cheeks flush and looked away.

Natalia eyed her daughter, then nodded. "Good." She reached for her skirt and cane, started to push herself to her feet. "I'll leave you to your practice then and take care of my leg."

"I'll take you, *mon cœur*," Leon carefully scooped the love of his life out of her chair, cane and all, cradling her as if she weighed nothing.

"Thank you for your help, Ma'am." Luca moved out of the way as Leon carried Natalia to the door. "And may I say, seeing you perform like that, even for a minute, was one of the greatest honors of my life."

Three Time World Champion Natalia Beauchene allowed Luca a small smile. "Flattery at my age," she said wryly, "is always appreciated."

Claire and Luca waited until her parents had made their way safely to their office.

"Shall we?" Luca held out his hand to Claire.

"Okay." She took it, feeling the lazy tingle sweep up her fingers. The same electricity she felt every time Luca's hand touched hers, the curl of nerves in her stomach as she looked up at his face. He was sweaty, had put in a full hour of practice before she'd joined him, and was no doubt tired from working a full shift at the bar. But the second the music started to play, he'd light up and dance the way he always did. Perfectly. She loved that about him, Claire realized as Luca guided her back to the center of the room. Loved the heart that he put into his dance, the smile that came to his face the second the music started, and, if she had to be brutally honest, the smell of him and the way he fit into his skintight tank top and sweats.

She would use that, Claire decided, taking her position in front of Luca, allowing herself to press against him, feel the brush of skin on skin. His spicy scent wrapped around her, all at once dizzying and exhilarating.

"Claire?" Luca's whisper, his warm breath in her ear, added a shiver down her spine. "Are you ready?"

Claire slid a hand up, feeling the silky-smooth skin of Luca's throat, the slight prick of stubble on his jaw. Felt Luca shiver slightly under her touch. Thorns and roses, she remembered. No, not thorns, they were sparks. Sparks on tinder, ready to make a flame.

"Absolutely," she whispered back.

Claire closed her eyes as the music began, familiar rhythm pulsing out of the speakers. Rolled her hips, felt Luca's fingers slide down her arm, down her torso. The lightest of touches, sending up sparks wherever they went. Her head snapped up and a slow smile crept across her face. She was slowly catching fire, everywhere Luca's hand touched, and as she stepped and spun, all Claire could see was Luca, his dark eyes gleaming as he pulled her in, whirled her around.

Was this *chispa*? Claire wondered, chasing Luca across the floor, felt the added confidence in her steps. She reached for Luca and pulled him to her, hungry, demanding. She was burning from inside out, the air seemed charged around the two of them and Claire could practically see the sparks as Luca lifted her, pivoting her, once, twice, three times. And as Claire rolled off his shoulder and dropped into a perfect split, it was a wonder she didn't crumble into embers.

* * *

As Claire was leaving for the day, she caught sight of a blur of red in one of the small practice studios. Peeking in, she saw Bethany stretching on one of the barres.

"Touch my face and I'll make you pay for my plastic surgery," Bethany warned, reaching for her toes.

"I'm not interested in doing you any favors," Claire retorted, turning away from the practice room.

"You're not here to gloat?" Bethany called after her, extending one long, slender leg along the narrow wooden beam.

Claire paused. "Why would I do that?"

"You didn't hear?" Bethany looked delighted and Claire guessed she had some particularly juicy gossip. "I've entered myself in the Blackpool Dance Festival, and Sebastian is going to be my partner."

"I didn't, actually." Claire tried to think about the last time she'd seen an episode of *Dance Craze* or searched for news on Sebastian. Not since the horrible day in the ballroom. She had done everything she could to focus on other things; her rehearsals, Bella's upcoming ballet auditions, Luca, her dance classes, costume fittings for Blackpool, Luca. "Does that mean he got eliminated?"

"Are you serious?" Bethany tossed her red hair over her shoulder and began stretching out the other leg. "Wow, you're really out of the loop. Thanks to your little hissy fit during the competition, the producers on the show decided he was unfit to continue and had him disqualified." She smirked, "which means he's free to compete with me."

"Disqualified?" Claire opened her mouth to say she was sorry to hear that, then realized she wasn't. "Well, at least he's not letting this setback slow him down. I guess I'll see you both in London, then."

"Oh, don't pretend to be a good sportsman about this," Bethany scoffed. "I'm sure you think being kicked off the show is an act of karma." She stretched backwards, then forwards. "Personally, that whole day was a win for me. I got to see you take a major spill in a competition and now I get to dance with Sebastian in Blackpool."

"You must really want that nose job." Claire took a step into the studio. "Seriously, what did I ever do to you? I've never been anything but nice, and yet you cheated behind my back with my boyfriend, and now you're actively trying to beat me at the Blackpool festival," she crossed her arms over her chest. "We might not have been besties, but I thought we were at least on the same team."

"God, do you even know how to be rude? You're so sweet it makes me gag." Bethany swung her leg off the barre and turned to face Claire. "Little Miss Perfect, who's liked by everyone, always getting the best of everything. The best costumes, the best shoes..." She paused. "The best partner. Always a winner, while I was lucky to get second place."

"Hey," Claire jabbed a finger at Bethany. "I worked hard for those awards. You want to get a first place, maybe you should try practicing more."

Bethany's eyes gleamed. "Yes well, I considered that, until I found out that there were some things…and some people…that didn't need as much effort to take." She snickered. "It was actually really easy to get him, you know Sebastian didn't like you bossing him around and making him practice all the time?" Bethany twirled a strand of red hair around her finger, reflective. "But he did enjoy playing the perfect boyfriend with you and the bad boy with me, because if I came over after you left…" Bethany chuckled. "Let's just say things got super hot." She cocked her head to one side. "Actually *all* the sneaking around was super hot. We weren't even trying to distract you during the competition, that was just a happy accident…"

She stretched contently, looking for all the world like the cat who got the canary. "Anyway, I'm really looking forward to going toe-to-toe with you at Blackpool. Do you think we can get you to fall on your face in front of all those world champions? Because I bet we can."

Claire stared at Bethany, her temper mounting. "You're doing all of this…for your entertainment?"

"Jeeze, I just explained it to you, are you a klutz and stupid?" Bethany rolled her eyes.

"You're the stupid one." Bethany's head snapped up in surprise. "Here's the thing," Claire took a step towards her. "We might never have been friends, but I still watched you dance from time to time. And you know what I saw?" Claire took another step towards Bethany. "You're second rate." Bethany's mouth dropped open in shock. "I've seen five-year-olds who put more effort into practicing," Claire continued. "Your technique is sloppy, the routines you put together are garbage, and even if you had been partnered with Sebastian from the beginning, you'd still be second to me." Claire took a breath. Her veins were full of adrenaline, and she could feel her heart beating in her chest. "So you can try to distract me, or cause drama to keep yourself entertained, but once you step onto that dance floor in London, you won't be able to sabotage me because you're going to be so out of your depth, it'll take everything you have not to be eliminated after the first round."

Bethany's eyes narrowed. "I'm a good dancer."

"If you took the time you wasted gossiping and trying to ruin other people's lives and applied it to dance, maybe you'd have a shot," Claire retorted. "But from where I stand?" She paused and leaned in close. "I bet you'll be the one to embarrass yourself."

Claire saw the slap half a second before it hit, felt the sting on her cheek and continued to stare Bethany down without flinching. "Is that the best you've got?"

"Bitch," Bethany hissed. Fury and hate seemed to radiate from every pore of the girl's body as she glared back at Claire. "I'm going to wipe the floor with you."

Claire took another step towards Bethany and the girl took a nervous step back. "You want to beat me at Blackpool?" Claire asked, keeping her voice quiet. "You're going to need a lot more than Sebastian to win. Because at the moment? You're not even a threat."

"Excuse me, Miss LaManna, I thought I made it clear you were not welcome here anymore."

Both girls turned to see Leon Beauchene standing, unsmiling in the doorway.

"I thought that was because I hadn't renewed my tuition payment," Bethany started. "But my mom just paid for this month, I should be—"

"Let me be clear. You are not welcome here, because *I* do not want you here. Your payment has been refunded." Leon's eyes were cold. "Now, if you will leave my studio…" He swept a hand towards the exit.

"This is bullshit," Bethany raged, but she walked quickly to the door. "You couldn't pay me enough to come back." She stomped down the hallway to the exit, yanked open the door and it slammed shut behind her.

"*Chérie.*" Leon moved quickly to his daughter, one hand stroking her cheek. "Are you all right? What did she say to you?"

Claire patted his hand. "It's not important, I handled it. But Papa, isn't it bad business to kick out one of our regular clients?"

Leon clasped her tightly in his arms. "Sometimes there are higher priorities to worry about. Mostly," he said, running a hand through her hair, "where you are concerned."

Claire threw herself in her father's arms. "Thank you, Papa."

Leon kissed the top of Claire's head. "You and your mama will always be my priority. If I must kick out a thousand students to keep you safe and happy, then so be it."

"You say that, but no matter how many times I complained about Luca, you never kicked him out."

Leon chuckled and Claire felt the vibration in her chest. "And aren't you glad I didn't? I would be hard-pressed to find a more exceptional young man." He kissed her head gently and pulled away. "I should get back to the office, plenty of paperwork still to do before we close."

"Papa," Claire reached out to grab his hand as he turned. Was it her imagination? Or were there a few more lines around his eyes? And did the hand with its missing fingers seem a little stiff? "If I had never wanted to dance, would you still have supported me?"

"Of course," Leon smiled. "We only want you to be happy."

"So, even if I decided I wanted to study to be a lawyer, or an accountant, or fly to Africa to study animals on the savanna, you still would have supported me?"

Leon's eyes narrowed. "*Chérie*, are you trying to tell me you don't want to compete in London? Because we already bought our tickets and our plane leaves tomorrow."

"No," Claire shook her head, "that's not what I'm talking about at all. I just…" She hesitated. "Thank you, Papa. For everything," she fumbled. "I never really appreciated how much you and Mama do for me. And I'm really lucky that you love dance as much as I do because for most people, wanting to be a dancer is a crazy dream to have, so I never really realized how lucky I was to be able to do what I wanted, until I met Luca's family and realized how hard he works to follow his dreams."

"Another good reason to keep him around," Leon murmured.

"What?"

"You're right, not everyone is as lucky as you to have parents who share your dreams," Leon said, patting her hand. "And having those who work a little harder to achieve what you've been fortunate enough to do your whole life… can offer perspective."

"He was also right," Claire sighed.

"About what?"

"I was a snob when we first teamed up."

"You were…" Leon hesitated. "Well, perhaps your behavior could have been improved," he admitted. "But I am proud that you have seen the error of your ways." He leaned in and kissed Claire again on the forehead. "No if you'll excuse me, I really do need to get started on some paperwork."

* * *

Stepping out the studio door, Claire walked down the steps, stopping as a slight breeze, warm and full of the scents of spring, ruffled the blossoms of the crepe myrtle trees that lined the streets. The evening sky above was purpling, with hints of orange and blue, and Claire stopped for a minute to appreciate the beauty outside her door. Tomorrow, she would be leaving with her parents for London, and in two days she would be competing at the Blackpool Dance Festival with dancers from around the world, vying for a prize she had been preparing for most of her life. How had time flown so fast? It seemed like just yesterday she and Sebastian were competing at the Paxton Regional Competition. Just yesterday that he had left, just yesterday that she had seen him making out with Bethany behind the stage.

Claire tried to shake the unpleasant image out of her head and focus on the next few days. Had she and Luca practiced enough? Would they really be able to win?

Sliding behind the wheel of her car, Claire began to drive, still fretting. Suppose they didn't win, what was the worst that could happen? They could always compete next year. With more practice, they'd be more ready, more experienced. There was no shame in coming back and trying again.

Claire sighed. She had been so confident that she was ready when she had been prepping with Sebastian. Now, she just had to hope that she and Luca would manage, given the amount of practice they'd had in the last two months.

Claire pulled over her car and laid her head on the steering wheel with a sigh. Worrying wouldn't help. Not with the competition only a few days away. She would just have to hope for the best and…

Tap tap tap…

"Claire? What are you doing here?"

"Nothing, just—" Claire lifted her head, blinked in surprise. Without realizing it, she had parked her car outside *Ragazzo's*. Luca was outside her window, a worried expression on his face.

"Is something wrong?" Luca asked as Claire got out of the car. "I thought you were going to get some rest."

"I thought you were too," Claire managed to arrange her features into a smile, even though internally, she felt like screaming. What had possessed her to come here? Did her subconscious have a built-in Luca locator? She noted the over-sized garbage bags Luca was holding in one hand. "Are you working another shift? What happened to resting before our trip?"

Luca shrugged. When he'd come home there was a hefty hospital bill waiting for him. Thankfully Chris was eager to have the extra help and tips were usually good during the week.

"I got a little nap, I feel fine."

"Are you sure?" Claire met his gaze, her blue eyes concerned.

A small smile twitched the corner of Luca's mouth. "I won two gold medals last year after working for twenty-four hours straight," Luca tossed the garbage bags in the nearby dumpster. "I'll be fine." Before Claire could object, he changed the subject. "Can I get you some lemon water while you're here?"

Claire hesitated, then nodded. "If it's not too much trouble."

"The day water and lemons are worth their weight in gold, I'll let you know," Luca said, holding open the door for her. "Come on in."

Chapter 20: Media Luna

"The man leads the lady from a backward ocho, via a side step to a forward ocho, creating a half moon. Hence the name."

"So, Bethany and Sebastian are going to compete against us at Blackpool," Luca handed Claire a tall glass of iced lemon water. The bar was quiet, empty but for Chris, who was sitting in a corner, sipping a beer as he stared blearily at the inventory list he was supposed to be filling out.

"Well, they're going to try," Claire took a sip of her water. "I'm not sure how much of a threat they'll be with only a week or two of practice."

"I've seen them dance together before," Luca shrugged, "they're not bad." Claire looked up in surprise. "But we're better," Luca added quickly. "We've practiced a lot and our routines are solid."

Claire looked down at her glass, studying the thin wedge of lemon floating among the ice. "She confronted me a little while ago. Bethany. She said she was going to try and get me to embarrass myself in London. And then I lost my temper and told her that she was a second-rate dancer and she wasn't even a threat to us."

"You did what?" Luca gaped.

Claire shrugged. "Maybe it was a mistake, but she just made me so mad!"

"It wasn't a mistake," Luca's grin was amused and a little wicked. "I just wish I could've seen the look on Bethany's face when you told her she was a second-rate dancer."

Claire felt a smile curve her lips. "It was pretty priceless," she admitted with a chuckle. She looked back down at her water. "What if I'm wrong though? What if they actually beat us?"

"Claire, for the past few months, all you've talked about is winning." Luca leaned on the counter; his dark eyes concerned. "Why are you letting Bethany get in your head now?"

"Because she's the reason I messed up the last competition," Claire pointed out, feeling a twist of panic in her gut that hadn't been there before. "What if she distracts me again at exactly the wrong moment and all this work is wasted? What if—"

"All right, first of all," Luca said, holding up his hands for her to stop. "We're going to be competing in London, in one of the *biggest* dance competitions in the world. How many people can brag about that? No matter what place we get, no matter what Bethany does to get in our way, that's an experience that can't be taken from us."

"But what if she manages to sabotage me again?" Claire pressed, her grip tightening on the glass. "What if I fall in front of the best dancers in the whole world? What if I become an embarrassing video online and that's all I'm known for?"

"Well maybe…" Luca hesitated for a moment then reached for her hand. "You should keep your eyes on me the whole time so she can't."

Claire let her fingers tangle through his, enjoying the gentle warmth seeping through her. "And maybe you should only look at me…so she can't distract you either."

Luca's lips curved as he leaned in closer, his dark eyes only a couple inches away. He had the longest eyelashes, Claire realized. Another unfair gift on his already perfect face. "That's…a good idea," he whispered.

He was so close, and Claire felt her heart speed up several notches. Claire started to close the distance, her lips parting…then they both jumped apart as Chris let out a giant belch.

Luca exhaled, dragging a frustrated hand through his hair. "I forgot he was there," he muttered under his breath. "Chris," he raised his voice, "take care of the bar, I'm going to take my break."

Chris looked up from his seat in the corner. "Wha? But it's not midnight."

"I'm still going on my break," Luca said firmly, still holding Claire's hand as he stepped out from behind the bar.

"Okay, but don't complain to me in four hours—"

"I'll manage!" Luca retorted, leading Claire to a door in the far corner of the bar. For once, Claire didn't resist, she simply allowed Luca to lead her through to the backroom. There, along with several mops, buckets, was a peeling-paint ladder. An open hatch led to the roof. "Up you go," he said gesturing.

Claire eyed the peeling-paint ladder. "You can't be serious."

"It's fairly private, and Chris won't be able to bother us. Plus," Luca tucked a strand of hair behind Claire's ear. "There's a great view."

* * *

A light breeze swirled the loose strands of Claire's bun as she stepped out onto the roof. Two stories above the ground, the night was silent with only the occasional honk and *rush-rush* of traffic down below. Bare except for a few vents, the concrete surface under her feet was surprisingly free of dust and grime, leaving Claire to wonder if Luca swept it regularly. Turning in a slow half-circle, she stepped closer to the edge. Between the buildings, the city of San Diego was a sparkling blanket spread out into the distance. Ambient light prevented all but the brightest of stars from being seen, but the illuminated windows of buildings twinkled in the darkness.

"It's a place where I come to think."

Claire turned at the sound of Luca's voice. He was standing by the ladder, watching her, his dark eyes inscrutable in the dim light.

"And to practice?" she asked. "I bet you feel like you're dancing in the sky up here."

How had she known that? Luca wondered. Could she sense that this was the place where he could breathe freely? The place where he escaped to when he needed a break from work, from the anxiety of taking care of his family? Claire's expression was rapt as she looked around the small rooftop, as if she was taking in a beautiful vista rather than a bar rooftop. "It is not so easy to book a practice room," Luca said instead, "when a certain person hogs the best one."

"I'll share the practice room if you share this place." Claire tried an experimental spin, her arms extending gracefully in front of her. "It's gorgeous. Does it ever get so foggy that you feel like you can dance on the clouds?" The streetlights haloed her hair, outlining her delicate figure in gold.

"Once or twice. But I never thought of it that way." She was beautiful, Luca realized, and took a few steps closer. Beautiful in motion and in stillness as she stopped, tipping her head back to feel the breeze on her face. "Perhaps I just needed someone else to see it in a new light."

"Look, the moon!" Claire pointed and Luca forced himself to look in the direction she was indicating. The full moon was peeking over the horizon, a celestial giant beginning its journey across the sky. "You're lucky to have a place like this," Claire said. "It feels like I could reach out and touch it, I'm so close." She rose on her tippy toes, her arm extended toward the moon.

"Perhaps you just need a little extra height," Luca wrapped his arms around her waist and Claire squealed as he lifted her easily off the ground.

"Put me down," she giggled, "there's no way I can reach."

"Well, it never hurts to try," Luca gently lowered her down and caught a whiff of her scent, both flowery and exotic that uniquely and only belonged to Claire.

"Thanks for the effort," Claire tipped her head back and her blue eyes, still sparkling with merriment, met his. Once again, Luca found himself on the edge of a precipice, poised, looking down. He knew it would take only the smallest push to fall into the deep and dazzling blue.

"No problem," Luca murmured. He was acutely aware of Claire still in his arms, of his heart beating furiously in his chest, and with no desire to do anything to change it.

"We should practice," Claire turned her head, the brush of her hair on his shoulder sending tingles across his chest.

"Why?"

"Because," Claire's smile was the enchantment of a fairy by the light of the moon. "I feel like dancing."

"Sure," Luca reluctantly loosened his hold, sliding one hand up to her shoulder blade. Felt her small hand slide into his, the other settling into place, resting in the curve of his bicep. There was music playing. Somehow, at some point, Claire had queued up a song on her phone.

A Waltz—the light, graceful melody lifted his arms and straightened his spine, as he encircled Claire within his frame.

"Shouldn't we be practicing our Salsa?"

Claire shook her head. "This roof was made for the Waltz."

Made for the Waltz, Luca mused as he shifted his weight and began leading Claire in a circle around one of the vents. Perhaps it was. He'd never seen it that way before, but then again, he'd never danced across the roof with Claire in his arms, her lithe form practically floating, light as a butterfly, the night sky a backdrop behind her.

At the edge of the roof, he lifted her, cradling her as he spun, a light and precious bundle against his chest. Once, twice, they spun, before he set her down in a graceful dip.

"That was fun," Claire smiled up at him, her eyes a deep blue in the moonlight. Luca stared down at her, his heart hammering in his chest. He was falling now, too late to stop. Her eyes were pulling him in and he was diving, down, down to the deepest depths.

"Claire…" he started to say. Then Claire's arms came up around his neck and she kissed him.

He was caught, frozen in place like a fly in amber, aware of the feeling of her lips on his, tingles spreading through every nerve of his body, unable to move, to breathe, then he was pressing her lithe body against his and kissing back with equal ferocity.

The small ember of desire that he'd never been able to squash sparked, became a hungry flame, devouring every hesitation and doubt like tinder. Luca's fingers traveled up her back to the nape of her neck, yanking away her scrunchie and letting her hair fall free. A few pins fell to the roof as he dug his fingers into her silken tresses.

"Hey!" Claire broke free and grabbed for the pins. Luca pulled her back.

"Leave them."

"But—"

"Leave them," he repeated, crushing his lips against hers.

She melted against him, all lean muscle and curves under his hands, while her scent of flowers, lemon and something that was delicate and uniquely her, wrapped around him, threatening to overwhelm his senses.

Below the city lights still gleamed, and a light breeze whipped around them, tugging at Claire's skirt and tangling her hair. Luca felt something hungry, primal stirring in his blood. He grabbed a fistful of her hair at the base and pulled her head back, her neck pale in the moonlight, so he could feast on the sensitive skin, thrilling in Claire's whimpers of pleasure.

"*Merde*," Claire arched her back to give more access, her fingers running through Luca's curls, pulling him closer. She was liquid fire, burning him from the inside out. He tried to fuel the need, the desire of the last few weeks into his kisses as he pressed her against him. No, maybe it hadn't been just the last few weeks, Luca admitted to himself. There had always been something there. Under the rivalry, the petty squabbles, there had been something deeper that they'd always skirted around.

"You're driving me crazy," he hissed, as Claire ran her hands over the hard lines of his torso and was surprised her nails didn't shoot up sparks. "I don't suppose you know how to say that in French?"

Claire paused; one eyebrow raised as she considered him.

"If you don't know, that's okay," Luca said quickly. "I know I understand more than I can say-"

"*Je t'aime à la folie,*" Claire interrupted quietly and Luca felt a jolt go through him at the sound of the sultry cadence. He hadn't anticipated Claire speaking in French would be such an enormous turn-on. He found her lips again, pressing her against the wall and kissing her fiercely. One hand sliding up to tangle in her hair, the other pressing into the small of her back.

Claire responded by twining her arms around his neck. In a quick movement, she wrapped her legs around his waist, pressing herself tighter against him.

"Claire," Luca groaned as she ground her hips against his, feeling the shockwave of heat shoot straight to his core. He pivoted, balancing her on a narrow ledge, shifting and pressing her up against the wall again, his hands sliding down to cup her thighs, the material of her practice skirt feeling tissue thin under his hands.

She was driving him slowly insane, the feel of her against him, the taste of her on his lips, under his hands. He moved with her, their breaths coming faster, bodies moving to the rhythm of a dance they'd only just learned.

"Stop." Through the haze of lust, Luca heard Claire say the word. He immediately froze, then pushed himself away, both of them gasping for air.

Claire staggered a couple steps back, leaning against the wall of the roof, her lips swollen and her hair deliciously mussed. Luca was tempted to run his hands through it again but stopped himself. "Things are getting very intense, very fast," she managed.

"Very intense," Luca agreed.

"And it's not that I don't want to keep going," she admitted, her cheeks flushing bright pink. "But maybe we could wait?" Claire hesitated. "Go on a few dates, not rush to do everything on a rooftop?"

"Of course," Luca's legs were horribly unsteady and he leaned on the roof railing for support, taking deep breaths to slow his galloping heart rate. "We can take it slow."

"Really?"

"Yes really," the feeling was starting to return to Luca's legs. "Claire, you're worth it at whatever speed you want to go. I'll let you lead, I promise."

"First time I get to lead," Claire's laughter bubbled up. She cast a glance over her shoulder toward the open skylight. "If we're hitting pause, maybe I should go home? See you tomorrow?"

Luca nodded reluctantly. "That'd probably be a good idea."

Claire turned toward the ladder and stopped. "Before I go…" she paused, biting her lip. "That phrase you had me say in French…can you say it to me in Spanish?"

How could he say no to the siren before him, her pale hair lit by moonlight? Luca stepped forward, taking Claire's hand in his. "*Estoy loco por ti*," he whispered. He tenderly kissed the soft white palm of her hand, before moving on to her fingers, kissing each one by one. "*Estoy loco por ti.*" He kissed her nose, her forehead, then her lips again, kissing her slowly, deeply. "*Estoy loco por ti.*"

Chapter 21: Embraza

"Prior to the dance, the couple engages into an embrace (embraza)."

Stockings, curling iron and hair nets. Claire checked the list in her hand one more time.

"Oh, and hair pins." She grabbed a spare pack and tucked it into her toiletries bag. She had a sudden flash of standing on the roof with Luca, the pins falling around her feet, his hands on her, his lips…

Claire touched her lips. They felt more sensitive somehow, tingling at the slightest touch. Maybe it was her imagination, but she could feel the heat of his lips on hers, the brush of skin on skin.

Estoy loco por ti. The memory of his voice made her knees weak. Claire could still see the way he had looked at her. Luca hadn't just said the words, he'd *meant* them.

"*Merde*," Claire drew a shaky breath. The thought was both thrilling and terrifying at the same time. Claire took another breath, trying to calm her racing heart. She'd never felt this way about anyone. Not even with Sebastian.

And in half an hour they were all flying to London for the next week. Claire both wanted to escape to the farthest part of the world and sprint all the way to Luca's house.

"Claire!" Natalia poked her head through the door. "We're packing up the car. Are you ready to go?" Her sharp eyes surveyed the state of the room and her blue eyes, so like her daughter's, narrowed. "Your room is a mess, and you don't look done."

"I am, Mama." Claire quickly zipped up her suitcase and carry-on bag.

"You look flushed." Natalia stepped through the doorway and laid a slim hand on her forehead. "What is the matter? Do you have a fever? I told you that you shouldn't have been out so late last night," she scolded.

"Mama! I'm fine, I—I'm just excited for the trip." It wasn't a total lie, Claire told herself as her mother eyed her suspiciously. There was a certain element about the trip that she was definitely looking forward to.

"Hmmph," Natalia frowned, unconvinced. "Well hurry up and bring your bags downstairs, we still need to pick up your partner."

Partner… the name resounded in Claire's head and her face flushed again. Luca was coming to London with her as her partner.

"Quickly with the bags!" Natalia's sharp order as she left shook Claire out of her daze. "Your papa is waiting with the car!"

"Coming, Mama!" Claire said, quickly grabbing both bags. The wardrobe bag was slung over a chair and she snatched it up as she headed for the door. Finally, after so much time preparing, she was on her way.

* * *

"Luca?" Elaina rapped on the doorsill to Reina's room where Abuela had been staying on a fold-out bed. "There is a car outside for you."

"Coming," Luca leaned forward and placed a kiss on Abuela's forehead. Her temperature was cool, thanks to the nearby fan, and a pitcher of water had been placed next to her bedside to keep her hydrated. "Make sure to drink plenty of water," he told her. "I'll be sure to bring you back a souvenir," he promised. "And maybe a big trophy."

Abuela shook her head. "Just dance," she said, reaching up to pat Luca's cheek. "Dance the way you were meant to." Her hand slid down, tapped Luca on the chest. "Dance from here."

"I will." Luca took his grandmother's hand and kissed it gently. "*Te quiero*, Abuela."

"*Te quiero, mijo*," Abuela whispered.

"Luca, they're waiting," Elaina prompted, and Luca rose to his feet.

"I'm coming," he repeated.

His duffle bag was packed and waiting by the door, as was a coat hanger with his costume, the expensive suit carefully covered in a plastic trash bag. Juan was by the door, his duffle of paint cans over one shoulder, no doubt off to work on his masterpiece.

"Off on your big adventure?" He dropped the bag to give his brother a bear hug.

"Yep, off to England." Luca hugged him back, ruffling his brother's hair. Juan definitely needed a haircut. Something to remember when he got back. "I'll make sure to call when I land to check in," Luca promised. He glanced back towards the room where Abuela was resting. "And if anything happens…" Doubt churned his gut. "I don't like leaving her here. If she faints again, or she has any health emergency…"

"I'll keep an eye on her," Juan promised.

"We both will," Elaina said firmly. "This is a great opportunity for you, you should go. Don't worry. If anything happens, one of us will call." She handed Luca a paper bag. "It's not much, just a sandwich, but at least you won't have to spend any money on airport food."

"Thank you, Elaina," Luca took the bag and hugged her. "For everything."

Elaina touched Luca's cheek gently. "Your mama and papa would be so proud of you. As am I," she added.

Luca swung his battered duffle bag over one shoulder. It was a gift from Joe and though one of the zippers often got stuck and showed a few signs of wear and tear, it was still sturdy enough to survive the trip. He stepped out the door of Elaina's house and immediately felt under-packed when he saw the Beauchene family car, loaded with luggage.

"Good morning, my friend!" Leon waved merrily from the driver seat. "Our journey begins!" He turned to Claire, who was sitting in the backseat. "Claire, help Luca with his bags."

"No, it's fine, I can manage—" Luca's breath caught as Claire stepped out of the car and her eyes met his. She'd tied her hair into a long braid and she was wearing a simple blue shirt and jeans, but the sight of her set his heart racing and blood rushing to his face. "Hi."

"Hi." Claire ducked her head shyly and scurried to open the trunk. "We uh—left you some space for your bags, you should have plenty of room."

"Thanks," Luca joined her. There was enough space left for three suitcases, making the duffle bag look even more battered and small among the sleek, matching suitcases and garment bags. Luca swallowed the self-consciousness rising in his chest. "I've never done a trip like this," Luca found himself making excuses, "so I just brought the essentials."

Claire's eyes lingered on the trash bag he was using to protect his costume. "You know," she said carefully, "we have a few extra garment bags if you need one. That is, if you want to borrow one," she added quickly. "What you have is perfectly fine, I'm just suggesting it since we have extras, and it's a long flight and I want your costumes to be safe. I'm not saying ours are better—"

"Claire," Luca held up a hand to stop her. There was a feeling building in his chest, terrifying in its intensity the more he looked at her. The girl who had once made fun of him for being a scholarship student was desperately trying to walk a tightrope between being considerate of what he had and trying to help him take care of his dance costumes. "If you have a spare bag, I would love to borrow it. Thank you."

"Really?" Claire breathed out a sigh of relief. "Good. Because," she said in a rush, "Like I said, we have tons of extras just in case and it's no trouble." Luca caught Claire's hand before she could grab the spare garment bag.

"You're adorable when you're flustered," Luca murmured. He ran a finger along her bottom lip, delicate and soft as a rose petal. Lifted her head, took in the delicate features glowing with a rosy blush. "I really want to kiss you right now," he murmured.

"Now?" Claire darted a glance toward the car behind them, where her parents were waiting.

"Just a quick one," Luca leaned in.

"Come on! Let us be going!" Leon's shout made both of them jump apart.

Claire cleared her throat as her cheeks blushed bright red. "Maybe we should put the garment bag over your clothes at the airport," Claire said.

Luca nodded, his heart pounding furiously in his chest. "Let's do that," he agreed.

* * *

In the front of the car, Natalia shared a glance with her husband. "She loves him."

"Yes," Leon nodded, then sighed, suddenly feeling old. "And he loves her. Possibly enough to take her from her papa forever. The *feu de la passion* in his eyes," Leon took his wife's hand and kissed it. "Much the same as ours, would you not agree, *mon cœur?*"

Natalia hmphed and patted her husband's hand. Their wedding rings glinted in the light as she linked her fingers with his. "You know he was going to kiss her."

Leon chuckled. "Why do you think I shouted out the window?"

Chapter 22: Wing

"Both partners take a step forward, and then the lady walks in a half-circle in front of the man from his right to his left side."

"Claire, you will be in room 1201, Luca, 1202 and your mother and I are in room 1203," Leon said, handing out keycards.

The hotel near the airport was elegant, full of marble floors and wood finishings. Outside, Luca could see the New York skyline rising above the treetops. They'd made it to their layover in New York, before word of a rare tropical storm had delayed the plane until the next morning.

"You two will take twenty minutes to get changed and meet us downstairs," Leon was saying. "I need to speak to someone at the front desk about reserving a room that we can use to practice."

"Yes, Papa." Claire took her key, flashing her father a smile.

"*Mon cœur*, you are not going to be helping me charm one of the best rooms?" Leon asked as Natalia followed Luca and Claire to the elevator.

"Charm is your strength, I think I will be more useful keeping everyone on schedule," Natalia said, hitting the button to go up. "I will see you in twenty minutes—unless I am needed to terrify someone at the hotel."

Luca chuckled and Natalia shot an inquisitive glance in his direction. "Something funny?"

"No ma'am," Luca said quickly. "I mean, the terrifying thing was a little funny—"

Natalia's elegant face remained serious. "I never joke about such things. I am—how you say—the big guns that get things done."

"This is totally unfair!" Luca turned at the sound of a familiar whine rising above the hubbub of travelers who had just arrived. Bethany, dressed in a bright green jumpsuit that complemented her red hair, pouted prettily as she crossed her arms over her buxom chest.

"Relax, it could be worse," Sebastian, dressed in khaki slacks and a deep blue V-neck sweater, patted her arm absently, his eyes glued to his phone. From a distance it seemed like whoever had fixed Sebastian's nose had done a decent job, though it never would be completely straight again. Light strips of bandage held the bridge of the nose in place. "At least we don't have to pay for accommodations."

"But I don't want to stay overnight in some random hotel, I want to get on another flight now!" Bethany's voice rose to a wail.

"Even if we get tickets for another plane," Sebastian's face twisted in annoyance, "all flights to London are grounded due to the weather conditions."

"You didn't even try to ask, how did you know that?"

Sebastian sighed and held up his phone. "Because I'm looking at the storm warnings right now."

Bethany scowled and tossed her hair over one shoulder. "You don't have to be such a know-it-all. I bet you never talked that way when Claire was your partner."

"Claire was smart enough to realize you can't get a plane when all flights are grounded due to weather!" Sebastian's shout had several more people turning in his direction.

Bethany had the good grace to look embarrassed. "Fine, get us checked in, then," she sulked. She pulled out a small compact and a tube of lip gloss and began touching up her lips. "I'll stay here with the bags."

"No surprise there," Sebastian stalked off, heading toward the front desk. He caught sight of Claire standing with Luca and Natalia by the elevator and paused, his eyebrows shooting up in surprise. "Claire." His mouth quirked up in an easy charming smile, and he made an immediate detour in her direction. "I didn't expect to see you here."

"Just our bad luck." Claire took a slight step closer to Luca and to his surprise he felt her hand slip into his.

"Well, not completely." Up close Luca could see make-up had been applied to hide the bruising around Sebastian's eyes. "I just wanted to say you had every right to lose you temper."

"Bethany driving you crazy already?" Claire asked, feeling a petty twinge of glee.

"No, of course not, we're fine." Sebastian's bright smile cranked up a couple notches in wattage. "Every couple has its rough patches and ours just happens to be now…" his eyes flicked down, taking in Claire and Luca's joined hands and his expression faltered. "But I see you're already on the rebound," he finished coolly.

"You're one to talk," Claire responded. "That's one of the reasons I broke your nose in the first place."

"The lightest little tap, I barely felt it," Sebastian's grin remained fixed in place. "Doctors said there was only minor bruising."

Claire smiled back. "I'd be happy to hit you harder."

"Well, that's us," Natalia said quickly as the elevator *dinged* open behind them. "Come on, everyone!" She stepped inside, dragging Claire and Luca with her.

The interior of the elevator featured more wood and marble, with cream-colored walls.

"Mama, I'm sorry, I shouldn't have—"

Natalia held up a hand to silence her. "A word to the wise. If you are going to threaten someone, make sure there are no witnesses." She sighed and ran a hand over her immaculately styled hair. "How unpleasant that he was rerouted here as well. I was hoping never to see him up close again."

"Me too, Mama." Claire stared up at the lighted numbers that showed their progress to their floor. Her thumb brushed over Luca's knuckles, light as a feather.

"Still," Natalia continued. "I took some satisfaction from seeing what you did to his face."

"Mama!" Claire laughed.

"What?" Natalia's eyes were cold. "He got off lucky he did not tangle with me." The elevator shuddered to a halt. "This is our stop." Natalia stepped off first. "Twenty minutes to change and get downstairs."

"Yes Mama," Claire nodded.

Natalia's sharp gaze flicked down to Claire and Luca's joined hands and her mouth twitched slightly. "Hmph. Don't be late," she said, unlocking her door and stepping inside.

"See you soon," Claire gave his hand a gentle squeeze, flashing Luca an apologetic smile as she let go, unlocking her room and stepping inside.

"Yes, Ma'am," Luca said, opening his own door and closing it behind him.

The hotel room was twice the size of his bedroom at home and three times as opulent. A king-sized bed with snow-white sheets was featured in the middle of the room and a bronze-colored sofa lined one wall, while screens in the same color covered the windows. A welcome basket on the dresser held a variety of coffees, cookies and nuts. Luca laid his borrowed garment bag carefully on the bed and raised the blinds to look out the window.

Outside the sky was still overcast, steel gray buildings rising up into the clouds, while down below, yellow taxi cabs darted in and out of traffic, picking up fares.

Never in his life had Luca imagined staying in a luxury hotel, preparing to dance in one of the most prestigious competitions in the world. His stomach twisted into knots and he snatched one of the cookies from the basket, nibbled anxiously. Did he really belong here? It had always seemed like Claire's world more than his.

A scruffy pigeon landed on the ledge outside the window and eyed the cookie in Luca's hand.

"Shoo, you can't have it." Luca waved a hand at the pigeon. Instead it ignored him and hopped closer to the glass.

What are you doing in there? The yellow eyes seemed to say. *You don't belong.*

Luca closed the blinds quickly and checked his watch. He still had ten minutes to change before he needed to meet the Beauchene's downstairs. He unzipped the garment bag, carefully taking out his costume. Unlike the simple black shirt and pants he'd been wearing for the last two years, this costume had been sewn especially for him. Sleeveless and skin-tight, the shirt opened in a wide V-neck to showcase his chest, the black material covered with glittering sequins in gradiating blues. The pants were also black, with a line of matching sequins along the seams. Luca felt his throat close as he took in the label neatly stitched into the waistband. *A Natalia Beauchene Original* he read and felt the knot of nerves twist even tighter. Did he really deserve all these things? He was a good dancer, but was he *good enough*?

Suddenly homesick, Luca dug out his phone and dialed Elaina. She picked up after two rings.

"Hello? Luca?" At the sound of her voice, Luca felt some of his nerves immediately settle. "Have you made it to London?"

"Almost," Luca said "The planes were grounded in New York due to weather conditions. We're staying overnight in a hotel. How is Juan?"

"He's still working on his mural," Elaina reported.

"And Abuela?"

"Fine, *mijo*, she had some soup earlier and she's napping now. Want me to wake her?"

"No, just tell her that I miss her and I love her and…" Luca bit his lip. "I wish all of you were here with me."

"We are there with you in spirit, *mijo*," Elaina assured him. "Us and your mama and papa and Abuelo and all your ancestors. We are there in your heart."

There was a sharp rapping at the door.

"Luca!" he could hear Claire calling from outside. "Come on, we have to go down to practice!"

"Elaina, I have to go," Luca said, cradling the phone as he leaned down to unlace his shoes. "Call me and give me updates -"

"You think I can't look after Abuela, *mijo*?" Elaina demanded. "Go enjoy yourself, I will call if there's an emergency."

"Luca!" Claire was still banging on the door. Luca slipped out of his jeans and into his sweatpants, grabbing the bag that held his dance shoes.

"I'm coming!" He bent down to stuff his feet into both shoes, and carrying his shirt, ran for the door. "I'm almost dressed," Luca said, yanking open the door.

"Umm… okay…" Claire took one look at his muscled, bare chest and turned bright red. "I just uh-wanted to let you know that we have to meet Papa downstairs," she stammered.

"Okay. Sorry," Luca found himself trying to juggle his shirt, phone and keycard as he closed the door behind him. "I had to call Elaina."

"Here, let me take that," Claire held out her hands.

"Thanks," Luca tried not to stare at the skimpy, blue two-piece practice outfit that showed mostly bare midriff. Her legs looked two miles long in three-inch heels. Luca dumped his phone and keycard in her hand and yanked the sweatshirt over his head as they hurried toward the elevator.

Natalia was waiting for them. "About time," she commented, pressing the down button. The doors slid open immediately. "Let's go."

Luca stepped quickly inside, running a nervous hand through his curls.

"You look very nice," he murmured to Claire as the elevator doors closed.

"You, too," she whispered back.

"Yes, yes, everyone looks nice," Natalia said as the elevator began to move. "We need to hurry; we are already late."

* * *

"Well, *mes amies*, I think we have done enough practicing for today." Leon turned off the stereo an hour later. "How about we change and take a few hours to relax and explore? We can meet back here at seven in the hotel restaurant for dinner."

"An excellent idea," Natalia stood, leaning on her cane. "I could use a nap myself."

"But Papa, the competition is the day after tomorrow," Claire protested.

"*Chérie*, we have been practicing long enough." Leon put a hand on his daughter's shoulder. "There is nothing more to work on, you are both as ready as you are ever going to be. Take some time to rest, explore New York." He pushed Claire and Luca toward the doors of the conference room. "The storm has passed, it's a beautiful day outside, and you should go and enjoy it."

Chapter 23: Walk

"The <u>walk</u> is probably the most basic dance move. It exists in almost every dance."

"There you are!" Bethany, wearing green leggings and a matching crop top, stomped over to Sebastian in three-inch heels. "I tell you we're practicing in the gym, and you leave me waiting for half an hour so you can go flirt with some waitress?"

"She was a hotel attendant, and she was flirting with me," Sebastian lied, giving a backward glance at the charming brunette who was hurrying away. A pity, but perhaps he'd run into her later.

Bethany laughed. "Please, you're not with naïve little Claire anymore, I know all your tricks." She crossed her arms and eyed Sebastian speculatively. "So, what were you trying to get her to do?"

"I was trying to get us the conference room so we didn't have to practice in that smelly gym," Sebastian said defensively. "It's free for the next two hours, by the way. You're welcome."

"See, this is why we're perfect for each other." Bethany ran a hand up his shirt. "We're always thinking of how to get something better." She grabbed him by the collar and yanked him down for a kiss before he could dodge.

"Oww," Sebastian hissed as she bumped against his sore nose.

"Oh don't be a baby," Bethany chided. "I'll just grab a nonfat latte and meet you there in fifteen minutes."

"Good idea." Sebastian forced a smile. "I'll see you then." He watched her trot off, red ponytail swinging, and sighed. A few months ago, their affair had been a deliciously guilty pleasure, but now the fun was fading quickly. Being disqualified from *Dance Craze* had led to a steep fall from grace in both his professional and social life, leaving him a dwindling amount of prospects.

His eyes recognized the flash of Claire's blonde hair as she went out the lobby doors, arm and arm with the scholarship student. For some reason she seemed happy slumming, maybe that was the reason she'd turned down the opportunity to join him in LA. Sebastian remembered with a slight twinge how it wasn't long ago she'd come running to him whenever he called. If she'd just said yes to the damn guest spot then he wouldn't be in this mess. It just showed how stupid women could be with the wrong person in their ear.

Focus, Sebastian told himself, he didn't have the luxury to agonize over the past. If he could eke out something that resembled success, maybe he could turn things around.

Making it to the final round at Blackpool might be just the thing to save his crumbling dance career…and convince someone influential to take his phone calls again. After all, everyone loved a good redemption story.

* * *

Outside the hotel, spring was in full bloom. A rush of balmy air that smelled like rain greeted Claire and Luca as they stepped out of the taxi that stopped at the main entrance of Central Park.

"According to the top ten list of things to do in New York," Claire consulted her phone. "Viewing the cherry blossoms is a must-see. Central Park is also the site of many famous rom-coms, which I thought would be fun."

"You wanted to pretend we were in a romantic movie?" Luca teased.

"Well, it's sorta one of our first dates." Claire was suddenly focused on putting her phone in her purse. "So, I wanted to get it right. Maybe it's silly, but when I saw the pictures, all I could think was I wanted to see it with you."

"Claire." Luca said gently. She was genuinely nervous and flustered, and he felt his heart warming at the sight. "It's beautiful, and I'd love to see the cherry blossoms with you. But there's one important thing we need to do while we're here."

"What?"

"You need to hold my hand," Luca said, interlacing his fingers with hers. "If this is a first date, there's a lot of things I'd like to do, too."

The sun beamed down, warming the pedestrians and tourists who were also in the park. Above, the sky was a vibrant blue, fluffy white clouds floating here and there like massive cotton balls. And then there were the cherry trees. Slender branches covered in lichen curved over the path in an archway, blossoms meeting over Claire and Luca in an explosion of pink.

"These trees are called Yoshino Cherry Trees," Claire read from her phone as Luca guided her around some tourists snapping photos. "They were a gift of friendship from Japan in 1912." A couple pushing a baby carriage ahead of Claire stopped to pick up a fallen twig with a few blooms clinging to it, and dangled it in the air over their offspring. Their baby, who couldn't be more than a few years old, cooed and tried to snatch the blossoms with a pudgy fist. "The blossoms only last a week or two, so we're lucky we happened to be here around the same time."

A gentle gust of wind blew through the trees, catching up fallen blossoms and swirling them into the air. A happy-looking puppy attempted to chase the dancing petals, and Claire laughed in delight as she watched it pounce on the blossoms, tail wagging furiously. Luca couldn't take his eyes off her. If he lived to be a hundred years old, he never wanted to forget the sight of Claire laughing in the park, her eyes as blue as the sky overhead.

"If this was a rom-com, which would it be?" he asked her.

Claire wrapped an arm around his waist, leaned her head on his shoulder. She smelled of sunshine and flowers, her hair falling loose to her waist. "Well, *When Harry Met*

Sally is definitely a classic," she said thoughtfully. On either side of the path, green grass grew in a lush carpet, and children of all ages ran and played with an assortment of toys and splashed in puddles, young voices shrieking and laughing. "And of course, dancing like Giselle in *Enchanted* is something we can and totally should do next time we're here…but I think the rom-com that would fit us best is…" she stopped walking and turned to face him. "Ours," Claire answered.

Luca's fingers lazily traced the curve of Claire's jaw, tilting up her chin. Her lips were soft as the petals that surrounded them, the kiss slow and sweet, making his senses swim. "I think so, too."

* * *

They bought lunch at a small pizzeria, which according to Claire's phone, had been around since 1905, and walked down the street eating their slices. Taxi horns blared, and people rushed by on all sides. Overhead, trees were in bloom, petals of pale pink, white and red carpeting the sidewalk.

Ordinarily, thoughts of her upcoming competition should have had Claire anticipating various worst case scenarios, urging her to go back to her room to check and double check her costumes and equipment over and over to make sure everything was perfect. But for once Claire was content to simply stroll along the sidewalk with Luca at her side.

"This pizza tastes even better outside," Claire commented, nibbling on her pizza crust. The cheesy was the perfect blend of gooey and savory, coming off in delicious strings. "I wouldn't normally eat carbs before a competition, but this way we can walk it off." She took another bite and sighed happily. "Plus, it smelled so good!"

"I think you got a little bit right there," Luca chuckled and dabbed at her chin with a napkin. "And you shouldn't have to worry about carbs, we've been practicing enough for you to work off a full pizza."

"And yet, there's a part of me that will agonize about how my stomach will look during the competition after eating this," Claire shrugged ruefully.

"Claire," Luca said firmly, "if anyone is looking at you while you're dancing, it'll be because you're an amazing dancer. One slice of pizza isn't going to change that."

Claire eyed her pizza for a moment. "You're right." She took another bite, closing her eyes as she savored it. "Ugh New York pizza definitely lives up to the hype," she swallowed. "Thank you. Sometimes I get too wrapped up in my own head."

"Well when that happens, I'll do my best to pull you out," Luca promised. He stopped, cocking his head to one side. "Do I hear music?"

Luca pulled Claire around a corner to find a group of street musicians, playing drums and guitars, the catchy melody causing onlookers to gather around and move with the beat.

"Come on." Luca finished the last of his pizza, and dusted off the crumbs on his jeans. "One last dance in the wild before the competition?"

Claire tossed the last of her crust to a pigeon and a veritable cloud of birds descended on the piece of bread. "Why not?" she smiled. "It'll help work off the carbs."

"We don't need to, you look beautiful just the way you are," Luca said, taking her hands and pulling her close. "We're doing this because it's fun and I want to dance with you in New York."

"Sweet talker," Claire murmured, twining her hands around his neck.

"You're not the only one who wants to dance in a rom-com."

"Really?" Claire's eyes twinkled and onlookers made room as Luca spun her around. "And what movie would you want to be in?"

"Like you said," Luca twirled her out, then pulled her back into a Sweetheart Embrace. "The best rom-com we could be in is ours."

"Come on," Claire teased, "if you could choose, what rom-com would you like us to be in?"

Luca took his time leading Claire through a series of complicated turns. "*Top Hat*," he finally muttered, looking embarrassed.

"*Top Hat*?" Claire repeated, intrigued. "You like Fred Astaire?"

Luca shrugged. "Mostly Abuela likes him. She always wants to Foxtrot around the kitchen to *Cheek to Cheek*."

"I love that scene," Claire gushed. "Did you know Ginger Rogers was the one who insisted on wearing that dress with ostrich feathers? The feathers started coming off during the filming and that's how she got the nickname 'Feathers.'"

"Promise me you'll never make us wear costumes that shed feathers," Luca dipped Claire up and around in a way that generated applause.

"I promise nothing, that costume was iconic,"Claire said. "I hope one day to have a dress everyone knows me for."

"There's something Fred Astaire said that reminds me of you," Luca rolled Claire out, then rolled her back in again.

"It's the backwards and high heels quote, I've heard it."

"Fred Astaire once said Ginger Rogers had guts. He was choreographing complicated dance sequences and all the women auditioning to be his partner cried because it looked too hard. Ginger Rogers never cried, and she never thought any routine was impossible." He rolled her out again. "You've got guts too. You decided you were going to compete in Blackpool and here we are, on our way."

Claire's cheeks flushed bright pink. "I don't have guts, I'm just too stubborn to quit."

"The same could be said for Ginger."

Claire eyed Luca speculatively. "That's some pretty specific info. You sure you're not a Fred Astaire fan?"

Luca shrugged. "I might have watched one or two of his other films."

"One or two?"

"Okay, maybe five or six," Luca's ears turned red. "For research. And because Abuela always wants me to dance with her."

"Mhmm. So when do we get to dance like Fred Astaire and Ginger Rogers?" Claire teased.

Luca lifted her up and spun her around to cheers from the watching onlookers. "Anytime you want," he said, setting her down gently.

"Any time?" Claire asked skeptically.

"Would you believe…" Luca dipped her low, "I enjoy dancing with you?"

Claire slid her hands up his chest. "All that practice time, and you still want to dance with me more?"

Luca lightly kissed her nose. "When it comes to you, I'm insatiable."

Claire cupped his face in her hands. "You're a charming man, you know that?"

"Guilty," Luca kissed her hard, to the sound of whistles and applause.

* * *

Juan sat back on the concrete, his arms and legs aching, and studied his finished masterpiece. He was finally done. And best of all, it would be seen by people coming to this store once it was sold.

Juan wondered if he could get Joe and Elaina to drive Abuela over here to surprise her. Maybe he'd bring the whole neighborhood over to see his finished mural, hold a small *fiesta* here to celebrate his finished work. He'd buy some of Abuela's favorite Coca-Cola, and they could dance all night long. No, Juan would wait until Luca came home from London, with a large trophy in one hand, and that hot dance partner of his in the other. Juan didn't mind sharing the spotlight, they could celebrate both Ortiz brothers at once and take a picture of the whole family in front of his mural.

Juan grinned, feeling celebratory. He really should sign it. Taking a can out of his duffle bag, Juan sprayed his name with a flourish near the bottom of the wall.   He was slinging his bag onto his shoulder when he became aware of a vibration coming from his pocket. Juan pulled the small, cheap phone Luca had bought him for *Navidad*, and answered it.

"Hello?"

"Juan?" Juan had never heard Elaina sound so terrified. "I need you to meet me and Joe at the hospital. Your abuela is vomiting blood."

Chapter 24: Closed Change

"Closed change is a basic step in the waltz. The leader steps forward on either foot whilst the follower steps backward on the opposing foot."

"To us." Leon held up his glass of wine. Dressed in a clean suit, his greying hair combed back, he cut a handsome figure, made all the more dashing by Natalia in a vivid green cocktail dress at his side.

They were sitting in one of the most elegant restaurants Luca had ever dined in. Rich red drapes framed tall windows that looked out on the twilight city below, the buildings silhouetted against the fading glow of sunset. Each table was covered in the same rich red cloth as the drapes and decorated by candles which winked like mini stars. Servers, dressed in neat bowties and vests passed by with trays of food, bottles of wine and pitchers of water, as elegant men and women laughed and chatted over appetizers.

"Tomorrow, we go to London," Leon smiled. "But whether Team Beauchene wins or not, I want you to remember how hard you have worked," he said to Claire and Luca. "And no matter what, win or lose, I am so proud of you."

"We are both very proud," Natalia corrected him. "When we partnered the two of you together, there seemed a better chance of you—how you say—duking it out. But you have succeeded in working together and have found that love is better than fighting."

Claire choked on the sparkling cider she and Luca had been served in lieu of wine. "Mama!" Dressed in a backless dress of deep blue, her hair tumbled loosely to her shoulders.

"What? What did I say?" Natalia looked to her husband for help. "Were we supposed to pretend we don't know? They have 'lovesick' all over their faces." Claire and Luca blushed furiously, looking down at the plate of appetizers they had been served. "See? They are doing it again right now."

"I'm going to the bathroom!" Claire jumped to her feet, red-faced, and rushed from the room.

Leon and Natalia shared a look. "Fine, I will go with her," she sighed, rising. "If our waiter comes back—"

"The salmon salad with vinaigrette. I'll order it," Leon said.

"Thank you." Natalia limped off through the dinners after her daughter.

"Can I refill your water for you?" Luca turned at the voice and did a double take. Dressed in a crisp white shirt, vest and bowtie, the waiter couldn't have been much older than he was, with the same wavy hair and dark skin. It felt as if he was looking into a mirror. And if he had been living in New York instead of San Diego, no doubt he would have a job just like this.

"Uh, yes, thank you." Luca held out his glass and watched the young man fill it with experienced ease.

"And have you decided on what you will be eating tonight?"

"The um… chicken salad." Luca named the cheapest item on the menu.

"Ignore him, he'll be having a New York Steak with roast potatoes," Leon said, "as will I. My wife will have the salmon salad and my daughter will have the zucchini linguini."

"Very good, sir." the server scribbled the order down in his small notepad. "And how would you like your steak cooked?"

"Umm…" Luca tried to ignore the price of the steak glaring up at him from the menu. He could feed himself and Juan for a week with what they were charging for one piece of meat. "Lightly seared, please," he said, closing the menu and handing it to the waiter.

"My friend here has good taste," Leon nodded in approval. "Make mine bleu. And bring over another bottle of wine and sparkling cider."

Was this where he belonged? Luca wondered as the server hurried off. Just last week he had been mopping up puke at Ragazzo's and now he was being treated to dinner at a five-star restaurant. Was his true place at the table with Leon Beauchene, who was nibbling at their appetizers, or serving the patrons that surrounded him?

"I know what you're thinking, *mon ami*." Leon took a sip of his wine. "Do I deserve to be here? Am I good enough?" he tutted reprovingly.

Luca looked down at his hands. They looked callused and rough against the expensive tablecloth and place settings. "How did you guess?"

"I used to ask myself the same question," Leon said, to Luca's surprise. "The truth is, I wasn't born much better off than you are. My mother was a housekeeper and raised me herself. As soon as I was old enough to work, I took every job I could in order to become a dancer,"Leon told him. "You see, I already knew what I wanted to be and I dedicated every day to practicing and taking lessons whenever I could."

"But… didn't your mother object?"

"She saw it as an investment. She sewed all my costumes and came to every competition and performance she could." Grief clouded his eyes for a moment. "She died before I bought my first dance studio, but she never stopped believing in my potential."

"How did you know what you wanted to do?"

Leon smiled, a far off look in his eyes. "When I was eight years old, a Russian ballet company came to the town where I lived. Of course, the ticket was more than we could afford, but my mother was hired for cleaning work and managed to sneak me into the theater during the performance." Leon sighed, a dreamy smile on his face. "Tchaikovsky's *Nutcracker*. I'd never seen anything like it. For two hours, I was completely transported to this whole new world. Everything, from the costumes to the set, was fascinating, but the dancers completely enraptured me. In particular, the dancer who played the young Clara. At first sight, I was smitten, and decided if I ever wanted to share the stage with her, I would need to be the best dancer in the world. I dedicated my life from that point to learning to dance, starting my own studio, moving to the United States, starting my second studio, and eventually making it here."

Leon picked up a slice of bread and began buttering it. "My point in all of this, *mon ami*, is that it does not matter where you start. A dream can get you far, as long as you have the dedication and passion to follow through." He took a bite and closed his eyes, savoring the taste. "Delicious." He swallowed and opened his eyes. He held out the breadbasket to Luca. "So, let go of your fears and try something."

"Thank you, sir," Luca hesitantly reached for a piece of bread. "But what if—" He jumped as his phone rang shrilly. Several diners looked disapprovingly in his direction.

The caller ID said Juan. The last time his brother had called, he'd been in trouble. Luca sighed and wondered if there was a chance Juan was calling to ask what New York was like. Probably not, he decided. Juan rarely called unless it was important.

"Would you excuse me, sir?" Luca said. "I need to take this."

"Take as much time as you need," Leon bit into his crispy slice of bread and hummed with satisfaction. "Tonight is a night to rest and celebrate."

"Yes sir," Luca hurried from the room, not noticing Sebastian and Bethany sitting a few tables away.

"Juan, what did you do?" Luca sighed, stepping out into the lobby. A cacophony of voices, all shouting at once answered him. "Juan? I can't hear you." Luca put a hand over his ear to quiet the hotel noises. "What's wrong?"

"Luca." Juan's voice was anxious and confirmed his worst fears. "Abuela's kidneys are failing and she's refusing treatment. You need to come home right away."

"Give me the phone," Luca heard Abuela's voice, firm and authoritative in the background. "Juan Esteban Ortiz, give me the phone." There was a pause and sounds of it being passed and a moment later Luca heard his grandmother's voice loud and clear over the phone. "Luca, can you hear me?" It was raspy and tired, but still determined.

Luca swallowed. "*Sí*, Abuela."

"Luca, the doctors say I am not long for this world, and I am at peace with that."

"How could this happen?" Luca demanded.

"Apparently my earlier accidents were signs that they were struggling. There were some other signs, feet swelling, aches and pains…" she chuckled quietly. "I just thought it was part of being old. But now it is too late."

"Don't say that!" Luca protested. He tried to remember the stuff he'd seen on medical shows. "Aren't there treatments or dialysis that you can do? I could donate one of my kidneys-"

"Absolutely not." Abuela's voice was raspy but firm. "I'm not taking one of your kidneys, mijo. You have a long life ahead of you and you're going to need both of them."

"Well then there's a transplant list and you can be on dialysis until something becomes available."

"No," Abuela repeated. "No transplant, no dialysis. I'm an old woman, and I deserve to choose how to live the rest of my life."

"This isn't a choice of how to live your life. If you don't do dialysis, you'll definitely die," Luca snapped. "Don't you understand that?"

"I know I will die." Abuela was calm. "You think that I do not understand what I am doing just because it's not being explained in my first language? I understand, *mijo*. I also understand I am old, and finding a kidney for me will not be easy. I understand that dialysis can extend my life, but it won't let me live forever and when I go, I'll be leaving you buried in debt. I can't ask you to do that."

"You can't ask me to let you die."

"What I'm asking is for you to go to London, and let me live out the rest of my days as I choose."

"Abuela!" Luca protested.

"Listen, *mijo*," Abuela interrupted. Her voice softened. "You are about to have an amazing opportunity for your future and I can't ask you to come back, just for me. I want you to go to London, and dance with your whole heart. And if you come home and I… am no longer here, that is okay."

"No—" Luca fought the lump rising in his throat.

"Because I will be watching you from above with your *abuelo*, and your mama and papa, and we will all be cheering on your accomplishments and watching you shine as bright as the sun. You are going to do great things—"

"No!" Luca said louder. "Abuela, you can't ask me to go to London and never see you again."

"*Mijo.*" Abuela sounded tired. "You are so close to your dream, and I am just an old woman whose time has come. I am not—"

"Stop saying that," Luca interrupted. "You're my *abuela*, how can I possibly put a competition above you? I'm going to get a plane home tonight. Just… wait for me, please."

"Luca—" But Luca was already hanging up.

* * *

At their table across the room, Sebastian and Bethany had a perfect view of the Beauchenes from behind a potted plant.

"Look at them, being happy and already toasting their victory," Bethany sneered, sipping her cocktail. "They won't be so cheery when their precious Claire loses to me."

Sebastian eyed his partner over the rim of his wine glass. Bethany might know how to have a good time, but she was wildly irrational, not to mention a bit delusional. Which was why he had to get rid of her as soon as possible.

"We're just keeping an eye on them right now," he reminded her.

"Ugh, boring," Bethany propped her head in her hands. The drink was making her deliciously relaxed. "I wish we could just keep them from going to London altogether. Can't we make them miss their flight?"

"How?" Sebastian noted Claire and Natalia had left the table, leaving Leon and Luca alone. "Do you think you can get your daddy to ground all the planes going to London?" he asked, a touch of sarcasm creeping into his voice.

"Hey, he knows people, maybe he could," Bethany pouted. "Or we could injure one of them."

"That would be very illegal."

"And grounding all the London planes isn't?" Bethany twirled a strand of her red hair around one finger. "Maybe we don't injure them, but we get them really sick-"

"Also illegal. Also, if you have a cold and you are planning to cough on Claire to get her sick, not only will that not work, but if you are sick and you infect me, I am going to be very, very annoyed."

"I'm not sick," Bethany scowled. "I was thinking of finding someone who was sick—"

"Unless that person has the Bubonic Plague, you're not going to stop them," Sebastian interrupted. "Claire once competed in a regional championship while fighting a fever of a hundred and two. She's a dedicated dancer, she'll power through."

"Fine. You don't have to sound like you like her so much." Bethany drained her glass.

"She takes her craft seriously," Sebastian retorted, "Which is more than I can say for you."

"Hey, you weren't complaining so much when I got you behind the stage," Bethany snickered. "In fact, I'm pretty sure you enjoyed it."

"It was briefly enjoyable," Sebastian acknowledged, flicking a speck of dust off his watch.

"That hurts my feelings." Bethany put a hand to her chest. "Would it have been more fun if we hadn't been caught?"

"Yes, of course it would've," Sebastian snapped. "I lost my place on the show. Not to mention…" he gestured to his nose which was still very tender.

"Hey, don't blame me for that, your ex-girlfriend was the one who broke your nose," Bethany protested. "Which is why I really think-"

"Quiet." Sebastian's attention was diverted when Luca returned to the table looking shaken. "I think something is happening."

* * *

"Luca?" Claire stood as Luca came back into the restaurant. It was clear from the look on his face something had happened. "Is everything—" She started to say, then Luca pulled her into a tight embrace.

"I'm sorry," he whispered as Claire's flowery scent enveloped his senses. For a moment he clung to her, a brief respite from what came next. "I'm so, so sorry."

"Luca, what's wrong?" Claire pulled away.

"Abuela's kidneys have failed and she's refusing treatment. I need to go home to try and convince her to go on dialysis, or at the very least, be with her when…" Luca swallowed. "I'm sorry, but I can't go to London anymore."

"Her condition is critical then?" Leon spoke up.

"Yes sir," Luca turned to Leon. "I'm sorry, Mr. Beauchene, I need to pack and get to the airport."

"Of course," Leon stood, tossing his napkin on the table. "I will call the airport and get your tickets changed so you can go home."

Luca blinked. "You're not mad?"

Leon gestured expansively. "If there's one thing I've learned, it's that family comes first." He clapped Luca gently on the shoulder. "My condolences," he said, and strode out of the restaurant.

"I'll see if this can be taken to go," Natalia said, gesturing at the food that was waiting on the table.

"I'm sorry," Luca said. Natalia shook her head.

"Do not apologize to me. I understand how life rarely goes according to plan. My daughter however..." Natalia jerked her head towards Claire who was striding away towards the elevator.

* * *

"Claire, wait!" Claire wrenched free from the hand that gripped her wrist.

"Go away, Luca."

"Claire, you have to understand. Abuela doesn't have much time."

"I know!" Claire burst out, and wiped at the tears rolling down her cheeks. "I know you have to go, and I know it's incredibly selfish to want you to stay, but dammit Luca, the competition is the day after tomorrow and we are so close!"

Luca's temper flared, and he forced himself to speak calmly. "You're upset, I get it. But Abuela is my family, and I would never forgive myself if I wasn't there for her." He cleared his throat. "There's always next year for Blackpool."

"Always next—" Claire threw her hands up in the air in frustration. "You know, when Sebastian left me high and dry two months ago, I thought that had to be the worst possible timing. But then I discovered how good you were and I started to hope and to believe…that we actually might be able to pull this off." She wrapped her arms around herself as if to push her frustration back inside herself. "And I get it, you have to go…but I just want to be upset for a little bit. Because of course Abuela had to get worse right before we leave for the biggest competition of our *careers*, and of course you have to go home and be with her!"

"Claire," Luca said softly. He pulled Claire roughly up on her toes, crushing her mouth against his. She tasted of tears and frustration, grief, and countless hours of practice all rolled into one. Dreams that could never be, and dreams that might be.

For another moment, they clung to each other, clung to the hours of blood, sweat, and tears that had gotten them this far.

"You should dance with Sebastian," Luca whispered as they broke away, and he felt Claire stiffen in his arms.

"What? Why would I do that?"

"Because next to me, he's the best. And he's opportunistic enough to jump at the chance to be back on the winning team."

"But I don't want to dance with him," Claire protested. "I want to dance with you."

"Claire, I'd give almost anything to dance with you at Blackpool, but this is the one time I can't be there. But just because I can't be there, doesn't mean you can't. You've been dreaming of this competition your whole life, and if you want a shot at winning, he's your best option."

"So, this is some kind of noble self-sacrifice?" Claire sniffed and wiped at her eyes, not caring if her mascara smeared. "Sorry Claire, I have to go, but why don't you see if this repulsive snake is still available?"

"Claire, wait," Luca seized her wrist again as she started to stomp off. "I just want you to be able to go after your dreams, even if I can't."

"You know what I wish?" Claire yanked at her arm. "That it wouldn't be selfish to ask you to stay. That you weren't the most amazing person in the world, because of course you have to drop everything and go home. That things could go according to plan for once instead of always falling apart at the last second. But I can't wish for any of those things because of course it's selfish to ask you to stay and of course you have to go and of course nothing ever goes according to plan." She let out a bitter laugh. "I'll see you around, Luca."

"Claire," Luca whispered.

Her face was pure agony. "I wish I'd never agreed to partner with you, Luca Ortiz."

This time, when Claire pulled at her arm, Luca didn't resist, and he watched helplessly as she ran away.

* * *

Claire had run then, blindly, tears streaming down her face, past families juggling kids and luggage alike, couples arm in arm, hotel staff rushing from one task to the next. She didn't care where she was going, as long as it was somewhere quiet where she could cry and no one would find her. Finally, exhausted, she slumped down by a large potted plant, dropping her head in her hands, sniffling.

First Sebastian's dreams, then Luca's priorities had cheated her out of her own dreams of Blackpool when she was so close to the finish line. She'd trained all her life to get to this point, she worked hard with Luca to learn his routines and dance style and now all that practice, blood, sweat and tears - not to mention flying across the country was all for nothing.

A hand holding a handkerchief reached into her field of vision. She looked up to see Sebastian bending down, one of his personal hankies held out to her.

"I keep telling you to stay away and you never listen," she scowled. In response, Sebastian laid the hanky carefully on the carpet near her feet and edged away. Claire eyed him warily. "If you came here to gloat, just get it over with." She sniffed.

Sebastian settled across from her on the carpet. "Why would I? We're both facing challenges in our respective relationships." He paused. "I did follow you though."

Unwilling to make eye contact, Claire stared in front of her at the cream-colored wall. At about her height there was a faint child-sized handprint that looked like it had been made with jam. For some reason, she was reminded of Reina smacking Luca's cheek. *Peso Tiss.* "So what do you want?"

"First, please take that handkerchief. You're dripping snot and that dress doesn't deserve to be used as a kleenex. Second, tell me what happened. I gathered your partner said something to make you upset but I couldn't hear the details."

Claire reluctantly took the hanky. "Luca's grandmother has been sick for a while, but he just got a call that she got worse and he went home to take care of her." Claire blew her nose. "It's horrible of course, and I feel selfish saying this, but it's frustrating to be so close to my dream and have to give up."

"Ah," Sebastian made a sympathetic sound. "It's difficult to give it your all and lose, but it's even worse to walk away without trying at all."

Claire shrugged listlessly. "Anyway, we'll probably be going home tomorrow instead of going on to London, so congratulations," Claire blew her nose again. "You now have one less competitor to deal with, so that should make you happy."

"Well, yes and no," Sebastian said thoughtfully. "On one hand I am a little relieved I won't have to face you at Blackpool but on the other…" he hesitated.

"What?" Claire asked.

"I wanted to see if you'd consider taking me back as your partner."

"Wow." Claire blew out a breath. "I broke your nose and you still want to partner with me? You must be really desperate."

"We need each other." Sebastian said simply. "I might not be the dancer Luca is, but he just went home. As for Bethany…" he shrugged. "Well, I admit, you're right, I'm desperate." He met Claire's gaze earnestly. "I know I messed up; I'm not asking for anything other than a partner. You need someone last minute to dance with, and I need someone who can actually give me a shot at a gold medal. It's win-win."

Claire stared forward again at the jam handprint. A few hours ago she and Luca had been kissing in Central Park, so happy, so in love. Now…

"Two months ago…I would've given anything to hear you ask me that. Now…" She turned back to Sebastian. "Can I sleep on it? If I don't give you an answer before you leave for London, then just consider that a no."

"You're not giving me a lot of wiggle room," Sebastian pointed out.

"Well you broke up our partnership an hour before you left for LA," Claire rose to her feet. "Consider us even."

Chapter 25: Apilado

"Milonguero style of embrace is danced in closed position, chest-to-chest."

"Abuela." Juan almost didn't recognize the woman lying in the hospital bed. There were tubes in her arms and chest like some horrifying sci-fi creature, her hair a tangled gray mess on the pillow behind her. She looked smaller, sunken, and when Abuela opened her eyes, Juan saw fear and pain, before she blinked it away and forced a smile.

"*Mijo.*" She held out a hand that was covered with tubes and looked as delicate as a twig. "What are you doing here? You should be at school."

"I told my teacher it was a family emergency, Abuela." Juan sat and carefully took her hand. He was afraid to hold it too tightly, her fingers looked as brittle as twigs.

"Juanito, you can't just skip, your education is important."

"So is spending time with you," Juan insisted.

Abuela patted his hand. "Tell me about your painting. Is it done yet?"

"It's done," Juan nodded. He felt the sting of tears in his eyes and forced them back. "If you'd consider treatment to get better, we can go see it together."

Abuela smiled slightly. "You're a sweet boy. Perhaps I will see it on my way up to heaven."

There was commotion in the hallway and Juan heard one of the nurses speaking. "Excuse me, sir, you can't go in there-"

"I'm a family member, let me through." And now, Juan really did want to cry, because Luca was standing in the doorway, wearing a shirt and jeans, looking tired and harried.

"Lu," Juan whispered, and he launched himself at his older brother so hard that Luca stumbled backward.

"Hey, careful there." Luca hugged him back, ruffling his hair. "You're getting big enough to knock me down."

"Sorry." Juan rested his head briefly on his brother's shoulder. The stress of the past day and a half made him feel like he hadn't slept in a week.

"Luca, what are you doing here?" Abuela demanded. "You were supposed to go to London."

"London can wait until you feel better," Luca released Juan and strode over to the bed. "Tell the doctors you will accept treatment."

"It's not your problem to deal with."

"*Mentira!*" Luca snapped.

Abuela's eyes flashed fire. "Don't use that language with me, young man."

"Abuela, be reasonable," Luca pleaded. "If we work together, we can pay for it."

"*Mijo*," Abuela reached for Luca's hand. "You might not think of me as a burden now, but the longer I am on dialysis, the bigger the burden I will become." Abuela grasped for Juan's hand with her free one. "I am old, with not much use for anything anymore."

"Abuela-"

"Hush," she said firmly. "If it is my time to die, then it is my time." Abuela squeezed Juans's hand. "I have lived a good life, I have watched my grandsons grow into fine young men, and I am ready to move on. You'll be alright."

***

Claire found Sebastian practicing alone in the gym.

"Claire," he said in surprise, turning away from the mirror with a smile. "Have you considered my proposal?"

"Yes." Claire glanced around the room."Where's Bethany?"

Sebastian managed a tight smile. "She mentioned something about getting a few photos in Central park for social media, she'll be back..." he waved an arm wearily. "At some point. So," he said, taking a sip of water from a stylish looking bottle. "What can I do for you?"

Claire took a breath. "I considered your offer and… I'm in."

"Really? That's great!" Sebastian rushed forward, arms open for a hug. Claire held out a hand for him to shake.

"Sorry," Sebastian took his hand in hers. "Old habits."

"It's fine," Claire pulled her hand free, and was aware she didn't feel the slightest tingle. "We have a lot of catching up to do and there's no time to waste." Claire walked to the center of the room. "Let's go over our waltz routine."

"All right," Sebastian queued the music and strode over to join her. The familiar sounds of the Waltz floated through the air as Sebastian took her hand in his. Claire sighed. It felt familiar and comfortable, like a well-worn shoe. At the precise moment, they pushed off together, spinning across the floor.

Finally, Claire thought, she was back in her comfort zone. The hours of practice, of engrained muscle memory, made the steps second nature and she felt herself whisked around the floor with very little effort.

"You've been practicing," she observed as Sebastian lifted her and spun.

"When I was first kicked off the show, I wanted to come back and ask to partner with you," Sebastian confessed. "After all, that was our plan."

"But?" Claire pressed.

"But, considering what happened last time I saw you, I figured that was a long shot," Sebastian gave a rueful smile.

"And yet you still practiced."

Sebastian twirled her and shrugged. "I've always been a sucker for long shots."

The music faded away and Claire and Sebastian bowed to the empty room.

"I don't want to celebrate too early, but I think we have a decent shot at winning," Sebastian commented.

"Yes, I think you're right," Claire nodded.

There was silence between the two of them.

"Well, we can practice the routine again if you want, but I think we nailed it," Sebastian smiled. "Want to grab a drink?"

"No… thank you." Claire shook her head. "I think I'm going to go back up to my room and make sure everything is packed."

"I'll see you at the airport, then?"

"Yes." Claire started to head for the door, but stopped. "Seb… just because we're partnered together, doesn't mean I forgot what happened between you and Bethany. You broke my heart," she stated quietly. "But I need a partner at Blackpool, and you're the best option I have now."

Sebastian was quiet for a moment, then he nodded. "I understand. I'll see you at the airport, Claire."

Claire opened the door. "See you, Sebastian."

Claire strode across the lobby, punching the button for the elevator. The doors opened promptly, and Claire stepped inside, leaning against the wall with a sigh. She should be happy. Ecstatic. The dream she had held onto for so long was finally coming to fruition. So, why did she feel so empty inside?

The elevator stopped on her floor and Claire stepped out. She wanted a hot shower and a coffee before she got on the plane. As Claire trotted down the cream-colored hallway, she saw the door to Luca's room was open. Her heart skipped a beat. Maybe Abuela had made a miraculous recovery, maybe he'd come back just in time…

"Luca?" Claire hurried to the door. "Is that you?"

A woman dressed in a crisp housekeeping uniform looked up, a bundle of sheets in her arms. "So sorry," she said in accented English. "There is nobody in this room yet."

"Oh." Claire fought the lump of disappointment in her throat. "Thank you anyway. Sorry for the interruption."

"Have a good day, miss," the woman smiled, dumping the sheets in her cart.

"Claire." Natalia was standing at the doorway to her room. She gave Claire a cursory look up and down. "Why don't you come inside."

Chapter 26: Final Bow

"Occurs at the end of a performance when one or more performers return to the stage to be recognized by the audience."

The tree outside Abuela's window was in desperate need of water, Luca decided. The dry branches reached towards the sun, so brittle that the slightest winter wind could turn them to dust.

Abuela's hand twitched in his, gnarled and brittle as the tree branches outside the window. She was sleeping peacefully for the first time since he'd come home, as she'd finally relented and accepted a morphine drip to dull the pain raging in her fragile body. It was only a matter of time now, the doctors had said, and Luca wanted her to be as comfortable as possible until the end.

He had failed in convincing her to accept treatment. She had insisted on being taken home, where she could be surrounded by her remaining family and friends, and photos of loved ones. Which was why Abuela's room was now filled with hospice equipment, and a nurse came by for a few hours every day to check on her.

Abuela's eyelids twitched, and for a second, Luca convinced himself she would wake up. Any moment now, she would smile and sit up in bed.

"What are these for, *mijo*?" she would ask. "I feel fine. Let me get dressed, and I'll make you some soup." They would get rid of the machines beeping all around her and Abuela would be miraculously healed, able to go about her day, without any pain, living forever. But the moment passed, and Luca remembered that Abuela was dying.

"Luca, have you been here all day?" It was Elaina, her favorite green sweater thrown over her work uniform. Reina bounced on her hip, sucking on one chubby fist.

"Nowhere else to go," Luca attempted a smile, rubbing his face. There was two days' worth of stubble growing on his chin, and he was in desperate need of a shower, but he only left Abuela's side long enough to use the bathroom and refill his water bottle.

"Here, *mija*, why don't you play here?" Elaina plunked Reina down in an armchair and dug a toy out of her oversized purse. She grabbed Luca's chin and clucked reprovingly. "You need to rest. Have you eaten anything?"

"Of course." Luca jerked away, indicating a handful of snack wrappers in the trash can. "The fridge was empty but I found a stash of snacks under Juan's bed."

"Crackers and chips are not enough," Elaina scolded. "Here." She dug into her purse again and produced a tupperware. "It's just leftover rice and beans, but it's better than nothing."

"Ice an eans," Reina crowed, and banged her toy against the chair arm.

"Thank you." For once, Luca was too hungry to argue. He dug in ravenously.

"Has anyone talked to you about her condition?"

"That she's got a week left, at the most." Luca pushed away the Tupperware, his appetite lost. "Juan wanted to stay home from school again but I told him I'd call if she got worse. Right now we're just… waiting."

"Do you want someone to sit with you? A lot of people have been asking how she's doing."

Luca shook his head. "Tell them thank you, but… I'm fine. I got the week off from work, I'll be okay."

Elaina laid a hand on Luca's arm. "You need a break. Let me take over for you. I can ask Joe to watch Reina so you can shower, buy groceries… sleep…"

"No." Luca clutched Abuela's frail hand in his. "I couldn't convince her to accept treatment, the least I can do is stay with her."

"Luca?" Bianca, dressed in her scrubs poked her head in through the screen door. "I just finished my shift, and wanted to see how she was doing before I went home." She walked over to the bed and checked Abuela's chart. "I'm sorry," she said, replacing it. "I'm sure this is tough for you."

"Is there anything you can give her to make her better?" Luca buried his head in Abuela's palm, kissing the delicate skin. "I just need a little more time, I'm not ready to say good-bye."

"Not without her permission." Bianca shook her head. "If she was willing to accept treatment we could put her on dialysis, but she's refused it every time I asked."

"Then please… leave me alone," Luca didn't raise his head. "I'm not leaving her."

"All right," Bianca sighed quietly. "I'll come back and check on you tomorrow."

Elaina stood and kissed Luca on top of his head. "I need to go home and make dinner. Call me if you need me to come back."

Luca heard the quiet footfalls of Elaina and Bianca leaving the room. The door closed behind them.

"You're not going anywhere," Luca whispered, holding Abuela's hand in his. It felt so cold between his fingers, so delicate. "I'll stay here as long as it takes, so please, get better. I'll be a teacher, and a dancer, the way you always believed I could be, and you can come to all my competitions." Abuela didn't stir. "Don't you want to see Juan graduate from high school? Or become a famous street artist?" Luca pleaded. "Or maybe you can come to London with me next year and watch me dance at Blackpool? There are so many things I want you to see Abuela, can't you stay a little longer?"

But Abuela didn't wake up. She stayed silent, and Luca fell asleep waiting, his head on Abuela's lap, while the machines beeped around him.

* * *

"We only have a little time before we have to go to the airport." Natalia closed the door and limped to the small coffee maker. "Can I make you something? Tea? Coffee?"

"No, thank you, Mama." Claire leaned against the doorway. "I don't need anything."

"Well, I could use a cup," Natalia said, opening a tea bag of chamomile. The coffeemaker hummed as it dispensed hot water into the pristine hotel mug. "I am sorry Luca had his emergency, but don't worry; when your father gets to the airport, he is planning to change our tickets. We can rest, go home tomorrow, and try again next year."

"There's no need, I'm going to fly to London." Claire met her mother's eyes. "Sebastian and I have decided to partner up for his competition. He knows I'm a stronger competitor, and we have enough history as partners to guarantee us a shot at winning."

Natalia picked up her cup. "I see. And what led you to make this choice?"

Claire looked down at her hands. "Luca told me I should dance with Sebastian, so at least one of us could achieve our dream."

"And you agreed?"

Claire shrugged. "He told me it was the best choice for both of us. And Sebastian is willing to change partners last minute. And considering I've been wanting to compete at Blackpool for as long as I can remember, why should I give up when I'm this close?"

Natalia regarded her daughter carefully. "That sounds very logical. You were fortunate to find a partner who could substitute at the last minute. Congratulations."

"Thanks," Claire stared down at her manicured nails. "I'm really lucky to have Sebastian be available again. A few months ago this was everything I wanted."

"Claire, come sit here with me," Natalia said, limping over to the sofa.

"No, thank you Mama, I think I'll just back to my room-"

"Sit. Down." Natalia was not to be refused. Claire sat.

Natalia sat down next to her on the sofa, sighing gratefully as she sat back against the soft cushions. "You're so much like me, you know. Ambitious, stubborn, with a love of dance most people can never understand. I remember being exactly the same, but right now you are making a decision between your head and your heart, and I think you are making a mistake."

"Why?"

Natalia regarded her daughter for a moment. "Claire, do you know what a *prima ballerina absoluta* is?"

Claire nodded. "It's even better than a prima donna."

"A title given to only the most exceptional of all ballerinas," Natalia corrected her. "An honor given only to the best of the best."

"Were you a *prima ballerina absoluta*, Mama?" Claire asked. Natalia chuckled and shook her head. "No, but that was my dream." She took a sip of tea, her blue eyes focused on something Claire couldn't see. "My parents were ballet dancers, and when I was old enough, I was accepted into the Bolshoi Ballet Academy and began my own training. At the age of twelve, I got my first role as Clara in the *Nutcracker*," She took another sip of tea.

"I was eighteen when I was chosen to be a principal dancer, by the time I was twenty, I was the *prima ballerina* for the Bolshoi Ballet in Moscow, but that wasn't enough. I desperately wanted to be the best dancer in the world by the time I was thirty." Natalia put down her mug of tea. "I practiced tirelessly for hours every day, pushed myself to be more than perfect, better than the best. Every ballet company wanted me to dance as their leading lady. I became something of a celebrity, touring all over the world, performing on the grandest stages."

Natalia looked wistfully into the distance. "For two years I was given everything I could ever want. And when I was twenty-one, I became engaged to a man named Sergio Konf. He was a rich patron of my ballet company, who could provide me with a comfortable life once I retired."

"So, what happened?" Claire asked.

Natalia sighed. "I came home one day, to find him in bed with someone else. You understand, I was mortified and rushed from the house with no idea of where I was going to go. It was winter, the roads were frozen and it was dark. I was hit by a driver who didn't see me until it was too late."

"Mama," Claire put a comforting hand on her mother's. Natalia patted it absently.

"When I…awoke…" she took a deep breath. "I was told that I had sustained broken ribs, a fractured arm – my leg was broken in several places, I needed pins in my knee and my hip…." A tear rolled down her cheek. "I knew my career was over. The papers wrote about the tragedy for a few weeks, and then…I was forgotten. No more fans, no more parties, I was just a ballerina who could no longer dance."

Natalia turned to face her daughter. "Can you imagine what that would be like? To no longer be able to dance? I sold my house, spent all my savings on treatments, experimental procedures, desperate for a miracle, but nothing worked. The last place I visited was an orthopedic surgeon in France. I had heard that they specialized in traumatic injuries, but after examining me, they told me the damage to my leg was irreversible.

I left the hospital with no hope, no money and no future. It was winter, and as the sun went down, I found myself on a bridge, ready to end it all."

"Mama," Claire stared at her in disbelief.

"I was preparing to jump, when someone grabbed me from behind." Natalia shook her head. "It was this young, French man with the most idiotic face I had ever seen."

"Papa."

Natalia nodded and continued. "I remember I screamed at him in Russian to let me go. I clawed at his hands, scratched at his face but no matter what I did, he held onto me and kept me from jumping. At some point, someone called the *gendarme*. I was taken to a hospital and put on what you call—suicide watch." She shrugged. "Your father visited me every day. He'd been brought to the hospital as well; in the process of holding onto me he'd lost a glove and he lost the tips of two of his fingers to frostbite." She brushed a hand over her own fingers.

"At the time, I was furious at this silly little man who wouldn't let me die. But he was stubborn and took it upon himself to learn Russian so he could talk to me. And somehow he convinced me to try ballroom dancing. It wasn't ballet, but with Leon helping keep the weight off my leg, I could reclaim a part of myself again." Natalia took a breath. "I knew I was never going to be the *prima ballerina absoluta*, but with your father's help I gained something even more precious: a reason to live." She took a sip of tea. "Your father saved my life that day. And he's made it worth living every day since."

Claire looked into her mother's eyes. "Why have you never told me this story before now?"

Natalia considered for a moment. "Because now, you are not a child. You are a young woman. More importantly, you are a young woman who has dreamed of competing not just at Blackpool, but competing with someone you *love*."Claire stared at her in surprise. "Again, you think I do not see. It is all over your face." Natalia shrugged. "You can try to convince yourself all you want that you want to compete at Blackpool to be the best, but I know you also dream about dancing there with someone who has a special place in your heart."

"Two months ago, all I wanted was to dance with Sebastian, but now… it's not the same."

"Of course it is not," Natalia nodded. "You have grown, changed, redefinitioned—" she corrected herself. "*Redefined* the kind of person that you want to dance with."

Claire sniffed and wiped at her eyes. "But Mama, I'm so close. I can't turn back now."

Natalia stood. "I have something to show you." Limping over to her suitcase, she pulled two heavy flat objects out of her carry-on bag. "Here," she said, placing it in Claire's hand.

Claire stared. "Are these…your medals from Blackpool?"

Natalia shrugged. "Your father wanted to do some sort of photo op," she explained. "He said when you won we could take a picture of two generations of Beauchene's winning at Blackpool."

Claire ran a hand over the embossed medal. A blue ribbon was threaded through the top and there was an inscription in blue that read, *UKA Dance Blackpool, First Place.* "It's beautiful."

"It is," Natalia agreed, taking it back. "But when you look at it in black and white, it's just a medal. It was an honor to win, and I am proud of the work we did. But the time I spent practicing and falling in love with your father, that is something I remember much more."

Claire's eyes stung and she carefully wiped away a tear. "I just wanted to be like you and Papa. I was so sure if I did everything you did, I'd have the perfect life."

Natalia's face softened with understanding. "Claire, our life is far from perfect. And even if it seems that way, it's not because of the trophies and medals we've won. It's because we have each other." She gently cupped Claire's cheek. "It's because we have you. You are worth more to me than a thousand *prima ballerina absolutas* and a million gold medals and if I had to do it all again I would. If I had to choose between a life with you and your father and a life of fame and fortune, I would choose you two every time."

"But isn't it a waste to give up now?"

Natalia's eyes met hers. "Isn't it a waste of your life to commit to something you don't want to do?"

The door opened and Leon entered, looking tired. "*Mon cœur, mon chérie*, I have returned." He kissed Claire on her cheek and his wife on the lips. "I saw Sebastian downstairs, am I to understand he is your partner once again?"

"I asked and he said yes, Papa," Claire said.

"He is lucky to get such an opportunity," Leon commented, though he did not smile. "I would like to take a few minutes to rest before our final leg of the trip. We have a long flight ahead of us."

"Almost there," Claire managed a smile. "I did it."

She was only a day away from the competition she'd dreamed about her whole life. She could practically see the dance floor, hear the roar of the crowd, feel the weight of the gold medal around her neck. Sebastian would once again be by her side, just like she'd always dreamed.

"Come on, help me up, we'll leave Claire alone," Natalia said, reaching for her husband's hand. Claire watched her father help her mother to her feet. The hand with the missing finger tips wrapping around her waist, lifting her up and supporting her, taking the weight off her mother's injured leg until she could support herself with her cane. Mama's injured leg. The injury that ended her career. The leg that never would've been able to dance again without Papa's help.

Papa, who had saved Mama's life by making life worth living. Papa's hand with his missing fingertips. The tips he had lost to frostbite. The hands that had held onto Mama, refusing to let her go then, and supported her now. Claire had seen him help her mother to her feet a thousand times, but now it felt like she was seeing them both in a new light. Seeing them for who they had been then, and now.

"Claire, *chérie*, what's wrong?" Leon asked. "Why are you sad?"

"I'm not sad, Papa." Claire was suddenly aware there were tears trickling down her cheeks. "I'm just happy that you and Mama found each other."

"As am I, *chérie*, as am I." Leon kissed his wife's cheek.

Claire thought of Luca supporting her when she was injured, how when she'd fallen during the competition he'd picked her up and carried her carefully, gently off the floor. Now, Abuela was dying and Luca was rushing home to be with her all by himself.

"Mama, Papa," Claire said, getting to her feet. She took a breath. "I know what I want to do."

* * *

Luca awoke to the sound of gentle voices around him. The air was filled with a familiar flowery scent that he knew all too well and a laugh that was music to his ears.

"Claire? What are you doing here?"

"Elaina let me in." Claire placed a bouquet of roses on Abuela's bedside table, then fussed with a few of the blooms. "I thought I could sit with Abuela while you eat and take a shower."

"Isn't she nice?" Abuela rasped. Her skin had taken on a yellowish tint but her eyes were bright and alert. "Came all the way to help. And she brought pretty *rosas*."

Luca gave her a cursory look up and down before looking away. Claire's clothes were rumpled, her hair was tied in a messy bun and she looked like she hadn't gotten much sleep. If he had to guess, she had just come from the airport.

"I feel like I should be looking around for a big fat trophy. Did you drop it off at home before you came over here?" Luca asked wearily.

"There isn't a trophy, because I didn't compete with Sebastian," Claire said. "He offered and at first I said yes, but… it didn't feel right. So, I told Sebastian that I couldn't compete with him, and came home."

Luca was half-convinced Claire would disappear like a mirage if he touched her. "I can't believe you gave up on Blackpool. I was so sure you were going to pair up with Sebastian and never talk to me again."

Claire's blue eyes met his. "I did too." She paused. "Right up until I realized that the victory wouldn't mean anything if you weren't there with me."

Luca swallowed. His heart was suddenly beating a little too fast.

"Sounds like you made a very smart decision." Abuela spoke up. "Don't you think, *mijo*?" Abuela looked meaningfully in Luca's direction.

"Very smart," Luca managed to say. He wasn't completely sure he was still dreaming.

"Your neighbors gave me some casseroles that you can heat up and eat." Claire gestured toward the kitchen where a mountain of Tupperware and Pyrex dishes were sitting. "It's almost noon, you should have something."

"I'm fine." Luca ran a hand through his greasy hair, and his stomach gurgled in protest.

"Take a break, *mijo*." Abuela patted his hand. "Claire and I can have some girl time while you get clean."

"Fine." Luca pushed himself to his feet and stumbled to his room to get clean clothes before he stumbled back to the bathroom to shower. He could hear Abuela and Claire talking and laughing as he stepped out twenty minutes later, feeling like he just scrubbed away layers of dirty skin.

"All my life, I've been working towards a single goal," Claire was saying as Luca stepped into the kitchen and chose a dish at random to heat up. "But maybe, it's time to make room for other things as well."

"I am glad to hear that. So what are your big plans for the future?" Abuela asked.

"I'm going to take classes at the local community college so I can have that college experience," Claire said. "I'll get a business degree so I can start helping Mama run the dance studio. And during school break, Bells and I are going to take a trip to South America, and learn about some of the dances there."

"How exciting," Abuela laughed, and winced in discomfort. "My husband and I loved our life there. I shall have to give you a list of places to visit."

"Or I could bring you along…" Claire started to offer.

"No, thank you *querida*." Abuela shook her head. "You enjoy your trip. I am just glad you are trying new things, living for more than dance. You are so young, and there are so many things you can do when you're young, and you should take the time to do as many as possible."

"You could do a few more things if you wanted, Abuela." Claire's lip quivered.

Abuela patted her cheek. "You are young, of course you should appreciate the long life you have in front of you. But I am old, and tired. My husband is gone, my daughter is gone." A tear ran down her cheek. "It's a comfort to know I will see them again soon."

"But what about us, Abuela?" Luca demanded, coming out of the kitchen.

"*Mijo*." Abuela managed a smile. "My talented grandson, watching you grow up and follow your passion has been one of the greatest joys left in my life." She reached for his hand, clasping it in hers. "But I don't want to be a burden to you anymore. I am so tired of being old and in pain. Can you understand that?"

"No, I can't," Luca whispered, as tears began to fall again.

"One day you will," Abuela said with a sad smile. "And I hope when that day comes, you have someone taking care of you with the same love you have given to me." She turned her head, meeting her grandson's eyes. "You know the thing I always wished I could see?"

"What's that?"

"The routine you two were practicing together."

* * *

It took a little time to set up. Elaina had to be called over to help, and she set up a chair and umbrella for Abuela as Luca carried her carefully outside. He took his time settling her in the chair, making sure she was comfortable, under the jacaranda trees where, just a few weeks ago they'd celebrated her birthday. Elaina sat next to Abuela, fan in one hand, and a cup of water in the other.

Claire brought out her phone with the music cued up and a portable speaker and placed it next to the chairs. Taking her practice heels out of her bag, she put them on, re-tying her messy bun into a neat one.

"Ready?" Luca asked.

"Ready." Claire pressed play on her phone and hurried to join him in front of Abuela. The first strains of music echoed around the neighborhood as Claire and Luca took their positions.

* * *

The music was something Abuela used to play for Luca when he was learning to dance. *Bless him*, Abuela thought, he was bringing bits of his past into his routine. The sun felt warm today, hints of summer heat in the air, filtering through the purple jacaranda blossoms overhead. Abuela watched as her grandson spun Claire carefully around, bringing her back into his arms.

He loved her, she could see it in his eyes, the way he held her, with the innocence and fervor that came from being young. She remembered what it used to be like to dance like that with her husband, Hector. To live, to love, to dance with enough energy to go all day and long into the night, without feeling tired. As long as Hector's hand had been in hers, she had felt she could do anything.

"Would you like to dance, *mi amore*?" Abuela turned. The sun must be making her drowsy. There was a man beside her, tall and dark, a twinkle in his eyes she knew all too well. The same face she had fallen in love with as a girl of nineteen. Hector smiled and held out his hand. "It's been a long time."

Strange that she suddenly wasn't feeling so tired. "I'll be right back, Hector is asking for a dance," she told Elaina, taking his hand. Somehow it was easy to get to her feet, her body did not seem so tired, so achy. Her hair fell down to her shoulders, rich and dark, her favorite dress swishing around her legs. There was music playing, the kind of song that made her move to the rhythm. Ahead of her was a floor full of dancers, women in colorful skirts swirling around men like tropical flowers. Abuela thought she caught a glimpse of her dear Serena, long hair flowing as she whirled around in her favorite red dress.

Hector looked over his shoulder at her grinning. "Shall we show these amateurs how it's done?"

Abuela laughed. She felt young, and vibrant again, with the energy to dance all night. "I thought you'd never ask."

* * *

Claire and Luca finished their routine, feeling slightly out of breath. Luca could barely remember if he danced the right steps. He was aware only of the music, the electricity that seemed to spark in his fingers every time he touched Claire. The sun was sinking down in the sky, and Luca and Claire turned to where Abuela and Elaina were sitting, expecting applause. But Elaina was clutching Abuela's hand in hers and did not seem to realize the dance was over.

"Elaina?" Luca hurried to her side. "What's wrong?"

Elaina looked up, tears running down her face. "She's gone," she said quietly. "She said 'I'll be right back, Hector is asking for a dance,' and then she was just… gone."

Chapter 27: Encore

"An encore *is an extra performance at the end of a longer one, which an entertainer gives because the audience asks for it."*

The house was too quiet. No telenovelas blasting out of the TV, no sounds of cooking from the kitchen. There were no smells of Abuela's soup, no glimpses of her moving around in the kitchen, dressed in one of her colorful mumus. The kitchen was empty. Drab and colorless without the woman who used to fill it.

The living room was empty. Abuela's possessions and photos packed away. And as Luca sealed up the final packing box and loaded it onto the moving truck, the house was empty. It was all part of the aftermath of Abuela's passing. The house Luca had grown up in was being sold to pay her medical expenses. Anything left would be put into Juan's education.

Luca had found a two-bedroom apartment for them to move into, that was a short distance from the dance studio and Juan's school—no easy feat.

Luca adjusted the cufflinks on his black dress shirt. They were his *abuelo*'s. Elaina had found them while she was helping pack up, tucked in the back of a drawer. There was a note attached to it with a rubber band, in Abuela's handwriting, saying that they were for him. Luca had stared at himself in the mirror as he'd put them on, trying to see his *abuelo*'s face in his, the fire in his eyes, that devilish smile. But all he saw was a scared kid on the verge of twenty, grieving and exhausted from sleepless nights.

They would be okay. Joe and Elaina were going to do their best to help out, so when Luca started his full-time job at the Beauchene Dance Studio, Juan would have someone keeping an eye on him. And if things didn't work out—like Chris hoped—there was always the bar to fall back on.

Luca walked through the empty rooms of his house one last time. He'd already checked three times before and knew there was nothing. But he just couldn't leave, leave his family house with all its memories yet. There was the doorframe with pencil marks where Papa used to measure his and his brother's height. There was the dent in the rug from the worn-out couch where they watched movies every Friday night. There, the squares of darker colored wall, where the family photos used to hang. Luca's eyes filled with tears. It was gone, all gone. And he was alone.

Juan had left after lunch, claiming there was some project he had to finish, Joe and Elaina had stayed until the last box had been packed and then they both left, as well.

"Luca?" For a moment Luca wondered how Claire knew when to come just when he needed her most. Then her arms were around him and he was breathing in the scent of flowers as the world that had been feeling so uncertain slowly steadied.

"I'm sorry," she whispered. "I can't imagine how awful this must be for you."

Luca allowed himself to rest his head on her shoulder. "I keep thinking I'm going to hear her voice or walk into the kitchen and see her there. But then I walk in and no one is there."

He kissed her, seeking comfort, one hand wrapping around her waist, the other tangling in her hair. Claire ran her fingers through his curls, and Luca felt the grief ease slightly, like a beam of sunlight coming through the clouds. He wanted to drown in her, dive deep into the scent and feel of her rather than face the world without Abuela. But Claire was already pushing him away, brushing away his tears.

"I'm supposed to bring you somewhere," she was saying. "It's a surprise."

* * *

Luca recognized the rundown grocery store as soon as Claire drove up.

"What are we doing here?" he asked.

"All I can say is I was asked to bring you at five," Claire said, getting out and locking the doors behind them. Luca caught a whiff of something cooking. Someone was cooking meat, and as he got closer he smelled pastry, sugar; it smelled like there was a backyard fiesta going on nearby.

And then Claire led Luca around the corner and he was surprised by the entire neighborhood yelling, "*Felicidades!*"

The empty lot was awash with color. Paper lanterns and streamers hung in every corner, and there were tables piled high with food and drink. Neighbors, young and old and dressed in their best clothes gathered, laughing and smiling.

"W-what is this?" Luca asked.

"We wanted to gather and celebrate Abuela one last time." Elaina stepped forward. "She changed all our lives, and it seemed right to have one giant fiesta in her honor." There were cheers and Elaina had to wave her hands to quiet everyone down. "But, before we start, Juan has another surprise. Juan!"

Luca turned and saw Juan sitting on the edge of the roof with Joe, grinning from ear to ear. Each held a section of tarp that was draped over the wall, covering the mural.

"Abuela," Juan said, "this is for you." Juan and Joe released the tarp and as it fell down, there was a collective gasp from everyone gathered as they took in the oak tree, the ocean view, and the family underneath. But one thing was different. Instead of sitting with the rest of the family, Abuela danced with Abuelo in her favorite dance costume, her grey hair flowing, her skirts whirling around her, a happy smile on her face. She seemed so joyful, so free, and as Luca stared, he felt tears trickling down his cheeks. Claire pressed a tissue in his hands as she dabbed at her own eyes.

"It's beautiful," she whispered. "The way he captured your family here. Now as long as this is here, a part of her will always be remembered."

"And the best news is," Juan swaggered up, looking tired but proud. "The grocery store is being bought by some new owners who have a whole chain of stores for a tidy profit. Not only do they want to keep this mural on their store, they want me to be on a team to design murals for *all* of them."

"Would you look at that—*Juanito*, the successful artist," Joe said, ruffling Juan's hair.

"Told you I'd make it," Juan grinned back. "The Ortiz boys got skills." He looked at Luca, who was still silent, and his grin faded slightly. "Do you like it?"

"Like it?" Luca grabbed his brother in a fierce hug. "This is amazing. Best thing you've ever done. It's perfect."

"Best I've done so far, you mean," Juan wheezed. "I've got tons of ideas for the other stores."

"I'm sure you do," Elaina said, "but in the meantime, I know everyone is hungry. Let's get this fiesta started!"

A cheer went up and everyone made a rush to the tables that were groaning under the weight of their dishes. Music began to play as people talked and ate, mingling together, laughing as they shared their favorite Abuela stories.

Claire handed Luca a plate piled high with food. "Eat something, apparently we're going to be dancing all night."

"Thanks," Luca hadn't had much of an appetite in the past couple weeks, but he dug in politely. Claire took a seat next to him, sampling the different food from her own plate.

"How long have they been planning this?" Luca asked.

Claire shrugged. "Not sure. Elaina called me this morning and asked me to bring you here. It's incredible though," she looked over the sea of faces in the parking lot. "All these people are here because of Abuela. She changed their lives, and all these people are here to honor her memory."

Something had been weighing on Luca's mind since she'd come back. "Are you still glad you walked away from Blackpool? I know it wasn't an easy decision."

Claire cocked her head, considering. "All my life I had choreographed a very specific routine for how my life was supposed to go. And I was so sure it was the perfect routine to ensure a perfect life because it was the one I thought my parents had followed too." She took a bite of food. "It turns out their routine wasn't that perfect either, it just seemed that way from the outside." She turned to look Luca in the eye. "You're the one who pulled me from my routine and forced me to improvise and adapt in the wild. But you're also the one who keeps me steady when things seem completely out of my control. It turns out, I needed that more than I needed a gold medal."

"But still, you gave up on your dream—"

"There's always next time. And until then," Claire shrugged and there was a twinkle in her eyes. "There's a World Latin Championship in four months, do you think that's enough time to practice?"

Luca stared at her. "You want to partner with me again?"

Claire rolled her eyes. "You're the best Latin dancer in the studio, who else would I partner with? Plus," Claire's eyes gleamed briefly with avarice. "My parents couldn't get past silver when they entered, it'd be a big deal to come home with a gold."

"My *princesa* has guts," Luca chuckled, pressed a kiss on her head. "It's going to take a lot of work, are you sure you're up for it?"

Claire laid her head on his shoulder. "You make anything possible."

* * *

One year later, London…

"I got our number." Claire hurried through the crowd of glittery, costumed dancers to where Luca was waiting. Dressed in a few skimpy pieces of fabric and feathers in gradiating colors of blue and black, a line of rhinestones tracing a glittery trail up her stomach, she didn't even stand out. But the look on Luca's face as she approached made her feel as if she was the only person in the room he could see.

"Thanks." Luca was dressed in matching colors of blue and black, rhinestones glittering up the bare V of torso not covered by his sleeveless dance shirt. Claire handed him a printed packet of papers as she pinned their number to Luca's back.

"Our first heat is in five minutes, we have another right after that and then we get a break for one heat before we start our third—"

"Claire, relax, we're ready." Luca turned around to cup her chin in his hands and kiss her carefully on the forehead, avoiding her heavy make-up and rhinestones. "We've been practicing all year, and now we're here. We've finally made it."

"I know, I know." Claire linked her fingers through his. "I just keep thinking about how my parents and our students are watching us, and I don't want to disappoint them."

"Don't forget Juan, Elaina, Joe, Reina…" Luca reminded her. "Joe actually asked for the day off, and Juan is taking a break from his newest commission to watch our performance on TV. So let's dance our best and make them proud."

* * *

"Ladies and gentlemen, number 233. From San Diego, California, here's Luca Ortiz and Claire Beauchene for the Salsa!"

Luca led Claire onto the floor to the sound of applause and spun her as they bowed to the judges on their raised stage.   Surrounded by international dancers, lights, and hundreds of cheering spectators, Claire felt her heart beating faster.

"Are you ready?" She whispered, and felt Luca's hands gently squeeze hers.

"Let's show these amateurs how it's done."

And then the music began, the pulsing rhythm that could be felt in her bones, integral as the air she breathed.

She was vaguely aware of the roar of the crowd, the swirl of skirts all around her, and the judges watching from afar. But in that moment, Claire didn't care about their score, whether they would advance to the next level, whether they would win.

All that mattered was the music, the applause, and Luca's hand in hers as he spun her around. Because regardless of how well they did, *this*, Claire knew, was the thing they would keep chasing every day of their lives. The passion burning in their center, the fire for the dance that burned in their core. This, Claire knew, as Luca lifted her and spun like a top, was *chispa*.

Acknowledgements

There are a lot of people to thank for the completion of this novel. First and foremost on my list are my dad and my sister Violet, to whom I read the first few pages of a story I'd just started to write, and when I stopped, they demanded I keep going because they wanted to know what happened next.

This was the spark that fueled a five-year long process that involved me carrying around the various notebooks that housed the scribblings of *Chispa* so I could write whenever inspiration struck. Sometimes it took weeks. Other times I shelved the project so I could focus on work and odd jobs that helped me pay the bills. But I could never put it down for too long because either Dad or Violet would ask, "what happened to that chispa story you were writing?"

Covid gave me a lot of free time to write. Suddenly the story that was struggling to find its legs was moving along in leaps and bounds. And when the final page had been written, I took a breath…and started the long process of editing.

There should be a saying that behind every writer, there is a talented team that helps get that book on the shelves. I am incredibly blessed to have all these people on mine.

Susan Lanigan, who has been my go-to editor since I started publishing my other series, *Mickie McKinney: Boy Detective*. God bless Susan and her red pen, she has always been patient and kind with her edits despite the multitude of corrections needed.

My cousin Jennifer Harris, with her gift of missing nothing and putting together a staggering amount of suggestions to improve the plot.

My sister Violet and co-founder of fINK PRESS who has done everything from editing, to formatting, to modeling for the cover with her husband, Jamie and designing the final product. I love you both for that—it looks amazing. I love Violet specifically for being such a huge driving force behind this novel. I can't wait to see what our next project will be.

My beta readers, Ellanore Molzhon, Andrea Frazier, Jessica Baehr, Jocelyn Wright, Suzanne Freyjadis, Kari Murphy and my Aunt Katy Johnson. Thank you all for taking the time to read and give notes.

My dance teachers, Jean, Wendy, Eugene and Jesse of the Arthur Murray Dance Studio in Valencia, who gave me real world experience into the life of a competitive dancer. I may never have been a champion, but you made me feel like one.

Lastly Orbelina Martinez, who was my Abuela in every way but blood. I never got to say good-bye to you, so I wrote a story where I could.

About the Author

Ruby Fink grew up a California native, the eldest of three. She is author of the award-winning detective series *Mickie McKinney: Boy Detective* as well as *The Dreaming Tree* and *Until You Grow Tall*. Ruby fell in love with ballroom dancing at the age of sixteen, and while she doesn't have half the skill of Claire or Luca, still enjoys a good Rumba on the dance floor. She is also the co-founder of fINK PRESS, a small writing company she manages with her sister Violet.